ACCLAIM FOR SUSAN WILSON'S EXCEPTIONAL NOVELS

THE FORTUNE TELLER'S DAUGHTER

"A compelling blend of romance, intrigue, and passion . . . a rich story, filled with likable, interesting characters who leap off the page."

—*New York Times* bestselling author Kristin Hannah

"A poignant drama. Susan Wilson builds characters that are deeply layered and quite compelling."

—*Romantic Times*

CAMEO LAKE

"As in her previous work, *Hawke's Cove,* Wilson uses a clear grasp of family and marital dynamics to bring us a touching story of people dealing with real problems in a very human way."

—*Library Journal*

"Wilson's tale is a sensitive scrutiny of one woman's struggle to discover what she wants in life."

—*Booklist*

"A deep and compelling read."

—*Romantic Times*

"This is a beautiful love story full of strong emotion; of tragic endings and beginnings; of healing and forgiveness. It touches something deep inside of us all. A great novel, Ms. Wilson."

—*Old Book Barn Gazette*

"*Cameo Lake* is a moving, unforgettable tale of the many facets of love. Delving deeply into the complexities of the heart, this powerful story of endings and beginnings, healing and forgiveness will strike a chord for all readers and resonate in their hearts. Susan Wilson is a superb storyteller, deftly weaving all the story's elements into a vibrant, richly patterned tapestry. . . . I highly recommend *Cameo Lake*. It's a book you will remember long after the last page is turned."

—AOL's Romance Fiction Forum

HAWKE'S COVE

"From the pen of Susan Wilson comes a gem of a story that can't fail to touch all who read it. . . . Wilson writes with compassion as she tells these stories separated by time and brought together by a common thread. Romantic and tender, *Hawke's Cove* will appeal to a wide variety of readers [who] will cry, be joyful, and be surprised at this story that proves love is timeless."

—*Under the Covers Reviews*

BOOKS BY SUSAN WILSON

Hawke's Cove
Cameo Lake
The Fortune Teller's Daughter

SUSAN WILSON

THE FORTUNE TELLER'S DAUGHTER

POCKET BOOKS

New York London Toronto Sydney Singapore

This book is a work of fiction. Names, characters, places and incidents are products of the author's imagination or are used fictitiously. Any resemblance to actual events or locales or persons, living or dead, is entirely coincidental.

 POCKET BOOKS, a division of Simon & Schuster, Inc.
1230 Avenue of the Americas, New York, NY 10020

Copyright © 2002 by Susan Wilson

Originally published in hardcover in 2002 by Atria Books

ISBN: 0-7434-4231-8

First Pocket Books printing February 2003

10 9 8 7 6 5 4 3 2 1

POCKET and colophon are registered trademarks of Simon & Schuster, Inc.

For information regarding special discounts for bulk purchases, please contact Simon & Schuster Special Sales at 1-800-456-6798 or business@simonandschuster.com

Cover art by Robert Hunt

Printed in the U.S.A.

Dedicated with love to my family, especially David, who built me a shed of my own.

Thank you to Marty Nadler, who offered insights into the film business, and Holly Nadler, who got me going in this business.

As always and forever, to my guiding lights, Caroline Tolley and Andrea Cirillo, thank you.

There is a fatality, a feeling so irresistible and inevitable that it has the force of doom, which almost invariably compels human beings to linger around and haunt, ghostlike, the spot where some great and marked event has given the color to their lifetime; and still the more irresistibly, the darker the tinge that saddens it.

—Nathaniel Hawthorne, *The Scarlet Letter*

PART 1

One

Thursday, September 21, 2000

South Congregational Church was rapidly filling up. Sabine Heartwood eased herself into a pew beside Moe Condon, the editor of the weekly *Pennywise Paper* and her boss. It was a tight squeeze and Sabine felt a little awkward as her rump touched the massive thigh of her curmudgeonly employer. South Congo, as everyone called the church, was a living antiquity; excepting the electricity in the ornate hanging chandeliers and central heating, nothing was different about the church than when it was built in the early eighteenth century. White-painted pews with shellacked coamings, a simple preacher's lectern to one side of the plain wooden cross at the front of the nave, massive multi-light windows—open now to allow in the slight breeze, a faint lick of which tickled the back of Sabine's neck, ruffling the loose curling hairs not caught up in her twist.

Sabine nodded to Moe, and he patted her hand in an uncharacteristic show of solidarity. The town had lost an icon and they all felt the loss. No, Beatrice Danforth had been more than a static icon, she had been Moose River Junction's matriarch. The overflow crowd at this funeral was testimony to a life well lived. Influence, imperiousness, expectation. She was the last of her kind. Everyone at the wake last night had used those words, or ones similar. Born with the century, living long enough to have witnessed wars and depressions, foolish politics and personal loss. Stoic, uncompromising Beatrice had indeed been the last of her kind. She'd witnessed the zenith of her town's heyday as it moved from agrarian to industrial, and then its inevitable decline as one by one the small manufactures closed, and the subsequent exodus of her town's youth to the siren call of city successes. The most personal of these was the departure of her only grandson, Danforth Smith.

The organist, hidden from sight in the loft above and behind the congregation, played a soft, sorrow-evoking prelude. Sabine smoothed the fabric of her dark blue silk dress and let her eyes rest on the pearl gray wall in front of her. The sunlight streaming in through the wavy, ancient window glass created an odd illusion of shapes against the wall, bending and blurred in such a way that she could make out faces, as if the light was exposing the crying out of spirits who once worshiped here. Nonsense, of course. Churches were seldom haunted. Sabine half-closed her eyes and let the images shift, shadow and light playing against the pearl gray, revealing to her alone the sad visages of perpetrators of cruel punishments. Sabine blinked to dispel the vision. There had been cruelty dealt out in the name of God within these marvelously preserved walls. Once a woman had been condemned to death for accusing a prominent citizen of rape. They had turned it against her and the magistrates, using these holy spaces as a court, had banished her from the fledgling town of Windsorville. Banishment, into what in those days was surrounding wilderness, was tantamount to a death sentence. As clearly as a photograph, Sabine saw the woman's face in the wall. "Stop it." Sabine widened her eyes to throw off the trance.

"What did you say?" Moe had been talking with his wife, to his right.

Sabine hadn't meant to speak aloud.

"Oh, just a little prayer." She blushed, annoyed with herself for letting the spirits so easily catch her attention. All of her life, Sabine Heartwood had felt the cold spots, sensed the disturbances, and heard the wind in still places which revealed the presence of the lost. As a busker, a street performer, her mother, Ruby, told fortunes, reading Tarot cards or tea leaves, or palms. When it became evident that Sabine not only had inherited her mother's small gift of second sight, but also had an enhanced psychic capacity to sense the mysteries beyond the knowable world, Ruby had imagined a ghost-busters-style mission, traveling cross country in their lime green Volkswagen bus. "Imagine it, Beenie. Heartwood and Heartwood, 'It's Not Your Imagination' Spiritualists and **Psychic** Communicators."

It had been their largest bone of contention. All Sabine wanted was to be normal. Which is why she'd come to Moose River Junction. To live like a normal person. To have a regular job, a permanent home, and people she could call friends. The ordinary things everyone else took for granted were the things her mother's peripatetic lifestyle had made exotic and charming in Sabine's eyes. She looked around the airy room, taking satisfaction in picking out all the familiar faces. There was Greta Sutler, and her boyfriend, Arnie Sokolowski.

Over there, also checking out familiar faces, was Lynn Miller, Sabine's closest friend in Moose River Junction. Sabine wiggled discrete fingers at her friend. Her coworkers from the *Pennywise Paper,* Teddy and Balto, were standing in the back of the room, looking odd in their Sunday best. Sabine was so much more used to seeing them in their rumpled workaday state. Had they known Mrs. Danforth? Had all these people really known her? More people than ever filled a town meeting crammed into the church, Moose River Junction paying final homage to the last of its aristocracy.

The prelude was over and the congregation ceased their soft, respectful murmuring. The only sound now was the slow footsteps of the pallbearers flanking the solid cherrywood coffin. Behind it followed Beatrice Danforth's prodigal grandson, Danforth Smith. Holding him by the right hand was her surviving offspring, her late-in-life, developmentally challenged son, Nagy. Beside his tall nephew, Nagy looked more gnomelike than usual. Like everyone else, he seemed out of context all dressed up in a dark suit hastily altered to fit his stumpy legs and short arms. His grizzled gray hair had been flattened into submission. As he drifted by Sabine, she felt the palpable confusion emanate from him. He'd had half a year to understand this was going to happen. And yet, as clear as speech, Sabine knew that he didn't really understand that his mother was dead.

The pallbearers brought the casket on its wheeled bier to a dignified stop, and the organist began the introductory measures of the opening hymn. Sabine let the words sink deep into her voice, laying them against the memories she had of Beatrice Danforth. *A mighty fortress is our God, a bulwark never failing; our helper he amid the flood of mortal ills prevailing.* . . . Admittedly, she'd known her only a little, but that little seemed enough for the sorrow Sabine felt at the old woman's passing. Sabine and Moe had worked on the obituary with Mrs. Danforth. Like everything else the dying woman did, she planned the details well in advance. Of all the good works she might have listed, from trustee of the library and founder of the historical society, to second soprano in the Windsorville High School Glee Club, class of 1921, patron of the small art museum, mother and grandmother, it was her owner-ship and love of the Palace Theatre which Beatrice wished to be her best-known legacy. "Tell them all about Frederick Danforth and how he built the Palace for me."

The Palace Theatre, an Art Deco–style building with a house that might hold 350, not counting the long-dis-used balcony, now dusty and threadbare. The only movie house in town. At one time, the Palace was Moose River Junction's entertainment capital. Vaudeville, live theatre productions, then, finally, simply movies. Sabine preferred it, with its full-sized screen, to any multiplex she'd been in. At least at the Palace, the rococo decora-tions were original. And Nagy was there to make sure you took your ticket stub. Poor Nagy, a child yet in a middle-aged man's body. He looked somehow even more vulnerable dressed up like he was today. Sabine watched his nephew Dan lay a comforting arm across his shoulders.

When Dan Smith took her hand yesterday at the wake, Sabine had felt his tiredness; layered within it, she sensed a disappointment, which felt to her a separate thing from the grief he displayed in the quick, "Thank you for coming," murmured as he held onto her hand. Noting the absence of his girlfriend last night and now at the formal service, Sabine intuited the source of this dis-appointment.

The locals had been all abuzz with the return of Dan Smith. And when his sylphlike girlfriend showed up now and again, the buzz became a clamor. With Moose River Junction being just to the wrong side of the popular Berkshire destinations of Lenox and Tanglewood, and down a little from the tourist-thick Mohawk Trail, there was little to attract celebrities. Karen Whitcomb, though not quite a bona fide star, was, nonetheless, as close as the town had ever gotten. It seemed, if you listened to the gossip in the Blue Moose, that everyone had loved her in *Six Pence for Sorrow* and *Sir Westover's Victory,* two British films that had played at the Palace several times over. Karen had that dewy quality beloved in film ingenues. Nothing hard or dirty about her. Even when she swore on-screen, she did so with a peppery charm. Frankly, Sabine didn't know what all the fuss was about. To her, Karen Whitcomb was interchangeable with any other twenty-something starlet moving up from a Broadway chorus line to her name below the title. Well, it didn't matter what sort of actress she was; she didn't make it to her putative boyfriend's grandmother's funeral. And he looked like he could use the company.

Looking at the two men alone in the front pew, Sabine hoped that they were taking comfort from the words spoken solemnly by the minister.

For the last ten years, Dan had been away. Away. That's what they called it around here. He thought he was making a life in New York, but to these old friends, he was simply away. His life in New York seemed so removed from his small-town boyhood. The people he knew there were of the present. Scarcely anyone spoke of their lives before New York; everything was immediate and forward moving. Not like Moose River Junction, not like

Gran. Here history was a living thing, evidenced by the very plaques on the church's foyer walls, commemorating people and events no one still living remembered.

As a child, his bedtime stories were drawn from family legends. Beatrice's tales of Indian kidnappings and bad blood between opposing branches of the Windsor family kept him with his head under the covers on many a night. Sometimes Dan felt as if keeping away, keeping in New York, helped lighten the weight of ancient history and modern secrets. Back within the valley, where nearly everyone knew him or his grandmother, or who his parents had been and what had happened to them, the past bore down on his shoulders like a burden.

Six months ago, Gran had conceded that she was dying. At age ninety-five, it was simply the acknowledgment that something was, indeed, greater than her drive and her controlling will.

He'd gotten the call on his cell phone, in the back of a cab.

"Danforth, I need you to be here, to take care of details and the business. And Nagy."

"What's the matter? Are you in the hospital?"

"Of course not. And I won't go there."

"Are you sick? Have you fallen?"

"Danforth. The time has come for you to come home and take up the reins."

"Look, I'll be home this weekend." Dan snugged his phone against his cheek and dug out his Day-Timer. Every day presented a clutter of meetings and appointments leaking across the month, heedless of weekends. If he moved the site visit to very early on Saturday and begged off going with Karen to her friend's gallery opening in the Village on Saturday night, he could fly into Bradley International Airport in Windsor Locks, rent a car, and be in Moose River by Saturday afternoon.

"Danforth. I'm almost ninety-six; I may not have until Saturday afternoon." Beatrice's imperious voice had thinned in the last decade—the voice that commanded attention at town meetings and demanded fealty from the staff at the theatre she had taken over at her husband's death. It was also the voice that had consoled him, chided him, raised him up to manhood. Whenever anyone asked him to describe his grandmother, Dan always said "crusty."

"Gran, what exactly is wrong?"

"That bastard Doc Phillips says I have cancer."

Dan felt the blood leave his face. At her advanced age, very little would be done. Mostly because she wouldn't stand for it, even if her frailty allowed it. Alone in the back of a New York City cab, Dan felt the implosion of impending grief. She'd raised him. Loved him. She'd swallowed her disappointment when he refused to take over the theatre from her, in that callous way of youth, demanding to make his own way, follow his own desires. Never mind that she had no one else to give it to without letting it out of the family. Never mind that it was Nagy's life.

"Okay, Gran. Hang on and I'll be there soon." Dan pressed the end button and sat staring out at the passing street, Day-Timer still open, cell phone still in his hand. As often as the abstract idea of her death had crossed his mind, Dan was amazed at his naïveté faced now with the concrete fact. He had thought that it would be sad but that he would be okay. He truly hadn't expected the pain.

Being in the film industry had given him a view of life as mise-en-scène. The scriptwriter bending to the will of the director, everything and everyone in their places.

And then Beatrice Windsor Danforth had called him home. Since that day, Dan felt that he was working blind. The scriptwriter of his life would not give him a rewrite. He was without a director, and the actors in his life would not listen to him. Worse, the script called for all the conceits of *It's A Wonderful Life*. He didn't want to be here, yet he couldn't abandon his responsibilities.

Dan kept his eyes on the place just in front of the altar. He didn't want to make eye contact with anyone, especially the minister, fearful that he would be unmanned by this outpouring of sympathy. Nagy's hand in his was sweaty, and he felt his own perspiration mingle with his uncle's. The September heat wave had become the stuff of legend. A week of unrelenting eighty and above. Not more than a warmish breeze off the hillsides to leaven it, warm even at night. And yet, Gran had been cold. He'd wanted to buy her an air conditioner, but she wanted another blanket. He'd sat in that room for days, the windows closed, the air so still you felt as if you could touch it, move it aside like a curtain. Downstairs he could hear the sounds of the neighbors, bringing dish after dish of casseroles and lasagna. Sometimes stifled laughter would reach his ears and he would smile, wishing he could be down there, mingling with whoever was taking care of "things" today, of Nagy. Of himself.

Dan let go of Nagy's hand and patted his back. At once he felt the absence of Karen and bit back the resentment. She'd been there, on and off, to help where she could. Not that there was much she could do; she was shy of Gran, a little nervous with Nagy. Her chief contribution had been reminding him that he had another life, one not filled with dying grandmothers and challenged uncles. One in which he was climbing determinedly upward.

Hopefully, he'd worked his last stint as first assistant director. There were murmurs that his work had caught the eye of a producer and his name was on the lips of those who could raise him from glorified grunt work to top dog. It helped, though he hadn't planned it, that he squired around one of New York's most interesting new faces. Karen Whitcomb, on the verge herself of moving from the stage to the big screen, was more than arm candy. Talented, bright, beautiful, she was in the same place he was career-wise. As she was one good film away from stardom, so he was one project away from a solid reputation as a director.

Except that he'd disappeared for six months. A very detrimental career move. Karen, however, had gotten a call to audition for Redford.

"Of course you have to go," Dan had insisted, relieving Karen of having to look bad. In his heart, he knew that there was no way she'd jeopardize this opportunity, no way she'd choose being by his side at this moment over a career move of this magnitude. He couldn't blame her and wouldn't put her in the position of feeling even the least guilty about it.

"Dan, if you're sure." She'd covered the tiny cell phone in her hand, and it occurred to him that her agent was still on the line.

"I'd go if it was me."

"Marty, I'll fly out as soon as I can get to an airport." Karen covered the phone again. "Dan, where do I fly out of? Logan or Bradley?"

Upstairs Dan could hear the shuffle of black-shod feet, the funeral director and his associate carefully bundling the frail, tiny form of Beatrice Danforth into a body bag. "Umm. I don't know. Logan."

Dan dragged his attention back to the moment and

opened his hymnal as the organist played the introductory measures of "The King of Love My Shepherd Is." The choice of music had been Gran's. As had been the selection of daisies and freesia, peonies and late roses. "No funeral flowers for me. I want garden flowers, the sort the flower guild picks for Sunday services."

She'd been pretty strong at first, and until late April he'd gone back and forth between New York and Moose River Junction, clearing his calendar Friday through Monday. Then, as the cancer took a firmer grip on her, he stayed. And, as the months passed, it seemed to Dan as if the town had taken a firmer grip on him.

Without meaning to, Dan glanced past Nagy to the coffin. Such a large box to hold the tiny remains of Gran. She had never seemed so small to him until that day he came back and she was standing in her kitchen, apron tied around her waist, a waist still so tiny, the apron crossed itself in the back. Beatrice had looked a long time at him before speaking, as if she was unsure he was actually there.

"Gran?"

"It's about time."

He'd bent to embrace her and all at once understood that though she loomed large in his history, she was truly a little scrap of a woman.

Arthur Bean, in his dual capacity as old family friend and unofficial town leader, now got up to give the eulogy. Arthur had been quick to recruit Dan back into the volunteer fire department once it became clear that Dan would be in town for a few months.

"You were a good fireman before you got to be an all-high-and-mighty city boy."

"I haven't put out a fire in nearly ten years."

"Then just drive the truck."

That was the first, and perhaps deepest, hook into him. Arthur knew that Dan Smith would be hard-pressed to say no where the volunteer fire department was concerned.

Arthur's message was short, filled with the accolades Beatrice Danforth had earned after a lifetime of service to the town, and even a little humorous. Dan smiled, glad that his fire chief had been willing to do the eulogy. He couldn't think of anyone he'd rather have had do it.

At last the service was over, and Dan and Nagy followed the casket back up the aisle. Dan felt the hands that reached out to pat his shoulder, nodded his head in gentle acknowledgment of the support, stopped along the way for quick hugs from his old teachers and former teammates.

As he reached the last pair of box pews he noticed Sabine Heartwood standing there, her brown eyes glittery with sympathy. Looking at him as if, beyond his natural grief at his grandmother's passing, she understood what difficult decisions awaited him.

Two

Saturday, April 22, 2000

"That's my elementary school. I bet if we went in, it would still have the same smell of chalk, paste, and floor polish that it always had."

"All schools seem to smell alike. Don't you think?" Karen ran an emery board along the underside of her manicured nail. She was annoyed that her fresh manicure had been so easily ruined when she'd tried to undo the clasp on her overnight bag.

"Yeah, probably. And it would certainly look smaller."

"Naturally."

Dan drove past the school with its ugly chain-link fence surrounding the paved playground. Things had been tight economically for years, and the few town improvements he could see were on the order of a new flagpole in front of the town hall and the four-bay fire barn just on the outskirts of town. He'd wanted to stop and poke his head into this new facility, but the bored look on Karen's face warned him off giving into his curiosity. Though Gran had told him nearly a decade ago that they were building it, this was the first time he'd been home long enough to take a look at it. He wondered for a moment if old Engine Three was still running. Dan was certain it was Engine Three's running board where he'd been left to sit, wrapped in a scratchy wool blanket on that cold January night.

Dan's memories of the fire that killed his parents when he was six were shocky images like vignettes, stylized impressions augmented by other people's memories. He remembered being carried. He remembered sitting on the running board, wrapped in the blanket. In his mind's eye he still saw the rotating lights of the fire trucks as they speared the darkness with lurid red. There was no sense of time passing. He might have sat there for a minute or an hour staring up at those lights, watching the tongues of flame lick out of the upstairs windows. His childish fascination was held by the methodical way the firemen kept the thrashing hoses on the fire, sweeping the streams from window to window, and by how the firemen hacked away at the doors with their massive axes. He simply hadn't realized his parents weren't behind him, watching with the same fascination.

Nagy had been sleeping at their house that night, as he often did. The boys, one a child, the other childlike, had been sleeping in the back bedroom over the kitchen. Dan's parents slept in the downstairs bedroom and were probably dead of smoke inhalation before the flames from the basement even reached the first floor.

Dan remembered being carried again, this time to his grandmother's car. "I can walk." Dan remembered saying that, probably the only words he'd said at all. A fireman, a man he now knew was Arthur Bean, carried him in his arms the short distance to Gran's Lincoln, where Nagy waited in the backseat, a blanket also wrapped around him against the January cold. Dan still hadn't been told that his parents were gone. It had been left to Gran to tell him that his mother—her daughter—and his father were dead. Arthur had placed him in the big car and pinned a little plastic "deputy fireman" badge on his pajamas. The fireman had then ruffled Dan's hair and closed the door.

Nagy had seen the badge and touched it with one finger. "Can I wear that sometimes when we play fireman?" Nagy, his eyes a little crusty from being wakened in the middle of the night. A twenty-something child, distracted from the fact his sister and her husband and their unborn babe had perished, by the gift of a plastic badge.

"I want to show you something." Dan signaled for a left and headed down Maple Street. He wanted to show Karen more than the ordinary childhood landmarks. It seemed to be the right time to point out something more significant.

"I really should be making some phone calls."

"It won't take long."

Maple Street dead-ended at the confluence of Windsor's Brook and Moose River. A winter of heavy snows and a mild spring had sent the brook into torrent, and its racing waters were audible beyond the tangle of vines and bramble that had grown up since the fire. There was nothing there now, just an empty lot slowly filling with woody regrowth and wildflowers growing in the remnants of foundation. "I've considered nailing a plaque to that remaining maple tree: FREDERICKA AND GARY SMITH MEMORIAL PARK." Dan took Karen by the hand and circled around to the former driveway, which was still passable. "It's still mine, as the surviving heir. I pay the taxes on it. Gran always says someday I'll build my house here and raise a family." He kept his voice slightly amused, not wanting to give credence to Gran's viewpoint or alarm Karen with such a wildly domestic suggestion. "I suppose that eventually I could build a summer house here."

"Why?"

"A getaway place."

"Won't you inherit the house she lives in?"

Dan let go of Karen's hand and bent to pick up a piece of paper caught in a branch. "No. That's Nagy's house. Or it will be."

"Wouldn't he be better off in a—you know—a school or something?"

Dan crumpled the piece of wilted paper and stuffed it into his pocket. "No." It suddenly seemed too monumental to explain to Karen just how determined Gran was about that. His whole life, he'd heard how Nagy was never to be institutionalized. He was just "slow," not retarded. Special. Sometimes Dan thought the reason she'd lived so long, and had been so strong, was because of Nagy. Her will to keep him at home and healthy was self-strengthening. Now, all that was coming to an end. Even so, she was a fighter, ordering him about, crabbing at the home health aid who came to help her bathe, demanding that Dan take her to the theatre every evening, just as she had always done. Her one concession to the insidious disease crawling up her spine had been to stop driving.

"Karen, I have to stay on here. I can't keep going back to the city."

Karen hadn't rejoined his hand with hers. She stood

at the bank of Windsor's Brook, staring down the winding length to its juncture with the Moose River. The water was muddy brown, cluttered with debris from the hills, a yellowy froth churned up along the bank. The April air was chilly in the late afternoon, moist with future rain. The early buds were a poor screen disguising the broken foundation of the house that once was there. "How long?"

"As long as it takes. I don't know."

"Can I remind you that out of sight . . ."

"Means out of mind." Dan threw a rock into the raucous water. "Whose mind are you thinking of?"

"I'm just saying." Karen took her hand out of her pocket and linked it with Dan's. "You have to be careful in this business. I know you have to do what's right for your family. Of course I understand that."

"So, as you say, out of sight."

"Look, I'm not trying to start a fight here. I'm just making an observation about the business we're in."

"I know." Dan squeezed Karen's hand in his. "We should get back." It suddenly didn't seem as important for Karen to see this place. What was past was past. Someday he'd tell her the whole story, instead of the edited-down version he had given her. He led her away through the tangled path and back to the car.

Gran called Karen the showgirl. "How's your showgirl?"

"Gran, she's an actress."

"But you told me she's been in musical theatre."

"Showgirls are more like what goes on in Las Vegas."

"In my time, any young woman who danced and sang was a showgirl."

It was one of their convoluted conversations. "She's

like all the rest I knew. Your grandfather worked with many of them." One hand cupping her mouth into a stage whisper, "Not very *nice*." Meaning they weren't virgins.

Dan tried to laugh it off, but sometimes it was more annoying than endearing, this bringing of early-twentieth-century sensibilities into the next century.

Karen wasn't unaware of Beatrice's disdain. With the tips of his fingers, Dan traced the tension in Karen's thin, rigid shoulders, her pearly skin illuminated in the late afternoon sunlight coming through the bedroom windows.

"Maybe if you tried talking theatre with her . . . I mean, she's an original. She's been there, done that, long before talkies."

"Dan, we're worlds away from any common ground. She sang operatic arias in concert halls, your grandfather danced in vaudeville. She quit when she got married. *She* was a nice girl." Karen rolled over to face him.

"Why do you make *nice* sound so evil?" Dan took one of her nipples in his mouth and gave a little growl.

Karen slapped him away and moved off the bed. "I can't do this here."

"Oh, come on. She's napping, and half-deaf."

"Dan." Karen sat on the edge of the bed. "I'm going home. You do what you have to do. But I need to be home."

"Will you come back?"

Karen smoothed back her russet-colored hair from her cheeks. "Will you?"

Dan watched Karen gather up her things and stuff them into the overnight bag. Underwear, cosmetics, her boar bristle brush, all gathered into her arms and then dumped into the hard case. A strange doziness kept him from trying to talk her out of going. He should have wanted her to stay, a comrade in arms against this invisible enemy, death. The truth was, he felt pulled with her there. Gran demanding so much attention, and Karen, by virtue of her profession and personality, needing equal time. Dan simply didn't have it in him. He closed his eyes.

"Can you tell me how I'm going to get home?" The practical issue of departure had finally arisen.

"I'll fly back with you. I can leave Gran's car in short-term parking, get some of my stuff, and come back tomorrow night." Dan flipped the sheet off and bent to retrieve his boxers. "I'm sure she's okay to leave for that long."

"Just take me as far as the airport. I'll send what you need." Karen's voice was actress-neutral. No emotion evident.

He looked at her to judge the disposition of this offer. Was she angry or compassionate? Karen had on her black jeans and grapefruit pink cashmere sweater, and was bending to zip up the side of her dangerously pointed ankle boot. "Karen. This isn't forever."

She fumbled a little with the second boot, then sighed and reached over to take Dan's hand. "I know. I know I have to be patient."

Nagy wanted to go with them to the airport. "Please? I like to see the planes."

Dan could feel Karen's instant stiffening up at the suggestion. One of two sisters from a cultured New York family, all East Side and private schools, Karen's experience with people like Nagy was limited to the occasional handout to a homeless person on the street. No eye contact. She was the same with his uncle, not unkind, just tense, as if what Nagy had might be catching. Karen didn't say anything, but her discomfort was obvious at having Nagy go with them. When Gran was younger she and Nagy had driven all over, but it had been years since he'd been beyond the borders of Moose River Junction. Even when Dan had come to visit, they'd pretty much stayed put.

"Please, Danny?" Nagy gripped his poplin jacket as if he were about to wring it out.

"Sure, hop in the back. I'll let Gran know you're with us." Dan walked away quickly, leaving the pair of them standing by the car.

"So, she's going." With her hands resting on the back of a kitchen chair, Gran was looking out the kitchen window where she could watch the bird feeder, but Dan knew it had been the three of them standing in the driveway that had kept her attention.

"She's got a lot of stuff to do in the city, and . . ."

"She's not very comfortable here."

"Gran, you don't try to make her very comfortable." Dan didn't mean to sound accusatory.

"Are you going to marry her?"

Six wooden pegs were attached to the wall beside the back door. Dan noted his old NYU baseball cap hanging there. He couldn't remember how long it had been since he'd seen that hat. He reached for it now and gave the bill a little inward flex. Putting it on, he turned to his grandmother, trying hard to keep in mind her age and condition. "Gran. I think I might. So be nice."

"She'll never be happy living here." Beatrice defined the word *imperious* with her lifted chin, but now a slight tremor moved it side to side.

"I wouldn't ask that of her." Dan grasped the back doorknob, desperate to get away before she made her

inevitable demand of him. As yet, the topic of the theatre hadn't been addressed. He was in no mood to get
into that conversation when he had so little time to deal
with it. The car doors had slammed; Karen and Nagy
were waiting for him. "I'll take Nagy out for supper,
and there's a plate of leftovers for you ready to
microwave. If you need anything, I have my cell phone.
Maisie said she'd check in before going to the theatre."

"How will I get there tonight?"

"Gran, don't. You know you have to rest."

"I'm dying, Danforth. That's rest enough."

Dan took a deep breath and let it out slowly. "Then go
with Maisie. I'll pick you up when I get back."

Beatrice let go of the back of the kitchen chair, coming around to sit in it. "I'll be fine. Go take your girlfriend to the airport."

Dan bent to kiss her paper-dry cheek.

Three

❧

Tuesday, June 13, 2000

It was finally warm enough for Gran to sit outside. Happily ensconced on the padded chaise longue, her own handmade afghan tucked around her and a pink bed jacket over her shoulders, Beatrice began to order Dan and Nagy around. "You've got to clean out all of that mulch before you set the plants." "Now, Dan, I want that old juniper out and a nice yew in its place." "Nagy, you've got to bend over to get all those mucky leaves out from under the bushes. You can do it."

The doctor had mentioned that Dan might see some personality changes, that she could become argumentative and combative as the cancer made its inexorable way to her brain. *I'll be hard-pressed to notice a difference,* Dan thought as the physician handed him some literature. All his life, those two adjectives seemed to sum up Beatrice Danforth. Of course, in public her combativeness had helped save critical conservation areas, and her argumentativeness had turned the tables on more than one ill-considered town project. Like the demolition of the old fire house. "Throw a little money into it. One of these days you'll be glad you have the space." Yet not once had Beatrice crowed about being right so often. Not even when it was suddenly apparent that the old fire barn was still needed for the newly purchased second rescue vehicle and, with the installation of an elevator, the upstairs meeting room was perfect for various community meetings.

Dan, incrementally finding himself in deeper than he wanted, began to see Beatrice's legendary involvement as her living legacy to him. When talk first came up about purchasing a defibrillator for the primary rescue vehicle, Dan agreed it was a good idea, then suddenly found himself chairing the fund-raising committee. Was it heredity that made his right arm go up and his voice, detached and alien, volunteer to be of service? Some insidious particle of DNA causing him to entangle himself in projects he'd be better off running away from? Three months in Moose River and he was back on the volunteer fire department, running its campaign to buy a defibrillator, ushering at the South Congregational Church one Sunday a month, and playing basketball one afternoon a week with the Holiday Crafts and Hobbies pick-up team. And that was all before the theatre demanded his attention. Gran had been running it for so long that it was a painful surprise to find that things had deteriorated so much.

In his mind's eye, the Palace remained a place of red-and-gold beauty; the flocked wallpaper vaguely Chinese in pattern, the massive central chandelier in the small lobby sparkling with its candle-shaped lights. In reality, the wallpaper was stained where the roof leaked and the chandelier was much smaller, and fully a third of its hard-to-replace lights were missing. The books were in worse shape.

Built in the midst of the Roaring Twenties, the Palace Theatre had been Frederick Danforth's dream. Originally built as a vaudeville theatre, it had attracted class acts from all over the world to the sleepy little Berkshire town. Even Houdini had played this Palace. In the thirties, a screen was hung behind the heavy red velvet curtains and the house filled to capacity night after night to watch romance and adventure for a little while. In the forties, newsreels kept the town informed about progress in Europe and the Pacific, and a bond drive was organized, offering free admission on Wednesday nights to those purchasing war bonds.

By now, the ancient screen had permanent marks on it from generations of jujube shooters and the velvet curtains were but a faded memory to the few seniors who came in. Dan wondered if he was inheriting a white elephant, outdated, crumbling, and playing to a diminishing audience. Many people would rather trek the twenty miles into Springfield and have six choices on a Saturday night—hence, the threatened pulling out of the distribution company. Dan had discovered their unopened letter on the broad partner's desk in the theatre office. By a quirk of the business, he knew someone who knew someone, and metaphorically put out the fire with a couple of phone calls.

But that begged the greater question. What was he going to do when Gran finally gave up her battle and he was left with the Palace? More important, left as custodian for Nagy.

It had taken her nearly six weeks to finally make her wishes known. "Danforth, will you make us a cup of tea and sit with me for a little while? I want to tell you what's in my will."

Dan knew better than to argue with her, to tell her it

didn't matter, that he could wait a long time to hear it. Beatrice wouldn't have tolerated such a line. Also, he didn't think he'd hear too many surprises. He expected her to describe some bequests to favorite causes, maybe a gift or two to friends of her treasured objects; a nice working up to the meat of the subject. So it did surprise him that she got right to the point without preamble.

"As you know, Nagy lives here, with you as his legal guardian. The house will then revert to you on his death." Beatrice's voice was firm and without the tendency of late to quaver at the end of the day. "You, as my only other heir, will have the theatre. Now, Dan, I know that you have other plans, but it is important that you keep the theatre a going concern. We owe it to Moose River Junction; we owe it to ourselves to keep it in the family. Do I have your promise?"

Dan shook his head. "How can I promise that, Gran? I have a life which you well know, isn't centered here. I'm glad to be here now, but I can't stay indefinitely."

"I have no one else to turn to, Danforth. You must take up the responsibility for Nagy, and for the theatre. It's all he has, it's his life. I won't accept that he be forced at his age into an institution. I can't accept that you, of all people, would abandon not only your family but your heritage. The Palace is your legacy." Beatrice sat forward in her wing back chair, the teacup rattling a little as her hands shook with the palsy of old age. They sat in front of the fireplace, cold now in the warm June night. "Your grandfather built that theatre for this town. At one time, it was the visual high point of East Main Street, the only building constructed since the mid-nineteenth century with an eye for style and architectural significance. It still is. Would you have it close and be boarded up simply because you think you want to be elsewhere?

Married to an actress." She spat the last word out like lint on the tongue.

"Gran. I am aware of all of this; I will do what's best for Nagy, and for the Palace. But I may not be able to do it the way you've done it."

"How would you do it?"

Dan set his cup down on the tea tray and leaned forward as well. He gently removed her teacup and grasped his grandmother's hands. "I don't know. But I promise I won't let anything happen to Nagy."

"A broken heart is something which happens."

"He's more resilient than you think." Dan picked up the tea tray. "Is there anything else I should know about your will?"

"I'm giving Maisie Ralston my diamond brooch. She's been a faithful friend all these years and she deserves something pretty."

"No argument there. I love Maisie, she's been like an aunt to me."

"Then don't take her job away from her."

Dan decided to pretend he hadn't heard that. It almost felt like sorrow, this grip around his heart caused by what could escalate into a very divisive last few months with Gran. It wasn't worth it. He'd make her last weeks happy by playing along. When she was gone, well, then he'd have time to figure out whether or not he could keep his promise.

In the meantime he'd keep the struggling theatre open, do some repairs on it during the day, and take his grandmother there every night to put up the deposit as she had been doing since 1924. Maybe that's why she thought the place was a going concern. Some nights, the deposit in 2000 was the same as the one from 1924. Except that in '24, the fifty dollars represented a full house and now it might be ten people. In '24, fifty dollars paid the mortgage and monthly salaries. Today, it didn't even cover the cost of doing business for one night.

Dan went back out into the yard to collect Gran from where she dozed on the chaise longue.

Four

❧

Saturday, July 15, 2000

The July afternoon faded slowly in a long succulent sunset, all streaks of red and gold, a band of royal blue threaded between the layers. The hills surrounding the town were verdant with summer leaves. Sabine lay in her bikini on a towel in her backyard and soaked in the last warm rays of sun. She felt mildly decadent, the warmth coddling her all afternoon as she read and napped. It felt good to do nothing, yet with plans ahead. Tonight she and Lynn would get a bite at the Blue Moose and then go see the second showing of the new movie at the Palace. It was a pretty ordinary way to spend a Saturday night, but it suited Sabine. When she'd first settled into Moose River Junction and begun making friends, those new friends loved nothing better than to set her up. It was as if nature, which abhorred a vacuum, also, in Moose River Junction, abhorred an unattached female. Cousins and step-brothers, friends of friends had been given her number until Sabine had put her foot down. It wasn't that having a companion wasn't important to her, it was just that the effort was tiring. Making small talk, trying to find common ground, mostly talking about the person who had set them up. Dissuading some from the assumption that a beautiful, unattached female was automatically interested in sex; persuading one or two that she was. But none had ever given her that little click of "yeah, this is the guy." Approaching thirty, she was philosophical about it. Without the click she wasn't going to settle for compatible.

Johnny Reid had been her last boyfriend before she'd packed up and settled here. Ruby was living in Revere at the time, and Sabine roomed with two other women in an apartment in Allston. Sabine had always liked the Boston area, and had been thinking she might stay there. She had a nice job at an ad agency, and an appropriate social life for someone in her mid-twenties.

A handsome if beefy computer programmer working for John Hancock, Johnny Reid had been a football star in college until he'd permanently damaged a tendon. He and Sabine had met, as it seemed all young Bostonians did, in a bar. Sabine was in the pub with chums from the office, and Johnny had come up to her as she sat at the bar waiting for her Sam Adams to be poured. "I'm Johnny Reid. Can I buy that for you?" He was so practiced at this, so self-assured, that Sabine knew right away that very few women said no to him.

"No, thank you."

"Then perhaps your next?"

"No. Thank you."

"I come with references."

Sabine slid off the bar stool, trying not to smile.

"You know, this is the general idea of coming to a

place like this. To meet nice people. I'm pretty nice."
Johnny didn't follow Sabine, but his voice rose over the
din of the happy hour crowd.

Sabine spun around, a little of the foam slipping over
the side of her glass and trickling down to her fingers.
"And as soon as I sit down with my friends, you'll come
up alongside the next woman who goes to that bar and
say the same things to her. I have no evidence that you are
interested in me as a person. You have come in here to
score, and I attracted you." Sabine still held a smile in
check. It was her stock response to a stock situation.

"How can I know if I'm interested in you as a person,
if I can't sit with you for ten minutes and talk?" Johnny's
voice had lowered and he'd come over to stand in front
of Sabine. There was something in his expression that
substantiated this remark with furrowed brow and
twisted smile. "Please?"

Sabine relented and gestured to her friends, watching
intently from the little table in the middle of the room.
"Ten minutes."

Ten minutes became almost a year, until one day
Sabine woke up and realized that the relationship was
going nowhere. Their routine had hardly changed from
when they first met. Bar hopping, and sports on
Sundays. He didn't like museums or movies, and Johnny
really didn't like Ruby.

"She makes me nervous." Coming from a traditional
South Boston family, Johnny couldn't comprehend the
free-spirited Ruby Heartwood. His mother centered
herself with her family. Ruby centered herself with candles and aromatherapy.

"That's ridiculous. She's a little outlandish, but harmless." Sabine hated defending her mother. She'd been
doing it all her life. *My mother's not weird.* How many

childhood experiences invoked those words? Well, her mother *was* weird, but she wasn't going to have this failed football player make her feel bad. "At least she likes you. Your mother barely tolerates me."

"That's so not true."

"Really. I know what she calls me." Sabine had from the first known that Mrs. Reid would never accept her as her son's partner. She'd taken one look at Sabine's olive complexion and curly black hair and made assumptions that could only have come from race memory, not experience. "Black Irish" she called Sabine. An epithet implying a Spanish Gypsy taint in her blood. Far from hurting Sabine, though, Mrs. Reid had only provoked curiosity. A curiosity that, as always, went unanswered by Ruby.

"Are we Irish? Are we Gypsy? You used to say that when I was little; you told me wonderful stories of being raised by Gypsies."

"Bedtime stories, Sabine, nothing more."

"Why the secrecy? I'm old enough to be told the truth."

"What is the truth? Anything is possible. We are blank slates on which to write ancestry."

All of her life, Sabine had been hungry for details of her heritage, not knowing who her father was, or where Ruby had sprung from. Ruby had been evasive and obtuse about the subject, leaving Sabine to ultimately make her own assumptions. Ruby had seemed a little rattled when Sabine confronted her with Mrs. Reid's accusation, though. It was enough to prompt her to press Ruby a little harder. "Mom, is it because you're ashamed of being a Gypsy that you won't admit that we are?"

"Don't be ridiculous. There is no shame in any race. There are just things which must remain in mystery."

"Why?"

Ruby, as always, had no answer but a stagy sigh and shrug. "When it is time, I will tell you."

Sabine gave up. Short of tying her mother up and torturing her, there was no point in pursuing the matter. Not now. Not yet.

In the end, Sabine and Johnny had broken up easily, neither one more than a little saddened to see the relationship dissolve. They promised to remain friends but lost touch quickly. Sabine had moved to Moose River Junction. Johnny had gotten married. Evidently he'd found the one with the click.

A tiny little part of Sabine worried that her disconnected upbringing had spoiled her from ever attaching herself too deeply to anyone. She simply didn't have the example of lasting friends or extended family to learn how to be attached. For as long as Sabine could remember, it had been only Ruby and herself. To this day, she could only recall anecdotes about neighbors or clients, not friends. When she began to make friends as a child, she would soon be whisked away. By the time she was in high school, Sabine had learned how to be friendly without giving her heart away. It was only when she was in college, spending the longest period of time in her life in one place, that Sabine allowed herself to form attachments. But after graduation, even those friends slipped away to their new lives, and Sabine and Ruby were once again all alone.

When Sabine and Johnny broke up, she knew that it was time to make a significant change in her life.

Ruby took a different spin on Sabine's declaration. "Absolutely, I think we should think about heading out somewhere we've never been before. It's more than time to go."

"No. I'm not going, Ruby. You go. Keep moving. I'm going to find the place I'll call home forever."

"You think that Boston is that place?" Ruby's voice was soft, yielding to irony over sarcasm. "Don't be mistaken. There's nothing for you here."

Sabine pulled her hands away from her mother's grip. "No. I don't know where I'm going, but I swear, once I get there, it will be the last time I move."

"Then choose carefully. Let me read your cards."

"Ruby, I'm going to choose by myself. No cards, no tea leaves, nothing but finding the place which . . ." Sabine hunted around for the words, none of which had ever been organized in her mind before. "I'm going to find my home." With those words, she suddenly remembered Moose River Junction and the little drugstore with the penny candy counter. Ruby had let her walk down the street by herself, a monumental event in seven-year-old Sabine's life. Her first taste of independence. She'd quickly fetched up in front of Carlson's Pharmacy, with its enormous display of penny candy. She remembered the proprietor leaning over the counter, holding out the white bag filled with her selection of goodies and saying, "Come again, little lady."

"Don't mistake sentiment with reality."

"How can you, of all people, question my reality?" Sabine hadn't even mentioned Moose River Junction and already Ruby was ready to argue about it.

"I just don't want to see you get hurt."

"By what? Living like a grown-up on my own, and in a place where I can stay long enough to register to vote?"

"By living against your nature."

Sabine sat up and gathered her blanket and books. It was getting late and she wanted to shower off the sunblock she'd used. Jerry the cat was sitting on the newel post of the landing for her second-floor apartment, waiting to be let in. Climbing up the outside stairs, Sabine felt again that oddly thrilling sense of being at home. This was her place, her nest. Her refuge. Hers alone, and she had filled it with the objects of permanency. When she had looked at the one-bedroom apartment in the converted attic of the Fishers' 1850s farmhouse, Sabine had loved its emptiness. She would furnish it with her own secondhand furniture purchased at the many antique stores in the area. No furnished apartment for her, never again.

Carefully selected vintage photographs graced one whitewashed wall. Sabine called them instant ancestors, and would have been surprised if anyone had pointed out that each woman had her oval face and each man her dark eyes. They stared out from the gallery, unsmiling, formal portraits and washed-out amateur candids captured by traveling photographers in the mid-nineteenth century with their boxy Kodak cameras. Ignorant of the relative fame or reputation of any of the photographers, Sabine just liked the pictures: farm families, and the apron-wrapped proprietor of a long-gone butcher shop; her favorite was of a woman sitting casually under a great maple tree, her skirts fanned out. She was holding a small dog in her arms and must have moved at a critical time because her face was blurred, her image softened into a wispy ghost.

The living room was the largest of the three rooms, and boasted two windows that overlooked the country lane and the farm's former hay field, now growing raised ranches in quarter-acre proliferation. By virtue of her job, Sabine had scored an almost-new futon before it was advertised in the *Pennywise Paper*.

A four-poster bed filled most of the small bedroom, leaving but a footstep between it and the bureau. On the bed was a small stuffed rabbit. Its brown-and-white head lolled to one side, the stuffing long since degraded into its lumpy body.

If Ruby had been disappointed at Sabine's decision to settle down, she was mystified at her daughter's choice of this tiny western Massachusetts town. Moose River Junction was a town they had stopped in once to have a tire repaired, as they were on their way from one place to another. Ruby said it was a place good enough for a pit stop, to eat and fill the tank of the Volkswagen bus, but not big enough to consider setting up shop. A town north of nowhere and south of somewhere else.

"What are you thinking, moving to that postage stamp of a backwater? How will you make a living? You can't waste your life like that. At the very least, if you don't want to go with me to California, then settle in some city." Ruby disdained the country. Wherever they had traveled, they always stopped to set up Ruby's fortune-telling business in large communities. Addicted to Laura Ingalls Wilder novels, Sabine implored her mother to find them a place in the country where she could ride a bike down country lanes and maybe learn to ride a horse. She'd play with other children on the banks of a stream, build a tree house, even have a pet. "Small towns aren't good for the business. You need lots of foot traffic," was Ruby's reply. Sabine, with adolescent cynicism, once told her mother that the reason she needed cities was so that she wouldn't run out of gullible dupes.

"Ruby, I need to do this. I don't want to spend my life on the road."

They had been sitting in her mother's vintage Volkswagen bus. Ruby's fingers gripped the steering wheel, her enormous glass-and-silver rings digging deep in her fragile flesh. Her cascading black curls shook with the force of her emotion, threatening to dislodge the wig she always wore.

"I can't do it without you."

"Yes, you can. You've done it without me before, like when I was away at college."

"But then I always knew you'd come home."

"Ruby, I won't even go into how I've never had a home. A proper home."

"A Donna Reed home. That's what you've always wanted."

"Something like that."

Maybe not Donna Reed, the quintessential mom, dad, and two point five children, but a place where she could hang her Abba posters without worrying how to get them off the wall without tearing them. A place where she might get to call someone a best friend.

Sabine felt Ruby's feelings enter her own. She unbuckled her seat belt and leaned over to kiss her mother's cheek. "Mom, it's for the best. You have always said I had great instincts."

"I meant for the business."

"Didn't you foresee that I would do this?"

"You know it's hard to read people close to you; there's too much clutter. I should have read your Tarot instead of your palms. Maybe I should have learned how to interpret astrology—I could have done your chart and then you'd know if this was the right move."

"Ruby, you're a fake but I love you."

"You'll be back."

"Check your cards, Ruby. Read them carefully and you will see that this is where I'll be happy."

To Sabine, Moose River Junction was perfect. Barely a

town, it was nestled in a narrow valley between two of the Berkshire hills of western Massachusetts. It was hard to decide if the town boasted a slightly forgotten-by-time appearance, or whether it simply had yet to be discovered. Not all that far from the draw of Tanglewood and Lenox, and the beauty of the Mohawk Trail, Moose River Junction still managed to be a widely unknown and unchanged little town. No Starbucks, only Dunkin' Donuts. No mall. Just a main street which split in two at the small green into East Main and West Main. It had ordinary businesses like Perrotti's Market and Drysdale's Hardware Store. At either end of the green were white steepled churches known as South Congregational and North Congregational, and in the middle of East Main was a movie theatre, the Palace. The green and its churches, along with the few remaining ancient homesteads arrayed alongside, made up a small historic district with a nearby burial ground filled with people who had lived, loved, and died right here.

Sabine touched one of her photos back into alignment on the wall and went to jump into the shower. Afterward, still a little damp, she threw on jeans and a sleeveless jersey. One of the best things of such a casual Saturday was not having to think about what to wear. No heaps of rejected choices cluttering the bed. Nothing but lipstick on her face. Sabine pulled a white cotton sweater out of her bureau against the cooling July evening.

Just as she was about to open the back door, her phone rang. Without having to be a psychic, Sabine knew it would be her mother, Ruby. "Hi, Mom."

"Beenie, I just wanted to touch base with you before you went out."

"I don't want to be late, so maybe I should call you tomorrow."

"You're just meeting a girlfriend, so I don't think you should worry."

It never surprised Sabine that her mother would be so certain of her plans. It was the bond between them, this *knowing*. "Okay. Two minutes."

Ruby's calls were mostly chat about clients and places. Right now she was in San Francisco, doing readings in a tearoom. Sabine expected the usual gossip about people she didn't know, and usually she looked forward to these chats, but tonight she felt edgy. Almost as if Ruby were preventing her from something important.

"I've been dreaming about you for the past few nights."

"I'm flattered."

"No, I mean premonition dreams. Not junk dreams." Sabine could hear Ruby inhale as she lit a cigarette.

"Okay, I'll bite. Good or bad?"

"That's what's so disturbing: a little of both. Happiness, unhappiness, and then something in between."

"Can you be more specific? Maybe I'm going to a movie I'll hate. But dinner with Lynn will be fun. Then maybe we'll get ice cream and I'll enjoy it but feel guilty."

"Beenie, I wish you'd take me seriously. Go out, but be careful. Something significant is coming along. I just don't know what or when."

"Mom, I'm not a client. You don't have to play word games with me." What Sabine found most distasteful in the whole profession was the way a reader couched terms in such profound generalities that a client was bound to view his or her fortune as coming true. You'll meet a man. You'll struggle, but then be okay. Yada. Yada. Yada. "Do you see danger ahead?"

"Not physical danger, no."

It was the most significant dichotomy in her life that while she disdained Ruby's fortune-telling, she knew that it was often accurate. This psychic phenomenon, this ability to perceive the unknowable, was very real despite Ruby's playacting and drama. Sabine, for all her chiding of her mother as a fake, knew there were certain truths to what she did. Sabine knew this because she, too, from a very early age, could foresee. Each time she dealt out the cards, Sabine imagined she heard her mother's cigarette-worn voice, whispering, "You have the gift. Don't squander it by denying it exists."

Ruby had always made it a policy to tell people what she foresaw, but only in terms muffled with vagueness. "You don't want them to be afraid, and you don't want them to expect specifics. You are as human as they are and you are not infallible. If you see something and misinterpret it, your credibility is shot. So, you must never be specific. And, if you see a death, you say nothing." Sabine knew that her own rate of accuracy was even greater than Ruby's. Sometimes she cluttered up the truth of what she was seeing with harmless predictions, when what she really saw was too painful or unpleasant for the client. Even yesterday, she'd edited herself as Greta Sutler offered her palm.

"Sabine, any chance you could do a reading for me?" Greta leaned over Sabine's desk at the *Pennywise Paper,* her stiff blond hair winging away from her small face. Greta worked at the Holiday Crafts and Hobbies factory and was delivering the weekly copy for their advertisement in the *Pennywise Paper.* "I think that Arnie's going to pop the question."

"Then what do you need me for? You already seem to have divined the future." Sabine couldn't help but tease

Greta. To her thinking, Greta was much too young to be hoping Arnie was going to propose.

"What should I tell him?"

"Greta, I can't take responsibility for your decision."

"Then just do it for fun. Just tell me if I'll be happy." Greta offered her right hand.

Sabine stared into Greta's muddy blue eyes, feeling like she was about to exploit this child's innocence.

"People will always tell you what they want to know with their expressions or their body language. They'll signal to you what they expect to hear from the tea leaves or the cards or their palms." Ruby's words, uttered like wisdom to little Sabine as her mother arranged yet another second-floor walk-up with candles and incense and gauzy curtains. Ruby's trademark flowing gowns completed the mystical ambience of MADAME RUBY, FORTUNE TELLER AND PSYCHIC. "You just have to ask the right questions."

Sabine decided to give Greta a freebie.

"Give me your left hand." Closing her own eyes in a preparatory moment, Sabine relaxed her face into what she hoped looked like the face of someone reading your future. Greta was only nineteen, a simple high school graduate who didn't have a lot to look forward to in a little town like Moose River Junction. Like so many of the girls and women at the Holiday Crafts and Hobbies, Greta's choices were pretty limited. A job putting together cutesy tchotchkes, marriage, babies, a trip or two to Disney World, beloved grandchildren, big family dinners at Thanksgiving.

Stroking her forefinger into the grooves of Greta's hand, Sabine felt a gentle fondness for the girl, whose mother and grandmother still worked shifts at the factory, their husbands retirees of the volunteer fire department. Greta wasn't a barn burner, having stayed behind when most of her high school classmates had moved away. She was a hometown girl who would perpetuate the small town skills of civic and church volunteerism, becoming one of the good people who manage to keep their ambitions on the simple things of life. Home, hearth, and children.

Sabine folded Greta's fingers over gently with a squeeze born of an affectionate jealousy. "Oh, Greta, it'll be wonderful."

Greta bounced away from Sabine's desk, and Sabine found herself fighting a sudden instinct that Greta's wonderful life wouldn't be with Arnie. Ruby always called those lingering doubts afterthoughts. Sabine shifted her rolling chair toward the computer. I don't read futures, she told herself, I make up stories based on what I know. I am a sensitive, not a seer. A good guesser. Greta will be fine.

Sabine looked at the clock and knew she would be on the verge of rude if she didn't leave now. "Mom, I'll be fine. And I promise to let you know if I'm not."

"Love you, Beenie."

"Love you, Mom." Sabine hung up the phone with the slightest flicker of sadness. It had been a long time since she'd seen Ruby, more than a year since a nice tax refund had made it possible for her to fly out to California. They talked nearly every day, but that didn't entirely alleviate the desire to share a meal and be in the same room together.

Maybe she could scrape up enough money this fall to head out for part of the holidays. Another glance at the perpetually slow clock above the stove galvanized Sabine into heading down the stairs.

• • •

"So then I said to him, 'Mister Perrotti, if you're going to charge that much for hamburger, I'm going to become a vegetarian.'" Lynn laughed at her joke, proud of her combative ways with tradesmen and shopkeepers.

Sabine managed to laugh at what must have been Lynn's punch line, though she was distracted by the entrance of a tall man with a very thin woman beside him. There was a tension between them, evident by the slight distance the woman kept from the man. He was clearly cajoling her. And she was just as clearly having none of it. Sabine would have put money on the fact they were in the middle of some argument that he was trying to put behind them.

"Lynn, who's that?"

"Oh, Dan Smith. And that's his actress girlfriend. I went to school with him, he's Beatrice Danforth's grandson. Nice guy. Couldn't wait to get out of MRJ. Now that he's something in the film business, he barely ever comes back here. I heard that he's home because his grandmother's dying." Lynn drained the pint glass in front of her. "Why?"

"Why what?"

"Why are you curious about him?"

"How do you know I wasn't asking about the girlfriend?"

"Oh, puleeze!"

So as not to give Lynn any more reason to suspect her interest as anything more than simple native curiosity, Sabine kept her eyes on her own beer. She'd seen enough. It wasn't just that he was attractive, with his lean form and sandy cropped hair, it was more the interesting tension between him and the woman. A tension that escalated as his beeper went off with a hee-haw sound. Three other beepers pierced the noisy bar and grill, and the other volunteer firemen rushed out of the restaurant. Dan hesitated for half a minute before following. The din in the bar had hushed at the sound of the beepers, and his words were audible to Sabine and Lynn in the far booth. "Look, Karen, I have to go. I'm on duty and that's all there is to it. Bob here will get you a cab home." He took her face in his hands and kissed her expertly colored mouth. "I'll be back."

Karen remained as she was, her lips moued into a semi-pout. It might have been real pique, or it might have been seduction, but it was wasted on Dan, who was out the door without looking back.

"Firemen," Lynn said. Her father had been one, and she knew about unfinished dinners and long nights waiting.

Sabine kept her eyes on Karen. "If any man kissed me like that and ran off to put out a fire, I'd be a melted pool of butter on the floor."

Karen Whitcomb stood leaning against the bar, her glass of freshly poured chardonnay pinched by the stem. Sabine watched as her face changed to dismay at her abandonment, then anger, then perplexity. A glimmer of fellow-feeling touched Sabine and she pulled Lynn out of her chair to make an overture of feminine solidarity. They fetched up beside the still-standing Karen.

"This happens around here. Do you want to join us?" she asked.

"No. Thank you."

"I'm Sabine Heartwood, this is Lynn Miller. We don't have dates either, although we didn't start off with any. Do you want to come with us to the movies?"

Karen lifted her chin. "No. I don't think so. I'm sure he'll be right back."

"Not if there's a real fire. Could take all night. Bob

will let Dan know where you are." Lynn shot Bob the bartender a look for confirmation.

The man quickly nodded, adding his own suggestion. "I bet Nagy will let you all in free if you go with them."

"Oh, no, I'm just the grandson's girlfriend." There was a bite to her statement that exposed the probable source of tension between herself and Dan. It didn't take much prescience to figure out she was up against it, with Beatrice Danforth needing Dan's attention. As she stood there in her DKNY jeans and Prada boots, looking out of her element in the grubby bar and grill, it was hard not to imagine the battle for Dan's soul taking place every time this young woman came to visit.

"Look, we're just trying to be friendly. No big deal." Sabine turned to leave.

Karen set her drink down on the damp bar and folded her arms across her middle. "I don't mean to take it out on you, but we've only got something like forty-eight hours together and he runs off to play fireman."

"I don't think he's playing. I don't even know the guy, but I do know a lot of firemen and they all take their duty seriously." Sabine felt an unaccountable annoyance at this woman's attitude. "Oh, and there are no cabs in Moose River Junction. You'll either have to wait or walk."

Lynn pulled Sabine away. The pair collected their pocketbooks and headed out the door.

"Someday when she becomes a big movie star, she'll look back on this and wish she'd been nicer to us," Sabine said.

"That doesn't make any sense, Sabine. She'll never remember us. And what makes you think she's destined to be a big star?"

"The usual vibes."

Lynn had long since gotten used to Sabine's predictions. "That and the fact she fits the model. Tall, thin, sculptured cheekbones. Perfect skin. I hate her. Hey, actually, you have all those attributes, except for the silicone boobs, but you're a nice person."

"Yeah, but I can't act my way out of a paper bag, and I'm not so sure they *are* silicone." The two friends linked arms and made their way across the green and on to the Palace Theatre. In the distance they could hear the wail of the fire engines.

"Bet she's stuck in that bar all night," Lynn said.

Sabine laughed and knew that she was right.

Five

❧

Dr. Phillips had become so used to being in the house that he let himself in, lit a fire under the tea kettle, and hung his beat-up leather physician's bag on the peg beside the back door. His stethoscope was slung around his neck and there was very little else he needed on this call. His patient was drifting slowly away. Her grandson had been adamant that the old woman's wish to die in her own bed be granted. Doc Phillips knew, in the way that highly personal details leaked out in such a small place, that Dan had had to remortgage the theatre in order to afford the daily nursing care. Dan had shackled himself to the old woman's dying dream in two ways. To die at home and to keep him responsible for the dying theatre.

Morton Phillips had known Beatrice since taking over the general practice in Moose River Junction thirty years ago, but had never known Frederick, who had died shortly before Phillips came to town. However, as everyone did, he knew the story of Frederick's gift of the theatre to Beatrice.

Beatrice Windsor had sung like an angel. Strictly chaperoned, she'd toured the East Coast, eventually meeting the handsome vaudevillian Frederick Danforth. Danforth was a dancer, partnering his younger sister, Adele. With the guidance of his business partner, Oscar Nagy, they were wildly in demand and had a national reputation. Often the featured performers on the bill, they enjoyed an adulation reserved now for movie stars.

The legend was that it was love at first sight. A charming conceit. Beatrice and Frederick bumping into each other in the dark, narrow hallway where the dressing rooms were. The instant and powerful need for one another. But Beatrice's parents would not let her marry a traveling performer. In one of those inexplicable twists of parental logic, it was all right for their daughter to travel to perform in proper concert halls, but not to marry a man who traveled with the hoi polloi of common comedians and fan dancers performing in music halls.

Frederick found another dancing partner for Adele, borrowed money from Oscar Nagy, and built Beatrice a theatre. He gave up performing, except on his own stage, and became instead an impresario, bringing some of that same hoi polloi to Moose River Junction, but more often bringing class acts, traveling opera companies, and Shakespeare.

"He loved me enough to give it all up." Beatrice had told the story so many times, it was burnished like a fine piece of furniture.

Doc Phillips mounted the back stairs to Beatrice Danforth's bedroom. The pervasive sickroom odor met him halfway down the hall. Despite the unusual

September warmth, the room was shut up and the tiny figure on the big bed was buried beneath the covers. The home health care nurse quickly gave him Beatrice's physical stats, then gratefully left the room to make the tea he had started.

"How are you today, Mrs. Danforth?"

"I've been dreaming about singing. I can remember all the words to every song I ever sang. Latin, Italian, and French." Beatrice began to sing, a thin whispery sound. *"Laudemus te. Adoramus te.* Vivaldi's *Gloria.* A lovely duet for sopranos. *We praise thee lord, We adore thy name."*

"Would you like to listen to some music?" Doc Phillips motioned to the portable CD player Dan had set up once Beatrice had become bedridden.

"No. Everything I want to hear is in here." One bony finger touched her temple. She began to stroke away loose hairs. "Oh, Frederick, there you are. Come tell me about your day." The hand came down to pat the side of the bed.

Morton Phillips was always a little afraid of this part of the dying process, the dementia that provided the dying with a view into the next world. He felt Dan Smith standing in the doorway and knew that Beatrice did not see her thirty-three-year-old grandson, but the face of her long-dead husband. He turned to offer a little paternal comfort, as he often had when Dan was a fatherless boy being raised by this woman. To his surprise, Dan wasn't there. The physician looked back at Beatrice. Then he heard Dan's voice in the kitchen, speaking to someone, perhaps the nurse, maybe Nagy. An unfamiliar woman's voice floated up the back stairs. No, must be the New York girlfriend. Good, Dan would need some support. The clock had started on Beatrice Danforth's last hours.

Doc Phillips called down the stairs, "Dan, I think that you and Nagy should come up here now."

The doctor had left Dan and Nagy to sit vigil as the long day progressed. There wasn't much more he could do, though he'd check in every few hours. He told them to call if they felt they needed him. Karen had settled into the parlor; plenty of phone calls and reading to do. The house grew steadily quieter, as if the lengthening shadows of the day were quieting down the bustle of activity that had kept it a living home all these years. From upstairs, Dan could hear only the faint ticking of the case clock in the hallway. The starlings that had lined up along the telephone wires outside Gran's window in the late afternoon hushed their squeaks and chatter, suddenly bursting away en masse like an exploded pepper shaker to roost in the hillside trees. Unasked, Nagy switched on the bureau lamp, acknowledging the passage of time from day to night. The dull yellowish light only enshadowed the room.

Dan thought that it was like watching the tide go out. So subtle, the diminution of breath and movement. Had an hour passed since Beatrice last opened her eyes, or two?

When they first entered the room she had been sitting nearly upright, her eyes closed, perhaps asleep, perhaps only resting. Nagy sat in a chair on one side of the double bed, close to Beatrice. Dan sat beside him, closer to the foot, his view of Beatrice framed by the ornate carved headboard. He had the random thought that she had never looked lovelier. The odd trick of light and shadows had revealed the youthful beauty Beatrice once had been. She opened her eyes, the color of Spanish olives, prominent in her face.

"Nagy, you be a good boy. No more mischief. What you did was very naughty, but we are taught that our Lord forgives us. We must never speak of it again."

Dan shook his head at Nagy, desperate that his uncle understand that Beatrice was in some other time, some other place. "Nagy," Dan held Nagy's head close to his ear, "she's not talking about now. You haven't done anything naughty."

"I know." Nagy pulled his chair up to the edge of the bed and lay his grizzled head down on his mother's lap. Beatrice caressed his temples, smoothing her fingers over his sparse gray hair.

It was in this room. It was in this room that Gran had said those words or similar ones to him. His pajamas stank from the smoke and he could hear the water filling the bath, a hollow, heavy sound that sounded exactly like he felt. "Danforth, what you did was a very bad thing, but you will be forgiven. I forgive you."

"Gran, what did I do?"

Her hair still had touches of gold in it then. But her eyes were as green, and as intense, as now. "You started the fire. It was an unfortunate accident."

"How did I start the fire?"

"It doesn't matter. Just promise me, as I promise you, that we will never speak of it again. I forgive you, and God forgives you. Promise that you won't speak of it again?" Dan remembered her hands gripping his small arms, shaking him a little.

"I promise you."

"Good lad. Now, go. Hop in the bathtub. I'll be right there."

• • •

Almost everyone Dan knew was in therapy of some sort, trying to overcome fears, compulsions, anger. A host of maladies to be talked out of. Despite the widespread belief among his peers that therapy was as ordinary as a trip to the dentist, Dan had never believed that he might benefit from speaking out loud the accusation laid at his six-year-old feet. A therapist might have helped him fill the hole in his memory that contained the explanation of how the fire started, but his Yankee upbringing had thwarted any move in that direction. Nice people didn't tell strangers their business.

What Dan did remember was playing with a lighter that had belonged to his grandfather Frederick. Even now he had a vivid memory of touching that silver metal rectangle, of holding its chilly weight, and of flicking it into life. Just not what he had done to ignite the fire.

In the end, Dan had done what Gran had asked and they'd never spoken of the fire or his culpability again. All his life he had held on to that promise; even Karen never knew his shameful secret. Dan imagined there were others in town who must know the truth about the fire that destroyed his home and orphaned him. It was this silent underpinning to his youth that made Dan realize if other people were privy to his pain, he must find a life elsewhere. Which is what he had done.

Dan now watched his grandmother, her hand on Nagy's temple still. They were both asleep. He roused Nagy, moving him back on the chair, and then eased Beatrice down on the pillows.

She looked up at him as he shifted her gently. She placed one hand on the side of his face. "You must promise me . . . Nagy will never be put away."

Dan caught the fragile hand and settled it on the freshly smoothed covers. "I promise you." An echo of another time, his childish and faithful promise to forever keep in silence his culpability in the fire that caused his parents' deaths.

The soft tap on the bedroom door startled Dan from his half-doze. "I brought you some sandwiches and a Thermos of coffee." A young woman leaned a little around the doorway, obviously unwilling to disrupt the scene. Dan recognized her, but only in that small town way of everyone being a familiar face.

"Thanks. Where's Karen?"

"Karen? Oh, your girlfriend. I didn't see her. I let myself in." The woman held a large tray in front of her, laden with plastic-wrapped sandwiches and a quart-size vacuum bottle. "I was having dinner with Lynn Miller at the Blue Moose and someone said that you were up here. Waiting."

"How do people know these things?" Dan helped himself to a sandwich. He nudged the sleeping Nagy to do the same.

She shrugged. "I'm Sabine Heartwood. I worked with your grandmother on her . . ." She hesitated.

"Her obituary. She told me. I didn't put your face to that name, but now I realize I have seen you around. Thank you. She was very pleased with the work."

"It was a little weird, but I'm glad she liked, likes it." Sabine blushed, and Dan thought that it was a rather attractive color on her pale olive skin. "Anyway, they needed someone to come over with something for you to eat. So I volunteered."

"I'm glad you did. I'm glad to meet you."

"It would have been nice to have met under more cheery circumstances, but I'm glad to have finally met you. Your grandmother spoke about you quite a bit as we talked about her obituary." Sabine blushed again. "I should go, but if there's anything else . . . I'm around."

"Would you like a sandwich?" Suddenly it seemed really important to have this new, neutral figure in the room.

"I've eaten, but I wouldn't mind a bite of that brownie."

"Have it." Dan winked at Nagy. "Nagy won't mind."

"Oh, Nagy, I couldn't."

"I'm not hungry. You take it." Nagy put his half-eaten sandwich back on the tray and went back to his seat.

Sabine moved to stand next to Nagy. She put an arm around his shoulders and gave him a little squeeze. "Nagy, I know this is hard for you. You're being very brave." She put the still-wrapped brownie back on the tray. "I should go."

Dan stood up, aware suddenly of how good it felt to stretch. "Let me walk you to the door."

Sabine placed a restraining hand on his chest, a soft pressure exactly where his heart was full. "No. I found my way in. I'll follow my bread crumb trail back."

Impulsively, Dan took the hand so gently holding him back. "Sabine, thank you. Thank everyone for me."

He watched her walk down the hallway, then turned to look back at his grandmother. Nagy held her hand again, his cheek pressed against it. Beatrice was smiling, not at Nagy, but at him, her eyes wide open and seeing. Gradually her eyes shut with a slow, easy closing. She raised her chin a little, and Dan heard her last soft exhalation.

Six

❦

Thursday, September 21, 2000

The post-service collation was set up in the new parish
house of South Congregational Church. Tables had
been arranged in the center of the big room and were
now laden with the cookies and finger sandwiches the
Ladies Guild had fashioned. Antique punch bowls sat
sentinel at either end. The silver coffee service with its
nearly faded etching, GIFT IN MEMORY OF MR. AND MRS.
SYLVESTRUS WINDSOR 1882, was on a separate table
against the north wall.

Though not an actual member of the congregation,
Sabine had, over the two years she'd been in Moose
River Junction, begun to take part in various nonreli-
gious events at the church. Her quilting club met there,
and she'd helped out with the Christmas Bazaar.
Inculcated from birth to be wary of organized religion,
Sabine had yet to take the plunge into attending regular Sunday services. Even so, she had been recruited to
monitor the coffee service and now threaded her way

through the crowd that had gathered, awaiting Dan and Nagy's return from the private internment.

"Hey there, Amos." Sabine dodged Amos Anthony's elbow, barely retaining control of the newly refilled creamer she was carrying from the parish hall kitchen. "Watch yourself."

"Oh, my. Sabine, sweetheart, you look good enough to eat." Amos, a whiskery denizen of the Blue Moose Bar and Grill, was notorious for two things: flirting and being a crazed Red Sox fan. "Give an old man a kiss?"

"So, how 'bout those Red Sox?" Sabine tossed out the challenge and quickly moved away. She could hear Amos winding up for his annual lamentation of a blown World Series contest and how the Curse of the Bambino was a whole lot of bull . . .

She got just out of earshot and busied herself tidying up the coffee area, pouring fresh cups for guests and putting the dirty ones in the rack hidden discreetly beneath the table's long white tablecloth. The crowd noise abated for an instant, long enough for her to realize Dan and Nagy had reentered the room. Then the volume of conversation zoomed back to its original level, and Sabine caught sight of Dan at the far side of the room, taking handshakes and hugs. He was smiling in that way of a good host, and she couldn't help but admire him for his gracious manner, greeting each condolence as if it were his job to console the speaker. She pulled herself away from watching and set to refilling the creamers.

"Sabine, thanks for helping out. I had no idea so many people would come." Danforth Smith was at her elbow. He looked very handsome in his good suit, despite the circles of exhaustion beneath his pale green eyes.

"You look about done in."

The gathering had shifted in such a way that for a moment they were completely alone in the crowded room.

"The truth is, I am. And the worst is yet to follow."

"Cleaning out."

"Yeah. I've been trying to get some of it done while— well—while I've had time, but it's been pretty minimal."

"Is there any need to rush?"

Dan picked up an empty coffee cup from the damask tablecloth. "I need to get back to New York." He sounded a little exasperated, or maybe just tired and frustrated. "It's just that I have so much to do here."

Sabine took the bone china cup and filled it, handing it back to him. "You know if there's anything I can do . . ."

Dan took the cup and saucer from her hands. He sipped the coffee and smiled, as if the caffeine had somehow made everything all better. "I'll let you know."

A reconfiguration of groups brought others close by, and Dan was swept away. Sabine poured coffee for the next person, but it was hard not to follow Dan with her eyes. He had recovered from his momentary downturn and was once again playing good host. Sabine felt a little flicker of concern that he'd allowed her, a near stranger, to see him with his guard down.

It didn't take a psychic to see that he was sad and tired. But beneath all that, Sabine would place money on the fact that a lot more was weighing on Dan Smith than the prolonged, but expected, death of his elderly grandmother.

Across the room Sabine could see Nagy, sitting by himself against the wall, like a wallflower at the dance. Then Maisie Ralston, the longtime cashier at the Palace

Theatre, came and sat down next to him. Sabine's eyes filled up with tears as Maisie handed Nagy a finger sandwich and then took his other hand and held it.

Two years ago, Sabine had come to Moose River Junction looking for a home. That Saturday afternoon in March, sitting in the coffee shop, being pleased in some way that the town had changed very little from her childish memory of it, Sabine had let herself imagine staying. Conditioned from birth to expect portents and signs, she sat in the bow window seat of the little coffee shop and waited for something to happen, observing the town as one might watch a tank of fish. People looking for parking places along the green, moms hustling children along to Miss Peggy's School of Dance. A whole team of pint-size soccer players being herded by two dad-type coaches. The waitress had filled her cup twice before Sabine got what she was waiting for.

A stout man carrying a bundle of newspapers came through the door. He dumped the papers on a flat news rack near where Sabine was sitting. "Thanks, Moe," the waitress said, handing him a Styrofoam cup of coffee. As the man turned to go out the door, he brushed against the papers with his wide hip, knocking the top one off the pile and into Sabine's lap.

"It's a gift, keep it." The man saluted Sabine with the coffee cup and went out.

PENNYWISE PAPER, MOOSE RIVER JUNCTION'S OWN WEEKLY. Sabine studied the front page and then opened the paper up. The bulk of the issue was taken up with advertisements for the businesses in town, want ads, personal ads, and a calendar of events. Pieced here and there were birth announcements, death notices, the box scores for the local school athletics, photographs of the quilt to be raffled off to benefit the South Congregational Church Scholarship Fund. A movie review. Sipping her lukewarm coffee, Sabine read every line, absorbing the flavor of Moose River Junction. Could she settle in a town that gave over three columns of newsprint to the firemen rescuing a family of opossums from a storm drain?

Then, buried in the classifieds, was her portent: LOOKING FOR A HOME? The ad with its prophetic headline had gone on to describe the home Sabine had imagined all her life. A rural setting, a yard, and pets allowed.

Sabine remembered every moment of that day. She had come back to Moose River Junction only to see if it looked as she remembered it from her brief childhood visit. Sabine still remembered every detail. The freedom of walking along the sidewalk alone, the purchase of Swedish fish and string licorice from Mr. Carlson. The kind smile, and "Come back soon."

And here, now, as she had seen over and over, were examples of the way people in a small town cared for one another, just as she had imagined. Maisie holding Nagy's hand, comforting him without fanfare. Amos sputtering on about the Red Sox, being politically incorrect and calling her sweetheart, commenting on her appearance at a funeral. The way even Dan Smith, home to tend his dying grandmother, had rejoined the volunteer fire department. A community. A place to call home.

The gathering had thinned out until only the church women were left to fold up the tablecloths and find the last misplaced cup and saucer. Sabine wiped her hands on a towel and took off her apron, which read in large blue letters, KISS ME, I'M CONGREGATIONALIST. She retrieved her Staffordshire platter, on which she'd brought her offering of finger sandwiches, and began to look around for her purse.

"Maybe you left it upstairs," Marge Davey suggested.

"I may have."

The parish house was connected to the church through a passageway that went up a flight of steps leading to the front of the nave, just right of the chancel. Tired and a little footsore from wearing heels, Sabine made her way slowly up through the modern facility to the ancient wooden door that separated it from the old church. There was some story about why there were two Congregational churches in the little town, but Sabine couldn't call it to mind. With fleeting regret, she thought that Beatrice Danforth would have been the person to ask.

Sabine expected the hush of an empty church, a stillness after all the sound and feeling so recently filling it. But she knew instantly that she was not alone in the room. There was someone else, hidden perhaps by the walls of the box pews. Out of habit, Sabine stood still and waited to determine if what she felt was human or not. The images of the faces in the yellow light moving across the gray walls came back to her. Flight of fancy, or another unguarded moment when what was imperceptible to most other people was obvious to her? She sniffed: a slight odor of wood smoke. Maybe the extinguished candles? Shaking off the moment, Sabine walked up the aisle to the last row where she was pretty certain she'd left her purse under the pew.

As she walked toward the back of the church she happened to glance up at the choir loft, with its massive tracker organ. Looking down on her was Dan Smith.

He waved, a little gesture to say he knew she'd seen him hiding up there.

"I'm looking for my purse." Sabine opened the door of the pew and retrieved her clutch bag. "I'm not used to carrying one without a strap." She felt a little foolish, explaining herself like that. Realizing she was holding her large platter against her belly like a shield, she quickly tucked it under her arm.

"Stay there, I'm coming down."

Sabine leaned against the pew. "How come you're still here? I thought you and Nagy left half an hour ago."

"Maisie took him home. I just needed a little quiet time."

"Of course. I'm sorry, I've interrupted."

"No. I'm glad you came in. I've just been indulging in trying to decide what to do next." Dan's tie was loosened and his collar button undone. He held his suit jacket. "Want to go get a drink?"

Once again, a faint whiff of wood smoke, but Sabine ignored it. "Sure."

They walked across the town green to the Blue Moose Bar and Grill, walking past the Moose River Junction war memorial in the center and taking the paved path in deference to Sabine's heels. Dan kept up a patter of small talk, deliberately keeping them off the subject of the last few hours, weeks, and months. He was saturated with it. He asked Sabine the obvious questions about her choice of Moose River Junction, how she'd come to live here, how she liked it. Personal but not probing questions, the questions of a curious stranger. After all, they'd met only twice before.

They found an open booth and slid in. The late September sunset was reddening the sky above the hills, illuminating their window booth and causing them to squint at their menus. When the waitress brought them their beers, Dan raised his, touching the thick rim of the pint glass to Sabine's. "To the future."

"I would have thought you'd lift a glass to Beatrice Danforth." Sabine sipped the pale ale. "She was a tremendous lady."

"I know. She raised me. And tonight I'm raising a toast to her in a more appropriate manner, since she was a teetotaler."

"So how are you doing it?"

Dan was suddenly struck by how the sunlight turned Sabine's brown eyes into the color of maple syrup. "Tonight the Palace Theatre will be showing, for free, *Gone With the Wind*."

"Her favorite movie."

"Of all time."

"That's sweet."

"It was her idea. 'Give them a treat, Danforth, show them what a real movie is like.' Her exact dying words."

"You aren't serious?"

"If you count everything she's said in the last six months as dying words, I am." Dan closed his menu. Sabine looked at him with one slightly raised eyebrow. "Sorry. I don't mean to sound flip, but I'm a little weary."

"I'm sorry that your girlfriend couldn't be with you. I know that had to be a hard decision for both of you, but you shouldn't be alone today."

Dan had heard that Sabine Heartwood was some sort of psychic, doing a little palm reading at parties. But this intuitive knowledge of his unexpressed disappointment at Karen's decision to pursue her career, in spite of his need for her, surprised him. "I'm not alone." Let her interpret that any way she wanted. He wasn't alone because Nagy waited for him at home. And,

Karen had phoned early this morning from L.A. Still on East Coast time, she had awakened early and called him before seven. She had talked with him about the service he was about to attend; she'd told him she was thinking about him. "Besides, it wasn't a death in her family, and she had an audition that will probably change her life." Dan hoped he didn't sound either sarcastic or petulant, or like he was trying hard to believe himself.

"I'm sorry, I have a tendency to put my foot in it." Sabine pressed her back against the bench, as if physically moving away from him to prevent any more mind reading. "It's just that you looked so alone up there in the front pew." She leaned forward again. "But this is none of my business, obviously, and if you're a kind man you'll forget I ever said anything."

"Done. Shall we order something to eat?"

"I think you have to, if you're sitting in a booth." Sabine motioned toward the approaching waitress.

"There's so much food at the house, this seems decadent."

"Freezer bags."

"I'm not sure I have any room left in the freezer."

"My instincts tell me that Maisie is probably rearranging things even as we speak."

"Your instincts?" Dan handed the plastic menu back to the waitress. "Someone told me at the wake last night that you have the second sight."

"Not where freezers are concerned. I just know that if I were spending a couple of hours in your house, I'd probably look to see what needed the most doing. Sounds like putting food away is a top priority."

"But you do a little fortune-telling?" Dan was genuinely curious.

"I sometimes do readings."

"What kinds of readings? Like barometric pressure, or palms?"

"Both, actually. I'm the psychic weather girl for the *Pennywise Paper*. Didn't anyone tell you?"

"What are you predicting for tomorrow?"

"Sun during the day and dark all night."

Dan laughed, and the laugh felt so good he did it again. The joke was poor, but the laughter was rich.

"The sordid little story is that it didn't take long before I was forced to conclude that my salary as assistant editor for the *Pennywise Paper* wouldn't be nearly enough to support me in the style to which I wanted to be accustomed. It was just enough to cover rent, car insurance, and food, but there was precious little left for wild entertainment and savings. It's a good enough salary for someone with another income, that is, a husband, but not for a single woman, though one without dependents unless you count Jerry the cat."

"Don't most people looking for second jobs pull a shift or two at the Holiday Crafts and Hobbies factory?"

"I grew up with a traveling fortune teller. It was the family business."

"Like Gypsies?"

Sabine shrugged, a fleeting glimpse of old pain on her lovely face. "I don't know. Possibly. Anyway, what had started as an occasional income booster has begun to look like the more lucrative job. I'm not quite ready to write *psychic* in the occupation line of my tax form, but I do dutifully report it on the 'other income' line."

"Are you any good?"

"You mean accurate? Look, the truth is, it's all smoke and mirrors. I have a certain sensitivity to signs and signals, which all people emanate. But if you want to ask me if you're going to win the lottery, no, I'm only as good as you are picking the numbers."

Dan leaned a little closer. "I wouldn't ask about the lottery. But I would ask about my future."

"A tuna club, extra mayo is about to arrive in your life." Sabine sat back as the waitress set down her Cobb salad, then Dan's sandwich.

"Wow, you're really good." Dan laughed again and wondered why it felt like he'd known Sabine Heartwood forever.

Seven

❧

A drink had turned into dinner and then a walk along the green. The evening had cooled from the unusual warmth of the day, and Sabine shivered a little.

"Do you want my jacket?"

Sabine smiled at Dan's gallantry but shook her head. "No, I'm fine."

Across the way they could see the marquee lights illuminating the title of the movie. "Are you going?"

"No. I think that Walt and Nagy can handle the crowd tonight. I'm going home to bed."

"Thanks for dinner. Is it inappropriate to say I had a good time?"

"Not at all, I had a good time, too. I really needed to decompress and I'm glad you were willing to hang out with me. You've been great."

"It was self-serving. Trust me."

"I mean about all the help you and this whole town have given me in the last few weeks. You've all

reminded me what living in a small town is like." They
had reached the parking lot of the South Congregational
Church and stood beside Sabine's Honda.

"Do you think you'll stay?"

"No. I'll be here for a while, tying up loose ends, but I
need to go back to my real life."

They stood in silence for a moment, each feeling a certain reluctance to end the evening, yet both knowing that
it was time. As if underscoring the moment, the clock
tower in North Congregational Church signaled the hour
with eight chimes.

"Well, good night then," Sabine broke the silence.
She let Dan open her car door and she slid into the dri-
ver's seat. "Thanks again. If you need anything . . ."

"I might. I'll let you know." Before shutting the door,
Dan bent to give Sabine a quick, grateful kiss on the
cheek, surprising himself and her.

Watching Sabine pull away, Dan didn't think about
his action, only how soft her skin was, and the scent of
her hair, loosened from the knot she'd captured it in.
With some effort, he pulled his thoughts away from
Sabine and recollected that Karen had her big audition
today. He should call her and find out how it went.
Maybe she'd already left a message for him at home.
Maybe Karen had achieved her big break and his was on
the horizon.

Before he headed home, Dan made himself walk to
the theatre. He should just check in. Nagy had been
insistent that he man the door even on this, the night of
his mother's funeral. "Mommy would want me to." He
was determined and almost righteous about it. Dan
knew that he was coping in his own way and the familiar was his comfort. Nagy had changed out of his suit

and was wearing his usual rumpled khakis and white shirt with THE PALACE THEATRE emblazoned on the pocket. Out of some deference to the day, he still wore his dark blue clip-on tie.

As Dan approached, Nagy greeted him with a big smile. "Go see."

Dan could hear the music swelling dramatically as Atlanta fell. Instead of going through the swinging doors to the house, Dan went up the back stairs to the disused balcony. The original plush chairs were long gone, the safety of the suspended balcony in question, but he still deemed it safe enough to sit, night after night, in one of the three wooden folding chairs along the rail. He could lean his chin on his hands as he had done as a boy and watch the movie or the twenty-five people who might attend on any given night. Dan glanced in at Walt, who was watching the movie from the booth, the reel in the second projector at the ready for the switch over. Walt didn't see him, nor hear his footsteps over the sound of the projector. Dan made his way in the pitch dark to the chairs, but didn't sit down. He looked out over the house and felt suddenly overwhelmed by it all. Every seat was filled. Moose River Junction's tribute to Beatrice Windsor Danforth. Her tribute to them. There in the comforting darkness, Dan let his guard down at last and, as sweet Melanie died on screen, Dan let his own grief out.

It was nearly midnight before Dan and Nagy got home. It seemed like a reenactment of the funeral as each person leaving the theatre wanted one more word with Dan, one more expression of what a great lady his grandmother had been. All too many expressions of the hope that he would stay in Moose River Junction and keep the Palace open. Had Gran prepped these people? His appreciation of their sentiments was degrading into annoyance.

As late as it was, Dan knew he had to call Karen. There were half a dozen messages on the machine, but none from her. It was only nine in the evening in California, the shank end of the day there. She might be out at a club, but he'd try her anyway. Karen answered her cell phone almost instantly, her voice a near shout as she was certainly in some sort of crowd. "Hello?"

"How'd it go?"

"Oh, Dan. Hi. I think it went well. I was hoping you were my agent telling me I've got a callback. They said they were making the first cut choices tonight."

"I won't keep you then."

"That's okay. How was the funeral?"

"Good. Fine." Dan didn't want to be shouting into a phone about the day. He was too tired to try to express how touched he'd been with the outpouring of support from his townspeople. It was just too hard to do over the phone to someone not equally as solitary as he was in the front parlor of the quiet house. "When are you coming back? I'll tell you all about it then."

"Can't say. Depends on the callback. Then, if I do get it, we go into production almost immediately. I may need you to send me some things from the apartment."

"I don't know when I'm going back."

There was a silence on the end of the line, and for a moment Dan thought that Karen had moved into a dead zone for the signal. "Karen?"

"I'm here. I just thought that once things were . . . over, that you'd head back to New York."

"I am. I just can't leave tomorrow. There are details to attend to."

"Dan, I know that you want to keep your promise to your grandmother." Karen had moved into a quieter area; the din was suddenly gone and her voice was clear. "But we have some understandings, as well. People are already saying we've broken up."

"What people?"

"The kind who write stupid little articles in rags."

"Since when have either of us been in the spotlight?" Dan couldn't imagine that they were big enough fish to catch the interest of the sharks of journalism. Not yet.

"I'm just saying that we should be seen together. I'm saying I miss you."

"I miss you, too." Dan didn't elaborate on how much he'd missed her during this particular day. How her absence had caught the notice of one sensitive observer. "Come to think of it, one journalist did notice we weren't together today. The *Pennywise Paper*'s assistant editor." Dan wanted it to sound like a joke.

Karen didn't take it as such. "Do they have a wide readership?"

"Karen, it's an advertising and local news weekly. No one outside of MRJ reads it."

"Oh. You're making a joke."

"Karen, good luck with the callback. I have no doubt that the part is yours for the taking." Dan wanted to end the conversation. He could hear that someone was talking to Karen, distracting her away from his voice. He hadn't the strength to take her attention back. The weight of the day was forcing him downward and he desperately needed his bed.

"Hold on, Carl, I'm coming." The din behind her

voice had returned as she moved back into the crowded
room. "I've got to go."

"Love you," Dan said.

"Me, too."

The phone against his ear buzzed with the disconnection.

Sabine touched the place where Dan had grazed her
cheek with his kiss. A kiss between friends. A grateful
kiss. A cordial kiss. A meaningless kiss. A kiss, nonetheless. A kiss from a man with a girlfriend, one who
planned on leaving very soon. She was half-tempted to
pick up the phone and blurt out everything to Lynn, to
enlist her friend in the campaign to drive this kiss into
its proper realm. But she really didn't want to appear
foolish. It was nice, that's all. The faint "click" was
probably just her sensitivity to his situation. Empathy,
not connection.

The ringing of her phone forced Sabine out of her
reverie. It was after nine-thirty, Ruby had already
called today, and it was too late for a telemarketer.
Reaching for the wall phone in the kitchen, Sabine
felt a trickle of premonition go through her, like an involuntary shiver. During their conversation this morning, Ruby had been reminding her of her increasing
sense that something significant was going to happen
to Sabine. So far, it had been a dry forecast. Sabine
shook off the feeling, telling herself she was being
silly. The emotions of the day, the funeral and the
aftermath, coupled with Ruby's daily reiteration that
her life was about to change, had made her susceptible to hope. She forbade herself to hope it was Dan
calling.

She was instantly glad of her self-discipline.

"Are you the psychic woman? The woman who does readings?" The voice was high pitched, a little imperious, but from nervousness rather than a natural superiority.

"I do readings, yes. Occasionally." Sabine thought that the call sounded long distance. "Who is this?"

"My name is Loozy Atcheson. My husband Drake and I have just finished building a vacation house in Moose River Junction, off Lower Ridge Road. Maybe you know the place. An authentic replica of a seventeenth-century saltbox?"

"No. I don't think so." Very few people chose Moose River Junction as a vacation destination, and Lower Ridge Road was pretty far out of town and well off her usual path. It wasn't surprising that she wouldn't know the place or the people building it. Sabine shifted the phone to her left ear and picked up the notepad she kept by the phone. "Do you want me to read palms at a housewarming?" It was an unusual choice of activity for such an occasion, but Loozy sounded a bit unusual. "Or are you asking for a private reading?"

"I guess the latter. You see, there's something wrong with the house. I—Drake and I—would like you to come see if you—I don't know—sense something abnormal."

The words brought to mind Ruby's ambitions when she realized Sabine could, indeed, detect the paranormal. It had begun around adolescence, this openness to things beyond ken. The first time it had happened was in an odd little house they had rented in Waterbury. Sabine had come downstairs one morning and seen an old woman sitting at the kitchen table. She was bundled in a flannel housecoat and was furiously knitting something. Her white hair was so thin that Sabine could see the pink skin beneath. When Sabine spoke to her, she smiled, raised her unfinished knitting in salute, and vanished. The terrified fourteen-year-old had fled upstairs to Ruby. Far from succoring her child in her moment of extremis, Ruby had been elated. She quickly decided they would add spiritualism to the repertoire. "There's nothing to be afraid of; they can't hurt you. They only want you to know their stories."

"How do you know that?"

"It's true."

Ruby had brought home a Ouija board, and they practiced for hours to let the knitting spirit spell out her annoyance that her brother had sold the house the day after she died. From then on, wherever Ruby had moved them to, she set up her revised sandwich board. MADAME RUBY, FORTUNE TELLER AND PSYCHIC, PARANORMAL INVESTIGATIONS A SPECIALTY.

Much to her mother's everlasting annoyance, by the time she was eighteen and about to attend college, Sabine resolutely refused to enter into the realm of spiritualism anymore. There were things that were just too weird. Still, sometimes it just happened. Like this morning, when the light drifting across the walls in the church had been filled with the images of long ago, like movies projected from the past. In a million years, Sabine wouldn't confess to having translated simple sunlight into ghostly images. Today she would admit only that she had been an impressionable teenager. Perhaps still a little fanciful, if she was seeing images on the church walls.

"Look, I don't read houses. I read palms and cards."

"Couldn't you just come and see?"

Sabine doodled on the pad. "I don't think I can help you. Even if on the odd chance I do sense something, what could I do about it? If you're worried about spirits, call a priest. Get the house blessed."

"You have to understand." Loozy's voice was growing more and more nervous. "I've seen things. I've heard things that aren't there. Voices. You can't tell me it's all in my head."

"Mrs. Atcheson, I won't tell you it's your imagination, but you're probably sensitive to such things. Some people are. There isn't anything to be afraid of." An echo of Ruby's words in her mouth, Sabine tried to sound as sincere. It was true, she'd never been harmed. This Loozy woman wouldn't be, either, but living with the unknown could be traumatizing for someone not raised to accept such things as normal, as she had been. New Orleans voodoo practitioners, Southwest shamans, palm readers, tea leave readers, Tarot card readers, psychics of all persuasions—these made up the peer group with which her mother consorted. "Besides, what could I possibly do to help?"

"You're helping already, because you are the first person I've spoken to who hasn't immediately told me it's all in my head."

"I'd never tell anyone that." Sabine was too much her mother's daughter to ever try to convince anyone they might be imagining the validity of Tarot revelations or ghosts in the attic. *One must always project a certainty that the illusion is, in fact, reality.* Ruby's constant counsel.

"So, will you come?"

"Let me think about it."

"We'll be there in October. Can I call you then?"

"I'm not making any promises."

"I'll call." Loozy rang off quickly, before Sabine could say anything else.

Sabine remained standing at the kitchen counter, suddenly wondering if that significant thing Ruby had predicted was upon her. She looked at her doodling and wondered why she'd drawn little tongues of flame.

PART II

PART II

One

∽

October 2000

Sabine set her book down on the coffee table and got up to let the cat out. Not for the first time, she wished she owned the place so that she could install a cat door and be able to finish a chapter without interruption. She bent over to stroke the big black cat before pulling the wooden back door open. "You never saw a door you didn't want to be on the other side of, did you, Jerry?" Jerry had once been part of a Tom and Jerry pair, but Tom had long since vanished. A waft of cold fresh air induced Sabine to grab her Polarfleece vest and go out with the cat. It was one of those impeccable fall nights, exactly right for an early October evening, the black sky hung with brilliant chips of stars. A late cricket was feebly signaling, alone in his universe.

Sabine instinctively hesitated on the landing leading down from her apartment, staring out into the dark yard for any sign of darker movement. With no discernible skunk in sight, she came down the twelve wooden steps and into the small backyard of the wood frame house. The maples still valiantly clinging to their leaves framed the yard in a semicircle. In the quiet of the late evening, Sabine could hear the chattering of Windsor's Brook along the stream bed of loose stone and fixed rock exposed by the long, dry summer. The brook ran behind the house and into the larger river, from which the town of Moose River Junction had taken its name. The railroad that had created the junction had long since stopped passing through the center of town, but no one had seen fit to revise the name, itself a revision of the original Windsorville.

Across the brook and through the scrim of brush and trees, she could see the downward-facing spotlights of the Moose River Junction Volunteer Fire Department's old fire barn. Long since replaced by a modern multi-bay fire-house closer to town, the two-story frame building housed one of the town's rescue vehicles and was where the fire department held its meetings every other Thursday night. In the summer, Sabine sometimes heard their voices coming through the second-floor windows as she sat on her narrow landing. Sonorous male voices determining unknowable details of the small department, bullets of laughter soon followed by the slamming of doors and the gunning of truck engines as the men headed home.

Sabine knew several of the volunteers, mostly through their wives or daughters who were her friends. In Moose River Junction being in the fire department was considered a civic duty, and of the men who stayed, who didn't flee the hamlet as soon as they were able, most served for at least a few years. As the assistant editor of the paper, Sabine collected the department's statistics every week, usually a dry enumeration of calls: two false alarms, one clogged culvert requiring the pumper, a car fire on the Mass Pike. If there was an actual structural fire, Moe Condon, editor, owner, and chief reporter, was on it. Too big and out of shape to be a fireman himself, Moe got his adrenaline fix by writing about the infrequent blazes.

Placing herself exactly in the middle of the semicircle of trees, Sabine stretched her arms over her head and turned slowly, enjoying the planetarium effect of the framing maples. She picked out Cassiopeia, once again grateful that Ruby had not named her for this, her mother's favorite, constellation. It was bad enough being named Sabine. At various times in her youth she'd told kids that her name was Sally or Susan or Sheryl. She remembered her mother coming to school and being told by the children that there was no Sabine in that class, the new girl's name was Sally. Sabine couldn't quite remember if she had done that at the school in Ridgefield or the one after it in Ronkonkoma. She'd spent part of fourth grade in both of those places, and one other besides.

There was no question that they loved each other, but the twin conflicts of who they were and where they were going had always endangered their closeness. On both questions, Ruby stood resolutely enigmatic. Ruby's background was a tabula rasa. No family photographs, no papers, no objects survived her childhood. It was as if, Sabine sometimes imagined, Ruby had dropped from the heavens fully formed, like some goddess in Greek mythology. Ruby had written on that blank slate, telling Sabine stories, which changed over time, until Sabine realized that what she was hearing was part fairy tale, part lie. Stolen by Gypsies, stolen from Gypsies. Once they had been descended from an Indian princess, then a Spanish one. It wasn't until a fifth-grade family history project that Sabine realized her mother would never tell her the truth.

"At least tell me about my father. Tell me his name." Sabine had been so excited at the assignment to interview "family members," to fill in the blank boxes on a tree the teacher had them color in.

She had stroked brown crayon on the trunk of the stylized oak tree at school. Tenderly she'd colored in each of the leaves, choosing to make hers a fall-colored tree of Crayola orange and red and yellow. Carefully, Sabine lettered her own name on the base of the tree: Sabine Heartwood. To the right, Ruby Heartwood.

"Now, write your father's name on the left. And what's your mother's maiden name? You'll need to know that . . ." Miss Robinson had a cheerfully helpful voice, and this was her pet project.

Sabine had sat for a long time with the crayoned tree and all the blank boxes beneath its many branches. She knew that she would never be able to fill in even the most basic of any of the boxes. She'd done all that she could. Still, she brought the tree home, ever hopeful that Ruby would stop kidding around and give her real information.

Ruby had stood in the dim kitchen of their third-floor apartment. Her caftan fluttered a little in the breeze from the oscillating fan that wafted the scent of incense throughout the three-room flat. Sabine watched her mother's lips purse as she held the school project in her hands. The heavy glass rings seemed to overweight her hands as she held the paper away from her. Slowly she folded it, in half and then in half again. "Don't worry about this. We're leaving this weekend. I've a good feeling that Hartford is going to be where we find our fortune."

Sabine had reached out for the unfinished project. When her mother got that spark in her eye, there was no persuading her to wait even until the end of the school year. Sabine thought of it as her escaping eye. When Ruby's eyes glittered like that, Sabine was certain of a quick move.

The oak tag project still lay in the bottom drawer of Sabine's bureau. Waiting patiently for the answers.

Shivering, Sabine left off staring at the stars and headed back up the stairs to her warm apartment. Ruby had called an hour ago. She was on her way east from California.

"What took you so long, Ruby?" Sabine jibed her mother. "Two years in one state is pretty much a record for you."

"Yes, but it is a big state."

"When do you think you'll get here?" Sabine was looking around her small sanctuary, mentally rearranging the two closets to make room for Ruby's clothes. The futon would serve as a bed. They'd shared enough tiny spaces over the years to know how to do it.

"Depends a bit on the bus, although she's in good shape; I've been good about keeping the mileage down while out here. By the end of next week, maybe. I'm all packed."

"What's sending you off this time?" Sabine had gotten no glimmer of imminent departure from Ruby's recent conversations. Generally a move was preceded by a laundry list of complaints. The current landlord was mean and wouldn't fix things, or the client base was dwindling, or the neighborhood was becoming dangerous. Ruby had moved twice while out in California, once from Los Angeles to San Francisco, and then back. San Francisco was too cold. The rents too high and the hills too steep. Sabine had liked that reasoning. A petite woman, Ruby had always worn spiky, high-heeled boots to enhance what nature had deprived her of. "Maybe if you'd wear sensible shoes, the hills wouldn't seem so steep."

"It's still too cold. Damp, you know. Foggy."

Now Ruby offered no reason for pulling up stakes again, except to say, "It's time."

"I'm glad. It'll be good to see you."

"I *will* tell you this."

"What?"

"It is because of you I'm coming east."

"Are you admitting that you miss me?" Sabine made her voice sound teasing; she knew her mother missed her. She also knew that their separation had given them both an independence she, at least, relished.

"I do, but no. I'm coming because you're going to need me."

"Is this prognostication or motherly intuition?"

"Is there a difference? I've got to go, I've got a client." Ruby hung up.

"Circle the wagons, Jerry, Mom's coming." Sabine snatched the black cat off the newel post where he'd been waiting for her, and went back inside.

Across the brook, the firemen's meeting was just breaking up. It had been a lively meeting, plans for the annual Fireman's Carnival coalescing at last. The rides concession was confirmed, the games planned, and the construction crew for the booths organized.

Dan Smith was helping to fold up the chairs when Amos Anthony sidled over to him. "Dan, what's playing tonight?"

"A comedy. You'd probably like it, Amos." Dan

started picking up the unused paper cups from the refreshment table. "Tell Nagy I said to let you in."

"Hey, Dan, you'll go broke you keep letting your friends in free."

"A couple of freebies mixed in with the ten people who'll show up on a weeknight won't be the final straw. It'll be the distributors or the inevitable cineplex going in close by. If I can't treat my friends to a movie, what good is it being saddled with the theatre?"

"Okay. I'll make it up to you in popcorn sales."

"Attaboy, Amos."

With Gran's mandate to keep the theatre still heavy on his shoulders, he was struggling to find a compromise between wisdom and loyalty. Wisdom would have him close the place down. Loyalty and a generations-deep sense of duty kept that choice at arm's length. There had to be other answers. In the wayward path of random thoughts, Dan bumped into his perpetual concerns about Nagy. For Dan, there was no separating thoughts of the movie house and thoughts of Nagy, dutifully sweeping the theatre, emptying the trash, wiping down the seats with Lestoil, and proudly taking tickets every single night. In his fifties, Nagy still perceived the world as a child, with the innocent assumption that if people made fun of him, they liked him. Any plan for the theatre involved Nagy in a far more profound way than simply finding him another job.

Dan was the last man out of the firehouse, locking the door with the key that hung on his key ring beside the theatre key. They looked alike, both brass colored and bigger, as befitted important locks. Locking the firehouse and locking the theatre seemed to Dan to be the parameters of his life. They were his two mistresses. They kept him here when he would be gone, pursuing his chosen profession.

Karen was not happy with him. She hadn't gotten the role in the Redford movie and would have liked to have Dan at home, a sounding board and a shoulder to cry on. He wanted to be with her, too, but it seemed as though every time he loosened up some of his responsibility, something happened. Just last week, with Ralph and Maisie Ralston all prepped to handle the theatre and stay with Nagy, Nagy got sick. There was no way, given Nagy's age and relative fragility, that he could leave his uncle.

"I can't leave him, Karen. It could go into pneumonia," he told her.

"Dan, you promised me months ago that, no matter what, you'd take me to this premier. I have to be seen. You do, too. What will people say when I show up—once again—by myself?" There was a tinge of weepiness to her voice, a brave attempt at not crying that pierced his heart, while at the same time he half-wondered if it wasn't an actress trick.

"Karen. What can I do? Leave my uncle by himself while he's so sick? He can't take care of himself."

"You said that Ralph and Mary were going to stay with him." Karen's voice was petulant now.

"Maisie. I can't ask them to stay with him when he's sick. Maisie has a hard time with stairs, and Ralph wouldn't know what to do." Dan was feeling hammered.

"Don't you think that it's about time he was in a home?"

Reasonable, rational. Probably right. "No. I will not put him in a home."

"Dan." Karen's voice had no longer been petulant or weepy, simply matter-of-fact. "The time is going to come. It's unrealistic to think otherwise. It's unfair to you. And, by association, to me."

Dan rattled the firehouse door to make certain that it was properly locked, then headed for the Ford F150 he'd bought secondhand. The four-year-old blue four-by-four truck was fitted out with a rack of fireman's flashing red and blue emergency lights on the roof. With no income at the moment, writing the check for this truck had pretty much wiped out Dan's savings. He just couldn't keep arriving at the firehouse in Gran's late-model Lincoln. Well, maybe he'd sell the Lincoln now. He didn't keep a car in the city, and the truck would serve while he was still in Moose River Junction. The money he might raise from the big car's sale would tide him over, especially as he was keeping his expenses to a minimum.

When he had graduated from NYU's Tisch School, Dan had been lucky enough to land a job with the Mayor's Office of Film, Theatre, and Broadcasting. His primary job was to scout locations for visiting film companies. About half a dozen ancillary jobs fell to him until he wised up and began to hand some of the bureaucratic tasks to the newer kids joining the staff. It had been exciting, working with known and unknown directors, sweet-talking business owners into letting upstart film companies use their storefronts, being young and in New York.

Then he'd begun working directly with the independent filmmakers, first as second assistant director, then first assistant. He knew the place, he knew the people, and he could charm the most egotistical star into seeing the director's point of view with as much ease as getting the Parks Department to move trees and build kiosks where none had been. He loved the work. He loved the frantic pace, the edge-of-disaster adrenaline rush of a missing actor or bad weather. Maybe that's why he liked being in the fire department. Maybe he was just an adrenaline junkie looking for a fix. That was when he'd met Karen Whitcomb.

Fresh from a relatively successful off-off-Broadway production of *The Bald Soprano,* she was making her debut in film. Fresh-faced and younger-looking than twenty-seven, she had landed the ingenue role in a twenties-era F. Scott Fitzgerald knockoff. The role was for a vapid and innocent victim, but, as evidenced in the daily rushes, Karen had pulled off such a sympathetic portrayal that, far from thinking her character the idiot she was meant to be, the audience was driven to compassion as she made her fatal mistake. And as the saying went, the camera loved her. Dan was smitten. Once the film was in the can, he asked her out.

In that way of significant moments, Dan remembered every detail of their first date. They'd been sharing a cab, heading uptown from the location where she'd just shot her last scene. Devoid now of the makeup that had given her the verisimilitude of the Roaring Twenties, she was a little pale, her chin-length, straight auburn hair still a little damp from washing out the spit curls of the bygone era. He thought she looked lovely.

They'd made the usual small talk, their experience of each other solely framed by the work. Common friends, wasn't this a great script, hopes for success. The chat dwindled.

"So, are you a native New Yorker?" Karen had breached the common ground first. She stroked on nail color, using the flat side of her handbag as a manicurist's table. Her lips pursed with each stroke, little kissing moues until he felt himself grow hard with the suggestion of those lips on his.

"No, a transplant like so many." Where he was from was irrelevant. It was the instigation of conversation that mattered. "You are, though, aren't you?"

"Born and bred. Right over on Riverside Drive."

"Are you hungry?"

Karen looked at him, her nail brush paused in mid-stroke. "A little."

"Do you like Indian food?"

"Very much." Karen recapped the bottle of nail polish and carefully placed it in her bag. "Are you inviting me?"

"I am."

Lingering over the memory, Dan drove slowly through the quiet lane that led from the old firehouse to Main Street. As he came along East Main, he could see that two of the marquee lights right over the center of the title were out. Add a trip to the hardware store tomorrow to his list of tasks. Clearly there was something wrong with the circuitry in the marquee; he'd replaced those same bulbs four times in the last month. Not only was half of the film title in the dark, but worse, so many of the letters were missing that he'd had to spell it out in shorthand. *Is this what it all comes down to,* he thought, *years of hard work, the sweat of hundreds of writers, actors, producers, best boys, and catering services, only to be half spelled out on the marquee of a run-down theatre in the middle of nowhere?* He so preferred the making of movies. The hope and excitement, the rush and the fulfillment of seeing the finished product. Maybe someday he'd even get that most coveted of prizes, an Oscar.

But not if he remained in this backwater. Karen was

right. He needed to be back in the saddle soon or else kiss his career goodbye. As it was, it would take time to rebuild the reputation he'd worked so hard to establish. It was an unforgiving profession. Unbidden, came the question: was Karen as unforgiving?

Gran had been right about his thinking of marrying Karen. Dan had actually been looking at diamond rings, with the idea that he'd pop the question on Karen's birthday. That birthday had come and gone, lost in the wasteland that was the summer, and he was still in Moose River Junction, the proposal still unspoken.

Now he wondered if it was too late.

TWO

Sabine checked off the last call of the day on her tickler file and stood up to stretch. Just as she reached for her jacket on the coat rack, the phone rang. It was well after five, and as she was the only one left in the office, she debated for a ring or two about answering it. She knew that Moe was adamant about customer service, living by his motto, "No call goes unanswered. It could be a big advertiser." Her conscience pricked, Sabine picked up the phone. Even before she spoke, Sabine knew who was on the other end of the line.

"Hello, Beenie. I'm here!"

"Mom? Where are you?"

"I knew you'd be working late, so if you look out of your window, you'll see me. I'm right out in front."

Sabine stretched the phone cord around the divider and looked through the plate glass window of the storefront newspaper office, right at the preternaturally long-lived Volkswagen bus she had known forever. Ruby sat inside, cell phone to ear, waving gaily.

"So you are." Before Sabine could say "Stay there," Ruby was out of the bus and entering the small office. As always, the scent of attar of roses flowed as loosely around her as her caftan. Just over five feet tall, Ruby nonetheless appeared larger than life. "It's all in the attitude." Ruby lived by aphorisms.

"How in the heck did you get here so fast?" Sabine looked between the blades of the venetian blinds to make sure she'd actually seen the lime green bus.

"I was already in Colorado when I called." Ruby stretched, as if to demonstrate her exertions. "So, show me your, what is it called? Cubicle?"

Sabine knew better than to ask how Ruby was so certain she didn't have an office of her own. Just as she didn't ask how Ruby knew she'd still be at work. Ruby just knew things, and that was her stock-in-trade. "It's right here, the front desk."

"The receptionist's desk? I thought . . ."

"There are four people working here. No receptionist. I'm frontline because I work most often with the customers. The advertisers."

Ruby sat down in Sabine's chair and took a deep breath.

Sabine felt her eyes roll heavenward reflexively. Ruby was about to "read" Sabine's space. "Don't do it, Ruby. Don't tell me about myself from my surroundings."

"Why not? Your surroundings will tell me more about you than you will."

"That's not fair. What wouldn't I tell you?"

"Hmmm. That you like your boss but think he's a bit of an idiot. That you are a little bored with this job. That you are thinking about taking me to see a movie tonight."

"Well, except for the last, you know all that from our conversations."

"And, secret out, I know about the movie because you wrote it on this Post-it." Ruby flicked the yellow square with a sharp red fingernail.

Sabine laughed. "You are such a fake."

"Only sometimes." Ruby wheeled the chair close to where Sabine sat in her visitor side chair. "Give me your hand."

Knowing compliance was inevitable, Sabine lay her open right hand on Ruby's. Ruby examined the lines and mounds, folding Sabine's hand over to examine the lines that appeared in her bent pinkie. She flattened Sabine's hand again. "How long has it been since I've read you?"

"I don't know; ages." Sabine had often resented Ruby's insistence that every decision be examined by palm or card. "Why?"

"No reason."

"Come on, Ruby. What does your divining eye perceive?" Sabine, who understood just how the deepening of certain lines, or the appearance of new ones, portended growing older more than a change of future, wiggled her fingers in her mother's hand. "What's this central mystery you keep alluding to?"

Ruby sat back and folded Sabine's fingers, giving them an affectionate squeeze. "I keep seeing indications that you are about to enter a new life."

"A new life. Like a new relationship? Or job? Or what? You know that I'm not leaving here to find any of those things."

"I don't think you'll have to."

"That's good to hear. But the truth is, I think *you're* the one coming into a new life. When was the last time you had your own palms read?"

Ruby's glass- and silver-bedecked hands let go of Sabine's. "I could do with a cup of tea. Can we go now?"

Sabine led the way home, conscious of the contrast between her conservative light blue Honda Civic and her mother's lime green 1968 Volkswagen bus. As they drove past the theatre, Sabine saw Nagy unlocking the side door. She hadn't been to the movies since his mother had died, so she didn't know from direct contact how the poor fellow was faring. She'd bumped into Dan Smith a couple of times, though, and he'd said Nagy was doing all right. "How are *you* doing?" she'd asked him, thinking that he seemed more rested, but no less tense. They were standing in the grocery store, their carts faced off in the cereal aisle.

"I'm okay. Still tying up the loose ends."

"Still planning on going back to New York?"

Dan had looked at her with a mix of expressions that might have included frustration or desperation. "As soon as I can. God willing."

"I'm sure everything will work out."

"Can I have your word on that?" He'd laughed, but the sound was hollow.

Sabine had made some noncommittal remark and gone back to her grocery shopping. The part of her that was Ruby's daughter thought of suggesting she read his cards. The rational part of her, the part which denied any of that was useful, kept her mouth closed.

Sabine now kept her eye on her rearview mirror, since there were two or three turns after the main road that led to her farmhouse apartment. She pulled into her half of the driveway and jumped out of her car to motion to Ruby to pull in behind. The rear engine of the Volkswagen rumbled into silence. Ruby hopped out, stood with her hands on her hips, and stared at the old house.

"Well, this is it. Come on in." Sabine guided her mother around to the back entrance. There was time enough later to introduce her flamboyant mother to the older couple who owned the house.

Ruby took silent note of Thumper, the totemic stuffed animal that had been Sabine's almost since birth. A chill of suspended regret watered through her at the reflexive memory of once leaving Thumper behind. So moved had she been by Sabine's grief, she had turned around after a hundred miles and gone back to Duluth to the angry landlord, and recovered poor Thumper from the heap of trash in the alley. It half amused her and half alarmed her that Sabine still kept the toy on her bed. As if she hadn't outgrown needing it.

"So, no more California?" Sabine slipped her jacket off and hung it beside Ruby's faux fur coat.

"If I'm going to be poor, I'd rather be poor in the East." Ruby turned away from her contemplation of Thumper.

"Have you ever considered getting a regular job? Something with benefits and regular hours? A steady paycheck?"

"Bite your tongue. I don't care how tempting security is, it's a trap."

"Oh, yeah. Knowing where your next meal is coming from is such a bad thing."

"Sabine, Sabine, Sabine. You are so rebellious."

It was a conversation they had had so often, each woman knew her lines without investing any emotion.

Sabine put water on to boil for tea and pulled a vegetable lasagna out of the refrigerator. "So how was the drive?"

"All right. Dull. The midwest is endless. The feng shui in this place is all wrong, Sabine. You've got to turn that futon east-west. The beam is cutting you in half."

"That beam will cut you in half; that's your bed."

"Hmmm." Ruby lay experimentally on the white cushion.

"When did you take up feng shui?"

"Oh, I really haven't, but its all the rage out there in La La land."

"I can't believe you couldn't make a living out there."

"Everything is Scientology and high colonics. Nobody sticks to anything; I couldn't keep clients for more than a month. Always looking for the next sure thing." Ruby got off the futon and leaned against the counter that separated the kitchen from the living room. "What about you? Are you building some clientele of your own?"

"Ruby, what I do is so removed from your calling that it's a completely different thing."

"You tell fortunes."

"I play at making bridesmaids think they'll be the next brides. I walk in with a big disclaimer on my lips and no guarantees. I don't read; I make stuff up. I act. Just like you. Only I do it in the privacy of their homes, and I don't ever make anybody unhappy."

"And I do?"

"What kind of tea do you want?"

"Got any loose tea?"

"Ruby. You're on vacation. Lemon Zinger or Tetley? Just tell me."

"Zinger."

Sabine poured the hot water over the two tea bags, hers the orange pekoe. The two women drank their black tea in silence. They each glanced casually in the other's direction to see the changes that two years had wrought. To her mother, Sabine looked the more changed. As always, her unruly hair was hastily knotted up, as if Sabine could barely stand having it loose on her shoulders. Her face seemed thinner, more pure oval than before. But then, Ruby's thoughts of Sabine were so often memories of her as a little girl, not as she was now, a grown woman.

Sabine in turn studied Ruby, marveling that Ruby still seemed so unchanged, so youthful. Her life had been hard, although Sabine secretly held the notion that Ruby was her own worst enemy, making things difficult out of some bizarre desire to live like a Gypsy. What normal woman dragged her school-age child around the country, unless she was a fugitive from the law?

When she was fourteen and desperate to be in the school play, *Oklahoma,* Sabine had accused her mother of exactly that.

"Are you running away from the law? Did you steal me and have to keep running to prevent my being brought back to my real parents?" She had begun in frustrated anger, but halfway through her diatribe, Sabine was struck with how possible it could be. Weren't the television news magazines filled with such stuff?

Ruby had said nothing for the space of several heart-beats. Then, coolly, with deliberation, she'd smacked Sabine across the face. "You have no idea how hard it has been for me to keep you safe. How dare you make such an accusation."

Shocked beyond words, Sabine walked away. Her mother had never struck her before. Two days later, they were on the road. Riding on the way to somewhere else, it occurred to Sabine that she should ask her mother from what exactly was it she was being kept safe. But, still angry, still emotionally stinging from the slap, Sabine bit her lips and didn't ask the question.

As she cleared away the tea things, Sabine felt herself bite her lip in physical recollection of that moment. Maybe it was time to ask that question again.

It wasn't as clear as it had been the last few nights. The stars were muted behind thready clouds. Ruby stood outside on Sabine's single chair-width landing and smoked. She carefully screwed the butt into the little pot of sand that Sabine had set out for her, and pulled the belt of her faux fur coat tighter against the growing chill of the October evening. She caught the sharp heel of her boot against the lower board of the rail and stared out into the dark. Ruby could hear the chattering of the brook that ran between the banks beyond the trees. It was a sweet sound, peaceful after the long days of talk radio and country western music on the inadequate radio in the bus. She felt in motion, as if the bus had entered her and its wheels were still spinning along that endless highway.

Glancing through the window where she could see Sabine scrubbing away at the lasagna pan, Ruby lit another cigarette. She exhaled a prolonged stream of smoke from her nostrils in the manner of one who claims she is giving it up but is dedicated to enjoying the last one like a souvenir. Ruby saw it as a sign of maturity that Sabine hadn't started in this time on quitting, but had silently handed her the little sand-filled pot. Maybe she'd fool her and quit without the badgering.

Maybe she'd fool her and settle down.

The truth was that Ruby didn't know when she might climb back into the bus, which was more home to her than any she'd set up along the way. Climb back in and head her lonely way to an unknown destination. To go, to keep moving was habitual, long after the need for it had expired. Intellectually, Ruby knew that she could do what Sabine suggested; plant herself in some charming place and take up a more legitimate business. Emotionally, Ruby had become a fugitive. Not from justice, but by habit. She had been running nearly thirty years. How can one stop after so long? The reasons and the secrets that had sent her on her peripatetic life were old and invalid now. Yet every time Sabine started in on wanting to know her history, they rose up, fresh and humiliating. Ruby stubbed out the second cigarette. She had been alone with her thoughts for too long. Without an answering voice, they simply circled around, like a dog nesting, always ending up facing in the same direction. It was time to let the past go. She got up and went back inside.

"Can I help?"

"No. Tonight you aren't allowed to do a thing. Tomorrow is another day."

"I'll make dinner then. I've learned some wonderful Mexican dishes in California."

"Sounds great. Now, do we stay in or do you want to go out to a movie?"

Three

❧

Dan hitched himself forward on the folding chair and leaned his elbows on the balcony rail. Twenty-three heads filled the seats, not too bad for a Wednesday night second show of a second-rate film. From his vantage point, in the sidelights not yet dimmed for the feature, he recognized certain heads from the top, including Amos and his wife, the long-suffering Peggy. Everyone wondered how she put up with his verbal lechery. It was the consensus of opinion that, given his generally grubby appearance and politically incorrect behavior, she figured it was harmless. They'd been married thirty years, so she clearly either overlooked it or put up with it.

As always, Dan had gotten to the theatre fifteen minutes before the beginning of the second show. The only night he watched the whole movie was the first showing of a new feature. Oblivious to the sound of the projector, just audible behind him, Dan watched with the eye of a film school graduate, noting camera angles and lighting from habit. Occasionally a delayed-release film would contain locations he'd arranged, and a thin smile of amazement would light up his face in the dark. He'd once had a hand in this—a more dynamic hand than simply showing the end result to popcorn-chomping, soda-guzzling moviegoers.

As always, the house was filled with people he knew. A few guys Dan recognized from the basketball team and their wives, Miss Hanson from his elementary school, eerily unchanged from his childhood, with her friend Miss Bennett. There, alone in his accustomed center left seat, was Chief Arthur Bean. Leaning a little farther over the edge of the balcony, Dan could make out two curly heads almost dead center of the house. As she tipped her head a little to speak to her companion, Dan recognized Sabine. He felt an unexpected pleasure at seeing her. Things had been so crazed recently that he'd only seen her once or twice, both times in the grocery store. It had been a little awkward for him. He was so grateful to her for being willing to distract him the day of Gran's funeral, to let him talk at that impromptu dinner about other things. And yet now, when they met, it was once again as near strangers. She asked after Nagy; he gave her surface answers to her questions about his plans. The intimacy of that night in September had faded away, a unique moment. Still, the scent of her hair remained.

Usually Sabine had her hair bundled into a loose knot, but tonight it swung free of restraint. Her companion could be her sister, and he wondered why he'd never seen her before. He couldn't tell if she had similar eyes, but certainly her hair was as beautiful.

The previews were over, the sidelights dimmed, and Dan left off his musing to watch.

The projector hummed a little too loudly, and the focus was woozy for a couple of minutes. Dan gave Walter a five-minute grace period before he went in to see what was the matter. The crowd, long used to the vagaries of the old machinery, was patient, but only up to a point. Miraculously, Walt got it operating properly and Dan felt himself exhale.

During the 106 running minutes of the film, Dan collected the evening's receipts from Maisie, wrote out the deposit, then jogged across the green to the night deposit box at the Florence Savings Bank. That done, his watch checked, Dan walked next door to the Dunkin' Donuts and slid onto a stool beside young Arnie Sokolowski.

"Hey, Arn."

"Hello, Mr. Smith."

"Rumor has it you're thinking about getting engaged."

Arnie's fair skin reddened in the bright overhead lighting. "Well, yeah, I guess so. I mean, we are engaged."

"Then you're old enough to call me Dan. Decaf, Hallie, and an old-fashioned."

Arnie nipped around the edges of his glazed doughnut. "The truth is, I don't know if I'm ready . . ."

Dan sipped his over-sweetened coffee and glanced sideways at Arnie. The boy didn't seem to be looking for advice, just airing some doubt. Dan listened as Arnie enumerated the pros and cons of marriage at age twenty. "I've got a good job, with benefits. But I haven't even been out of the country. Not even to Bermuda. I suppose we could go there for our honeymoon." Arnie went on in this vein for some time before Dan interrupted him.

"Arnie. Do you love her?"

"Sure. Sure I do."

Dan suddenly thought of his own relationship with

Karen and realized that, should he ever be asked that question so bluntly, he might answer it in exactly the same passionless way. Candling a comparison to his grandparents' love affair, he knew that his fell far short. Frederick Danforth had built Beatrice Windsor a theatre so that he could be with her. He'd stopped performing in vaudeville, which he loved, and became instead an impresario because he loved Beatrice more. Dan, on the other hand, couldn't extricate himself from an obligation he resented. But then, Karen hadn't shown any inclination to sacrifice on his behalf. If she truly loved him, wouldn't she be here? Dan slammed the mental brakes on. It wasn't Karen's fault for not engendering that kind of passion in him, it was his for believing in a family myth. He should be moving mountains to get back to her. Dan raked his left hand through his hair. "But is she the love of your life?"

"How can I know that?" Arnie licked some glaze off the corner of his mouth and stood up, looking a little sorry that he'd gotten into this conversation. "She's the only girl I've ever been with. We've known each other all our lives."

Dan wanted to press the rewind on his mouth. What right had he to ask such a question? "Arnie, don't listen to me. You'll be fine."

Hallie wiped up the sprinkles left behind and asked Dan if he wanted more coffee. Dan shook his head. After Hallie turned around he shook it again, surprised at himself. *Is she the love of your life?* Too many romantic movies. Like the legend of Frederick and Beatrice, an impossible expectation. Maybe Karen wasn't the "love of his life" in the mythical sense, but they did have a relationship.

Dan dropped a tip on the counter and headed back to the theatre.

• • •

As always, Sabine and Ruby waited until the last credit rolled. Even with mediocre movies, and this was one, the credits deserved reading. With so few in the house, they were among the last to leave. Nagy was already pulling plastic bags out of the trash bins.

Chief Bean greeted them with a courtly tip of his hat, and Sabine made the introductions. "Mom, this is our fire chief, Arthur Bean."

"Ruby Heartwood. A pleasure to meet you." Ruby surprised Sabine by keeping her hands in her coat pockets. Generally Ruby grabbed a person's hand as soon as introduced, to "get a reading."

"How do, ma'am. What'd you think of the picture?" Arthur, in his blue chinos and serviceable tan poplin jacket, seemed so at odds with Ruby in her faux fur coat and stiletto-heeled boots.

Sabine found herself behind the pair as they chatted easily about the film, until his beeper buzzed discreetly at his hip and Arthur broke away from them, with another courtly tip of his hat, to bolt out the door.

Dan Smith waited patiently for them at the top of the aisle. Sabine felt herself smile, then quickly pulled her grin back into a cordial greeting.

Ruby took Sabine's arm as they neared Dan. "He's cute; who is he?" she whispered almost too loud.

Sabine extricated her arm and hoped for a miracle against the impending embarrassment. "Dan, hello. How's it going?"

"Can't complain. Nice to see you here." Dan let them pass through the doorway, then shut it, following the two women out into the small lobby. Sabine had Ruby by the arm again and was hustling her toward the doors, acutely aware that Dan's eyes were on Ruby. She'd changed out of the flowing garment she'd arrived in, in favor of her other trademark attire, a leopard print miniskirt over black tights and a peasant blouse tucked in beneath a large vinyl belt. Sabine had vivid memories of wishing her mother would dress like all the other mothers, in standard blue jeans or cowl-neck sweaters over leggings. "Be glad your mother can still wear this at my age." The implication being that Sabine would age equally as well. Except that she had neither inherited her mother's short stature nor her large breasts. The feature that tied them together was a classically oval-shaped face and the long, curly black hair. Except that Sabine's was natural and her mother's a wig. Ruby's natural hair was mousy brown and thin. She kept it clipped short and hidden beneath a succession of turbans and wigs because it didn't fit the image of a fortune teller to have such ordinary hair.

"Sabine, don't be rude. Hello, I'm Ruby Heartwood." Ruby pulled away from Sabine and turned to grasp Dan's right hand, not in a shake, but to hold it, combining their temperatures so that his warm hand was cooled by hers and hers tempered by his.

"Mom, this is Dan Smith. He owns the theatre."

"You're very conflicted about that, aren't you?"

Dan gently pulled his hand away. "I suppose so."

Sabine felt that oh-so-familiar rush of annoyance at her mother. "Mom, stop it. Dan, don't mind my mother, she's playing parlor tricks on you."

Dan smiled. "Yes. She's tricked me into thinking she's your sister, certainly not your mother."

"Oh, you are lovely." Ruby had heard that line too often to blush at it.

"Mom, Dan needs to lock up. Let's go."

On impulse Ruby took Dan's left hand, noting he

didn't pull it away. She turned it over, palm up, and ran a long nail along the prominent lines. "You can't always get what you want."

There was a pause, a stillness so brief it couldn't be timed. Dan turned his hand back over and grasped Ruby's. "But if you try sometimes, you'll get what you need."

Ruby caught the reference first. "Mick Jagger."

Dan snugged Ruby's hand close. "A pleasure to meet you, Ms. Heartwood."

Outside in the sharp October air, Ruby linked her arm again with Sabine's. "He's delightful. Very conflicted, but very charming."

"He's got a girlfriend."

"Are you certain?"

"Mother." Sabine unlinked her arm to open the car door. "Please don't start on me."

"Beenie, I am the last mother on earth to press for her daughter to be tied up with a man. You know I never liked Johnny."

"He was a shit."

"I knew that before you did."

"You're the fortune teller."

"I don't care if you are a grownup, don't be flippant."

"Sorry. I just mean, don't start. I like my life the way it is."

In silence they got into the car, both amazed that it had taken less than six hours before they had started scrapping. Halfway back to Sabine's apartment, they both tried to make amends. "Mom, I've had a long day. I don't mean to be snippy."

"I've had a long trip."

Silence.

"So, tell me about Mr. Smith."

Sabine sighed dramatically. "There's not much to tell. He's here temporarily, until he can get someone to run that theatre, or sell it. He takes care of his developmentally delayed uncle, Nagy. He's got a girlfriend in New York who's an actress."

"Have you spent a lot of time with him?"

Sabine glanced over to her mother in the passenger seat. "No."

"Odd. I'm getting a sense that you two are . . ."

"Ruby, I beg you. Please leave off forecasting my love life. We are neither destined to be together, nor linked mysteriously. He lives here, I live here, that's it."

"I'm not sure it was your love life I was forecasting. If I could sit with you over your cards, we could maybe get a sense of what's coming along. I told you I was coming because of you, because something significant is going to happen soon. I was born with a sixth sense of knowing this sort of thing, but, as you well know, it's never obvious what's going to happen. I won't really know what it is until I see it."

"Mom, based on that reasoning, you could claim foreknowledge of anything that happens."

"Well, be that as it may, something is cooking and my gut tells me that Dan Smith is part of it. Obliquely. That's what's so odd. The minute I put my hand on his, I felt this heat. This turmoil."

"Ruby! Enough!" Sabine pulled into the driveway.

The little red light was flashing on Sabine's answering machine. Its appearance was almost as welcome as a third party in the room. A new voice, a new topic. Sabine hit the button.

"Sabine, this is Loozy Atcheson. I called you a couple of weeks ago, about the house. We'll be in town on Saturday. Can you come then? I'd really appreciate your help." The intense voice left a New York number and a local one.

Sabine pressed the erase button on the machine.

"Don't you want to save those numbers?" Ruby's voice was behind her.

"I have them."

"I'm going to have a cigarette." Ruby bundled her coat around her and went out onto the landing.

Through her kitchen window, Sabine could see the exhalation of her mother's smoke stab the cold October air. She knew Ruby was desperately curious about the phone call, but some devil in her was making her mother wait for an explanation. She knew that Ruby would make a much bigger deal out of this than was necessary, thrilled that Sabine was, in Ruby's mind, living up to her potential.

"Beenie, you can't just give up letting the ghosts talk through you. It's not something that you can shut off. It's your God-given gift that you have this ability. Don't turn your back on it." Ruby's admonition from long ago, when Sabine refused to attend a séance the day before she was to leave for college.

"I don't have to do it. I'm through with it. Don't you understand?" Sabine heard her own voice, distant with the years, crying out. Knowing then, as never before, that as long as she lived with Ruby, her life would never be conventional. She would have to separate herself from the only person she loved if she intended to live outside of the psychic, soothsaying, paranormal milieu she had been raised to believe was normal. "I can't live like a freak anymore!" Her words had been wounding, both to herself and Ruby.

Gathering her dignity around her, like the folds of her caftan, Ruby had answered, "I have known true freaks, my dear, and they were good people. Honest and loving and kind. You would do well to live like them. But I understand what you really mean. Go. Live like an ordinary girl. Live without magic."

Sabine now watched her mother light a second cigarette. For a decade, she'd lived without the magic. Sabine opened the window. "Mom," she called. "When you're finished, I'll tell you about Loozy and her house."

Four

∞

As he had been doing for some time, while he waited for Nagy to finish sweeping after the second show, Dan was methodically going through the three massive four-drawer file cabinets in the old office of the Palace Theatre. At first it had seemed a breach of trust, rummaging through those files, uncovering the details of his grandparents' lives beneath the surface of the legends. Bills, paid and overdue; tax records; pay stubs for employees long in their graves. Lists of movies shown, deals with distributors. The popcorn purchases. A slow history of the rise and fall of the Palace Theatre. Correspondence between his grandmother and Oscar Nagy. Dan remembered Oscar, who came annually to visit them, an old man with an unfortunate toupee. He'd give Dan a five-dollar bill and take Nagy, his namesake, out to lunch. Now, here was evidence that Oscar had done more than pay his respects: he'd made an offer to purchase the theatre, an offer which Beatrice had dismissed out-of-hand.

"Jesus, in today's dollars, I'd take that offer in a heartbeat," Dan whispered to the empty room. The date of the letter, 1977, coincided with the last year Dan remembered Oscar coming to see them. He remembered that because it was the year he was ten and Oscar had brought him a Yankees cap for his birthday, in honor of Dan's being in Little League.

Dan shoved the letter back into the file folder. A lumpen feeling, like personal regret, settled in his chest as he read bills of sale for the land his grandmother had been selling off to support the old theatre. The noncontiguous acres, scattered around the rural outskirts of the town, had been family-held property since the beginning of time. Dan hadn't even known about them, as they were sold off about the same time Oscar Nagy had made his offer. The sale of a three-quarter-acre lot caught his eye and he smiled. The new firehouse sat on that parcel, which made him feel nominally better. The rest seemed to have been developed into building lots.

"Hey, Danny? Can we go home now?" Nagy stood in the doorway of the office.

Dan shoved the drawer closed. All of this history might as well be burned. "Everything under control, chief?"

"Yes, sir, all under control." Nagy loved pretending the theatre was a ship, or a mission to Mars. They'd played such games when they were real games to Dan, not just humoring Nagy's perpetual childishness. Dan sometimes thought Nagy's inner life was more fulfilling than his own real one. They'd been of an age when Dan was seven or eight, and Nagy in his early twenties. When Dan had come to live with his grandmother, Nagy had been not only his playmate, but an oddly compassionate friend in the dark, when the terror of the fire and the loss was so magnified. When Dan felt himself lose patience with Nagy, he reminded himself of his uncle's clumsy hugs and sympathetic tears. Over and over Nagy would say, "I'm sorry, Danny. I'm sorry that happened."

With those memories unaccountably freshened, Dan affectionately patted Nagy on the back, then snapped a salute. "Dismissed." Snagging the pile of unopened mail from the desk, he followed Nagy out of the office.

They walked home. The fresh air after the stuffiness of the theatre felt good, just cold enough. Once considered outside the town limits, the old house they shared was now the cornerstone of the town's small historic district. With a large tract of conservation land around it, the Windsor Homestead still maintained its rural character. Its actual proximity to town was only given away by the meandering asphalt sidewalk that passed in front of it and served to get Nagy on his own to the theatre every night. The two men followed that cracked path now, quietly enjoying the still night. The farther away from the town center they got, the more brilliant the sky above them became. It was impossible for Dan not to compare the Moose River Junction sky to the skyline of Manhattan. The jewels there were man-made and multicolored, muting the natural brilliance of the night sky, but not less beautiful for it. It wasn't awfully late; he'd call Karen when they got home. She liked to watch Letterman and would most likely be up.

In the old days, everyone in Moose River Junction knew where a fire was by the coded beats of the fire horn. Five short blasts and one long, and everyone piled into their cars and headed over to the school. Three long and two short, and everyone went to West Main Street.

There were only twenty alarm boxes in town, and the insurance company handed out cardboard sheets with the codes listed. Growing up, Dan remembered the four-by-eight strip with its black type pinned next to the telephone on the kitchen wall. By the time he was ten, the system had been revamped and modernized and the beats meant nothing, but the card remained where it was today, still pinned to the wall. He had studied it so many times while on the phone, trying to decide whether the call to his parents' home would have been the Four Two of Upper River Road, or the Four Three of Center Street. Their house on Maple Street had been halfway between those boxes.

Dan stood with one hand leaning against the doorjamb, now, his eyes on the alarm code card, the sound of Karen's answering machine in his ear. "Hi, it's me. Just calling to see how you were. Any chance you could come for the weekend?" He paused long enough so that if she were in the loft apartment, she might pick up when she heard his voice. Dan looked at the case clock in the hallway. Nearly midnight. Maybe she had turned the ringer off to get some sleep. It also wasn't hard to imagine she was out—she had lots of friends; or maybe she was at her parents' apartment. He couldn't think that she might just not answer him.

Ruby flexed her feet at the ankles and poked Sabine's rump. "They want you to read it." Ruby never phrased anything as a question if she could help it.

"I told her I read palms and tea leaves, not houses. But, listen to this, the oddest part of this is her name. Loozy."

"Probably comes from money. A derivative of Louise or Lucy. There is a certain social group which delights in giving meaningless nicknames to their young. I saw something about it on the *Wild Kingdom*."

"Drake and Loozy Atcheson."

"Bespeaks pots of money."

"Fits the type. Well-to-do dot coms. Lots of money and eager to spend it. Vapid lives unfulfilled by meaningful relationships. All *New York Times* Styles section manqué."

"You could tell that by one phone call. I knew you were good."

"Mom, I'm making it up. Except the dot com part. Loozy told me they built this authentic replica as a weekend home, but they can't bear to stay in it. She hears and sees things."

"What are you going to do?"

"I'm not going to do anything. You know how I feel." Sabine stretched, and got up off the futon. "These people are delusional. What they need to do is hire an engineer and get to the bottom of whatever physical problem this brand-new house has."

"Then why did you let her call you again? Why didn't you put a stop to it?"

"She wouldn't take no for an answer."

"Girl after my own heart."

Sabine smiled. "She's the one getting the vibes. She needs to deal with it."

"Not without professional help." Ruby shifted on the futon. "Sabine, you have a calling. You can't hide from it forever. You need to help this woman." Ruby set her feet down, toeing into her mules. "Besides, you certainly can use the money."

"You're so crass."

"We don't take vows of poverty in our line of work. Not like nuns." Ruby spat the last word, as if it was a contemptible thing. "I'm thinking you could go in with a Ouija board. You were very good with that as a girl."

Sabine leaned down to give her mother a kiss good night. "If I were to do it, and I'm just saying *if,* I might try automatic writing."

Ruby put a hand to her chin, like a mechanic contemplating a difficult problem. "Why?"

"From what I've read about it, it can, with a proper trance, open the medium up pretty broadly to the spirit's communication. Besides, it's quicker than that stupid Ouija."

"Sabine, it sounds to me like you've been considering doing this thing without realizing it."

"Good night, Ruby." Sabine went into her room, but before closing the door, she stuck her head back out. "And, if I do it, you're not going."

The bedroom door shut with a tiny click. Ruby sat back down on the futon that would, for a while, be her bed. She felt with stronger and stronger assurance that this was what had brought her back to Sabine's side. This was the significant event.

In her own mind, Ruby was a flyweight compared to Sabine. Sabine's divination abilities were, on occasion, quite amazing. Effortless. Not like her own, which were common garden variety prognostication: mild warnings against travel, a new man in your life, a rough patch, then success. Palms told her stories and she was their interpreter. Sabine, on the other hand, *saw.*

Ruby had first realized that Sabine had the gift when she'd contradicted Ruby on a reading.

"Mommy, why did you tell Mrs. Atkins that she was going to meet a man soon who will take great interest in her?" Five-year-old Sabine's voice mimicked Ruby's mystical intonation. "She's not."

At first Ruby thought Sabine was just carping on the basic fakery of the fortune. Of course Mrs. Atkins would meet a man who would take a great interest in her. All Ruby's readings announced ambiguous statements like that. The man could be a future suitor for the widow or the insurance salesman who might call on her.

But then Sabine had said, "She's going to die next week."

"Sweet Jesus. What are you saying?"

"It's all over her. She's very sick. Her heart's very sick."

"She told you this?"

"Mommy?" Ruby watched the dawning of realization come over her little daughter. "She didn't tell me. I just know it." Sabine had started to cry, afraid of what she knew and how she knew it.

Ruby knelt and scooped Sabine close to her. "Darling, it's all right. There's nothing to be afraid of. People like us sometimes just know things."

People like us. Transient bastard daughters.

Mrs. Atkins had dropped dead on the next Sunday of a massive heart attack. Fell while standing in line to receive Communion, within ten feet of grace.

And Ruby had a new and more compelling reason to keep on the road. It was a very dangerous thing to be a child with such a gift. Ordinary people did not understand these things. Like the man who'd fathered her, Sabine could see a person's death. It had ruined him, made him into a monster. Ruby did not intend for it to destroy Sabine.

Ruby got up and went out onto the landing to smoke a cigarette. The memories kept sliding into her awareness, no longer willing to be held in abeyance. As long as she stayed on the road, thinking only of the future, planning only the next stop, they stayed locked in the mental cell where she had remanded them. But lately, it had been harder and harder to keep them there. It was almost as if they were up for parole, demanding a new hearing in the courtroom of her heart. Maybe it was time to let those sad little facts of her life out into the open. To let Sabine know what she had clamored to know for years.

It had been no picnic, raising a daughter in the circumstances Ruby had often found herself. Raising an articulate, smart, sensible, and down-to-earth daughter from the child born of complete chaos. Staring into the muddy eyes of her newborn, Ruby Heartwood had promised her baby that she would protect her from the vulnerability of dependence on others.

Ruby involuntarily sighed with the memory. Well, Sabine certainly did seem independent. Except that permanency engendered dependence in some fashion or other. On a paycheck, or on a routine. On someone else. One needed to keep unencumbered. Unfound.

Crystal stars hung above the tree line in front of Ruby. Beyond the tangled banks of the brook, the lights of the old firehouse illuminated the front of the building. Sabine had mentioned that Dan Smith was a fireman, and Ruby had asked several nosy questions about him. It wasn't important what she asked, or what Sabine said. She only wanted to hear the tone of Sabine's voice as she spoke about him. It revealed much to her, how a simple question had given rise to a whole story of a dead grandmother and a handicapped uncle. How he had been so wonderful to the old woman, but now he was saddled with this theatre. None of that mattered. Ruby had seen the way he'd looked at Sabine, and the way Sabine had looked at him. Like two explorers eyeing the same territory.

Dan's hands had come as a surprise to her when she

grasped them the other night; she hadn't been expecting roughened workman's hands. Ruby stubbed out her cigarette. The man who'd fathered Sabine had had strong hands, too. Buck Fontana had held her down and covered her mouth with a hand that smelled of sick. A man not strong like this Dan Smith, but rough and painful and insistent. Ruby shook the memory away, like shaking out the match lighting her cigarette.

It had been almost twenty years before Ruby had allowed any man to touch her again. She thought of that man, a fat, gentle client with sweet eyes. He had helped her overcome the scars of the rape that had been Sabine's conception when Ruby was fifteen, a runaway who thought she had found security with a carnival. Eddie's soft, pudgy hands had helped ease her fears and taught her that being touched by a man didn't have to be painful. Buck Fontana had been a man made evil by his own weakness. He hadn't understood his second sight and it had driven him to drink, and the drink had destroyed his humanity.

Abruptly, Ruby stood up to physically move away from memories she had kept at bay for years. Why did looking across a pretty stream suddenly bring those evil days back so vividly? What was past was past. In the end, all she had ever wanted was to see her daughter happy and safe. Leaning her elbows on the rail, Ruby breathed deeply of the October air at midnight. Maybe it was time to tell Sabine the facts of her background, the truth of her birth. There was more of significance about to happen to Sabine than a haunted house. Two key elements were converging in Sabine's life, and she would help her daughter in any way she could. Even by telling her the truth.

Five

❧

"You done?" Nagy gestured toward Dan's half-empty plate.

"Yeah."

"You didn't like it?"

"No, it was good, Nagy. You make great meat loaf. I'm just not very hungry."

"Okay, Dan. I'll save it for you."

"Thanks." Dan watched his uncle carefully dump the half-eaten meat loaf into a container and then struggle a little to get the top to stay on. Nagy's tongue protruded from the corner of his mouth, a barometer of his concentration. Forcing himself to stay put, to watch and see if Nagy could manage without interference, Dan's thoughts returned to what had preoccupied him throughout dinner. How could Nagy ever live on his own?

"You've got to be responsible for your uncle, Danforth. You're all he has once I'm gone." Gran had gripped his hand in hers, the sharp, pointed nails grazing the back of his hand. "It's not fair, I know. But I don't want him institutionalized." At the end of her life those words became a daily litany. More than a concern, it had become an obsession, a fear in the old woman.

"Gran, I won't." He could feel the ball and chain of sincerity on his soul. Of course he'd never do that to Nagy. Besides, people like Nagy were no longer put in institutions, at least not the type that had haunted her conscience—brick and ironwork estates with white-coated attendants. But in making Dan promise to be Nagy's guardian, she might as well have imprisoned him.

Dan stood up and clapped Nagy on the shoulder. "Nice dinner." He hurried out of the kitchen and upstairs so that Nagy wouldn't see the surge of resentment coloring his face. Everything was growing more complicated. Karen was becoming more and more difficult to communicate with. She either didn't return his calls, or needed to be someplace else when she did answer the phone. "Dan, I've got to go." The five words he'd become used to hearing in the last few weeks. It was almost as if she was punishing him for attending to his responsibilities; as if she was demonstrating to him that he was becoming a nonperson in their world. It would be so much easier if he thought she believed he *was* working hard to get back to their life together.

Although he might have done it over the phone, Dan had gone into the *Pennywise Paper*'s office this morning to place an ad for a theatre manager. The newspaper had been around all of his life; he'd even been one of its paperboys back in the day of such things. It had been years since he'd been in the little storefront office and it had remained so unchanged that he felt as if he'd slipped into a time warp. The smell was even the same, something like a cross between old wood and wet paper. The vague green wall color and even the four lithographs of scenes around nineteenth-century Moose River Junction were precisely as he remembered them.

But Sabine, sitting at the front desk, was a complete change from plump Mrs. Condon, who had been the paper's advertising and social news doyenne until she started having children. Mrs. Condon used to give him candy along with his paycheck, always saying the same thing to him. "Here you go, Dan. Don't spend it all in the same place. And here's a Hershey bar for being such a good boy."

Sabine was a treat for the eyes, if not for the tongue. Dan blushed at the image that this brought to mind. He'd been going to mention how Mrs. Condon gave him candy bars then, kid Sabine about expecting something from her, but the words were too evocative of his sudden fantasy and Dan was a little afraid that any word out of his mouth would be fraught with double entendre.

"If we put a box around your ad, that would give it a little pizzazz to catch the eye." Sabine was like a counselor. "We can only run this weekly, so you may want to get an ad in the daily papers, maybe even the *Boston Globe*. Don't you think?"

"I think I'm not going to find anyone willing to work for what I can pay, much less move out here to the back of beyond, but I have to do something."

"The right person will come along." Sabine laid one hand on his. It felt smooth and cool against his own skin, and his renegade thought returned.

"Is that a prognostication or are you just being nice to me?" Dan thought that his tight voice surely gave away his imagining.

"Both." Sabine smiled at him and patted his hand, for all the world like she was an old friend.

He needed to change the subject and lit on the first thought he had. "I enjoyed meeting your mother. You two really do look alike, sort of the long and short of it."

"Don't think you're the first person to make that joke. But we're not that alike." Sabine stood up. She was dressed in what served as business casual for Moose River Junction, dark green wool trousers, white turtleneck, and matching dark green fleece vest. She wore Dansko clogs on her feet and horn-rimmed glasses perched in the welter of her knotted hair. Katharine Hepburn in clogs. "Want some coffee?"

He didn't but said yes. She brought back two mugs from the newspaper's kitchenette, hers black, his cream and one sugar. He wanted to ask how she knew how he took his coffee, but let the moment pass.

"I hope that you weren't offended by Ruby. She can be a little strong sometimes."

"No, not at all. She only spoke the truth. How can I be offended at that?"

"Still, she meddles. Be warned."

"Will she be here awhile?"

Sabine shrugged. "Who can tell? She's like the wind, you never know when she'll blow. I never lived for more than half a year in any one place until I was eighteen and at college."

"You sound a little bitter."

"I'm trying to grow out of it."

"Is that why you're here, in this hole?"

"Dan, it's not a hole, and yes. Unlike you, I love being in a small town. Settled. I like sitting in a room full of people and knowing half of them."

"What I like best about the city is that no one knows

you, who you are, who your grandparents were, what genealogical strand you descend from."

"Too intimate?"

"Yes. Exactly." Dan set his coffee cup down. "I should let you get back to work."

"Yeah, I probably should." They were standing now, facing each other in her small space. Sabine reached out to place one hand on his upper arm in a comradely yet utterly feminine motion, soothing him with a gentle stroke. "Don't worry, Dan. It will all work out."

"I hope you're right."

Back home that afternoon, Dan couldn't shake a new awareness of a loneliness he hadn't realized he'd been suffering. The few minutes of conversation with Sabine had reminded him of his unrelenting bachelor existence. From home to theatre and back, the biweekly firemen's meeting, all male, and the occasional call to put out a blaze. More and more, it seemed to have been another man who had lived in New York and made movies. Another man entirely who had slept with Karen, rooting for her career rise even as his own blossomed. Another man who wore expensive suits and drank Perrier. That man bore no relation to the one wearing flannel shirts, jeans, and work boots, with calluses forming on his hands. Drinking water from the tap.

Dan had long ago fallen in love with movies. With the making of them. As a boy, his favorite game was playing director. He'd set up his pals in scenes and then, holding a cardboard tube to his mouth, shout "Action!" The summer that he'd broken his leg and couldn't play outside, he'd become addicted to reading back issues of trade magazines his grandparents had stored in the attic. He absorbed the industry's names and numbers as he had box scores and players' statistics in baseball. But he'd never wanted to be the purveyor of the end product. It was the film itself he loved, not the theatre.

Dan looked at his face in the bathroom mirror. In two years he'd be thirty-five. If he failed in his goal of going back to New York, returning to the career he had so hastily abandoned, he'd end up as the middle-aged bachelor with the struggling movie house and the odd little uncle. The most exciting thing would be the occasional major fire. "Get a life, Danforth." He pointed to his face in the mirror. "Get a fucking life."

"Dan, I'm going now." Nagy was shouting up the stairs.

"Okay. See you at the second show." It was dark by now; should he give Nagy a ride? "Be careful." *He's got to be treated like an adult.*

"I will."

Dan went back downstairs and found the oven still on, the plastic container of meat loaf on top of the stove.

Six

❧

Saturday mornings were Sabine's favorite. After a quick cup of coffee, she'd slip into loose clothes and go for an hour's hike. A path led off Windsor Farm Road through the thickening woods of the conservation land and eventually to a small pond. No one ever seemed to walk there, and Sabine loved the intense privacy, the cathedral-like vault of the trees, lending themselves to thoughts that her daily life obscured. Especially now, with Ruby staying in the apartment, Sabine longed for some contemplative time.

Here in the woods, she didn't keep thoughts of Dan Smith at bay. Yesterday in the newspaper office she'd felt that little click again, the one she shouldn't be feeling. He was attached. He was only temporarily part of this community. As soon as he could, he'd be gone. So why did she allow herself to touch him, to let his overwarm skin radiate through her cool hand?

Sabine walked through the leaf-strewn path, scuffing up the fallen oak leaves like a child, relishing the rustling sound so evocative of youth. She could ask Ruby to read her cards, and see if there was some reason she felt this link to a man she knew so one-dimensionally. Or she could read his palm and see if his future was the one he planned—that's what Ruby would suggest.

Sabine slapped the trunk of a beech tree as she passed it. Maybe it was the fact that he was as frustrated with his current situation as she had been with her past life. There was an oddly kindred spirit there, in that they both knew what they wanted and had been, in her case, held back from it. In his, taken from it. There had been something else, too; the same kind of loneliness she knew. Not the loneliness of friendlessness, more the lack of a companion who understood the inner workings of one's heart. But he had his actress girlfriend. Surely she was a source of comfort to him, even from a distance. No, it was his damned dimples framing his sexy smile, and his quick laugh. Maybe she was just plain horny. She should ignore it and move on.

A little sweaty from her long walk, Sabine had just gotten back into the yard when she heard the phone ring. She dashed up the stairs to catch it before Ruby did, but was too late. She had no doubt it was Loozy Atcheson, and that Ruby would be milking her for details, encouraging belief in the unlikely haunting. New houses were very rarely haunted.

She could hear her mother. "So, have you got a lot of antiques in there? Something that might have come with an attachment, so to speak."

"Give me the phone," Sabine hissed, her hand out to snag it away.

"Oh, here's Sabine. Bye, now." Ruby smiled her I-told-you-so smile as she handed over the phone. "She needs you!" she mouthed as Sabine took it.

"Hi, Loozy. Are you in town?" Sabine deliberately turned away from Ruby, like a teenage girl talking to a boyfriend.

"We're at the house. Is there any chance you can come today? I'd love to sleep here tonight. It's such a long way from New York, and there's no good motel in town."

"Hold on, Loozy. Even if I come to check things out today, there's no guarantee you'll feel any more comfortable sleeping there tonight."

"You mean if you find something?"

Sabine wished she'd phrased her remark more judiciously. "I mean . . . okay. How about after lunch?"

"Great." Loozy spoke to someone behind her. "Drake says to use the back driveway. Don't park in front."

"Sure. Whatever. See you then." Sabine hung up and shrugged. "Evidently Drake is a control freak," she told Ruby. "Wants me to park behind the house. What do you suppose he's concerned about?"

"Being blocked in, in case you discover something." Ruby was rooting around in her massive duffel bag. "Here, I knew I still had it." She handed Sabine a long thin cardboard box. "The Ouija board."

"No, thanks. I told you, I'm not going to spend hours there. I'll use an ordinary pen and paper and see if these supposed spirits can write."

"Why don't you want to use the tried-and-true?" Ruby took the box back, gently brushing the cover as if an old pet.

"Mom, I don't really want to find anything."

"Beenie, you know as well as I do that if there are spirits, you won't be able to ignore them. Whether writing with a pencil or a planchette, you'll be touched."

"You think this is the thing. The significant event."

Ruby placed the Ouija board back in her duffel and

brushed imaginary lint from the front of her robe. "Yes."

"How so? I've communicated with ghosts before."

"I don't know. Maybe it signals a return to your calling. Maybe it's just an interesting interlude in your life. If I knew, I'd be a better fortune teller." Ruby reached across the space dividing them. "I only know that you need to do this, to do it honestly."

"I will. I promise." Sabine took her mother's hand and held it.

Ruby smiled at Sabine. "So, what will you wear?"

"Ruby, I can tell you right now, no caftans." Sabine let go of Ruby's hand and went to pour herself a cup of coffee.

"It's just that a little costuming can sometimes lend the right atmosphere to a reading."

"Mom, no. I'm doing this in broad daylight, nothing up my sleeve."

The subject seemed played out, and Ruby busied herself with tidying up the kitchen. Then, apropos of nothing, she turned to Sabine. "You seem a little flushed." In the time-honored way of mothers, she laid a hand across Sabine's forehead, then smiled knowingly. "You should take a cool shower."

"Thanks, I will." Sabine had to wonder if there was anything subliminal in Ruby's suggestion. A quick reading might help to settle her unruly imagination, which had been running roughshod over her heart for the last hour. If Ruby saw nothing, she would be more disciplined in her thoughts about Dan. If Ruby saw something, well, let the games begin. Pulling her thoughts up short, Sabine set down her coffee cup and went into the bathroom. What was she thinking! She despised women who moved in on other women's territory. She would not behave like that, no matter how much click she felt when she was around Dan Smith. Of course, if the cards spelled it out, who was she to fight the course of nature? Sabine twisted the shower faucets on, letting the water run cool.

She had promised Dan that everything would work out. But she hadn't been reading his future then; she'd been saying what he needed to hear.

Nagy worked furiously to scrape the leaves into a big enough pile so Dan would be pleased that he had gotten so much done. The wind had died down enough, Dan said, to rake without having to do it twice. Even so, the top leaves quaked and little eddies of uncollected leaves were touched off by the northeast breeze. Nagy was warm under his NYU jacket but he didn't take it off. A blister was rising where his thumb and pointer met, and Nagy wished Dan would hurry up so he could go get a Band-Aid. It never occurred to Nagy to just stop. Dan had asked him to do this, and he'd keep at it until it was done.

Finally Dan's truck pulled into the driveway.

"I'm almost done." Nagy gestured toward the big pile. "I need a Band-Aid."

Dan reached for the paper bag in the back of the truck and opened a new box of leaf bags. "Where are your gloves?"

Nagy shrugged in a marvelous comic gesture. "What gloves?"

"The ones I bought you last night."

"I don't know." Same gesture.

"Go get a Band-Aid."

Dan adjusted the NYU cap on his head and tried not to let the exasperation hiss out. It was a small thing. One of many small things. Nagy was blessed or cursed, depending on your viewpoint, with an inability to grasp concepts except by constant reminding until the idea took hold. Dan had not reminded him about the gloves, ergo, Nagy never gave them a thought. Any errand became a litany. "What do you want?" "Where are you going?" "What are you getting?" A child would learn and take that learning with him. Nagy could not, and sometimes Dan thought it was just easier to do those errands himself. But Gran had had infinite patience, and it was with her in mind that Dan held back his exasperation and praised Nagy's work. "You've done a good job, Nagy. Nice work."

"I'll be right back."

Dan picked up the discarded rake and began pulling the leaves out from under the shrubs that hid the old stone foundation. He got down on his hands and knees to reach the wet mulch and was reminded of playing in those bushes as a child. Hours of hide-and-seek with playmates and Nagy. There had been that little girl across the street—what was her name? Patty. And his best friend, a rough kid, not the sort his grandmother liked him to hang out with, but a decent kid underneath his blustery exterior. Dan pulled hard at the leaves and wondered whatever happened to Jeff. His family had moved away when they were about to go to junior high. Never heard from him again.

In the way that stream-of-conscious thoughts light on forgotten memories, Dan suddenly remembered a couple of buddies picking on Nagy. He couldn't quite pull up exactly what they had done, just that he not only hadn't made them stop, but had joined in. In that unconscionable way of boys, he'd teased Nagy along with them, happy to be on the winning side. Boy, had Gran been mad with him that day. Dan felt residual repentance heat up his cheeks even as he tried to suppress the memory.

"Danny, I can't get it on." Nagy stood with a Band-Aid held out, the sticky parts folded over and useless.

"Here, give me a new one." Gently, Dan layered the bandage over the burst blister on Nagy's right hand. Nagy's tongue poked out of the corner of his mouth as he watched in concentration. As Dan looked down on Nagy's head, with its sparse gray hairs sticking out, he felt that ancient remorse fire up again. Sometimes he forgot that Nagy wasn't a child but an aging man. "Why don't you just hold the bags for me?"

"Okay, Danny."

Nagy held open the big black bags and Dan filled them. A car horn made them face the road, and they waved to Sabine Heartwood as she went by. It was common for acquaintances to wave as they drove by; still, Dan felt a lick of pleasure that she had done so.

"She likes chick flicks."

"You just like saying 'chick flicks.'" Dan tossed a handful of leaves at Nagy.

Seven

✑

The Atchesons lived off Lower Ridge Road. The driveway went up a sharp incline, then turned abruptly left. A second dogleg and suddenly the large house appeared, an uncanny replica of a seventeenth-century saltbox, right down to the flat black hinges on the plank front door. The authenticity was quickly compromised by both the satellite dish under an eave and the Range Rover out front. As instructed, Sabine pulled around to the back of the house.

Before Sabine could reach the back door, it opened and a tall thin woman about her own age came out. "I'm so glad you're here. I really hope you can help us."

"You must be Loozy."

"Yes. And this is my husband, Drake." Loozy waved him over. "Drake, darling, this is our psychic."

"Let me tell you right from the get go, I don't believe any of this." Hostility fairly oozed from his impeccably clean pores.

"Neither do I." Sabine stuck out her hand, forcing him to take it or be rude. It was cool to the touch, despite the layers of Polarfleece the man wore. "You think that I'm going to try and separate you from some of your money without producing anything you deem a result."

Drake looked a little sheepish. "I suppose I do."

"Then I'll leave." Sabine turned back to her car.

"No!" Loozy grasped Sabine's sleeve. "Please ignore him. He's a skeptic."

"Most sane people are." Sabine attempted to extract her arm from Loozy's panicked grasp. "Tell me about the house."

Loozy, not yet relinquishing Sabine's arm, led her around the house to the front door. Drake, silent, followed behind. A central hallway led from room to room and Loozy gave Sabine a tour of each, keeping up a stream of chat, most of which was centered on the extensive decorating job and how much it had cost. The place looked like a set for a *Masterpiece Theatre* episode. A working fireplace in every room, real antiques offset by good fakes. The lighting was appropriately dim until they got to the one room that bore traces of real living. The den, clearly Drake's hangout, was comfortably furnished with what must have been their prewealth furniture: a soft couch, faded recliner, maple coffee table with rings staining the finish, and a television of suitable size. A wood stove jutted out from the fireplace hearth. A box of kindling and several logs lay beside it, but the October day was too mild to have a fire going. The kitchen was the last room they entered, and Sabine beat back jealousy at the sight of the Aga stove.

"Have you ever spent the night?"

"Oh, yes. Until I realized that the sounds I was hearing weren't normal."

"Describe them."

Loozy had begun setting out homemade cookies on a cobalt blue plate. Sabine watched her hands, French manicured and laden with heavy gold. Three bracelets rode up and down her arms with every action. *Clink, clink, clink. There is a very special sound to real gold,* Sabine thought. *Very special indeed.*

"Well, like voices. High-pitched. Low-pitched. I don't know. It was as if someone was having a conversation in another room. But if I went to that room, it stopped or moved on to another room."

"And you've had all the mechanical stuff checked out?"

"Pipes?"

"Pipes, location of the dryer. Stuff like that."

"Of course."

"No rodents?"

"Ugh, no."

"Wind in the trees? You've got a lot of woods around you."

"That's what Drake thinks it is. He says sometimes branches actually squeak. But it's not. They aren't that close."

There was something about Loozy, despite her gold and her manor house, that reminded Sabine of Greta Sutler. A simplicity of spirit. She just wanted to hear that everything was going to be okay.

"Have there ever been physical manifestations? Things moving around? Visual contact?" The dark irises of Loozy's eyes dilated, and Sabine remembered reading somewhere that at the sight of a loved one, a lover's pupils will do the same.

"Yes. I saw someone."

"Jeez, Loozy. You did not."

"Drake, you know that I did."

Drake stood at the Italian marble-topped island counter, where he was struggling to get the espresso maker assembled. "Loo, what you saw was a figment of your free-wheeling imagination. Ms. Heartwood, my wife is a creative genius. Sometimes it gets away from her."

Sabine ignored the husband and turned to the wife. The women were seated at a massive, oval country pine table that boasted a Martha Stewart—inspired centerpiece of artfully arranged dried flowers and ceramic fruit, all of which matched the hand-painted table runner in colors and shapes.

Drake got the espresso maker together and began to operate it. "That centerpiece is Loozy's. She painted the cloth. She's a wonderful artist, but like all artists, a little . . ." Drake tapped a finger to his temple to indicate some oddity within his pretty wife's brain.

"Drake, that is so unfair."

Sabine was surprised, given the insulting nature of his comments, that Loozy was actually laughing.

"He's such a tease."

Sabine thought he was rather mean-spirited. "Well. Be that as it may, what do you *think* you saw?" She emphasized the word *think* as a sop to Drake.

"A shape. At first I thought it was someone sitting in the rocking chair in our bedroom. It was dim in there. We were just, well, you know. Getting frisky."

"Were you in bed?"

"Not yet. Anyway, I had my eyes closed, and then opened them and there he was. Sitting in the antique rocker. In another second, he was gone."

"Ms. Heartwood, what her passion-induced sighting was, was simply our clothes tossed on the rocking chair."

"That's what I wanted to believe it was. Except that there was a face. A man's face, and he looked right at me."

"Loozy, have you ever looked at clouds in the sky, or seen faces in wallpaper?" Sabine had taken Loozy's hand in hers as she asked this. The soft hand was clammy to the touch, only warming as Sabine held on.

"Yes, of course."

"And when you did, did you ever experience the rapid heartbeat you experienced that night?"

"No. I was very frightened. I made Drake take me to a hotel. We had to go all the way to Springfield." Loozy extracted her hand from Sabine to scratch her chin. "How did you know I had a pounding heart?"

"Because you have one now just relating the story."

"It was so *real*. I saw his face and he blinked. He moved. He looked at me and he was so sad."

"Can I offer you a cup of espresso, Ms. Heartwood?" Drake set a tiny cup in front of her. Sabine heard the tiny cup chatter against its saucer.

"One more question." Sabine fingered the tiny spoon Drake had laid beside her cup. "What do you expect of me? What do you expect I can do?"

"Well, frankly, I don't expect anything. Loozy here hopes that you'll be able to divine whether or not this, this thing, is . . ."

"In my head or not." Loozy wasn't smiling now; she stared into her tiny espresso cup as if reading its contents. "I just want to feel safe here."

"Without doing any readings, I can guarantee you're safer here with or without a ghost than in the city." Sabine waggled an eyebrow at the suddenly too-serious pair and sipped the bitter coffee. "Look, I can take a stab at it, but I want you to know that I will not guarantee anything. Nor, if something happens, can I tell you what should be done about it."

"I just want to know if there's something here."

"Okay. Here's what I propose to do. Drake, could you find some paper and a pen?"

He rifled through a drawer in the island counter and pulled out a yellow lined pad and a Bic ballpoint pen, half used. "Will these do?"

"Perfect." Sabine flipped over the first page of the yellow pad. "I'm going to do something called automatic writing. Are you familiar with it?"

"Isn't that what nineteenth-century fakes did during séances to fool people?" Drake threw himself down on one of the harp-back chairs, and leaned back until only the back legs were on the floor. His arms were crossed over his belly and he glared at Sabine with challenge.

"Yes. But what I'm going to do won't be manufactured. I'll enter a trance and let my fingers do the walking, so to speak. If there are true ghosts in this house, they will speak through me via the pen. At least that's the idea. I will only guarantee that nothing will happen unless it's real. I won't even pick up the pen unless my hand is guided by a spirit."

"Sweet Jesus, you expect us to believe this shit?" Drake snatched the empty espresso cup out from under Sabine's hand. "How gullible do you think we are?"

"Not at all. I didn't offer to do this. You called me." Sabine felt a growing anger at this pompous, puffy man.

"Drake, please. Please let her try. What have we got to lose?" Loozy looked imploringly from Drake to Sabine. "Please go ahead. Do you want us to leave?"

"No. I think that it's best for both of you to be in here with me. I only ask that you remain very quiet. I'm a little out of practice in trances."

Sabine had learned at her mother's knee how to hypnotize herself. A parlor trick, really. Simply an exercise in relaxation. She should probably teach it to Loozy and forget about contacting spirits. As illusion is another level of delusion. Sabine also knew how to fake a trance and fully intended to do so if need be. Not for the first time, she was glad she hadn't handed this couple over to her mother. It would have been too much for Ruby to resist providing the nervous Loozy with proof of haunting. She would have justified it by saying it was what Loozy wanted in the first place. Besides, Drake deserved to be haunted.

Sabine shook off the mental voice and pointed the Atchesons to the other side of the table.

Bright afternoon sunshine backlit the pair so that she could not see their faces, only their silhouettes. "Now, I must warn you, don't expect much out of this exercise. This will just open the door to see if I can detect any sort of disturbance."

Loozy pushed her artfully tousled blond hair back with her perfect fingernails and then folded her hands like a good girl in Catholic school. Drake affected a more supercilious pose, one arm flung over the back of the chair, an admixture of disdain and amusement on his rather florid face. He was maybe thirty-five, yet already had the look of a man past his peak. The years ahead would not be good to him. Sabine had a hunch that if she read his palm, his lifeline would reveal a brief, cranky sojourn upon the earth.

Sabine laid one hand over the other and focused on the knuckles of the top hand. Breathing deeply, she tried to clear her mind of detail, opening up her inner eye to lose the physical surroundings and see only the interior world of her beating heart. Akin to meditation, almost like falling asleep, Sabine slowly allowed herself to loosen from the corporeal world and be released into dream. If anyone had sneezed or coughed, she would have heard it, as she did the ticking of the banjo clock on the wall. She slid deeper into the soft world of trance, letting go of thought and waiting for message. The ticking of the banjo clock diminished. In her early adolescence, it had been very easy to open up to the spirits. She hadn't even needed a trance state. Like seeing the old woman with the knitting, the spirits simply revealed themselves to her. As she'd grown out of adolescence, it had become nearly impossible to achieve the same easy state of communication. The sunlight-induced faces traveling across the walls of the church at Beatrice Danforth's funeral had been a surprise, and probably only her imagination. The trance began to feel good, like sleep. Slowly her mind gave up the clutter of thought, and then there was the blanketing nothingness of deep trance.

From somewhere outside came the sound of angry voices. They called to one another in words she couldn't quite make out, and on some other plane Sabine wondered if the Atchesons still had workmen on the property. Then she heard a woman's frightened voice, and a man's garbled response. They should be quiet, she thought—and was suddenly aware of the smell of smoke. The scent was so strong that she felt herself rise out of the trance. She heard a cry, a high-pitched, anguished cry. Sabine felt her skin crawl with the alarm. Then, a man's voice clearly saying, "Say naught."

Annoyed, she lifted her head and looked at Loozy and Drake. "I asked you to please be quiet."

"We haven't said a word. We haven't moved since you started writing." Loozy sounded a little hurt, a good girl falsely accused. The sunlight behind the Atchesons had dimmed from golden yellow to muted gray. No longer backlit, their faces were clearly visible and equally curious. She must have been entranced for over an hour. They were both looking at her hand, now gripping the pen. On the yellow pad was line after line of halting scribble, like a three-year-old makes pretending to write. Drake and Loozy came around to her side of the table to look at it. Nothing was legible until halfway down, when one clear word stood out. *Hide.*

Reading the word, she heard again the cry that had so prickled her skin. Sabine shot out of her chair, her heartbeat rapid, as if she had woken up frightened. Having stood up too fast, she felt a faintness come over her and she sat down, dropping her head between her knees to overcome the wooziness.

"Are you all right?"

"Fine. Fine. You should go check your wood stove."

"Why?" Drake had moved to the sink to get her a glass of water.

"I smell smoke."

Loozy and Drake sniffed the air and shook their heads in exactly the same manner. "The stove's not going."

"Oh." The odor of wood smoke had been such a strong influence, strong enough it had pulled Sabine from her trance. She sniffed the air again and smelled nothing but the potpourri in the centerpiece. The olfactory sensation had been a predominant part of the trance, the voices almost secondary. Sabine felt as though she were in the path of a light electrical current; her fingers, which still gripped the pen, tingled. Her pulse was as racy as Loozy's had been relating the sighting. *Something horrible has happened here.*

"So, what's the verdict?" Drake handed Sabine the glass of water.

"I'm not sure what to tell you." Sabine took a sip of the water, trying to calm her beating heart. "I didn't want foreknowledge to clutter an open mind, so I didn't ask before, but do you know any of the history of this place?"

"Not really. We got the land in an Internet auction,

then built the house. We always wanted a weekend retreat, but this place is turning into a nightmare." Loozy refilled Sabine's glass. "I spent a lot of time and energy to make this place the home I always wanted, and now it feels like something wants to take that away."

"Loozy, it's a beautiful place and you shouldn't be afraid of it." Even as she said those calming words, Sabine felt they were anything but the truth.

"I think you're both a little nuts." Drake began to take the espresso maker apart. "I haven't spent a fortune building the perfect place just to have my wife's overactive imagination prevent me from enjoying it. And I won't have some half-baked psychic feeding her delusions." Drake's face was flushed.

Sabine would have walked out without another word, except for the distraught expression on Loozy's face. "I think that something happened here. If not in this house, somewhere near it."

"Can't you please find out what it was? Can't you go back into a trance and try again?" Loozy had a tissue crumpled in one hand. From time to time, she'd touch a corner of the tissue to her eyes.

Sabine wanted to be out of that house and home with Ruby, to beg Ruby to tell her that she had fallen victim to her own imagination. But Loozy's distress touched her heart, and she knew she had to do something. "All right. Why don't you check in at the Historical Society and see if there's anything to find out about this property."

"No can do. We're out of here in half an hour." Drake pointed in the general direction of Boston. "We've got tickets to Blue Man Group tonight."

"We only came straight here today to meet you." Loozy's voice was still a little churned up. "Can't you check it out for us?"

"I really don't think so." Sabine was getting more and more annoyed with these people. "Why not just sell the place and find another house?"

"No. I love it. We'll pay you."

"Loozy, maybe she's right. Let's let it go."

His wife dabbed a fresh tissue against her red-rimmed eyes. "You don't even understand, do you, Drake? I want to stay here. I put my heart and soul into making this my dream house. I can't just let it go because of some noises."

"Then stay in it!" Drake was growing more flushed.

Compelled to put an end to it, Sabine stood up. "All right. Let me do a little research and see if there's some historical event that might have occurred on this location."

"Oh, sure, and charge us what?" Drake behaved like a man afraid of his money. Having made it, he was afraid of losing it.

"The going rate for ghost busting." Sabine ripped the top yellow sheet off the pad and stuffed it into her pocketbook. "If you don't want me to, that's fine with me. Nice meeting you." Sabine zipped up the front of her fleece jacket.

"Oh, please, Sabine. We want you to, don't we Drake?" Loozy's pale eyes darted from Sabine to Drake and back again.

"Yes. Of course we do." Drake snagged Loozy's hand in what looked to Sabine like an uncomfortable grip. "But I'll only go so far."

Despite a lingering syncope, Sabine took Loozy's hand away from Drake and patted it. "Just relax." She then offered her hand to Drake, once again making him take it or be rude. "I'll be in touch."

Fighting the sense that her legs were about to go out

from under her, Sabine got to her car and pulled away from the house. At the end of the dogleg driveway, she put the car into park and rested her head on her hands, gripping the steering wheel until she felt the slight faintness pass from her. There had been no workmen near the place. No other cars in either driveway, besides the Atchesons' Land Rover. No fire in the fireplace and no leaves burning.

The warmth of dawning awareness slowly filled her and the shaking ceased. Sabine lifted her head up off the steering wheel. "This is why I'm here." The spoken thought, so random and unbidden, was nonetheless true.

Ruby was right. There could be no question but this was her significant event. Even as she'd argued with that pompous Drake, she knew that she was invested in this mystery and would never be able to walk away from it. In the few seconds that she had touched Drake Atcheson's hand, she had felt that his fear of this thing, this entity was as great as Loozy's. Still, it wasn't his need for answers or even Loozy's now. It was her own.

Beyond the voices and cries, more mysterious than the single legible word *hide,* it was her powerful realization that the odor of wood smoke that had brought her out of her trance was precisely the same scent she'd smelled the day of Beatrice Danforth's funeral. She remembered it so clearly, a light whiff of smoke she thought might be extinguished candles, just as Dan Smith was looking down at her from the balcony.

A wafting scent of distant fire.

In Sabine's mind, the similar scents inextricably linked Danforth Smith and this house. Now she needed to find out why.

Eight

❧

When she got home from the Atchesons', Ruby was waiting for her with a hot cup of tea. The flavor was unusual and Ruby waved away Sabine's reluctance to drink it. "It's fine, you need a little calmative after your experience."

"If I were in the mood I'd ask how you knew I'd need a calmative, but I can't argue with you now. Mom, it was bizarre. I was in such a deep trance and then, pow! It was as if I was just sitting there and all these sounds were audible only to me. Garbled language, almost foreign sounding. Then the cries. That was very real. Mostly the smell of smoke. That was so real, too, as if I was sitting in a room with a fireplace. Then I was out of the trance, woken by what I thought were the Atchesons' voices. No sounds, no smells, no nothing except these two faces staring intently at me and this scribbling beneath my hand."

"The way I see it, there can be only two or three things to account for a haunting. One, the house had some curse put on it. Two, they brought in a haunted piece of furniture, an antique with a spirit attached; or, three, the land the house sits on is haunted." Ruby tapped her newly painted red nails against the counter-top.

"We could also say that, as predisposed as I am to suggestion, I imagined the whole thing."

"Sabine, you have the proof right here." Ruby indicated the sheet of foolscap with the scribble on it.

"What if that's my own thought?"

"I'm not saying it might not be. We both know that our own suppressed thoughts can cloud someone else's reading, but think of the word. What instant image comes to your mind?"

"Just the sense of a dark, closetlike place."

"Like any of the rooms in the house?"

"No. Older."

"There. Something happened on that land. I guarantee it."

Sabine yawned. "What is this stuff? A narcotic? I'm suddenly dead on my feet."

"That's the aftermath of a reading that powerful. Go to bed."

"It's only five o'clock."

"Don't be a baby. Do as your mother says."

"How am I going to help these people?" Sabine headed on unsteady feet toward her bedroom.

"Like you told them, start with research. You can't help them until you know what it is you're dealing with."

"I'll go to the Historical Society tomorrow." Sabine yawned and fell on her four-poster bed, instantly asleep.

Ruby stood a long time in the doorway, watching her daughter sleep, amazed at the power of Sabine's gift.

Her senses were being engaged selectively. Hearing and smell. Next should be vision, or touch. Probably not taste. That would be odd. Ruby sighed. When Sabine had turned her back on this gift, Ruby had argued with her, but understood. Each time Sabine had been brought in to do a reading, it had grown harder and harder for her to make that connection. It was as if adolescence had somehow opened up a window that closed as soon as she'd grown up. Partly hereditary, partly hormonal. This reading was so different. As a girl, Sabine had seen the spirits, always engaged in some household task, or simply standing or sitting. They were benign, as if memory, not emotion, had brought them into being. This reading was a mature connection, a true communication with something that had left a psychic residue into which Sabine had been invited.

Ruby softly closed the bedroom door and got out her tattered Tarot cards. It was time to see if Sabine should pursue this mystery or let it go. Ruby was no less convinced that this was the significant event in Sabine's life, but she intuited that it was only part of the story. The cries and voices, smoke and writing, might only be a conduit toward the true event.

The third card she turned up was one often associated with difficult relationships.

Nine

❧

On Sunday, Dan took Nagy to the cemetery where his grandparents, parents, and ancestors lay. Together they would tidy up the family plot, and then sit for a little while, gathering their thoughts and sharing lunch. The two men sat with their backs against the sun-warm limestone of a faded headstone and passed a bag of chips back and forth.

"Nagy, what would you like to do if you didn't work at the theatre?"

Nagy shrugged and punched Dan in the shoulder. "I don't know. I only know how to work in the theatre. It's my job."

"The craft factory needs help. Wouldn't you like to work with some other people, make some friends?" Last week Dan had spoken with a woman who arranged for people like Nagy to work in places like that. Six or seven men and women of varying mental disabilities already worked there, happily van-pooling together every day.

A supervisor made sure they were safe and self-sufficient. The woman had been very nice, assuring Dan that the clients were well supervised and had a good time despite the repetitive simplicity of their tasks. It was the only business within a twenty-five-mile radius that had places for people like Nagy, and only within the last month had an opening occurred.

The woman had been sweet but firm. "We need to know before the end of the month if we can expect Nagy to join us. Otherwise, I'll have to give the job to someone else."

Dan now cleared his throat. "They have a lot of fun. Besides, wouldn't you like to work in the daytime?"

"No. I like Maisie and Walt. I have lots of friends. They come to the movies."

Dan rolled the sandwich wrapper into a tight baton of white paper. "But what if there was no theatre?"

A little stiff from sitting on the ground, Nagy got to his knees. "Mommy said there would always be a theatre. It was our theatre. Why wouldn't there be a theatre?"

Dan didn't look at Nagy, only at the bag into which he stuffed the remnants of their picnic. "I'm just worried about your future. When I go back to New York, someone else will run the theatre . . ." Dan let the sentence die as he looked up into Nagy's stricken face. It was always the same; whenever he tried to suggest things might change, Nagy grew frantic. Nagy had no concept of the struggle it was to keep the theatre open, to keep up with the maintenance, to keep his grandparents' dream alive. His uncle had no idea what a toll it was taking on him.

"Danny, why would you let someone else run the theatre?"

Dan got to his feet. The yellow October sun was

bright in his line of vision and Nagy invisible in front of him. "Sometimes things aren't the way we want them to be."

"They're the way I want them to be. I want them to stay the way they are."

"It's okay, Nagy. Nothing is changing tomorrow. But you have to understand that things might."

"Don't you want me to work in the theatre?"

"Nagy." Dan put his hand on his uncle's shoulder and bent to look him in the face. "As long as I own the Palace, you'll work there."

"Are you going to sell the theatre?"

Dan was always a little amazed when Nagy went from child to adult. He knew it was only imitative behavior, but sometimes Nagy did seem to have a grown-up grasp of things, and it was to this momentary understanding that Dan replied. "I'd like to, Nagy. It's losing money faster than I can earn it. But right now I'm just trying to find a manager."

And then the child returned and Nagy began to weep. His bottom lip quivered and great dollops of tears slid down his cheeks. Dan felt his own eyes moisten and he put his arms around his uncle. "Nagy, don't worry. No one has wanted it yet. Don't think about it."

Dan led Nagy back to the truck, for the first time wondering if he was looking at life backwards. Maybe, like Nagy, he *should* devote himself to the Palace, to saving it. Last night he'd been working on a critique of one of his friend Paul Krest's film students. He tried not to think of it as a horrible mishmash of unconnected trick shots but as a fledgling's first attempt at making the film medium her own. Yet there were too many glaring technical oddities for it all to be deliberate. Unlike reviews, these critiques were meant to offer constructive criticism so that the student might improve on the work begun. Rarely, very rarely, had Paul sent him anything remarkable. Most of it was pretty typical, everyone trying to be an auteur without experience.

But watching the video, writing the comments, Dan had been overwhelmed with homesickness. He needed to be away from the sound of the projectors and back with the sound of the rolling camera. Nagy had no facility for understanding that. His cosmos was contained within the borders of Moose River Junction. He saw the outside world only as it was presented night after night on the screen. It's where he saw anger and greed, lust, violence, and love. Beatrice had created a world for Nagy in which he could move safely, unthreatened by the outside world. She had brought him up to believe that the Palace was the center of the universe.

Dan had called Karen again this morning, thinking that she'd be home on a Sunday morning, albeit sleeping in after a busy weekend. When the answering machine message came on, Dan steeled himself to say something, rather than hang up in frustration. "Karen, I'd like to talk to you about . . . about this situation. If you're there, please pick up." He waited a heartbeat, nothing. "Okay, you know where I am, please call me." He slammed the phone down. That, it seemed to him, was that.

Leaving her mother to pursue her own Sunday afternoon entertainment, Sabine walked the short distance to the former one-room schoolhouse that now served as Moose River Junction's Historical Society Museum. Behind the museum was the ancient burial ground, its other boundary the white clapboard South Congregational church which squared off the green. The three-quarters of an acre between the two buildings was filled with limestone, marble, and granite headstones in varying degrees of decay and tilt, some even flat on the ground, the battle with the elements and frost heaves lost.

The volunteer on duty was delighted to have Sabine come through the front door and willingly took her two-dollar suggested donation, handing Sabine back a tri-folded brochure describing the collection.

"I'm actually interested in finding out about some land off Lower Ridge Road."

"You'll want to start with the town ledgers. What are you interested in? Ownership? Transfer of property, that sort of thing?"

"Well, I'm not exactly sure what I'm looking for. I'm on a special project for the owners and just want some idea of its history."

"Land is funny. Buildings are easier." The volunteer led Sabine from the main room of the museum to a back room that might have been a cloakroom in the old days, now set aside as a library. "When the courthouse was remodeled, they gave us all of the deed books dating from the early eighteen hundreds clear back to the first title deeds of the colonial era. For anything more recent you'll have to go to the county courthouse. Unfortunately, we haven't the finances to get them properly archived, so here they sit." A phone rang and the volunteer excused herself, leaving Sabine to figure out where to begin her hunt.

"If only I knew what I was looking for." Sabine ran her finger down the stack of brown leather-bound ledgers and squinted to read the faded titles. The scent of old paper tickled her nose, and she felt a little afraid to touch the crumbling books. In the bright afternoon sunlight the dust motes sparkled in the air like faint snow.

Even knowing whose hands the land had passed through might not reveal anything to explain what might have caused the manifestation. It was an historical event she was after. Still, she had to start somewhere. Hefting the top three ledgers off the stack, Sabine headed into the main room and the big map table there.

Dan Smith and Nagy were chatting with the volunteer. Dan was quick to see her come through the library door and stepped up to take the heavy books from her. "Hello. What brings you here?"

"If I told you, you wouldn't believe it."

"Nagy, go use the rest room." Dan gave his companion a gentle push. "Nagy needed to use the bathroom. We've just been out back." To Sabine's puzzled expression Dan added, "We visit the cemetery every couple of weeks. We tidy up the plot, have lunch."

"I see."

"So, what do you think of our little museum?" Dan made a broad gesture encompassing the small building.

"It's lovely."

"I used to spend a lot of time in here doing school projects." Dan gestured to the left where a row of glass cases stood. "Have you seen the colonial armament display?" The glass case was full of antique muskets and powder horns.

"No, I'm actually here to look up something."

Dan touched the topmost ledger. "So I see. What are you looking for?"

Sabine flushed, embarrassed to admit she was back to practicing ghost hunting. It was okay for him to know she read palms and cards as a sideline, but it was another thing entirely to say she was acting as a medium. It didn't bear contemplation that he might think her an oddity, a member of a fringe society. "Well, there's this piece of property which might have an interesting history."

"Which one?" Dan glanced back at the men's room door, but it didn't look like impatience to Sabine, it looked more like he was pleased that the door remained shut.

"Some property off Lower Ridge Road. The Atchesons' property, about a half-mile from the intersection."

"On the right, driving west?"

"Yes. With the dogleg driveway."

"Newcomers. Built a big house there not long ago. So, what do they think might have happened there?"

Sabine slowly sat down in a hardwood library chair and leaned her elbows on the table. "Something which has disturbed the house."

Now Dan sat down, taking the chair beside Sabine. He leaned his left elbow on the table and rested his head there. He smelled good, not of any cologne or aftershave, but a good, manly smell like raked leaves and fresh air. A hint of wood smoke. Sudden dimples showed in his cheeks and his olive green eyes brightened with amusement. "Are we talking ghosts?"

"I didn't say that." Sabine felt herself blush a little, embarrassed that he'd caught on so quickly and might tease her. She certainly didn't want Dan Smith to imagine she believed in all this nonsense. In all of her experience, she had no one she could safely let into her secret life. Always she had pretended that none of it was more than a joke, or a game. "Sometimes things happen that are hard to explain. Noises, cold spots, shadows. Sometimes I can help."

Dan's dimples deepened but he didn't laugh at her. He ran his hand over the cover of the ledger. "I imagine the first thing you'd need to know about the land is the title, deeds, all that, going back to the original town survey. Do you have the map and lot numbers?"

Sabine nodded.

"Then once you've got all the names, go through other sorts of records to uncover the marriages, births, and, naturally, deaths. Who lived there, who died there, and who died unhappily."

"Sounds like a whole lot of work for an unrealistic expectation." Sabine slid back in her chair and looked over her shoulder to see Nagy coming out of the men's room.

"Did you wash your hands?" Dan asked him.

"Yes. See." Nagy held his hands out for inspection like a little boy, turning them over front to back for Dan to see.

"Good fellow." Dan handed Nagy his baseball jacket. "Sabine, would you be interested in some help?"

Sabine was surprised and a little charmed by Dan's offer. She covered his hand, which rested on the back of her chair, with hers. "I'd be a fool not to take some help, but honestly, I don't think I'm going to pursue this quixotic quest much further. I'm simply trying to justify the hundred bucks I charged this yuppie couple. And I wouldn't want to impose on your time." She gently tapped his hand, a little gesture meant to convey gratitude and release.

"You wouldn't be." Dan stood up but kept his hand on the back of Sabine's chair. "If you change your mind, I'm pretty well versed in local history and I know my way around a plot plan. Give me a call."

"Thanks. Maybe I will." Sabine felt that flush rise up her throat and deepen the color in her cheeks. "Change my mind, I mean."

As he left, she was uncomfortably aware that her

heart was beating a little faster than it should, almost as it had done after she'd been at the Atchesons'. It beat with the same excited wallop. Her rational self argued that Dan wasn't flirting, but just being nice. Probably he really liked historical research. After all, he was a native son. Dan Smith must be one of those rare, charming men who sincerely make you think you are amazingly interesting when all they're really being is polite. Still, if she hadn't known about Karen, hadn't actually laid eyes on his New York girlfriend, she might have succumbed to wishful thinking. Sabine inhaled slowly, exhaled, and then, back in control of herself, she opened up the first of the ledgers. The handwriting looked like encoded script. Her eyes were on the faint and spidery writing, but her mind was elsewhere, distracted by the unexpected meeting with Dan, and wanting to play with the idea he had been glad to see her.

After leaving the museum, Dan and Nagy headed for the market to pick up a few items. Dan gave Nagy his cold-cut order, making his uncle rehearse the pound of boiled ham and half-pound of turkey and one-half pound of cheese, American, white, three times before letting him go. Pushing the cart, Dan meandered down the aisle, trying to remember what they were here for. Sabine's voice kept coming to mind, the way she blushed when he made his feeble joke about ghosts. The way she touched his hand. Raisin Bran or Cheerios? Why did he feel like he'd been flirting? He wasn't a flirt. Whole wheat or pumpernickel? Sitting so close together, he might have reached over and kissed those lips.

"Hello, Dan, how nice to see you again."

Ruby Heartwood startled Dan sufficiently that he

jerked his hand away from the bread as if he was thinking of stealing it. "Ruby, hi."

"Don't let me interrupt your shopping. And don't forget mustard."

Dan watched her clip down the aisle in her preposterous high-heeled boots. "Why do you think I need mustard?"

"I have a gift."

Dan pushed his cart after her. "I just bumped into Sabine."

"At the museum." As usual, Ruby kept her inflection just this side of a question.

"Yeah. The Historical Society." Of course she'd know where Sabine was. No mystery there.

Ruby had turned around, her arms filled with the few items she had come into the store for. "I think that Sabine will take up your offer to help."

"How did you . . ." Dan had only just left Sabine sitting at the map table, ledgers in front of her.

"Dan, if you are to know Sabine better, and me, you have to know that we—to put it simply—know things. We have a bond that goes beyond words."

"A mother-daughter bond?"

"A psychic bond."

Dan almost laughed, then thought better of it. This little woman clearly worked the fortune teller schtick pretty well. "I see." He started to reach for the bread again, then something occurred to him. "Could it also be the bond of cell phone?"

"We have ways." Ruby didn't seem put off by his skepticism—rather, amused by it.

Another thought crossed Dan's mind. "Ruby, can I ask you a favor?"

"I'd be delighted. Shall we say seven o'clock?"

"For what?"

"A reading."

"No, no. That's not it. Well, not exactly. Would you be willing to help us out at the Firemen's Carnival? Would you do fortune-telling for us, as a fund-raiser for the defibrillator?"

"I never do carnies. Too many unsavory characters. Bad business."

"No, it's our own carnival. We do everything, except the kiddie rides."

Ruby considered his question for a moment. "Why don't you ask Sabine?"

"I could, I suppose. It's just that . . ."

"I fit the image better." Her voice was just this side of sardonic.

Dan tucked the loaf of bread into the child seat of his carriage. "It was only an idea. No big deal."

"When is it? I don't know how long I'm in town."

"Two weeks from Saturday."

Dan might have thought that Ruby would take out a calendar to consult, but instead she pressed the tips of her fingers to her forehead as if consulting an internal Day-Timer. "I'll do it. But I can only offer you half the take. It is my living, you know." Ruby tossed her springy black curls a little and gave Dan a sideways look, putting him instantly in mind of Sabine.

"I wasn't aware of that."

"You are a sweet liar. And this is a very roundabout way to get a reading done. So be it."

"That wasn't my intention, but thank you, Ruby. I'm sure you'll be a great addition to the day." Dan started down the aisle.

"Oh, and Dan, a friendly warning." Ruby looked dramatically left and right to make sure they were alone in the aisle. "I won't tolerate Sabine being hurt. Be careful how you proceed."

It might have seemed a non sequitur, except that Ruby had touched on his growing awareness of Sabine, and Dan understood her warning though he quickly denied its validity. "I don't believe that I'm proceeding with anything, Ruby. You must know that I'm with someone. And Sabine knows that I am. We're just friends."

Ruby's lips curved upward in an eloquent rebuttal of Dan's statement. "See you anon." She fluttered dainty fingers cluttered with glass and silver and vanished to another aisle, leaving Dan with an odd sense of being in an Ionesco play. Conversation with Ruby was like theatre of the absurd.

"And I don't need mustard," he said under his breath.

When the mustard jar in the fridge proved empty, Dan muttered an epithet before throwing the plastic jar into the recycling. "That was just a good guess, Ruby Heartwood."

Ten

❧

"Dan, what are we?" Dan had answered the theatre phone, never expecting Karen's voice on the other end.

"We're a couple."

"Couples see each other. Couples progress in their relationships. We are not only stagnant, but going backward. When are you coming home?"

Dan ran a hand over his newly trimmed hair. "I don't know."

The silence on the other end of the line was the silence of disapproval, skepticism. Contempt.

"Karen, why don't you come here for the weekend? We'll figure something out together."

"Are you saying that you're not coming back, ever? I'd like to be clear on this." Now her voice oozed sarcasm.

"No. I'm just saying, as I have been for a month, that things are going very slowly here. I've gotten exactly two responses to my ad, neither one viable, the roof is in dire need of replacing, and I'll have to do it myself because I can't afford to hire anyone. I'm saying that I miss you and I need you here."

Again the silence, but behind it Dan thought he could hear a ragged breath. "I'm not coming to you, Dan. You have to come to me."

"Okay, maybe I can get away for a couple of days. Midweek would be better than a weekend."

"No. I'm not talking about a couple of days. I'm saying come home now or it's over."

Dan held the phone out, almost as if trying to see if such words could be a mistaken transmission. "An ultimatum, Karen? It hasn't been that long."

"In case you're not keeping track, Dan Smith, it's been exactly seven months since you and I were together for more than forty-eight hours at a time. That is not a relationship. That is an acquaintance."

"Are you working right now?" He knew she wasn't, knew that he was being provocative.

"That's irrelevant."

"I am working. Maybe not in the job I want, but I am responsible for this theatre, the people who work for me, and Nagy. I can't just abandon them."

"But me. You can easily abandon me. You say you have responsibilities; well, what of your responsibility to me?" Karen's voice had a slight catch in it, as if at any moment she'd break down in tears.

Dan had the choice of provoking those tears or backing down. "I'm just saying that there's a little dinner theatre work in this area. It's not movies, but it's a living. You could come and spend the winter here, honing your skills."

"What?"

"Come to me."

"Dan, no. I will not step backward just so we can patch things up. I will not go backward so that you can stay in that shit hole of a town, playing with your little theatre and keeping your retarded uncle happy. You may have given up your dreams, but I will not."

Dan knew that there was no saving this conversation. "Karen, did you call to break up with me?"

There was a very deep sigh on the other end, a silence so profound there could be only one answer to his question. "Yes."

Dan very quietly set the phone back in its cradle. He felt slapped, and the most ringing blow was not her breaking it off with him, but her use of the word *retarded*. No one called Nagy that. Not since childhood. It was so mean-spirited that all else Karen had said in anger paled. She might deride him and his situation, but she shouldn't say such things about Nagy.

Karen had always been standoffish about Nagy. Not speaking directly to him unless she had to, or ignoring his presence on those rare visits she'd made to Moose River Junction. She'd neither been kind nor cruel; people like Nagy were of no interest to her. Like the old Vietnam vet who sometimes panhandled near their building. She'd stuff a dollar bill in his paper cup but not meet his eye or acknowledge his thanks.

Still sitting at his grandmother's desk in the theatre office, Dan looked up at the photograph of Frederick Danforth, slicked-back hair and smiling face. He wished that there was a matching portrait of Beatrice to hang beside it here in the theatre they both loved. Well, Gran had certainly been right about Karen. Why was it so hard to listen to the wisdom and instincts of our elders? Or maybe it was just a self-fulfilling prophesy. After all, it was Gran who had put him in this untenable situation which had cost him Karen. Dan felt sick. He was just so tired. Not physically, but emotionally. Sometimes he just wanted a moment's peace when he could stop being responsible; an hour when his wish to be a good boyfriend, his concerns about Nagy, his struggle with the theatre, would just stop.

The phone rang, the shrill, old-fashioned ring of the rotary instrument startling him out of his deepening contemplation. "Palace Theatre."

"Dan? I hope I'm not disturbing you . . ." Sabine Heartwood's cheerful voice caused an involuntary smile.

"No. This is a great time for you to call. I was just getting ready to jump off the roof."

"That never solved anything. Why so glum?"

"Never mind. I'm just being stupid. So, what's up?"

"Were you serious about helping me with this silly investigation?"

"I don't think it's silly, and yes. If I can, I'd love to help." Dan raised his eyes to meet those of the long-dead Frederick Danforth. It crossed his mind that he didn't know what color those eyes were; he'd only seen black-and-white photos of the man. Right now they seemed to be bright and encouraging. "What can I do?"

"Have lunch with me on Saturday and help me go over some of these entries I've photocopied out of the ledgers and some other sources. I'm so over my head here that I'm throwing myself on your mercy. Will you come?"

"I'd love to. Where do you live?" Dan shoved a pile of bills out of his way and found a scrap of paper.

"Thirty-nine Windsor Farm Road. Do you know where that is?"

"My dear, I'm a fireman in this town; I know where every property is. That's the Fishers' house, isn't it?"

"Second floor. Noon."

"Can't wait."

Dan settled the phone down gently. He had the oddest feeling of comfort, as if the unexpected conversation with Sabine mitigated the angry one he'd had with Karen. He felt vaguely exonerated.

Sabine leaned against the counter, her hand over her mouth as she still couldn't believe she'd called Dan Smith to help her. What had possessed her? "Jerry, what have I done?"

Jerry the cat wound himself around and between Sabine's legs in mute suggestion that she had done nothing extraordinary and should be feeding him.

"Mom is going to flip."

"Mom is going to flip why?" Ruby bumped the back door open with her hip, her arms full of bags. "Perrotti's was having a sale on canned vegetables. I bought him out of asparagus." Ruby set the heavy paper bags on the counter and dusted her hands together as if having done dirty work. "So, what have you done?"

"I called Dan Smith to help with the research. When I bumped into him at the museum on Sunday, he mentioned that he knew a lot about the town and how to read a plot plan."

"And now you think you're sending out mixed signals?"

"No, I think I'm getting them. He sounded so happy to help."

"Why wouldn't he be?"

"He's got a girlfriend."

"So he's said. So where is she? Where was she when he needed her?"

"That's not the point. I just don't want to be the agent of change, if you know what I mean."

"Sabine, what will be will be, and there is nothing you or anyone can do to change the inevitable."

"What *is* the inevitable?" Sabine folded her arms and tilted her chin, challenging her mother to wiggle out of that. It was so like Ruby to make these inscrutable and unprovable statements.

"I'd have to read his cards or palms to tell you that."

"Ruby, you are a piece of work. Now, what are we having for dinner?"

"I'm not sure, except that we'll be having asparagus with it."

Ruby put the groceries away while Sabine thawed some hamburger in the microwave. They moved easily around each other in the tiny kitchen, used to small quarters. No place Sabine could ever remember had a kitchen larger than six by six. Some had cupboards, some shelves, some had nothing more than a metal cabinet for food storage. No wonder she was struck speechless with envy at the sight of Loozy Atcheson's massive kitchen. A woman could really cook in there. Her own space was adequate and carefully laid out, but still there was only an illusion of separation by the island counter that divided it from the living room space. A living room now converted to a bedroom. Ruby had been with her for a whole week and, as yet, hadn't mentioned her next move. It was like waiting for the proverbial shoe to drop. I'm here, I'm gone. Little by little, the bus was being emptied out. Over there, a cardboard box of shoes. In that corner, the duffel bag full of the miscellany of a fortune teller's trade: gauzy curtains, fringed tablecloths, the rejected Ouija board. Sabine molded the thawed hamburger into meat loaf, all the while casting glances at Ruby, who was reading the evening paper. "So, what's your plan, Ruby? Will you stay with me awhile?"

Ruby looked up at her daughter and nodded. "As long as it takes."

"As what takes?"

"For you to live through your significant event."

"I thought the house was the event."

"Part of it. The rest is cloudy, but connected."

"You're making this up to make me crazy."

Ruby shook the paper into submission and laid it back down on the coffee table. "I'm here to make sure you don't avoid your fate."

"You've always told me you can't avoid your fate."

"That's just fortune teller schtick. Haven't you read Frost? 'The Road Not Taken'? Come on, Sabine. You know very well that the human will is far stronger than random fate. People make choices."

"So you've got some idea that you need to be here to help me make my choices?"

"No. I just want to watch."

"Rice or potatoes?"

"Rice."

"See, you've already made me make a choice." Sabine laughed. Ruby joined her on the kitchen side of the counter and they hugged, pleased in some way that their sparring was half jest and all a sign of affection.

Eleven
❧

Quarter to eleven on Saturday and Dan still had things to do. If he hurried up and got the light fixtures in the bathroom changed, he'd still have time to go home and change his stained work shirt for a clean one, and get to Sabine's on time. He opened the storage closet door.

"Nagy, have you got my toolbox?" Dan shouted up the short steps that led behind the screen. Nagy liked to sit behind it, eating his lunch at a small table that had been there from the beginning of time. The table was drizzled with paint from various projects, and had a long drawer that had been jammed shut from the time he was a little kid. Posters that Dan knew had more value than the whole theatre were hung on every available space. *Gone With the Wind, The Wizard of Oz, The Magnificent Seven*—all vied for space against Nagy's preferences from recent years, *Big, Toy Story,* and *The Lion King.*

"Yes."

"Can I have it?"

"Yes."

"Nagy, what were you doing with my toolbox?"

"Nothing."

Dan was beginning to think that with Nagy, he'd never need to have children of his own.

"Exactly what kind of nothing?"

"Fixing things."

Dan sighed and went up the stairs. Nagy sat with the toolbox open on the table, several screws and three screwdrivers out, and his chair upside down. One chair leg was off and in Nagy's hand.

"Did your chair leg come off again?"

"Yes. I can fix it. I know how."

"Yes, you do, Nagy. I know. Would you like me to find the right screw for you?"

Nagy poked at the selection on the table with one finger. "I can choose."

"Okay. But can I have that screwdriver? You don't need the Phillips head."

"You can have it, Danny."

Dan retrieved the screwdriver and left Nagy to repair the chair, which regularly wobbled. Nagy hated the wobbles, and yet wouldn't let Dan buy him a new chair. "I found this one. I like it." Dan had never quite been able to find out where Nagy had come across the old maple kitchen chair, but Nagy was proud of his find. One of Nagy's chief joys in life was finding things. In the last few months, Dan had discovered that his uncle had a propensity for keeping the lost and found items. Dan had uncovered a veritable tag sale of umbrellas and hats, spectacles, and even shoes in Nagy's back room.

He stood aside and watched as Nagy carefully set the screw into the hole. Nagy had been there that night, the night of the fire, one of dozens of nights he spent with them. At odd hours of random sleepless nights over the years, Dan had marveled that he hadn't cost Gran everyone she loved. His mother, Freddie, and the unborn child. His father, Gary, himself, and Nagy. If Nagy hadn't wakened . . . those thoughts could not bear weight and Dan kept them locked away.

"Thanks for the screwdriver, Chief."

"Just doin' my job." Nagy had picked that phrase up, like he had "go ahead, make my day," from some movie and never let it go. He was full of phrases from movies, drilled in like language rudiments from the weeklong, twice-a-night showings.

Karen didn't know what she was saying when she accused Dan of taking these responsibilities too seriously. She had no idea what kind of debt he owed.

As always, minor repairs revealed major ones. The light fixture wasn't broken; the wiring was shot. He'd have to get an electrician in here. It was a miracle the whole place hadn't burned to the ground. Though that would certainly solve his problems. A quick mental slap, followed by a contrite silent prayer, "Please don't let anything happen to this place." Dear God, how could he live with himself if he caused two buildings to burn? Dan heard the double blast from the firehouse horn signaling noon. He'd be late getting to Sabine's, but he knew that Craig Olsen would be home for lunch and it was the best time to track down the elusive electrician. The best he could probably hope for was that the guy would come sometime in the next two weeks.

"You caught me at a good time. I'll come right over."

Dan was instantly in that miserable place where workmen hold customers hostage. If he said "not now," he might never see Olsen again. "Okay. I'll leave the side door open." Dan immediately dialed Sabine's number.

"Sabine, can we move lunch up to maybe one o'clock?" Dan explained his situation.

"No biggie. We can do it another time."

"No, I really would like to do this. I'm just stuck waiting for Olsen."

"Dan, I understand." Sabine sounded like she did understand that he wasn't deliberately blowing her off. "These things happen. Let's just postpone."

"Maybe tomorrow?"

"That's fine."

Hanging up, Dan was struck with how he was making a habit of disappointing women. Granted, Karen's disappointment in him was more serious, but somehow he felt worse about letting Sabine down.

He checked on Nagy and found his chair fixed, and Nagy bored. "I want to go home and play with my PlayStation."

"I have to wait here, Nagy, I can't give you a ride."

"That's okay. It's nice out."

Nagy was right, it was a beautiful mid-October Saturday, and here he was, trapped in the musty theatre waiting for a man who could only give him bad news. Trapped inside when he could be sitting in Sabine's kitchen, enjoying the company of a lovely woman and talking about history. He'd figured out where the Atchesons' lot was and knew that a terrific trail rose above the property. He was in the mood for a hike, a return to an old pastime. Karen had not been very outdoorsy, preferring a workout on the treadmill to a walk in the woods. Fresh from their breakup, Dan found himself silently enumerating the flaws of their relationship. He'd given up a lot to be with her: hikes, camping, rafting. She'd liked skiing, though. Was it nearly a year ago that they'd spent a week in Telluride? Was it only a year ago his life had been so settled? They'd loved film. They'd devoted their careers and their common ground to it. Sitting in the dark of his office, Dan concluded that it was his breaking away from the set piece of their life which had frightened Karen. In the end she hadn't trusted him, trusted him enough to believe he'd come back.

"Hello? Dan?" Sabine knocked on the office door with its old-fashioned frosted glass window, FREDERICK DANFORTH, MANAGER, still lettered on it.

Once again she had saved him from his thoughts.

"I figured Olsen would be taking his time, so I brought lunch. I hope that's all right." Sabine had an antique wicker picnic basket hung over one arm, a plaid wool blanket over the other. Dan took the basket and set it on his cluttered desk. "Let me give you the Cook's tour." He made a wide gesture. "This is my office, indistinguishable from the closet to its left."

Sabine looked around the small, dark room with its wooden file cabinets and ancient hardwood desk. A rolling chair with its back canted slightly to the left was tucked beneath the desk, which itself was heaped with piles of organized clutter. A man in a tuxedo smiled down from above the desk. "He looks like you."

"My grandfather, Frederick Danforth. He built this place in the early thirties. Imagine, smack in the middle of the Depression, my grandfather sticks his neck out like that."

"He must have been very certain it would survive."

"He was. And, mostly, it did."

Dan wouldn't go into the current state of things. He wanted to show Sabine just a little of himself, not everything. "Of course, vaudeville was a dying form and so he changed with the times. Turned it into a full-time movie theatre." They moved out into the lobby. Without the percussive popcorn machine going and the display lights in the candy shelves off, the place seemed museum-like and serene.

Dan carried the heavy basket. "Let's skip the projection booth." Walking her into the darkened house, he pointed to the bare stage with its silver matte screen. "How about a picnic under the pine trees?"

"Oh, yes. I see them, swaying ever so gently in the light summer breeze." Sabine laid the blanket down on the splintery dark floor and began to pull the sandwiches, chips, a flask of coffee, and a plate of brownies out of the basket. "I feel like I'm at the Teddy Bears' Picnic."

Dan immediately hummed the childhood tune. "I can't think of the words, but the tune sticks like glue."

"Oh Lord, now I'll have that stuck in my head all day."

"No. I can improve on the theme music. Wait there." Dan ran off to the projection booth and a minute later orchestral music heavy on the schmaltz emanated out of the speakers above the stage. Dan jogged back down the aisle and leaped up onto the stage. "All-purpose background music, courtesy of John Williams."

The tape played as long as they were eating. The prevalent *Star Wars* theme seemed to highlight the adventure of an impromptu picnic in an unlikely place, with two people as yet unsure of where this adventure would take them. The empty theatre was still redolent of the audience lately there, and from where they sat, they could see the places Nagy had missed last night where the popcorn still lay mashed underfoot. Eventually

Craig Olsen would appear, but for now the theatre was empty except for the two of them. A curiously intimate and confessional atmosphere.

"So where are you from, Sabine? What brought you here?"

"I'm from a lime green Volkswagen bus. Really. All my life I was on the road, one perpetual road trip. My only constant was Ruby, and the green bus. There is a small benefit to such a life; you get to see a lot of places and you find you can deal with a variety of personalities. But the flip side is that your laundry is never quite dry and you have no friends."

"She is unique, your mother."

"Thanks for the compliment. She used to tell me we were Gypsy. It might even be likely, since we certainly have lived like Gypsies, except for one major difference."

"What?"

"Travelers, which is what they're commonly called, travel as family units, never alone. Clans, not couples. And we stayed far, far away from any place we might have encountered them."

"So now you live here." Dan poked Sabine's arm. "Will you ever get the traveling bug back?"

Sabine shook her head. "I don't want to ever again live like that, like her. I'm here, and I'm here to stay. Nothing will make me ever give up this place, this security."

"Why here? Why settle for this podunk town in the middle of nowhere?"

"That's what Ruby asked."

"And your answer?"

"If I could tell you, I could tell myself. We stopped here when I was a child, and from then on I just wanted to come back. I guess that I feel as though this is home. Moose River Junction seemed familiar even that first time, and always figured in my imagination as the place I could finally stay put. What we in the fortune teller trade call Destiny, capital *D*."

"I do understand."

"Because this *is* your home."

"No. I understand because that's how I feel about New York. My life, my intended life, is there. In your words, my destiny."

Of course, his life with Karen. Sabine lay back on her elbows, his words reminding her that Dan Smith was only a temporary manifestation in her life. A temporary and romantically attached manifestation. Her spontaneous decision to bring lunch to him suddenly seemed not only misguided but stupid. Feeling a slight blush grow, she hoped that he didn't view her action as some sort of romantic play for him. Willing the faint heat to diminish, she began to second-guess her motive in doing this. Kindness for a guy too busy to eat. Ha!

Dan seemed oblivious to her embarrassment. "So, what about the fortune-telling stuff? Ruby certainly seems to be able to put a finger on a person's thinking, even before they know they've thought it."

Sabine paused to collect her thoughts, grateful for the change of subject. "She has a gift. It may be simply an uncanny ability to interpret small, unknowable signs from a client, but it could be that she has some legitimate gift to connect, to see with an inner eye." It was a rare thing to speak of herself and her mother so openly. Even to her last serious boyfriend, she had spoken rarely of her mother's confounding ability to know a person's mind before they knew it.

"She told me to stay away from you. No, that wasn't exactly it. She told me to proceed with caution. She wouldn't tolerate my hurting you."

Sabine sat up straight and looked into Dan's face. "When?"

"In the grocery store, when I asked her to do fortunes at the carnival."

"The nerve. Were you embarrassed?"

"Maybe a little. The truth is, I had been thinking about you just as she spoke. It was a little weird."

"She's a pain in the neck." There was no harshness in her remark, only a gentle matter-of-factness.

"And you love her very much."

"That doesn't mean she has a right to say such things to you." She wanted to ask, "You were thinking of me?" but didn't. "Just ignore her. I do."

Dan poured a little of the leftover coffee into Sabine's cup, then the rest into his. "So, tell me something?"

"What?"

"This ghost hunting. Is it for real?" Dan looked at her over the rim of the coffee cup.

Though his olive green eyes were mildly challenging, she could also see that he might actually be willing to believe her. Sabine reached into her handbag and pulled out the paper on which the single legible word, *hide*, was written. "In the Atchesons' kitchen, in broad daylight, I wrote this while in a self-imposed trance. I heard voices and I smelled smoke that wasn't there. I came out of it knowing that something happened in that place. Something dreadful."

"You're saying this—for lack of a better word—this entity, communicated all this through you?"

Sabine got to her knees and began clearing up the detritus of their meal. Her hair had loosened from the scrunchy holding it and she wrestled it back into a knot. "Dan, I don't know if that's what happened. The power of suggestion is pretty active in people like me." The

John Williams sound track medley was over, only the soft hiss of the speakers audible above their heads.

"People like you are . . . what?"

"Susceptible to forces not necessarily available to others. I'm a sensitive. On the one hand, I'm skeptical, and on the other, there are times when I truly do believe what I see."

"See what?"

"Images of things I should know nothing about."

"Ghosts, or people's futures?"

"Both. Sometimes."

"Do you see mine? My future, I mean."

"Not unless you want me to."

"What do you see?" He didn't give her his hand, only met her eyes with his.

Sabine stared at him, looking for the teasing, looking for the challenge. "Your ghosts."

Dan got up as she packed everything back in the wicker basket. He reached down with one hand and pulled Sabine to her feet. "I want to show you something."

Dan took Sabine behind the screen, a place few people besides Nagy had ever been. It was the only place left in the theatre that bore the untouched traces of its vaudeville past. Overhead remained the kleig lights, unpowered now. The pulleys and weights for the massive curtain dangled impotently with its absence. Sabine walked around. She did a little tap-dance step on the blackened surface of the stage and then closed her eyes.

"They're still here."

"Who?"

"The performers, the dancers and comedians. A singer."

"No one died here. Well, maybe not physically," Dan joked.

"No. Their performances are here. What they did."
She opened her eyes and laughed out loud. "Listen."

And, for a moment, he thought he heard the sound of
laughter and tapping feet. Then sultry music began to
play in his ear, as clear as if it were really there. He
looked at the woman standing close to him, as if the
music emanated from her. Dan was suddenly very glad
to have Sabine Heartwood there, in his theatre, seeing
the thing that formed him, the thing from which he
would escape. With her reluctant admission that she was
chasing ghosts, Sabine had touched a dormant whimsy
in him. He was released, at least for a moment, from
rational thought; allowed for an instant to believe in
something outside of his constrained world.

"Dance with me?" Dan asked and Sabine went into
his open arms. For the space of twenty imagined bars of
music, they danced a brief tango across the empty stage.
His grandfather's genes spoke through him, and Dan
skillfully guided Sabine through the imaginary measures, ending with the classic and seductive cheek to
cheek, Dan's body arched over hers. They paused, each
savoring the forbidden touch of the other's skin. Sabine
felt Dan's breath, a little sweet with brownie, warm and
so close to her lips. A tantalizing closeness that made her
aware of a sudden arousal she hadn't enjoyed in a long
time. And a faint suggestion of wood smoke.

"Hello, Dan! Olsen here!"

Abruptly they both pulled away.

"Damn." It might have been the exertion, mild
though it was, to cause Dan's voice to seem so breathless.

Twelve

꧁

"Robert Winsor, his land." They had seen the Windsor name over and over, hundreds of names listed like roll call, confusing variations in the spelling and contradictory records of ownership.

Yesterday Sabine had dashed out of the theatre so quickly, he'd barely had time to call out that they should still take a look at the ledgers. "Tomorrow?"

With her picnic basket clutched in one hand and the wool blanket tucked under her arm, she'd looked so girlish and pleased. "Okay. Great. See you then."

The area where the Atchesons owned their house had at one time been the epicenter of now-vanished colonial Windsorville. Where the post road had gone through, there once had been a small tavern, but little else to distinguish the place as a town. As a boon for some long-forgotten favor, the King of England had deeded the first Windsors what amounted to half of today's Moose River Junction, which lay on the south side of the highway. They had purchased or bartered for the other half, then judiciously sold it or rented it to tenant farmers until the Revolutionary War. Now most of that area was built up, the farms long since converted to half-acre lots fanning out to blend with the borders of surrounding towns in the county.

"They said that they found it on the Internet." Sabine set a sandwich down in front of Dan and opened the cupboard to look for potato chips to go with it. "Apparently there was some Web page with land sales on it." Finding the chips, she sat on the bar stool across from Dan and took a bite from her sandwich.

"It fries me, and I know it shouldn't. A beautiful parcel like that, so close to the Appalachian Trail, should have been put into conservation. We're losing our access. Moose River Junction doesn't have a lot going for it except the natural beauty surrounding it. No industry, no tourism, not even close enough to the next major city to be considered a suburb."

"You sound like you should run for selectman."

"Bite your tongue. Selectman is just a Mohawk word for unappreciated." Dan snagged the chip bag away from Sabine. "It pisses me off to think that only some outsiders knew enough to buy it. No wonder they're being haunted."

"Hey, I have never used the H-word."

"You know what I mean."

"Do you know of any incidents on that parcel which might lend credence to such a thing? The H-word thing?"

"No. I mean, there have been stories passed down, but nothing substantiated."

"Like what?"

"Indian raids. Kidnappings. The stuff Gran used to

tell us as bedtime stories, designed to keep us in bed and under the covers."

"Do you remember any?"

"Not really." Dan considered the question a little longer. "Well, there is the story, pretty well documented, about the defense of Windsorville. Sometime before the French and Indian War when, if I remember my history correctly, there had been a series of kidnappings, or 'takings' as they called them. The story goes that the colonists repulsed an Indian attack."

"Was this one of your grandmother's stories?"

"She always told us about how the white man prevailed against the savage. I suspect most of what she related was culled from James Fenimore Cooper." Dan finished his sandwich and stood up to take his plate to the sink. "I guess what I'm most annoyed with is that I have a hunch that land was in my family. I'd have to go back and check it out, but as I was going through Gran's papers, I came across bills of sale for land I had no idea she owned. Parcels all over the place. Turns out Gran was selling off the land to maintain the theatre. I shouldn't let it get to me, because I suppose it was what the land was meant for, investment. But I still wish she'd told me. I might have been able to help her. Before I had to leave the city, I mean, when I was still earning a living."

"So, ultimately you were left with only the theatre and the house."

Dan's back was to Sabine, but she saw the way he frowned by the set of his broad shoulders. "And Nagy."

"He's great. It must be like having a child and yet not."

"How aptly put. He's been my childhood playmate, and my painful embarrassment when I was an adoles-

cent. He's been needy and he's been uncannily support-
ive. Of all the things working to keep me here, his situation is the most challenging."

"But you love him." An echo of Dan's words to her
yesterday about Ruby.

"Yeah. I do." Dan came back to sit beside Sabine at the
counter. He needed to change the subject quickly before
she made him give away too much of himself. "Do you
think we could walk that property? I'd love to show you
the view from the trail that runs above it."

Sabine grabbed her fleece off the peg and bent to
write a quick note to Ruby. "Gone for a walk. Be back
soon."

They spent Sunday afternoon on the Atcheson property, following deer paths through the bramble. "Some
house," Dan had commented as they pulled up in front
of the seventeenth-century replica.

"You should see the inside. All I can say is, it must
be nice to have money." Sabine led the way to the backyard where they would begin their hike. The yard was
well tended, but not in the least authentic to the style of
the house. No kitchen garden grew, and only the most
modern of fertilizers had been used on the grass. No
rich manure here, only weed-killer-filled, scientifi-
cally balanced fertilizer. The black heads of an under-
ground sprinkler system poked up here and there. Not
an oak leaf disturbed the pristine yard. A gas grill was
tucked up against the house, further testimony to the
century.

"What did you say these people do?"

"Made a ton of money in a dot com startup."

"Nice." The rich October sun warmed the wild
grasses that sprang up beyond the manicured backyard

and before the woods. The sound of insects busying themselves before winter filled the air with an unmistakable fall sound.

"I'm not sure what we're looking for." Sabine unzipped her jacket.

"A nice walk on a perfect day."

"No, I mean, is there something I should be looking for?"

"If there ever was a house on this property, we'll find some remnants of habitation. Stone walls, bottle dump. Evidence of clearing. Assuming, of course, that when they built this house, they didn't destroy all the evidence."

"You sound like an archeologist."

"Like every kid, I went through a stage when I wanted to be one. Of course, I imagined Giza and pharaohs' tombs. But I've always had a natural interest in the history of Moose River Junction."

"Because your family goes so far back."

"Yes. I suppose."

They had gotten to the edge of the property, where it suddenly became sharply uphill through laurel and beech trees. A rich humus-y smell came up from the damp ground. Dan and Sabine walked for a while in silence, enjoying the birdsong and the quiet of the deepening woods.

The day was mindful of the impending winter, and a fresh breeze chilled Sabine's cheeks. As the deer path narrowed, she fell in behind Dan. He wore an old green barn coat, tattered around the edges like an old teddy bear grows tattered with loving use. He'd turned his white baseball cap around, and Sabine could see the NYU logo on it. Following Dan up the increasing grade of the hillside, Sabine wondered again what would have happened yesterday if Olsen hadn't walked in when he did. She hadn't told Ruby about the picnic or the spontaneous dance. Long experience kept her from giving Ruby any ammunition. Certainly none regarding this sweet but singular moment with Dan. Ruby would have said it was destiny. That overused word. Even she'd used it yesterday. The fact that the electrician had walked in at exactly the right moment was portent enough for Sabine. Some things were simply temptation, not meant to be.

Sucking in a great breath of the fresh air, Sabine let it out in slow frustration at herself. There could be nothing between Dan and herself. Not only was he taken, and by a sexy and talented woman, but he was at the opposite end of her dream. She meant to live in Moose River Junction. He meant to leave it. She had found a home; he was extracting himself from his. Sabine paused to zip her jacket back up. Dan kept moving, unaware of her stopping.

As promised, the deer path debouched onto a clearly marked Appalachian Trail offshoot. Following it, they soon crested the ridgeline of the hill. At the very top of the hill was an enormous boulder, jutting out over the precipice, and flat at the top.

"Wow! Is this what you wanted to show me?"

"Almost. The local lore is that this is called Indian Maiden Rock, where lovelorn maidens launched themselves off in desperation after their braves were killed in battle."

"Maybe that's the cause of the disturbance."

"It's all nonsense. Romantic drivel." Dan's fingers found the slight depressions and grooves that allowed him to climb up the boulder. He leaned back over the edge and grasped Sabine's hand. "The grooves are probably man-made, put there for toeholds." Dan brought Sabine up and to her feet and then, with a sweeping gesture, said, "This is what I wanted to show you."

The last of the colors of autumn stood out in the distance, but the spiky bare branches of the denuded trees lay in gray relief around them, punctuated by the dark green of fir trees. From where they stood, they could look down on the whole valley and across to other Berkshire hills. An intense blue sky, utterly cloudless, lent a perfect backdrop to the colors. Sabine felt as if she was suspended in air. "I didn't realize we'd climbed so high." She stepped back a little from the edge of the boulder, suddenly a little dizzy. A hawk lazily riding the air currents spiraled just above.

Dan slid an arm around her. "Listen."

More conscious of his arm around her than the sounds, Sabine cocked her head. "What am I listening for?"

"The sound of silence. You can't hear civilization. From up here, the highway is soundless."

Like the perpetual waves on the seashore, the Mass Pike was always audible, yet scarcely noted. It sundered Moose River Junction in two, an ancient grudge against the state still commented upon.

"This has got to be one of the only places where what you hear is exactly what my ancestors heard. Cardinal and crow, the wind through the pines, and not much else. That's it."

"It's wonderful." Sabine wasn't sure if she meant the quiet, the view, or the feel of Dan's arm holding her securely. Why did the simple act of holding her safely in place feel like a pledge?

"When I lived in the city, it was hard for me at first to get past the constant noise. It seems funny, but it didn't take long before it was a comfort to me. I miss it. All the sirens and horns. Vital sounds, like people are living their lives." Dan hadn't meant to hold on to Sabine, but he felt an overpowering desire to keep her near him, to keep her under his protection.

"Sounds more to me as if people are in danger of losing them. I hated living in the cities. To me, the smaller towns always seem more real, more personal. When a siren goes off here, it means something; it's not one of a thousand alarms you hear in a day until they become as much background noise as that highway is. Surely you must feel that way being here, being in the fire department. You must worry at each alarm that it will involve someone you know."

Dan didn't answer Sabine right away. "There have been a few."

In his silence, Sabine felt a thread of anxiety. What was she doing, letting him hold her like this? His nearness obfuscated the clear rules under which they could be friends. As if suddenly having the same thoughts, Dan let her go and slid down the steep side of the boulder.

Sabine looked to Dan to help her down from the awkward height. He may have held on to her hand a moment longer than necessary; he may have drawn her closer than need be. Dan coughed and motioned to Sabine to lead them back down the narrow path. He didn't want her to see the confusion going on in him. Confusion that was only exacerbated at the sight of Sabine wending her way down the steep incline. She slipped a little and he thrust out a saving hand. He couldn't make himself release his hold on her, and all of a sudden everything was balanced. Everything was different. He was suddenly afraid that she would misunderstand him, but he would not let her go.

Sabine recognized the change in Dan as clearly as the spoken word. His hand on hers bespoke a hesitant step. If she was gifted in any way with clairvoyance, she knew that this was a very difficult moment for him. Like frightened children linking hands, they continued down the hillside.

Just as they broke through the woods Dan stopped. "See it, over there?" He pointed to the right of the Atchesons' house, now visible as they stepped through the heavy brush. A low, lichen-green row of rocks could be seen between several trees. Sabine might have missed it; the grasses and determined oaks obscured them from all but the most discerning eye. "I think that's a foundation, or at the very least, part of a stone wall. Walls were pirated all the time, so it wouldn't be surprising not to have more of it in evidence. If it's a foundation, there may be a cellar hole."

No longer holding hands, the pair walked to the rock wall.

Sabine touched the rocks with her fingertips while Dan walked around them. On one side was a depression that might have been a cellar hole or simply topography.

"This is where I can't be of much use; I don't know enough."

"I think it's amazing that you can decide these rocks aren't here by nature."

"Nature doesn't stack them like this."

The sun had begun its rapid descent and the yellow autumnal light graced the greenish rocks. Sabine stood in what might have been the cellar hole of a small house. Instinct or compulsion made her close her eyes and let the place speak to her. Protected from the cool fall breeze by the surviving wall of stones, the place was warm in the late sunshine. Sabine let it play on her face while she took long, slow breaths. She couldn't drop into a true trance. Her senses were distracted by the presence, not of ghosts, but of this man. If there had been spirits there, they were being held away by a more powerful entity.

Dan came up behind her and placed his hands on her shoulders. She could feel his breath against her cheek, not brownie-scented now, but metallic with desire.

"You have a girlfriend in New York." The statement sounded more like accusation than raw truth.

"I did. She's broken it off." Dan couldn't imagine what ill Sabine might think of him, but he wanted her to understand that what had happened between himself and Karen had nothing to do with what he was feeling for her. "I couldn't get back to New York soon enough for her. She got tired of waiting."

"Do you still love her?" Sabine allowed herself the bluntness.

"Oddly enough, I asked Arnie a similar question, about Greta. I asked him, 'Is she the love of your life?' I don't know why I asked it, or asked in that way, but I think I was thinking of my relationship with Karen. Questioning myself, I suppose."

"So what's the answer?"

"I thought I did." Dan kept his hands on her shoulders. Through her fleece jacket he could feel her shaking. "I just hadn't seen how flimsy the whole thing was."

"How so? Because she wasn't willing to put her life on hold for you?"

"You sound like you're taking her side."

"I'm sorry. It's really none of my business."

"She wasn't willing to meet me halfway. She couldn't understand that I have things which need sorting out. And she didn't like Nagy."

"Like I said, it isn't any of my business. None of it."

Sabine took a deep breath. "You smell like smoke."

"I shouldn't. I haven't worn these clothes to any fires."

"Not even this jacket?"

"No. This is my hiking jacket."

"Maybe it's not you." Sabine stepped away from Dan and sniffed the air again. "No, it isn't you; it's this place. Do you smell it?"

Dan took a deep breath, and shook his head. "No." All he smelled was Sabine, the lightly floral scent of her shampoo, the clean smell of her skin.

"I smelled smoke the day I did the reading."

"Might have been someone burning leaves. The odor can travel for miles. But I don't smell anything now."

As strong as the scent of burning wood had been a minute before, it now vanished. They stood in the hollow, safe from the wind. Even the oaks were still. There was no sound, not even of roosting crows in the October sunset, or the perpetual rasp of late-season crickets. Sabine and Dan faced each other, straining for clues to this sudden mystery of need.

Dan stepped closer, then bent and placed his lips against hers. The kiss was an answer to their need. Dan felt Sabine's corresponding excitement, her arms around his neck, her mouth open and willing. They drank in the very essence of one another.

And then Sabine pulled away and held up her hands. "Don't. I can't do this."

Thirteen

❧

"Mom. I'm not sixteen. I am not going to give you details."

"I'll just caution you . . ." Ruby had been waiting for Sabine to come home, sitting in the near dark for all the world as if Sabine had missed a curfew.

"No, you won't. I won't have it. Keep your prescience to yourself. Okay?"

In the car, Dan and Sabine had sat quietly, each mired in a welter of conflicted emotions as he drove her home. After her words he'd stepped back, holding his hands out from his sides like a man showing himself unarmed. "Sabine, I'm sorry. I shouldn't have done that. I really don't want you to think . . ."

"That you're on the rebound? That she broke up with you? That it wasn't a mutual breakup and your pride is hurt?" She knew she sounded mean, but the truth sometimes was harsh.

"No. That's not it. This, this wasn't any of that."

"What was it? Compulsion? The woodsy air?"

Dan said nothing for a few moments. "Please forgive me. I acted out of what I thought was mutual attraction."

Sabine sniffed. "You have too much on your plate right now to take on another doomed relationship. We are opposites. If Karen left you because you could not leave Moose River Junction, I will not be with you because, ultimately, you *will*. Your desire to go back to your old life will always supersede any other desire in your life."

"You're condemning me without knowing me."

"I know enough."

The "if onlys" traipsed around Sabine's mind. If only he'd told her sooner that his relationship with Karen was over. If only he could realize that his soul belonged in Moose River Junction. If only she could forget the attraction she had for him.

Ruby came up behind her and, in unintentional mimicry of Dan, placed her hands on Sabine's shoulders. "Why don't you let me read your cards? Sometimes there are solutions to these problems just on the horizon."

"Mom, knock it off. It was a stupid mistake to try to be friends with an attached man." Sabine pulled away from Ruby's hands.

Ruby knew when to stop. She busied herself making a pot of tea, without suggesting she read the leaves. "I think I've found a good place in Springfield. A guy who owns a crystal shop has some space he'll rent to me. It's cheap and has a good walk-in clientele. It's near a couple of other hippie shops." Ruby, who still might be mistaken for a hippie, always used the word with disdain. "One sells Indian clothing and the other botanicals. It's a nice venue."

Sabine felt the pressure of tears behind her eyes. "You're leaving again?"

"I have to make a living. At least I'll be close."

"I thought you were going to stay 'as long as it takes.' Does that mean I've had my significant event?"

"I think you've begun it."

"Then why go now, when it's still happening?"

"Sabine, I need to make a living, that's the pragmatic side of fortune-telling. I'll still be around when you need me."

"What about your carnival readings next weekend? You need to be here for that."

"I'll come back for that weekend. You don't ever remember me reneging on a promise."

"I remember you blasting out of some town before a lease was up."

"No one is chasing me for money today."

"Is that why we kept leaving?"

"Mostly. Surely you knew that." Ruby swirled hot water in the ceramic pot. "Get some cups down, will you?"

Sabine got the cups from the glass-fronted cupboard. When she was a child, they had only owned two mugs. Sabine remembered them so clearly: one had a green-and-white hospital logo and the other was plain white, like a cup found in a million cafeterias. Inside they were deeply stained with thousands of cups of strong tea. The teacups Ruby used for readings were delicate, porcelain things, prized among their few possessions. After each client, Ruby washed them, careful that the tea stains came out. At each move, they were tenderly wrapped in layers of tissue and placed in a wooden box that had a space for the box of loose tea Ruby used for those sessions. The wooden box always sat between Ruby and Sabine on the front seat of the bus.

"Where did you get these, Mommy?" Sabine was in one of her curious moods, questioning Ruby about all sorts of things. She might have been six, maybe seven. "Who gave you that box?"

"A very gifted woman." Ruby placed Sabine's hands on the box with its precious contents.

The child Sabine laid her hands flat, letting the fine grooves and lines of the parquet press into her soft palms. An image. The image of a face, crumpled over a toothless mouth, slightly hairy on the chin. Sabine closed her eyes tighter and let the image grow. The face was at first kindly, then angry. The anger was so powerful that Sabine opened her eyes and started to cry. "She wants it back!"

"It is mine. I paid for it." Ruby took the box away from Sabine. "You have the gift. You have her gift. And his. Don't waste it."

Sabine now handed her mother the two sparkling clean Port Merion mugs from her cupboard and shook away the memory. "Whose gift do I have?"

They were so connected, Ruby didn't have to ask what Sabine was talking about. "Your grandmother's."

"Your mother?"

"No, your father's. I never knew my mother."

"You've never told me that before. You've never told me anything about your history. Why now?" Sabine heard her own voice rise in challenge.

"You've never been in this situation before."

Sabine was momentarily confused. Was Ruby speaking of the spirit in the Atchesons' house or of Dan's unexpected kiss? "What situation?"

"Where you needed to know how powerful your abilities are. I believe that this divination is going to be more powerful and significant than any other you've experienced. But you need to rally your resources, dedicate yourself to breaking through. This house, this ghost, this haunting, that's what you need to focus your attention on." Ruby grasped Sabine's hands. "Not on how a man hurt you."

"He hasn't hurt me." Even to herself, she sounded defensive. "You can't hurt someone if they won't let you."

"That's quite true." Ruby knew that a window onto her past had been opened, but thought that Sabine was so distracted by her abortive relationship with Dan Smith, she might not take advantage of the opportunity. Ruby sipped her tea and knew that she was out of luck.

Sabine returned to the earlier topic. "Why didn't you ever know your mother?"

"Because she abandoned me to the sisters of no mercy in Sault Sainte Marie."

"Canada?"

"Yes. Hence my distaste for the cold."

"Do you know anything about her?"

"Do you mean, did she have the gift? No. All I know is that I was a foundling, raised to believe that I would follow in my mother's footsteps and become a whore if they didn't beat me into obedience. When I began foretelling, they beat me harder. 'Beat the devil out of her.' That was their justification. Of course, it might have been my father who had the gift. Who knows? It isn't always women who have it."

"But mostly."

"Yes."

"My father's mother?"

"Yes. And your father."

"Who was he?"

Ruby closed her eyes, willing herself to begin the story. Sabine should know. But the words wouldn't come; her mouth felt taped shut. The self-inflicted prohibition against speaking his name, revealing the sordid specifics of Sabine's conception was too strong. It was unfair and illogical, but Ruby's instincts held her back. It wasn't time—but the time was coming. The time when she couldn't run away from her own truth. Sabine had been right about this town. There was something powerfully attaching here. It was a belonging sort of place.

The phone rang, making them both jump. Sabine remained where she was.

Ruby was relieved by the interruption. "Aren't you going to answer that?"

"The machine will get it."

Pulling her most clairvoyant face, Ruby shook her head, eyes closed and fingers pressed to the bridge of her nose. "It's important. It's Loozy."

Before Sabine could chide her mother for fakery, Loozy's voice came from the answering machine.

"Ruby, you're not off the hook." Sabine reached for the phone.

"Sabine, do you think you can come back and try reading again?" Loozy's voice was far less imperious than it had been the first time she'd called.

"I've been planning on it. I've done a little research. Stuff like ownership and metes and bounds." She pulled a leaf off her sweater. "I've been walking the property and I think that there's an old cellar hole nearby." Unconscious of the motion, Sabine touched her lips.

"That's great." Loozy was clearly anxious to move the conversation along. "Can you come tomorrow night?"

"I guess so. What time?"

"I'll leave right after my yoga class, so I should be there by five. I'll make dinner. Will you come?"

"Of course, that would be lovely." Even after Loozy had rung off, Sabine held the warm receiver to her ear. The absolute sense of Loozy's ulterior motive fed through the wire to Sabine's mind. She had no doubt that Loozy was coming alone and that she'd want Sabine to stay with her. Well, that was out of the question. She didn't mind reading other people's fortunes, but she wasn't about to be a baby-sitter to them.

"So, Ruby . . . where were we?"

Sabine spoke to an empty room.

Fourteen

❧

"I thought this might be of use to you." *Jacob's History of Windsorville* sat on Sabine's desk at work, with the unsigned Post-it note stuck on the dry leather cover. The bookplate inside left no mystery as to the lender. Dan had brought it to her from his grandmother's bookshelf. After pulling the note off the book and throwing it in the wastebasket, Sabine stuck the small volume in her bag to look at over lunch.

She took a late lunch, already behind in her day's tasks, as she'd started the morning at the dentist having her teeth cleaned. She hadn't had time to make lunch and so went across the street to the same little coffee shop where she'd lingered that March day, pondering the auguries for staying in Moose River Junction.

With only a half hour to spend, Sabine opened the book right to the chapter on Robert Windsor, as his was the predominant name in all the deeds and records thus far. Seeing his name in the little history was like finding a familiar face in the crowd.

"Orphaned as a babe, Robert Windsor was brought up in the household of his paternal grandfather, also Robert Windsor. Robert the younger attended Harvard College, where he studied law. Returning to Windsorville in 1703, after a distinguished career in Boston was shortened by ill health, he set up the law practice which bears his name to this day." Sabine glanced again at the date of publication on the history, 1825. She smiled to realize that there was still a Windsor, Tuthill and Meeks law firm in town. It didn't seem possible a firm could last through three centuries, but at least the name had.

Sabine scanned through the dry paragraphs, noting that Robert had been married three times, with issue from all of the wives. He'd had a total of fifteen children, leaving little doubt in Sabine's mind about what had killed his wives off. Of the fifteen, four boys survived into adulthood and the Windsor name lived on.

She flipped back to the chapter about Robert Windsor the grandfather, from whom the town took its original name. As she'd discovered in the Historical Society archives, this Robert Windsor had owned nearly all of the land now on the other side of the highway. A vast tract of the New England Town Survey of 1651, bounded on one side by the Moose River. A "Proprietor," granted his land by the King of England, Robert Windsor had been born in Exeter, England.

Still not satisfied that any of this had any bearing on the Atchesons' land, Sabine thumbed through the volume on either side of the elder Robert and the younger. She could find no mention of the orphaned Robert's father, except as listed in the names of elder Robert's enormous brood of mostly girl children. Thankful,

Sarah, Mary, Grace, Elizabeth, a second Mary, Ruth, and on and on the names went, birth dates aligned, many with the same date of death beside. Finally, almost like an afterthought, a last baby, the only living son, called Christopher, born 1650, died 1668.

Something tugged at Sabine, and she flipped back to the orphaned Robert. Born 1668. The same year his father died. Sabine closed the chapter over her finger and thought for a moment. The only references to Christopher were his birth and death dates. As if his life was as brief as those of his siblings who were born and died on the same day. Obviously he had married; thus the youngest Robert born. But nowhere was there a record of the baby's mother. No name, no birth or death. As if she hadn't existed. Every other woman mentioned, always in the context of her parentage and her husband and children, had at least those dates.

Sabine felt a tiny flicker of recognition, as if this story was somehow familiar to her. She fished around to try to grasp the elusive comparison and finally caught it. This could be her mother's story. Her mother was as anonymous as this baby's unrecorded mother, an orphan of unknown parentage.

Sabine sat up and stretched. She'd been hunched over this book for the better part of an hour, far longer than she should have. She handed the cashier her check and money, and then went back to drop a tip on the table. Preoccupied, she gathered her book and bag together. There was something there in the unwritten that touched her. This meticulous historian had essentially glossed over the life and death of one of the founding family sons, through whom the family name had stayed alive for several more generations. Whereas he had painstakingly recorded every move of the grandfather and the grandson, it was as if there were no records of the son. Sabine dug the book back out of her bag and flipped to the last chapter: "The Windsorville Defense." Dan had mentioned this yesterday. Before their nascent friendship blew up.

A quick survey corroborated Dan's thin account. Like Deerfield to its northeast, Moose River Junction had a checkered history with Native Americans. She vaguely recalled seeing the plaque in the center of the small town green, dedicated to the "Heroics of the Townsmen Who Defended Windsorville from Indian Attack." It had to be the same event.

She stood outside the coffee shop for a moment, certain the date on the memorial plaque was 1668, the same as the death of Christopher and the birth of Robert the younger. Impulsively, she walked across the street to the town green and over to the tiny memorial garden. A mauve-colored granite obelisk had been placed in the center of the decorative, iron post-and-chain-bordered garden, a testimony to a long history of Moose River Junction veterans. The ancient memorial stone had been incorporated into the garden, a little east of the monolith.

Sabine squatted beside it, pushing down obscuring grass to read the faint words carved there. She was right, the date was 1668. Maybe Christopher had died during the defense of the town. Maybe it was just coincidence that the child's mother died the same year, possibly even in childbirth bearing the orphaned child Robert. Suddenly aware she'd been out of the office too long, Sabine hurried across the street.

Dan had been hoping that Sabine would be at her desk when he came in with the book. It had been an odd find, sitting there all that time on the bookshelf in the parlor he'd taken over as his own when Gran died. He supposed it was like seeing a world filled with blue trucks when you've just bought one. A newly heightened level of awareness, in this case of his own hometown's history.

Finding it was almost like a reprieve. If he could bring her this little volume as a peace offering, maybe they could find that comfort zone they had been enjoying before he'd lost his mind. It didn't feel like rebound, but it must be. He thought that his friendship with Sabine would withstand scrutiny, yet maybe she was right, maybe the tension and subsequent breakup with Karen had been exacerbated by her quiet comfort to him in those days.

Dan almost wrapped the book, making a present of it to her, but thought better of it. At the end of the day, it would be selfish and wrongheaded to attempt to push this friendship into something it could never be. He was, as she said, ultimately going to leave. And she would not follow. The best he could hope for was to patch up the easy friendship he had jeopardized with his impulse to feel her lips on his.

"Sabine's gonna be a little late this morning, Dan. Dentist appointment or something," Balto told him. "I'll give it to her."

"That's okay. I"ll leave a note." Dan had pulled a Post-it off the pad on Sabine's desk and then stood for a decade, thinking of just the right blend of words to convey contrition and hope of friendship without strings. "I thought this might be of use to you. Call me if you would still like some help." That was the best he could come up with, then pondered how to sign his name. She'll know who left it, he thought, and walked out of the office in a sudden hurry.

Back in his own office, Dan was shuffling through the unrelenting bill pile, picking and choosing which ones he could manage this week, when the phone on his desk rang with its old-fashioned shrillness. He answered it with the hope that it would be Sabine calling to thank him, calling to say things might be mended.

"Hello, Dan." Not Sabine, but Karen.

Fifteen

❧

"I'm so glad you could come." Loozy had rushed out into the chilly evening as Sabine pulled up behind the Range Rover. Sabine knew immediately that Drake wasn't in the house by the warmth of the atmosphere within. As she had suspected, this was Loozy's idea and her journey.

"I brought some wine. I hope it's all right. You didn't mention what we were having."

Loozy took the bottle without a look and slipped her arm beneath Sabine's. "I'm sure it'll be fine. I've made lamb."

"I've brought chardonnay. You can see that my reputed psychic powers have failed me. Be warned."

Loozy laughed, but the grip on Sabine's arm showed she was only laughing out of politeness. Her preoccupation with being in the house alone stiffened her into a revealing posture of tension. She released Sabine only when they had reached the kitchen, where she suddenly thought to ask for Sabine's coat. She hung it on a hook near the back door. The small mudroom held antique tools but no mud. A tiny bathroom was squeezed in near the door.

"Did you find any of these tools on the property?" Sabine picked up an ax head, long since separated from its handle. She hefted its weight and ran a finger along the dulled edge. Pits of corrosion pocked the surface, as if it had been a long time out in the elements.

"The builders found a few items. That ax head, yes. And one other thing, I forget which. They were pretty close to the vest. If certain kinds of artifacts are dug up, well, then there's the whole archeology issue to deal with."

"You mean Native American artifacts."

"I suppose. I guess. Anyway, they didn't find any."

"Any that you know about."

"Yes. Is it important?"

Sabine shrugged, some inner voice telling her to keep her own counsel. Loozy was so clearly a fragile creature; to add Indian wars and kidnappings to the mix might not do anyone any good. Besides, she reasoned to herself, You have no real information at all about this place. She kept the ax head in her hand as she came back into the warm and fragrant kitchen, setting it down on the island counter, where she touched it from time to time as she sipped her chardonnay and watched Loozy fuss with a complicated sauce.

"So, Drake isn't with you?"

"No, he's in L.A."

"You're being very brave to come up here by yourself, knowing how this place disturbs you." Sabine lay her whole palm against the ax, wondering if the warming of its metal was from simply being moved away from the cold back door.

"I know. Believe me, I've been playing loud music and talking to myself to keep me here. But Sabine, you have to understand that deep down, I really love this place."

That's what she herself kept saying to Ruby. *I love this place.* It made no sense that she had chosen it, but it's where she wanted to be. It made no sense that the Atchesons had chosen this place, either; they had even less connection to the town than she did. *What calls a person home?*

"If it's any comfort to you, I know exactly how you feel. Sometimes you just feel connected to a place and no amount of dissension can make you change your mind."

Loozy nodded but didn't seem convinced.

"Has anything happened recently?"

"No. But I've only been here a little over an hour."

"All quiet when you arrived?"

"Yes. But like I said, I kept the music up loud." Loozy stirred the sauce, dipped a delicate finger into it, and proclaimed it done.

They sat at the big country table, set with the cobalt blue plates on Loozy's hand-painted placemats.

"You are a fabulous cook, Loozy. Are you a professional?"

"No. But I like to take cooking courses."

Sabine knew that if she was to read Loozy's palm, it would tell her that Loozy pursued cooking as she did all of her domestic arts, with a passion born of boredom and frustration. "It's wonderful." She would have read that Loozy had to seek out meaningful activities to fill the holes in her life.

Following the braised lamb and fresh asparagus, Loozy brought a bowl of fruit to the table. "I didn't have time to make a dessert."

"There goes your tip." Sabine chose a plum from the bowl and bit into it. The tang of its slightly under-ripe juice brought to mind the taste of disappointment. Some things had a taste. Disappointment did. She shouldn't let it bother her; she was the one who had put the brakes on with Dan. The appearance of the book on her desk this afternoon had opened her up to reconsidering her stance on beginning a relationship with a man on the rebound. Maybe she was being misguided about not letting their friendship grow. What was to say that little click she'd sensed two months ago had to be a false alarm? Sabine remembered the first time she'd seen Dan. Karen had been with, but not with, him, as they came into the Blue Moose. She recalled the observable feeling of tension between this pair of strangers and being fascinated by it. That night things had already been uncomfortable between Dan and Karen.

Holding that thought in mind, Sabine had called Dan after work to thank him for the book, and perhaps to apologize.

"Danny's not home. He's getting gas in Mommy's car. He's going to New York tomorrow." Nagy had nothing else to say on the matter except that he didn't know when Dan would be back. "He just says he has to go." Sabine had heard Nagy's own disappointment in the tone of his voice.

Sabine now set the half-eaten plum down on the corner of the dessert plate. "Let's get to work."

The two women quickly cleared away the dishes, then returned to the table. Sabine ripped the sheets with her scrawled research notes off the yellow pad and stuffed them in her bag. She took the pen Loozy handed her. Laying the pad and pen down on the cleared table, Sabine simply put her hands on either side of the objects. Opposite Sabine, Loozy sat very still, her own hands folded in her lap. The kitchen light was dimmed, the candles on the table still lit. The warmth from the cooking was beginning to dissipate though the odor of the lamb seemed to grow stronger. Sabine took deep, even breaths until she could no longer smell the lamb, or feel the cooling air, or sense the troubled woman across from her. She allowed the trance to develop, tracing its spread through the weightiness of her limbs, until all sense of now was muted and there only lay the open sensation of being a vessel.

Loozy Atcheson watched as Sabine's lids slowly closed over her extraordinary golden brown eyes. As had happened the first time, Sabine's left hand floated over the pen and pad, then dipped as if reaching through water for a lost object. As she grasped the pen, it floated upward, as lightly as a balloon and with about as much control. Eventually her hand seemed to recover its weight and it dropped, clutching the pen, onto the table. Sabine's face remained an impassive blank. Apparently of its own volition, the hand began to twist until it had arranged the pen between thumb and forefinger. This was different: the last time Sabine's hand had clubbed the pen in its fist, like a little child might hold a crayon.

As she watched, Loozy heard her own heart loudly beating as Sabine's hand started to steadily write across the page. Sitting opposite as she was, she couldn't make out the writing, only that this time it looked readable, real letters forming one after the other. Every few words, the hand would make a little dabbing and shaking motion. It came to Loozy that whatever was doing the writing was dipping the pen in ink and shaking off the excess. The motion was so clear, it seemed that she could see the ink pot sitting there on her table. It came to her then, what the excavators had found. A little green glass ink pot. Pulling her rapt gaze away from the moving hand, Loozy glanced over to the window that looked out over the backyard. There, along with several other antique bottles aligned on the wide windowsill, was the little greenish ink pot. The air seemed very cold just then; a wafting of icy air made the candle flames bend in her direction. Loozy could no longer suppress her frightened wail.

"Loozy!" Sabine's eyes snapped open. "You can't make noise. Please."

"Look." Loozy pointed to the yellow paper, now completely covered in copperplate handwriting.

"Wow. How long was I out?"

"I think it's been over an hour. It felt like forever." Loozy was shivering, and Sabine noticed that the room had chilled.

"That's a long trance." Suddenly dying of thirst, Sabine helped herself to a glass of water from the tap. "It didn't seem that long." He knees were shaking badly and she leaned her elbows on the cool surface of the marble-topped counter. "I kept smelling the lamb, and didn't think I was that under."

"Can you read it?" Loozy pointed to the yellow pad. Her face was an interesting mixture of curiosity and skepticism. She knew what she had seen, but she desperately wanted Sabine to prove it wasn't real, that she'd been doing the writing and that it was all a big joke, that maybe they just needed to get different storms on the windows. Abruptly Loozy stood up and blew out the candles, tiny spatters of melted wax hitting the tablecloth. Picking up the yellow pad by the edge as if it was distasteful or dangerous, she brought it over to Sabine without looking at the handwriting. "Can you make anything out?"

"Let's see." Sabine set her glass down beside the yellow pad. She still felt a little twitchy, the images that had been visible to her mind's eye just fading. As curious as she was to see if the written words would reflect those images, she was a little nervous. What she had seen had been a complicated pastiche of impressionistic colors. Like her sense that some emotions had flavors, these seemed to be the colors of fear and panic. Muted reds and golds suddenly overwhelmed by gray and black, as if the colors had been sucked dry of pigment. As if fire and flame had become smoke and ash.

Sabine picked up the yellow pad. What seemed like straightforward writing was a morass of connected letters, bringing to mind one of those word search games she'd played so often on her long road trips with Ruby. Buried within the letters were some identifiable words, which she read out loud to Loozy. *"They come. They come. Hide in . . .* something I think is *butry.* Buttery, that must be it. Old houses had rooms for storage called butteries." Sabine looked up from the pad to Loozy's face, which was a mask of worry. "Does this house have a buttery?"

"No, but the plans called for one. It would have been used as a pantry, but I wanted more space in the kitchen."

"There are a couple more I can see. *The babe . . . hide the babe. They come . . . keep still."* Sabine felt a wash of exhaustion. "I'd like to take this home, if I could. I'll make a copy and send it to you. What's your New York address?" Sabine picked up the pen, then looked at Loozy's face. "There's nothing haunted about this pen. What happened just now would have happened with any writing instrument."

"You're right-handed."

"Yes."

"You . . . *it* . . . is left handed. Your hand kept dipping and shaking." Loozy went over to the window. "As if you were using one of these." Loozy reached for the little glass vessel, then pulled her hand back as if slapped. "I can't touch it. Maybe that's what's haunted. The men found it when they were digging the foundation." Her voice rose in pitch, her words coming out as choppy as an exhausted runner. "Maybe we were being warned."

"Hide. They come. Words of warning." Sabine moved to Loozy's side and picked up the green glass ink pot. She held it with both hands, waiting to see if the cool glass would warm to her touch. "I can see where that might make sense. But I don't think it's you the spirit is talking to. And, Loozy, let's keep things straight: I wasn't using an ink pot, the spirit was."

Sixteen

Hanging up after Karen's call, Dan had felt a world-weariness force itself across his shoulders with such weight he was compelled to sit down. "I'll be away all day tomorrow. You need to come and get your things and get out before I get home." Karen had not called to apologize for her silence but to give him a small window of opportunity to collect his things from her place. The loft was Karen's, although he'd always split expenses down the middle, even while he'd struggled to keep the theatre open and Maisie and Walt paid. "I don't want to see you."

"How have I been so terrible that you can't even bear to be in the same room with me?"

"Are you coming?"

"I've got to first make sure I can get someone in for Nagy. And tomorrow is one of my on-call days at the firehouse. I'll have to get someone to switch."

"Are you coming or do I throw everything out?"

"Yes. Of course."

"See how easy it is. Why couldn't you have done that before?"

"Karen." But he spoke to a disconnected line.

Dan finished changing the sheets in the guest room. Maisie never seemed to mind being asked to come stay with Nagy, and Dan suspected she enjoyed being in Beatrice Danforth's house without Beatrice in it. He knew his grandmother had intimidated Maisie, as she had everyone. The regal hauteur, the high expectations, the ramrod bearing of her posture even as the cancer ate its way through her—she had been every inch a grande dame. Only to him did she ever show the slightest bend. As he ran the edge of his hand under the pillows to smooth the spread, Dan remembered Gran's laughter at some silly television show. *All in the Family* or maybe *Barney Miller,* later *Seinfeld.* As poised and sophisticated as Gran was, she had a penchant for shows like that. If he teased her about it, she'd always retort, "Comedy is the meat of vaudeville. You could have your jugglers, or your song and dance men, but it was the comedy which brought people in night after night." She didn't seem to think it at odds with her persona that she should love mindless TV.

Finished with Maisie's room, Dan headed for the parlor. He wanted to make sure he had all of the student tapes his film school buddy, Paul Krest, had sent him, collected together to return. While Dan had moved on to learn the directing profession, Paul had become an academic, teaching film studies to students whose tapes Dan now occasionally reviewed for his old friend. He carefully placed the eight student videos in a cardboard box. It was nearly ten P.M. He needed to get to the theatre to finish up the deposit and collect Nagy. More than that, he needed to speak to Sabine. Setting the box down on his desk, he picked up the phone.

Ruby answered. "She's with a client."

"Oh. Will you have her call me?"

"I thought you were on your way to New York."

"Tomorrow." Dan didn't even rise to the bait as to how Ruby knew this. It was a small enough town that she could know that bit of gossip without psychic intervention. "Tell her I called?"

Ruby seemed to be deciding.

"Ruby?"

"All right. But she probably won't be back until late."

"I'm at the theatre until at least eleven-thirty. She can call as late as she wants."

"When she does these readings she comes back exhausted. I can't guarantee that she'll call."

"Just tell her . . ."

"What? That you're thinking of her?"

"Yes."

"Will you be all right here alone?" Sabine was fighting the exhaustion her trance had dropped over her like a shroud. Loozy's revelation of the left-handedness of the entity had spooked her. Despite the unflustered appearance she presented, she was desperate to get home, where she could enlist Ruby's pragmatic help in sorting out her feelings about this. Should she be afraid or should she be open to continuing this experiment? Ruby had spent many years in the company of fakes and shams. At the same time, she'd encountered what she called the real McCoy, people with the true gift of prophesy and psychic sensitivity. "You're the real McCoy. You have the gift." Over and over Ruby would tell her that when she'd know something ahead of time, or have those uncontrolled visions she tried mightily to ignore. Moments when she could see a Band-Aid on a friend's finger an hour before the cut occurred. Those awful times when she saw a person's death.

Sabine drank down another glass of water. "Will you be all right?"

Loozy shrugged, her lovely painted mouth drooping just short of petulance. "I guess so." She looked up at Sabine. "You wouldn't consider . . ."

"No. I have to go to work early tomorrow." Sabine almost smiled at the stock one-night-stand phrase. She didn't want to tell Loozy that nothing could induce her to stay another ten minutes in this house. But looking at Loozy's pale, intense face Sabine caved in. "Look, do you want to come home with me?"

Sabine wasn't surprised at Loozy's quick acceptance of the invitation. Shoving regret aside, hoping Ruby would behave, Sabine gave Loozy directions and promised to have the hot chocolate ready.

Loozy was barely five minutes behind her, and Sabine had only a quick word with Ruby. "Don't ask me why or how, but Loozy is coming along to spend the night. You can sleep with me and we'll put her on the futon."

"How did the reading go? Tell me everything."

"I will, but it will have to wait. Promise me you won't go all psychic on her? She can't take it."

Ruby heaved a dramatic sigh and nodded. "Okay, I'll be a *normal* mother, just for tonight."

Sabine hugged her and went to meet Loozy's knock.

It was only momentarily awkward when Loozy of the Martha Stewart house entered Sabine's little garret. Sabine was reminded of the rare times she brought friends home to one of the shabby apartments she and Ruby had occupied over the years. The worst of these would be the years they couldn't afford a separate space for the business, and she'd had to walk her new friends through the "parlor" that Ruby would have decorated in an odd combination of Gypsy and Middle Eastern styles. Candles, gauzy curtains, and astrological signs mixed with scimitars and samovars.

"What a lovely place you have, Sabine." Loozy seemed genuinely impressed, and Sabine began to relax a little. "Thank you so much for being nice to me."

"Should you call Drake and let him know where you are?"

"I'll talk to him tomorrow. I don't have his itinerary with me."

Sabine detected a tension in Loozy's voice which was only slightly different from her usual high-strung manner. She seemed as nervous in this safe place as she was in her allegedly haunted house.

Ruby stepped right in. "You're safe here, you know that?"

"Oh, yes. I'm not afraid here."

"Then what's upsetting you?" As her mother asked the question, Sabine knew they were dangerously close to a long night of listening to Loozy's woes.

"I think Drake . . ." Loozy sat on the futon and reached for a tissue from the box on the coffee table.

"Go on." Ruby placed one hand on Loozy's wrist.

"I think Drake is going to sell the house."

"Because you think its haunted?"

"Yes. Because he's tired of me obsessing about it."

Sabine could understand that and felt a momentary sympathy with the man. Trying to settle her guest down, Sabine offered her the box of tissues. "Have a good cry, Loozy. Then we'll talk."

Loozy settled in to oblige, Ruby offered her maternal

shoulder as comfort, and Sabine slipped around the island counter to the stove to make the hot chocolate.

Sabine reached down her favorite Port Merion cups and saucers. Loozy was done weeping, reduced now to sniffling and laughing self-consciously. Sabine poured her a cup of the chocolate and handed it to her.

Ruby, looking at Loozy over the rim of her cup, felt compelled to comment. "If you want to stay in that house, you'll have to accept that it has something odd about it."

"How can I?"

"Loozy, what harm has been done? Whatever it is can't hurt you."

"Then why does it keep saying, 'Hide'?"

"It's not talking to you. Think of yourself as the audience." Ruby set her cup down on the saucer with a tiny clink. "Maybe you are one of those with the special sensitivity which allows such entities to contact you."

"Mom, you promised," Sabine hissed. She was finding it hard to stay awake. The trance had sucked all of her energy dry and she had no resources left to comfort Loozy or defend her from Ruby's sort of help.

"If you face facts, they can't hurt you." Before getting up from the end of the futon where she still sat beside Loozy, Ruby took the young woman's hand. "You'll be fine." Sabine held her breath, waiting for Ruby to turn Loozy's hand over for an impromptu reading, but her mother caught the annoyance in Sabine's eye and simply squeezed Loozy's hand before going into the bathroom.

"Look Loozy, sleep here tonight, go back to the house tomorrow, and try to think of it as street noise in the city." Sabine got up to fetch Loozy sheets and a blanket. "I'll leave the kitchen overhead on dim so that you have some light."

"Thank you, Sabine. I'll make sure you get compensated for this." Loozy slid under the bedclothes.

Sabine sat on the edge of the futon and let Loozy hug her. "Hey, I don't run a bed-and-breakfast. This is a girls' sleepover, not a job." Loozy's hug filled Sabine with a flood of imagery. She gently disengaged herself, but not before the images could form. It wasn't just Drake's selling the house that troubled her; there was a stronger disturbance emanating from Loozy Atcheson. A hole where her self-esteem should be. Drake, no doubt, was a loving bully; Loozy, his child-wife.

Ruby was right in one way: Loozy was a vulnerable person whose frame of mind opened her up to the other side. She was someone to whom ghosts attached themselves, being as empty of body as she was of meaning. Shaking off her thoughts as preposterous, yet too weary to challenge them, Sabine crawled in beside Ruby without even brushing her teeth.

Ruby glanced at the bedside clock before closing her eyes. Eleven forty-five. "Sabine?" Only the sound of a sleeper's deep breathing answered her. Ruby smiled. "Good night, my love. Sleep tight."

Seventeen

Dan heard the hall clock chime with its rhythmic twelve strikes and told himself to quit overvaluing the meaningless. It meant nothing that Sabine hadn't returned his call. She might have stayed at the Atchesons. She might have other things to do besides jump at his calls. It wasn't a signal that she wouldn't want to speak to him.

He'd left his offer of continuing to help with her research, and she hadn't thrown the book back at him. Sabine didn't seem the type to shut a guy down just because he mistook a touch, a smile, a laugh, for a lifeline in a choppy sea. Nor was she anything like Karen, who used silence as a weapon.

Dan got up and dug another blanket out of Beatrice's hope chest. A stiff wind was blowing down from the north, and his north-facing bedroom was chilly despite the rumbling of the furnace trying valiantly to heat the odd angles and drafty spaces of the old house. With oil prices the way they were, Dan was adamant about never turning the heat up over 68 degrees. The little trust fund Beatrice had arranged for Nagy hadn't allowed for the whopping rise in fuel and maintenance costs. Dan tried not to use that money, not as long as he lived in the house.

There had been no mortgage on the theatre until Beatrice had gotten sick and insisted on staying home to die. Despite Medicare and her small life savings, the cost of home care was stiff, and Dan had no choice but to remortgage the theatre. It seemed a better idea than mortgaging the house, especially since that would belong to Nagy. And, at the very least, most months the theatre paid the note. The mortgage had forced Dan to raise the admission prices, though, the only variable at his disposal. God, how he hated to do that. It had been his greatest pleasure as a kid to bring in his buddies, and on days when they were showing a popular kid's movie, they could be legion. They'd gather upstairs in the old balcony. Walt would shush them, and they'd lean over the edge, their little boy bottoms barely grazing the edge of the hard wooden seats. Now he had to charge those same buddies and their families more than the average guy wanted to spend on a movie he could rent six months from now for three bucks. *Catch-22* had been a great movie, but now he felt as if he were living it. If he charged more for movies, fewer patrons might come; fewer patrons meant the distribution house would cancel his contract. No big movies, no patrons, no theatre. Maybe that was his way out. Unintentional closure, by default.

Pestered by his random thoughts, Dan tried to harness his thinking into images of New York and the visit ahead. When Dan had called him to beg a place to crash tomorrow night, Paul had been thrilled. He'd asked few questions when Dan gave him the thumbnail sketch of his ended relationship with Karen. "That's too bad. You guys looked good together. Look, Marcia and I are going to a party tomorrow night. It'll be just the thing, Dan. Get you back in circulation and get your mind off, well, off stuff."

"I don't know . . ." Then, "Sure, why not." It would feel like being back in the saddle again to attend a premiere and after-party. It would also get his name and face back on the circuit, even in a small way. Besides, it would feel real good to leave the flannel shirts and jeans here and slip into the Armani suit Karen had insisted he buy.

An "investment," she had said, and was insistent about it. The Yankee in him blanched at paying that amount for a suit, but he knew that Karen was right. "In that, you look like a player." The very thought turned her on. That night, she made aggressive love to him, the heat and immediacy reminding him of their first coupling. He lay awake long afterward, wondering at the magic of an expensive suit, wondering equally if it was the man or the suit she wanted. Now he knew. Karen wanted the man in the suit, not the man in the jeans.

Dan rolled over, tugging the blankets around him and slamming a fist into the feather pillow. The sound of his fire department beeper startled him with its insistent alarm. It was a welcome relief to have to bolt out of the house, hop-stepping into his boots and hauling on his old Irish knit pullover. There was little chance he was going to sleep tonight, anyway. The fire siren began to bleat its public alarm to the still town as Dan sped away from the house and his sleepless bed.

As he turned the corner to the firehouse, Dan could

see the glow of a well-fed fire in the distance. For an anguished instant, he thought that it was in the area of Sabine's place, but quickly realized it was in the hills beyond the Windsor Farm Road house.

"Looks like a rite of passage is about to become history." Arthur Bean jumped into the front seat of Engine Three with Dan.

"The Old House?"

"Looks like it."

The Old House had for generations been a hangout for the rebellious youth of Moose River Junction. Perfectly concealed by new-growth woods, the abandoned farmhouse was the place where first beers were drunk and virginity was lost on the straw-stuffed mattresses scattered on the floors in all four rooms. Although he'd drunk his first beer there, and smoked a joint or two, Dan remembered being squeamish about the mattresses, and had gone a different route with his girlfriend. In the privacy of the theatre at noon, Dan and Jaymie Dawn Marino had utilized front row center. In many respects, the theatre had been his erotic awakening. He'd seen the R-rated movies legally denied to his brethren, except when he could sneak them past Nagy and up to the balcony. It seemed a perfectly natural place to have his first sexual encounter, certainly more conducive to romance than the Old House with its filthy mattresses and stink of spilled beer. Every few years some citizen would demand its demolition, but somehow the old place survived.

Nothing more than a cart path led to the two-story building, which by the time the fire department arrived was fully engulfed and sending showers of sparks onto the tinder-dry growth that surrounded it. While the others set to work to prevent more of the woods from going up, training hoses on the roof and surrounding brush, Dan lifted the portable breathing unit out of the truck.

"I sure hope there's no one in there." Arthur Bean stood beside Dan. "Look, don't go too far in, Dan. No heroics."

"Ten minutes, Arthur. Just a quick look around."

Hefting the Scott AirPak onto his back, Dan adjusted the face mask to make sure he could breathe and see. Raising his ax in front of him, he kicked in the door. The heat met him head-on, and it took a moment before he could forge his way into the main room of the house. Broken glass crunched under his boots as he moved through the room, the burning walls an eerie image of hell. He called out, but without much hope that anyone could survive in this conflagration. Dan fought his way through the boxy house, each small square room potentially holding a transient who fell asleep while warming himself with a sterno stove, or a pair of drunken teenagers, the match from their cigarettes carelessly dropped. Or maybe a cigarette lighter, monogrammed silver, accidentally dropped from stinging fingers. Dan slammed his ax through the burning wall into the last room and took the stairs to the second floor.

He could see the sky through the holes in the roof. In an oddity of fire, only the eastern wall was in flames, illuminating the one-room attic, revealing its empty state. Breathing deeply within the mask, Dan backed down the stairs, relieved that no one had died.

Eighteen

At first light, Loozy had gone home, not to Lower Ridge Road but back to New York. In the light of day she was less weak and much more the Loozy Sabine had first spoken with on the phone.

"Thank you so much, Sabine. You've been very kind. I'm looking forward to seeing what you can figure out about the writing. No, no coffee please. Don't trouble yourself."

"When will you be back?"

"I don't think I'll be back anytime soon. We're off to New Zealand in a couple of weeks. I'll call before we go."

Loozy had slipped away quickly, leaving the bed-clothes on the futon rumpled and a slight odor of Chanel.

Sabine looked at the kitchen clock. Six-thirty. The sheet of yellow lined paper lay on the island counter where she'd put it last night. The top edge, where it had been torn from the pad, had begun to curl. Sabine flattened it out and tried to pick out a few more words. The only pencil she could find had a dull tip, but was adequate to the job of circling the readable words. There were some she thought might be those oddities of antique spelling: *peple, fyre, crost at eving, Punishment.* That last word was distinct against surrounding gibberish and spelled perfectly. Who was being punished? The question teased at Sabine. It would have to wait; with a quick glance at the clock, Sabine put down the pencil, hurrying now to get ready for work.

"The ghost did some more writing last night." Ruby's disembodied voice came from under the comforter on Sabine's bed.

"Yes. Quite a lot, and it's like trying to read a word search without a topic clue."

"He's trying to tell you a story."

"No. I think he's living an incident. I don't know how to explain it. It's almost like there's no narrative, just dialogue." Sabine held the paper up to the sun coming in the bedroom window. "*'They come . . . Now. Hide.'*"

"What else?"

"There's a lot I can't make out. Scribbles, really. Then, *'Butry, safe, babe.'* Then a lot of letters squashed together, and the last thing I can make out is . . ."

"*'Help.'*"

Once in a while her mother did truly surprise Sabine with her prescience.

"Yes. *'Help us.'* Written over and over until the words dribble off the page." Sabine went in to brush her teeth. Over the foam in her mouth she called out to Ruby, "Did I tell you that the dates of the so-called defense of Windsorville and the death of Christopher and his wife seem to coincide?"

"Just the year, right?"

"That's all I have to go on." Sabine spit into the sink, then wiped her mouth.

"Busy year for Windsorville."

"I'm beginning to think that Christopher and his wife were maybe killed by Indians." Sabine rummaged around in her bureau for something to wear.

"It sounds plausible. But Sabine, I have to say, I have a sense it's something else. Something more heinous."

Sabine rolled her eyes. As usual, Ruby had to make more of something than was necessary. And yet. She'd come up with the same sense of undiscovered tragedy herself. Obviously an Indian massacre was pretty awful, but modern sensibility recognized that awful or not, it was likely justified. This whole business felt more like a true injustice had taken place. *Punishment.*

"Tell me what else you notice when you're at that house."

"I keep smelling smoke."

Ruby made the same sound a doctor makes when a patient lists an important symptom. A *hmmm* of interest. "And no obvious source?"

"The first time, I assumed it was a whiff of smoke from the wood stove, but it wasn't on. The second time was when Dan and I walked the property. That was very strong, but only lasted a few minutes." Sabine felt herself color a little at memory of that moment. "We found what might be a foundation or a wall, and then I got a definite whiff of smoke."

"And the third?"

"I guess that was the third. The first time I actually smelled the smoke was at Beatrice Danforth's funeral. I thought it was extinguished candles, but the odor is so similar each time. In the church, in the house, in the cellar hole."

"Interesting that twice the smoke can be associated directly back to Dan Smith."

"How so? I mean, he was only there twice when I smelled it. Not when I did the actual reading." Sabine declined to admit she'd had the same instinctive coupling of Dan Smith and the house.

"His emotional state on both those occasions had to be pretty powerful. Grief and desire."

"Please. Let's not confuse the two things in my life. The house is one thing, my acquaintance with Dan another."

"But you didn't smell it this time, last night when you read?"

"No, but Loozy had cooked lamb and the smell was quite strong."

"Maybe that wasn't the lamb."

"Mother!"

"No, I mean the evidence suggests a fire in the past. You smell smoke, the word *fyre* is printed three times in the handwriting. All of this is part of the haunting."

"Maybe there is no haunting. The fact is, Loozy is a ditsy neurotic whose real problem is an overbearing husband." Sabine yanked a skirt out of the closet and pulled it on over her slip. "I'm being as suggestible as Loozy."

"And the words are yours?"

"No, of course not."

"You can't have it both ways."

"That's how Loozy wants it. She loves the house but is afraid of it. What can I do for her? Really?"

"Find out more about the Indian attack. Find out where it happened and how."

"Who knew being a psychic was so much work?"

"It is if you're going to do it right. If I were you, I'd spend a night there alone, entranced. See what happens.

You're halfway there now. Your sense of smell and touch are there already. You just need to start seeing."

"Ruby, sometimes I think you really believe this stuff."

"Sabine, you know you do, too."

Sabine fastened her skirt and hunted around for a sweater. "I don't know what to think or how far I want to go with this."

"As far as it wants you to."

"Mom, what if it's only Loozy herself somehow transferring to me her inner turmoil? Giving me a false reading?"

Ruby threw back the covers and trudged past Sabine to the living room, where she found her fuzzy bathrobe. She put it on, checking the pockets for a pack of cigarettes, then went out onto the back porch, leaving the door open a crack. Her disembodied voice picked up the conversation. "It's always possible. What did Loozy say about the handwriting, about you writing with your left hand?"

"Mom, I can't talk to you through the door. Finish that damned cigarette and come back in." Sabine set up a new pot of coffee for her mother and then hunted through the refrigerator for some leftovers to reheat at work. "Loozy insists that not only was I writing left-handed, but that I was making little motions like someone using an ink pot. She was pretty freaked out. She realized that she had an ink pot on her windowsill which had been found on the property."

Ruby shut the back door, then reopened it to let Jerry in. "I'd say that points directly to pure channeling. You're the medium, my pet, not Loozy." Ruby moved Sabine's big handbag to one side of the counter and sat down. Under the bag was a book. "What's this?" She held up the history Dan had loaned Sabine. "You haven't shown this to me before." Curious, Ruby opened the book, taking an especial interest in the bookplate with Beatrice W. Danforth's name stamped on it.

"I just got it. He left it at the office for the research."

"Yesterday?" A simple word fraught with significance.

"Yes."

Ruby smiled that infuriatingly knowing smile she had graced upon Sabine since childhood. The smile that mixed I-told-you-so with amusement.

"What?"

"Beenie, whether you like it or not, he's in your life."

Sabine snatched the volume out of Ruby's hand and jammed it into her capacious bag. "How clear do I have to be? He's only and ever going to be . . ."

"What, Sabine? What is he going to be?"

"Nothing. I have to go to work." Sabine jerked the back door open.

"He called last night. Wanted me to let you know he's thinking of you."

Sabine felt the blood leave her cheeks. "Did he also mention he's on his way back to New York?"

Nineteen
෴

After all these months driving the Ford F150, Gran's Lincoln felt like it was driving itself. Dan eased himself into a relatively safe seventy and pressed the cruise control. The danger was, as tired as he was from last night's lack of sleep, he could very easily nod off.

He'd gotten home before dawn, barely. With that curious last shot of adrenaline that often came to him at the end of long nights, Dan didn't feel he could sleep at all. He was also afraid that if he did, he'd wake up more groggy than if he just sat still for an hour reading last week's *Pennywise Paper* and then showered. Karen had given him a very short window of opportunity to collect his things and he dared not risk being late. It was a good four, four-and-a-half-hour drive to the city, and he needed to be there before lunch. Paul had been relentless in his insistence that they have lunch at one of their old watering holes.

Feeling the newspaper slip from his lap, Dan woke

with a start. He shook off the sleepiness and peeked in on Nagy, sleeping flat on his back, mouth open and snoring. His eyes burning with the combination of lack of sleep and smoke, he was momentarily tempted to bag the whole thing. *Keep the stuff, Karen. I've lived this long without it. No,* he told himself, *just jump in the shower, and get over to Dunkin' Donuts for a big hit of caffeine.* This was Karen's way of coping with their breakup. He wouldn't deprive her of it.

Dan kept moving the radio dial around now, raucous pop to country to talk show, until he found the public radio station strong enough to stay with him from the Mass Pike down Interstate 91 through Connecticut. He couldn't remember Gran ever playing the radio in the car, and it was almost a surprise that it worked. As he passed through Hartford, tight only where I-91 interchanged with I-84, the radio station was playing Schumann's Rhenish Symphony, which Schumann had written with images of his honeymoon on the Rhine. In Dan's weary state of mind, the piece was softly evocative of the emotions he'd been waving off now for days. Sabine entered so easily into his thoughts, like a whisper. He smiled to think of her, then drew his mouth down and punched the radio button off. Taking the car off cruise control, he let his muscles determine the rate of speed.

Something had come over him Sunday afternoon in the cellar hole. Maybe he lived too much in the world of movies, where people could recognize instant and mutual attraction; where the overpowering connection would be heralded by sweet and crescendoing music. But this was life. Sabine Heartwood had more integrity than to believe a man just rejected by his girlfriend had legitimately fallen for her. Dan pressed a little harder on the gas pedal. It was later than it should be; he should be nearly to New Haven.

Beatrice had brought Dan to New York for the first time when he was eleven. Every time since, as he came along Interstate 95 and the sudden familiar skyline hove into sight, Dan felt that same heart-thumping excitement. They'd stayed at a hotel, the Lexington, he thought, and taken in several shows. When they went to Radio City Music Hall, he felt overwhelmed. The massive theatre, the great organ, and the amazing Rockettes. "This is what Vaudeville was like, Danforth. A smorgasbord of entertainment."

That visit had opened up a world for Dan that never left his imagination. He was one of only two or three other kids who'd ever been to New York by the sixth grade. He begged his seventh-grade teacher to make it their class trip; then lauded it over the others there by pointing out the restaurant in Chinatown where he and his grandmother had eaten, and all the theatres they'd attended. Finally somebody clocked him in the back of the head with an orange and Dan wisely shut up.

He never came into the city without remembering that trip. And the solitary journey to NYU. By eighteen, Dan had chosen his course. He loved New York. He loved the movies. By attending New York University and its film school, he'd have the best of both of his favorite worlds.

The traffic thickened, the skyline beckoned, and Dan felt a slight nervousness, an excited tension that mutated quickly into anxiety. He wasn't here for fun, he wasn't here to stay. Not yet. He was here to clear out his things from Karen's life. And to do it before she got home, like he was some kind of unwelcome guest. Dan dodged a slow-moving vehicle and signaled for his exit.

Luck was with him as he found a parking space on the right side, within several feet of the building. For a few minutes he sat in the Lincoln, gathering himself for the task at hand. From his pants pocket, he pulled out a single key on a leather strap. His key to the loft. He'd kept this key separate from his Moose River Junction keys, as if it would be forgotten among the jangle of theatre, house, fire barn, truck, and mailbox keys. There were so many more keys in his Moose River Junction life. Here, only this one. Karen had given it to him, with the stylishly embossed key chain bearing his initials, the day he moved in with her. There had never been any question of her moving in with him. His flat was a sublet so tiny that the bathtub was in the kitchen. He hadn't needed more, had seldom been there. His life in those halcyon days was held on the outside, at clubs and parties, at Starbucks and on location. Karen had the invisible support of well-to-do parents and had skipped the starving-artist training ground of her profession.

Dan gathered the boxes he'd put in the trunk of the car and made his way into the building. There was no one else in the slow elevator, just his own reflection in the murky mirror. Maybe it was the cloudy glass, or maybe he truly looked gray and tired, like a ghost. Just the thought made him smile, thinking of Sabine and her ghost hunting. Maybe *she* was the ghost, haunting him with her gentle spirit. The elevator clanked to a tentative stop and the door opened. By a habit he hadn't known he had, Dan waited until the elevator settled to proper alignment against the floor before stepping off. Walking down the hallway, its odor of cleaning solvent and damp rug instantly familiar, he yanked his thoughts away from Sabine.

The key in the lock turned easily, and Dan pushed the

door open. Karen had piled all of his belongings in the middle of the floor. Books splattered open, rolled-up posters crushed, CDs, city clothing, all heaped as if she'd tossed them from a distance. Dan stood in the doorway and stared at the anger-built pile. It looked like the beginning of a bonfire. "Well, no need to rummage around."

He hadn't allowed that Karen was so mad. Their couplehood had been fraught with spats, with arguments over going out or not, and with whom, and how his career took him in one direction, while hers set another course. Fights that simmered, exploded, and settled. Most contentious of all, his professional derailment as he remained away from her and in Moose River Junction.

Dan began to pick up his books and place them in the cartons. Maybe this was really for the best. He didn't want to use the words *high maintenance,* but there was a little relief in knowing that he wasn't going to spend the rest of his life with someone who could do this to his belongings. The books and CDs took up most of three boxes. The clothes he crammed into three more. Maybe he could take them to the Krests and beg for storage space? Or bring them home and put them in the attic, laced liberally with mothballs, and wait for the day of his New York return. Maybe he should just toss them into the nearest Salvation Army donation box. Or would that express a secret doubt that he would ever be back to wear these clothes again?

Everything boxed, Dan sat on the white couch where he'd sat to watch so many basketball games and old movies. Midday sun streamed in the big loft windows, highlighting the small treasures Karen had placed about the room, little expensive collections of glassware and ceramics. Nothing of his. Nothing of his had ever sat on those shelves. He'd been a guest. In that way of familiar places left behind, it felt off-balance to be there. The pictures on the wall seemed to stand out in a way they never did when they were part of his daily surroundings. If this had been a scene in a movie, he would have delighted in the way the sun streamed in through those huge windows, touching the sofa with a band of yellow light, as if highlighting the emptiness. Was there a word the opposite of *noirish*? *Whitish,* exposing the bones of the scene. What would happen, in his imagined scene, is that Karen would walk in. She would be dressed in red, a bold color, the color of passion. She would be angry that he was there, then relent. He heard her voice. "I was wrong." He couldn't hear his reply. Then he heard Sabine's voice, so real she might have actually been there. In his mind's ear he heard her say, "Dan."

Dan reached for the phone. He'd promised Nagy to check in at noon, so that's who he intended to call. But his fingers dialed Sabine's number. No answer. What was he thinking? Of course she was at work. Probably at lunch. He disconnected before the answering machine kicked on, and this time dialed his own number.

Nagy answered on the first ring. "I'm good. Don't worry about me."

"Did Maisie give you your lunch?"

"She's making it now."

"I'll be home tomorrow night."

"I know. Do you want to talk to Maisie?"

"Sure."

Dan double-checked everything with Maisie Ralston, until she chided him about being a worrywart.

"Well, thanks again for being there."

"Dan, I'm glad to help out, you know that. I always helped your grandmother."

Dan sat for a few moments after ending the call. How in God's name was he ever going to break free if he had such angst in just going away overnight? He had been alone in his thoughts for the long drive in and had hoped hearing other voices would ameliorate his tension, but instead it felt refueled.

It took four trips to get the boxes down and into the car. Dan took a final trip up to the loft, feeling as though he should leave Karen a note. What could he write that wouldn't annoy her more? He could write an apology, yet he wasn't certain he had anything to apologize for. If she'd only been a little more understanding. For just a little while longer.

He could say, let's be friends, but he wasn't certain she would take to that idea just yet. He could tell her he was staying at the Krests. Maybe they could have drinks. He still pictured her in the red dress and suddenly remembered it was the one she'd worn on their first official date. Karen's dark hair was cut to frame her face, accenting the sharp angles of her cheekbones. Her magenta-colored dress was made of some shimmery stuff, and made him think of latex poured over her sculpted body. She moved one hip and he knew she was exquisitely aware of the effect she had on him. Except that once you took the sexy clothes off, her angles and bones made an awkward tangle of dry love. Karen didn't like sex; she liked being sexy.

In the end he only wrote, "Here's your key. Thanks for everything." He knew she could read it as sarcastic or contrite. Maybe it was both. Closing the door behind him, Dan left the building.

Twenty

Sabine set her grocery bag on the counter and began to empty it. Jerry insinuated himself around and between her legs until she poured new crunchies into his bowl. For some reason, none of the choices for dinner appealed, and she decided she wasn't really hungry. Moe had treated them all to lunch at the Blue Moose, and her bacon cheeseburger had been enough to hold her past dinnertime. She'd just have some cereal. Ruby had left this morning to set up the new shop in Springfield, so there was no one there to comment on the inadequate meal.

It was a blend between odd and comforting to be getting her space back to herself. Ruby was equally a joy and a burden. They might be said to have a tumultuous relationship, but the fact was they enjoyed being together. For when you came right down to it, each was all the other had in life. As much as Ruby drove Sabine crazy with her way of life and her mysterious past, she was her mother. And Springfield was a good choice. Close enough for a quick visit, far enough away so they could each have a little space. Sabine finished putting away the groceries and poured herself some cereal.

Even before she heard Loozy Atcheson's voice, Sabine knew who was calling. "Hi, Loozy."

"How did you know it was me?"

"It's what you pay me for, Loozy. To know things."

"Sometimes I forget."

Sabine felt a little bad about her cynical tone. "I have caller ID; no tricks."

Loozy laughed and Sabine felt a little better. "Remember that I told you we're going to New Zealand?"

"Sure."

"I was wondering if you might stay in the house. I mean, if you wanted to stay overnight now and again. See what happened."

"See what happened?"

"See if you might get a clearer picture of what's wrong with it." It seemed very difficult for Loozy to get the words out, as if she didn't want to articulate the fear.

The idea of being in the house alone intrigued Sabine, even if it didn't appeal to her. After all, any trance is compromised by having people nearby. Just as dreams take on the sounds and scents of the world around the dreamer, so, too, can the trance be altered by the sounds and emanations of the observers. The scent of the cooked lamb or the cough in the audience. Yet without the observer, there is no proof of the trance.

At the same time, there was a yawning hole of the unknown, and Sabine wasn't entirely willing to enter it.

"I don't know, Loozy. I'm maybe not ready for that."

"Please. You said yourself it can't hurt you."

"How will I get a key? If I decide to go?"

"I'll FedEx one to you. Go anytime, stay as long as you like. The guest room is the one to the left of the stairs."

"I may not do this, you know." Sabine felt the failure of her own courage, negating almost everything she'd tried to convince this woman was all right.

"I think you will. I think you are brave enough and curious enough to actually do it."

"Let's hope so." Sabine ended the phone conversation, uncomfortable with Loozy's faith in her intuitive abilities.

What Loozy couldn't know was that this whole thing was beginning to creep her out. It had been all right, until this last time. Before then, it could have been any subconscious thought rising from the self-hypnotic state. Now she was frightened. She felt like inside she was the Cowardly Lion, muttering, "I do believe in spooks, I do believe in spooks," while on the outside she had to behave cool-headedly like Dorothy.

Sabine had just gotten up to rinse out her cereal bowl when the back door opened. Jerry rushed over to wind himself around Ruby's ankles.

"Thank you, Jerry, for being so happy to see me." Ruby scooped the black cat up. "Maybe I'll just take him with me."

"You will like heck. He's my baby." Sabine pried the animal out of her mother's arms and nuzzled him dramatically. "So, all moved in?"

"Almost. If you can stand it, I'll take one more night here with *my* baby."

On the counter lay the yellow-lined pad with its inexplicable notations. Beside it was the Windsorville history book Dan had loaned her. Loozy's call was fresh in her mind, and the fear of what she might discover still made

Sabine queasy. Maybe it was time to bring in the cavalry. "Mom, before you go, can I ask for a consult?"

Sabine had tried hard not to involve Ruby in this, painfully aware of Ruby's proclivity for drama and exaggeration. Without Sabine's caution the other night, Ruby would have had poor Loozy running for her life. With her artfully flowing gowns and the ridiculous mass of fake hair, Ruby could be a rather convincing actress.

What Sabine did believe, though, was in her mother's abilities to divine certain things. Some things simply can't be faked, and time and again Sabine had witnessed Ruby discovering some truth about a client, a specific thing that person might never have spoken aloud. She knew that wasn't the same as being a medium, which was what Sabine had been practicing, but certainly Ruby would be able to put her intuitive finger on the answer to this strange manifestation of an unhappy house. It might make sense to let her come along. It had been all right to do the automatic writing, it had been interesting to do the research. But a night alone, entranced in a house with such a disturbance . . . Well, maybe she did need to call in reinforcements. At the very least, Ruby would love the opportunity to see this *House Beautiful* home for herself.

Ruby Heartwood sat on the back porch and lit a cigarette. She exhaled slowly and considered exactly what she could do. That Sabine had asked for a "consult," as she'd called it, was more interesting to her than the mystery of the haunting itself. That still sounded, in Ruby's experience, rather a mundane thing. Some unhappy element wanting closure. And that's what she'd told Sabine. "Let it tell the whole story, don't write it down, just get under and listen."

For too many years she had kept company with the psychic community—seers and sages, fakes and legits— to think she herself had more than common garden-variety clairvoyance. Annually, since Sabine was old enough to stay on her own, she'd journeyed to various conferences, picking up ideas and honing presentation skills. It was a far cry from the carnival she'd been with in her youth.

The seedy trailer life, the moth-eaten robes, the funky odor of mobile poverty were still too easy to bring to mind if she let them. The carnival life had given her an escape from the religiously justified abuses of the convent orphanage she'd run away from. Illegitimate girls were subject to strictures intended to prevent them from repeating their mothers' mistakes. Little girls who were caught touching themselves, or each other, were caned with glee. Little girls who knew things without being told were beaten with even more energy. *Liar, troublemaker. You can't know what you know. Second sight is the devil's doing.* Beat the devil out of her indeed, thought Ruby thirty-four years later. Beat the devil *into* me.

Carnival life had proven abusive too, in an entirely different way. Phyllis Fontana's "Madame Fontaine"'s exploitation of her limited gift, in return for a bed in their trailer. The dirty hands of her middle-aged son scrabbling to feel her childish breasts while his whiskery lips wandered over her face. Catching her behind the carnie workers' trailers, forcing himself on her. Her abandonment in a strange town when she became visibly pregnant.

Sometimes Ruby woke up in the middle of the night, sweat-bathed from some unremembered dream. Her heart would beat against the fear her dream had renewed, fear that the nuns had been right, bred in the bone, brought out in the blood. Maybe Ruby *had* followed in her unknown mother's footsteps. Maybe her mother, too, had gotten pregnant at fifteen. What Ruby could not know, despite her abilities, was whether her mother, like herself, had been a victim, or if she'd simply been a love-struck teenager making a mistake? And had Ruby's clair-voyance come from her . . . or from the equally unknown father?

What of Sabine? Her gifts were so powerful that any ability Ruby might have, paled into mere parlor tricks. Ruby had watched her little daughter communicate with spirits. Watched the invisible dialogue take place, but was deaf to the conversation.

No, Sabine would have to do this on her own. This was Sabine's adventure. Her destiny.

Ruby got up and went in. "Sabine, no. This is what you have been called to do. I don't think I can help you by being there, as much as I'd like to." Ruby took up a tattered set of Tarot cards and began shuffling them slowly. "This is something you need to do, because the entity is comfortable speaking to you." Ruby laid one card over another.

"Mom, Loozy is the one the spirit is bothering."

"No, no. Loozy is just the alarm. She would never in a million years be able to understand more than the ran-dom sound or near-sighting." Ruby slid another card out from the deck. "You are the messenger. Whatever it is that this spirit is experiencing, he or she wants you to be there."

"So you won't come?"

"No. This is your journey."

"I can't believe you. I thought you'd be jumping at the opportunity."

"Beenie, it's not my opportunity."

Sabine stroked Jerry as he kneaded against her thigh. "Mom?"

"Yes?"

"What else do my cards say?"

Ruby slid a third card out from the deck. She studied it for a moment against the others laid out. "You will be told a secret."

"By whom?"

"You know better than that. I can't be specific. I've shuffled three times, and each time I can see that you'll be the recipient of secrets."

"Your secrets, maybe?"

"Like I say, who can tell?" Ruby bundled the deck back together.

If Sabine was to divine secrets, perhaps *she* was meant to tell them.

Twenty-one

⁂

Dan Smith walked into the kitchen of his uncle's house and saw Nagy, one rubbery cheek smooshed down against the kitchen table, sleeping a slightly drooly sleep. "What am I going to do with you, Nagy Danforth?" Dan muttered as he shook his uncle's shoulder.

"Hi, Danny. I waited up."

"So I see. Go to bed now, Nagy. It's very late."

Nagy stood in the doorway of the kitchen, one fist knuckling a sleep-gritty eye. "Did you have a good time?"

Dan nodded, a weak half-smile on his lips. "Yeah. I did. Now go to bed."

As Nagy made his way up the narrow back stairs to his room, Dan sat heavily down in a kitchen chair. The effervescence of being away, of being in the city he loved, the glimmer of hope of a potential job, had begun dissipating even as he'd merged onto the highway and set his course for Moose River Junction. It had been the most bizarre twenty-four hours.

After lunch with Paul, they had headed home to the Krests' 79th Street apartment. Dan kissed Marcia on the cheek and scooped up the babies, holding one in each arm. At two-and-a-half and eighteen months, the little girls were too young to remember Dan. They each looked at him out of Paul's dark blue eyes, studying him with babyish intensity to judge if this man looked like the name they had heard a lot over the last couple of days. "Say Hi to Uncle Dan," their father cooed, but the girls remained skeptical and squirmed to get down.

"They're as beautiful as their mother." Dan released them to run off to a safe distance to observe him.

"You haven't lost your city suave, despite your banishment to the backwoods," Marcia chided, directing Dan to leave his bags in their bedroom. He'd bunk on the foldout couch, a place he'd occupied once or twice during the occasional spat with Karen. He and Karen, Marcia and Paul, had never quite formed a couples bond. He'd known the Krests for far too long before meeting Karen, and somehow the fact of their old and close association had prevented the foursome from gelling. As often as the four of them might have dinner or meet at some party, the Krests were always *his* friends.

Dan waited until Marcia had her back to him. "She's broken it off with me, you know."

"I'm sorry, Dan," Paul said.

"Well, you know what they say. It's probably all for the best."

"Is it too painful yet for me to say, it probably is?" Marcia turned to face Dan, arms crossed, ready to defend her position.

Dan shrugged. "No. I don't think it is."

Marcia was distracted by the sound of some mischief the little girls were causing in the living room and so didn't probe Dan for more details right then. Before she dashed off to investigate, Dan caught her arm and leaned close to Marcia's cheek, giving her a tiny, grateful kiss. When they were at film school together, he'd been the one with the crush on Marcia, who was petite, blond, and knowledgeable. The three of them had teamed together for every major project, acted in each other's films, critiqued each other's work. They'd fallen asleep across each other's laps on couches at three in the morning before exams. They'd competed for the same awards and celebrated equally, whoever might win. They drank and smoked together, but they did not cross the sexual barrier. Then one day, Marcia asked him to meet her privately. Dan had felt a rapid heartbeat. For a very little while, he hoped she was going to tell him she felt the same way about him as he did her. But she hadn't. It had taken every fiber of his post-adolescent soul to smile and hug Marcia and say, "Go get him," when she confided that she was in love with Paul.

Watching Marcia extricate one blond child from the grip of the other as they fought over a toy, Dan congratulated himself on keeping the secret of his erstwhile crush on Marcia to himself all these years. He would never have made her as happy as Paul had. As in referencing his failed relationship with Karen as "for the best," Dan also chalked up what might have been with Marcia as an example of the mysterious hand of God. His ardor for his best friend's wife had long since evolved into brotherly love, which told him the passion he had felt for her ten years ago had undoubtedly been the passion of proximity, the passion of youth, and not to be trusted.

So what of Karen? Had his long absence awakened in her the same realization?

Out of sight out of mind. She'd said it back in April.

The film had been refreshingly unique, or maybe it had been so long since he'd seen a decent indie film, it just looked unique to his eyes. The short feature boasted a well-defined plot, good acting, and an outstanding soundtrack. What it lacked in editing perfection was more than made up by all the other elements. The applause was enthusiastic and the young filmmaker, who looked to be about sixteen, stood modestly at the front of the small screening room and bowed with self-conscious humility.

"Were we that young when we started?" Dan whispered to Paul.

"Younger. He's twenty-six."

"No way."

"Way. We're elder statesmen now, my friend."

"Maybe you are, Paul. But me, I'm eternal youth."

"That's just because you don't have a wife and kiddies making you behave like a grown-up."

Dan laughed, but there was a pinch to his laughter. As true as that might be, Paul wasn't thinking about Nagy and the awesome responsibility Dan had in keeping him safe and happy. Nagy and his back-room tinkering; Nagy leaving plastic dishes on the hot stove. Dan pulled himself back to the moment and stood to help Marcia on with her coat.

The after-party was held in a massive private ballroom. The young director's father was someone in the business and this was his opportunity to show off, network, and also manage a little payback. The ballroom glittered with over-bright chandeliers and jewels. Dan was very pleased he'd chosen to bring the Armani suit, although he had to borrow a pair of Paul's black shoes as, in his exhaustion, he'd brought only his trusty Hermann's Survivors. He had been able to snatch a quick nap while the babies were sleeping in the afternoon. Although a siren had awakened him, his pulse responding and his hands fishing around for his beeper, he thought he had managed to wake refreshed enough to handle a late night.

A server in black and white offered Dan a flute of champagne. Other servers were offering canapés and crudités, winding through the clusters of guests with skill, silver salvers held high. Suddenly famished, Dan snagged an hors d'oeuvre from a passing tray. A delicate scallop puff, with cheese melted within the pastry. It was hot and burned his tongue. He took another glass of champagne.

Dan knew a lot of the people here. He'd even met the boy's father once or twice. Malcolm Drexel. Back when Dan was a rising contender in the film industry, Malcolm Drexel had tried to hire him for a documentary, but Dan had been committed to another project. The last project he'd worked on, before Gran . . . before his life was derailed.

Dan downed the second champagne and reached for another. He felt the sizzle in his belly, and knew that loosening up he seldom allowed himself anymore. Between the fire department and the theatre, especially with Nagy so dependent, he rarely had more than one beer.

Tonight was different. Tonight he would climb his Everest; he would mingle and charm and remind the film world that Danforth W. Smith still lived. And maybe, maybe someone would tell Karen and she'd realize she'd tossed away a good thing. Hell, maybe he'd tell her so himself. The champagne was lifting his spirits as effervescently and as fleetingly as his one sweet kiss with Sabine had done. And as temporarily.

"Dan Smith. Thought you'd vanished off the face of the earth."

"No, only to western Mass."

"Dan Smith, good to see you."

"Dan, I don't know if you remember me . . ."

On and on it went, a marvelous, dreamlike reunion with people he'd known a lifetime ago. More champagne was handed to him; the room warmed and the faces bloomed. Finally Paul came up and took his arm. "Dan, I'd like you to meet our host."

Malcolm Drexel pumped Dan's hand with drunken enthusiasm, and Dan made the right comments about his son's film. "Clearly he has talent. You don't generally see that in someone so young."

Drexel had heard a variation on the same theme all night and wasn't a bit tired of it. "Paul here tells me you've established a theatre in the Berkshires."

"Not quite. It's my family's movie theatre. A nice former vaudeville venue, big screen, comes with staff. Do you want it?" He must be more drunk than he thought.

"Well, I don't dabble in real estate. I make movies." Drexel seemed suddenly sober. "Occasionally I think it might be nice to have a place to show the kinds of things these hot young auteurs bring out. But then I say, where will the audience come from?"

"Yes." Dan set a half-empty flute back on a passing tray. "That's exactly the problem with a theatre in the middle of nowhere."

"So, are you available? I've got a couple of projects in the talking stage."

"I've had some family matters to take care of, but I am definitely available."

"Good. Come see me."

Dan had wondered if at last the wheel of fortune had been given a good spin.

With a champagne headache pounding the next morning, he'd awakened to the realization that Drexel was probably saying the same thing to all the other out-of-work directors and assistant directors heaping praise on the boy's first work. Nothing would come of it.

But that wasn't the end of the evening. Not by a wide mark.

Turning away from Drexel, D saw Karen coming up the sweeping stairway into the ballroom.

He shouldn't have been shocked. This was exactly the sort of event she'd be invited to. He realized that part of him had been expecting her, hoping that Karen would be here.

Marcia had said something to that effect before they left. "Are you sure you want to go?"

He'd been a little abrupt in his attempt to satisfy Marcia with his assurances. "Of course I do. I've got to get back out there."

"You know, she could be there." Marcia seemed to be avoiding the use of Karen's name.

"I'm a big boy; I can handle it." He purposefully evaded the look of doubt Marcia shot at him.

Karen's presence in the crowded room left Dan with a choice. He could duck out now and dodge the awkward moment, or, having the advantage in knowing she was there while she had no idea that he was, approach her and see what might happen.

From his vantage point at the room's far corner, Dan watched Karen ascend the last three steps into the ballroom. As she had in his imagining of her, she wore red. A simple slip dress, showing to advantage her slim legs, boyish hips, and stunning breasts. Her dark hair was freshly cut in the chopped, uneven look becoming popular with models and actresses. She was animated, chatting to those near her, waving to those less close.

Dan stood at the side of the room and admired her. It was as if he were watching Karen on stage. She had the ability to transform herself into any character, and the character she was portraying tonight was the star on the rise. Thinking about it, Dan wondered if maybe he'd been attracted to the ingenue she had been portraying that year they'd met. It was a phenomenon inherent in the business of film and theatre. Actors were not their characters—but there was always a fine dust of disappointment when they weren't. Once off the set and out of the clothes, the spit curls washed away, the ingenue was gone. In her place was Karen, once a debutante, but never an ingenue.

What was to say that this relationship might not be repaired? A momentary regret took him; he hadn't done any of the right things to mend this breach. He should have just come back. If she meant anything to him, he should have made an attempt. What did that say about him? About his feelings for Karen? He'd been about to ask her to be his wife, and yet he was so easily turned away. No wonder Sabine had the good sense to send him packing.

Dan knew that with all the people they knew in common in this room, there was no way he could simply slip away. It would be cowardly. Last night, he'd chopped his way through a burning building without fear. With one more glass of champagne, gripped by the stem as if it were an ax, Dan strode across the ballroom floor.

He moved through the crowd, twisting this way and that to avoid elbows and tight groups of chattering people. No one seemed older than forty. Everyone was intent on impressing everyone else with their insider knowledge and their affinity for the latest craze in bottled water. At the far end of the room stood Karen, her champagne glass held artlessly between casual fingers. One hand stroked the opposite elbow, as if she enjoyed the feel of her own skin. Dan moved closer and watched her as she recognized his face. A wave of surprise, then, with a slightly raised eyebrow, her involuntary appreciation for the way he looked, and finally, brows lowered and knit together, disapproval.

"Hello, Karen." Dan wondered if he should air-kiss her, take the hand not clutching the glass, or simply stick his hands in his pockets and wait for her to react. She had not moved either toward or away from him, but stood fast, as if deciding what the appropriate greeting should be. Dan wondered if she'd been talking about their breakup. Or was it not yet on the gossip mongers' radar screen?

"Hello, Dan. What brings you here?" *Ah, it would be icy disdain.*

"The same thing that brings you: a need to be seen."

"Did you get everything?"

"Pardon?"

"From the loft? Did you get everything out of my apartment?"

"Yes. Thank you for sorting it out for me." They had locked eyes, bull and bullfighter. Dan noticed that a tiny flake of mascara had fallen from her lashes onto her cheek, like a tiny paint chip. Dan looked away first, unable to keep his eyes on that little flaw in her perfection. "Good party."

"Yes. I hope you've gotten reacquainted with people. It's probably not too late for your career, Dan."

"Just for us."

Karen put a hand to her hair, running her fingers up and under it to embellish its odd shape. She nodded. "It was time."

"You mean, like an expiration date?"

Uncomfortable, Karen moved a little away from him. Two or three other people were nearby, their own conversations muted as they strained to listen. Rumors, then, were in full flower. "I really don't want to talk about this."

"Let's go someplace else."

"No. I mean I don't want to talk about it at all. It's over, Dan. Move on."

"Is there a problem?" Taking Karen's thin arm in his hand, stood an actor Dan had worked with once or twice. An actor who had successfully transitioned from TV to movies in the last year. His proprietary hold on Karen was too familiar to be a recent phenomena. As Dan watched, his hand left her arm and traveled to her behind, where it lingered.

"Dan, do you know Carl Langstrom? We're working together on Malcolm Drexel's new project. I play opposite him."

"I bet you do." Dan stuck out his hand. "Dan Smith."

Langstrom's hand felt weak and Dan was tempted to give it a bone-crushing, masculine squeeze. He kept his eyes on Karen. "Congratulations, darling. All the best."

Karen let Dan kiss her cheek.

The scent of expensive perfume tickled Dan's nose, and he knew that he'd never be able to smell that particular scent again without some association with this moment. "Carl, a pleasure. I hope you have better luck with her than I did."

Leaving the future Hollywood couple standing with mouths slightly agape, Dan left the party. Halfway down the sweeping stairs that led to the lobby, Dan heard Karen call his name. The image of Rhett Butler crossed his mind, proud and decisive. *Frankly, my dear, I don't give a damn.* Dan stood on the third to last step to the lobby.

"Dan, I'm sorry. I should have told you that I was seeing someone."

"For how long?"

"I was hurt when you wouldn't come home. Carl was there."

"So, a month? What?"

"A little less."

A little less than a month. Since Gran's death. Since he'd seen Sabine and begun to know her. Since Sabine had thought him a jerk for hitting on her when, presumably, he had a girlfriend. "Why didn't you tell me?"

"I don't know. It would have seemed mean, I guess, given the circumstances."

"So, rather than tell me you've moved up the food chain, you let me believe that it was my fault?"

Karen frowned and lifted her chin. "It would have happened anyway."

For the first time, Dan realized that it had never mattered if he came back from Moose River Junction; Karen had spun out of his orbit a long time ago. Women like Karen weren't in it for the long haul. They moved, bumblebees on blooms, from man to man. Always looking for the next step up in their careers. In Karen's case, from an unemployed assistant director to a leading man. "You have a part in a movie, then?"

Karen smiled, relieved to move away from the unpleasantness. "Yes. A good one. Leading lady."

"You deserve it. You've worked hard."

"Thanks. Thanks, Dan." Karen had been coming down the stairs one at a time until she reached his side. "When you do finally come back, call me. We'll have drinks." She kissed his cheek and went back up the stairs.

Dan touched his cheek, brushing the place gently, as if making sure none of her lipstick had remained behind. A buoyancy subsidized by the amount of champagne he'd consumed lifted Dan's feet as he walked out of the hotel and flagged a cab. He was free.

PART III

PART III

One

All week long the town green had been undergoing its
annual transformation from green space to a carnival. The
firemen had been building the booths that would house the
familiar food vendors and game stations. On Thursday,
the amusement ride company arrived and began setting up
the Tilt-A-Whirl and Flying Swings. The Moose River
Junction Volunteer Fire Department had been doing this
carnival for as long as anyone could remember. It was
equal parts goodwill and fund-raising, harvest home and
farewell to the vehicular intrusion of leaf peekers. Initially
just from bobbing for apples and ring toss, with a pie-eat-
ing contest thrown in, the event had expanded into a full
weekend, complete with music and the Dazzling
Derrick's Magic Show. From time out of mind, the carnival coincided with the first cold snap, and everyone would
show up in their wool sweaters muttering about how the
firemen should change the date to September. More hot
chocolate would be sold than lemonade.

Ruby drove the lime green bus over the flattened grass and pulled up next to a little cardboard sign nailed to a stake with MADAME RUBY written on it.

"If I'd thought how cold it was going to be out here, I'd never have volunteered."

"It'll be fine in the tent, Ruby." Sabine lifted the hatch of the bus and grasped the end of the bagged tent.

"We aren't talking L.L. Bean here."

The tent was hardly more than a conical gossamer setting for the fortune teller. Vaguely medieval, it sported colorful purple, pink, and yellow nylon streamers at every point and a banner at the peak. After years of sitting at street fairs under a wobbly beach umbrella stuck in a pail of sand, Ruby had invested in the tent, calling it her upscale business expense. It had lent a certain sophistication to her presentation and she'd quickly made back the money spent. People seemed to like to come into a tent to have their fortunes told.

"So, wear long johns under your caftan. No one will be the wiser."

"It wouldn't be the first time I've done that." Ruby grabbed the end just emerging from the bus, and the pair hefted the rolled-up tent. "Thankfully it isn't too windy."

"Can I lend you ladies a hand?" Arthur Bean trotted over to where they stood grappling with the tent.

"Thanks, Chief. Yes, you certainly can."

Arthur quickly picked up Ruby's end of the bundle, and she joined Sabine at the other. They had the tent up in no time, and Ruby went back to gather the tools of her trade out of the bus.

"Hey, Sabine?" Arthur stuck his thumbs into the tool belt around his hips. "Can I ask you something?"

"Sure, what is it?" Sabine noticed that the chief had

stepped back a little ways, out of Ruby's earshot. A tiny flicker of nervousness revealed itself to her by the way he rubbed the palm of his left hand over the head of the hammer hanging from his side. Back and forth, as if calming himself with the feel of the cold hammer beneath his hand.

"Do you think your mother would be willing to . . . ummm."

"Do you want to ask her for a date?"

"Not in so many words. Maybe . . ."

". . . Ask her if she wants to go get coffee?"

"You really do read minds." Arthur let go of the hammer and rubbed his bristly chin.

"Just making a guess. I don't know what to tell you, except go for it."

"She's not involved, is she?"

Sabine shook her head. "No. As far as I know, she's not involved." As far as she knew, Ruby had never been involved. Not even with her own father. "It can't hurt to ask."

"You don't mind?"

"Chief, I'd be a pretty awful daughter not to want my mother to go out with the town's most eligible bachelor." Sabine made her intonation flirtatious.

Like some mythical cowboy about to enter the OK Corral, Arthur hitched up his tool belt and approached Ruby. He had at least ten years on her, and a pot belly, but he was a good man, a true pillar of the town and a longtime widower. Ruby could do a lot worse. Or, as always, do without.

Sabine couldn't watch, so she busied herself dressing up the round table with its dark blue tablecloth with the gold crescent moon and stars on it. Ruby had said she would mostly be reading leaves; people would like to come in for the sip of hot tea. Sabine opened the wooden box with the fragile teacups in it. As a child, she was seldom allowed to hold them. Even now, Ruby was tense the minute she touched the gilt-edged china. Sabine set the cup and saucer down on the table and sat on the three-legged stool Ruby used. The sorcerer's stool, Sabine had always called it. Opposite the stool was a simple, black rush-bottom chair with vaguely mystical symbols painted on it in gold and silver. Clients sat there. One of the legs was slightly shorter than the others, intended to keep the client off balance, Ruby said. Sabine thought she'd probably been able to get the pretty little chair cheaply because of the flaw. A low second table held the little spirit stove that heated the tea water, an ordinary aluminum saucepan on it. The teapot was also very ordinary, something with no magic attributed to it.

There was some indefinable difference in Ruby these days, some anticipation distracting her. It was more than the sudden decision to move to Springfield; that was vintage. Sabine knew it was tied to this repeated declaration that a significant event was taking place in her life. It lay more fully in the few tantalizing facts Ruby had let slip about her history. Sabine could not remember, in all her life, when Ruby had been truthful about her past. Always it was born of the Gypsies, or stolen from them. Or stolen by them. Fantastical stories designed to entertain, not to explain. *Why now, Mom?*

Sitting on her mother's stool, Sabine held an empty china cup in both hands. She listened for Ruby's voice, half expecting her to burst in between the flaps of the tent and rant about the nerve of that man asking her out. Hearing nothing, hoping for peace, Sabine gently held the little cup with its lilac blossom pattern. An image floated by—other hands holding this cup, not her own and not Ruby's. Soft, white hands, the nails very long and purple. Like Ruby, a ring on every finger. Other than that, they were not like Ruby's hands; these were much blunter, the nails a color Ruby had never favored. Sabine stared down until she could see plump wrists. She let the image deepen until she saw those hands rolling out bread dough, shaping it into crescents. Her own hands felt sticky. Then the virtual hands were holding the teacup again and Sabine strained to listen as a low, accented voice began to speak.

"Sabine!" Ruby stood in the entrance, hands on hips, startling Sabine out of the trance and causing her to almost drop the teacup. "What are you doing?"

"Nothing." Sabine let a little coyness creep into her voice. "Just trying to communicate with my grandmother."

She thought Ruby would laugh. Instead, Ruby stormed over to the round table and grabbed the fragile cup out of her daughter's hands. "Please don't."

"You told me the cups belonged to my grandmother. That was the first time you've ever mentioned a relative. Don't I deserve to know who she was?" Sabine had never had any intention of starting this argument, but now it seemed let loose upon the air like a curse.

"Not that way."

"Oh, so there is a possibility you'll actually tell me about her?" Sabine knew she sounded sarcastic, and hated herself for it.

Ruby settled the fragile cup into its bed of tissue paper and closed the parquet box. "When it is time for you to know, I will tell you."

Sabine got off the sorcerer's stool and pushed past Ruby. "I'll be back at the office."

Ruby fought the urge to take the wooden box and smash it against the ground. She hated being reminded of Madame Fontaine. Of how, while the old woman rolled out the dough for the crescent rolls she was making that last night, Ruby had stolen the parquet box, tucking it into the pillowcase thinly stuffed with her few clothes. She knew what Madame Fontaine intended, and she would not go without some compensation in return.

More than the hundreds of light bulbs burning white against the growing darkness, more than the pervasive odor of fried dough, more even than the music pumped out of the merry-go-round, it was the sound of the generators that brought the memories. The little Firemen's Carnival on the green in Moose River Junction certainly wasn't the same as that traveling troupe of rides, games of chance, and freaks, but it felt the same the minute the heavy drone of the generators powering the rides tickled Ruby's ear. For a quarter of a century, Ruby had avoided carnivals. They were small communities, roustabouts going from one to another, taking stories and gossip with them. It would only have been a matter of time before someone she'd known would have recognized her. There was no way she would ever let herself into that kind of danger again.

Her gossamer tent fluttered in the building evening breeze. Setting up her little easel with her hand-painted sign—MADAME RUBY, FORTUNE TELLER AND PSYCHIC—written on it, she shook out her deep blue caftan, touched a hand to the fanciful turban wound round her head, and entered her place of business.

Tonight she'd concentrate on tea leaves. She liked reading the leaves, the intimate act of pouring tea for a client, and that person sipping gently from the fragile cups to reveal the signs and portents in her life. Like a little tea party, as children might play. When Sabine was a little girl, Ruby had watched from the distance of the kitchen as she'd poured imaginary tea for Thumper. Ruby had had to clasp a restraining hand over her mouth to hide the amusement as Sabine had spontaneously taken Thumper's tiny plastic cup. "Let's see what we see," her daughter had intoned in a perfect imitation of herself. "You'll soon have an adventure."

Ruby poured a little bottled water into the aluminum pot and lit the spirit lamp. She heard the first rustling of a hesitant customer. "Enter and discover." It always seemed to take a few minutes to talk the first one in. After that, they tended to line up. *Never make them afraid; never worry them. Always give them something to consider.* Ruby's borrowed adages, as stolen as her china cups.

Ruby felt a double agitation. If the unexpected overtures of Arthur Bean had unsettled her earlier, this quarrel with Sabine had definitely set her nerves on edge. Her hands were trembling, not with the cool air, but with an inner chill. She thought it unlikely she would be able to read anyone's leaves correctly tonight, let alone her own. Still, she poured a little water into her own cup and sipped, then looked down at the signs.

What she had been intuiting for weeks was verified in the tiny yellow-brown leaves. It was time.

Dan and Nagy came along the midway. Nagy clutched a cone of cotton candy in one hand, the pink fluff stuck to various parts of his face and hands. They'd played all of the games and eaten at each of the booths. Dan felt his pockets emptied out and was glad that the whole thing was running so smoothly. Teens from all over the area moved through en masse, dropping small fortunes on the games of chance. Couples pushing strollers lined up to get on the merry-go-round. The first-aid booth was dispensing only Band-Aids. Tomorrow they'd be dealing with bee stings, as the October sun awakened the yellow jackets that always seemed so attracted to events of this nature. Having overseen the setup, Dan was exempt from manning any particular booth, though he'd help relieve various volunteers tomorrow as the day wore on. Tonight was Nagy's opportunity to go to the carnival. As long as Dan could remember, the Palace closed on the Friday of the Firemen's Carnival. Dan wondered if the tradition had started when Nagy was first standing in the door. Maybe it was Gran's way of making sure he got to go to the carnival at night, when it was the most exciting.

"What do you say, Nagy? We've done it all. Some of it twice. Ready to go?"

"Maybe one more . . ." Nagy held up two red ride tickets, a little sticky with cotton candy, but sufficient for the Tilt-A-Whirl.

"Nagy, I'm whipped. You can come back tomorrow afternoon."

"It's not the same."

Dan looked at his watch; nearly eleven. He'd been up and working since six. Well, he wasn't so old that he couldn't push himself a little. "Okay, one more ride, but then that's it."

Watching Nagy scamper off to jump on the ride, Dan was struck by how spry he was. He seemed blessed by an energy that never diminished. Here he was, not yet thirty-five, feeling every tired muscle in his body, while his fifty-seven-year-old uncle trotted away like a boy. Youth and innocence. Maybe they were the same thing. Right now he felt he had neither.

"Dan. I was beginning to give up hope you'd come in."

Dan turned in the direction of the voice. "I can't say I was planning on it."

Ruby stubbed out her cigarette in a little ashtray in her other hand. "No one ever does." She held the flap of the tent aside and waved him in.

Dan shook his head. "No, I don't think so, Ruby. Thanks anyway."

"What are you afraid of?"

"I'm not afraid of anything. Nagy will wonder where I am."

"No, he won't. He'll know. People like Nagy have their own sensory capabilities."

"Now I know you're full of it."

Ruby didn't leave her place at the front of the tent, but somehow Dan was now close enough that she could take his arm. "Then humor me."

If anyone had asked him at that moment, Dan would have been hard-pressed to explain what compelled him to go inside the little tent. Ruby didn't tug at him, certainly not. Nonetheless, Dan felt pulled inside. He would have laughed and said he was being a good sport, supporting the carnival with his ten bucks. But Ruby just waved his money away. "I only give true readings to people I feel need them."

"What if they don't believe?"

"Everyone believes. On some level."

"Okay." Dan sat himself gently down on the black-and-gold chair. It wobbled slightly, and he leaned against the unevenness, which placed him very close to Ruby. He could smell the remnant cigarette, and the Altoids mint she'd placed on her tongue as they entered the space.

Ruby took both of Dan's hands in hers. She closed her eyes and then announced, "I'll do your palms. Then maybe your cards. You aren't meant for leaves."

"Not a tea drinker."

"Hush, now. Let me look." Ruby took up Dan's right hand in hers. Her fingertips grazed his palm in a subtle sensual way that surprised him. Just as quickly, the feeling passed and he relaxed a little. Ruby glanced up at him with a slight smile. "You are a very conflicted man."

"You said that the night we met."

"Yes, but now I see part of what disturbs your heart."

Dan knew better than to speak. He'd make Ruby work for this.

"Here I see devotion. Could be to a person or to an idea. Very strong." Was it his imagination or had Ruby's intonation changed, and was there a slight indefinable accent? "Here," and her red-tipped nail grazed a line in the center of his palm, "here I sense a very deep . . ." Ruby traced the line, cupped Dan's hand a little to force it deeper, then touched where another line bisected it. "A very deeply held secret."

There was a secret. One that he'd carried for as long as he could remember. Dan shifted on the wobbly chair, moving his body away from Ruby even as she held his hand.

"An oddity here." And again she touched a line, which, as she folded his hand over, dented into the side of his hand beneath the little finger. "There is something misunderstood about this secret." She laid his hand flat again. "Do you know what it is?"

"I might."

"Whatever it is, you have been holding on to a lie."

A prickle of sweat erupted beneath Dan's collar. The small tent seemed overwarm suddenly, and he wanted to take his hand away from Ruby and open up his jacket.

"I thought maybe you'd tell me I'm taking a long trip." Dan tried to laugh, to back away from the closeness.

"You will. You'll keep running until you face this secret, this fact, which has kept you running for a long time. Your devotion and your misplaced guilt are in great debate over your heart."

"Misplaced guilt?"

"In my initial analysis, that's what I see."

"I should go find Nagy."

"Yes. I think we'll keep your Tarot for another time."

Dan stood up, knocking the little black chair aside. "Will you tell Sabine that I . . ."

"No. I won't pass any messages along from you. You have to do it yourself."

"You don't know what I was going to say. Not even you could know."

Ruby was on her feet and moving to shoo him out of the tent. "Don't bet on it. Tell her yourself."

Dan turned around to stand face-to-face with Sabine. There was a split second when the most natural thing would have been to embrace, and Dan reached out a little, but Sabine backed away.

That split second was shattered as Greta Sutler stormed up to Dan, finger wagging. "Dan Smith, what did you say to Arnie?"

Dan looked from Sabine to Greta, confounded. "What?"

"What did you say to Arnie about the love of his life? He broke our engagement off!"

The prickle of perspiration Dan had felt inside the tent suddenly bloomed into a cold sweat. "Greta, I'm sorry. He was . . . it was . . ." Dan backed away, but Greta kept coming. "I'm sorry. I never meant to interfere. I only asked him because he was expressing some doubts."

"Doubts! Doubts!" Greta threw her hands into the air. "What can you know of doubts?" She turned to Sabine. "And you, you said I would have a happy life."

"And you will, Greta. But I never said it was with Arnie."

"Oh, my God." Greta strode off, her mass of blond ponytail shaking with the force of her departure.

"I can't believe that he broke it off with her because of some idiot remark of mine."

"It really is all for the best, Dan. She'll realize that soon, so don't beat yourself up. I knew they weren't meant to be together. But you don't tell people those things."

Again he reached to touch her, and again she moved away. "Sabine, I feel as though we should talk. About Sunday."

"I thought we had. Dan, I'm not mad. You and I are human, the setting was pretty. It was nice, but forgotten. Okay?"

"No. That's not what I want to say at all. Things have changed."

"Don't make it complicated, Dan. Whatever your relationship with Karen is or isn't, it won't change anything."

Dan would swear she hadn't moved, yet she was out of his reach. "Why?"

"You're not a free man, Dan. Not in any respect."

Dan spotted Nagy coming back from the Tilt-A-Whirl, yet another cotton candy in hand. Ruby stood just inside the tent. All around them, carnivalgoers laughed and called out to one another. The music from the rides blared overhead. In the corner of his eye the spinning carousel caused a mild vertigo. Dan felt as if he'd been filleted. Between them, Ruby and Sabine had ripped him open with their razor-sharp intuitions, and exposed feelings and conflicts he hadn't allowed to the surface in years. He was freezing, the October air suddenly bitter as the night. How could Ruby have touched so pointedly on his deepest secret? Misplaced guilt? Surely he was leaping to conclusions, falling prey to the fortune teller's guile? Anyone could have a secret, and guilty was simply what secrets generally were, misplaced or otherwise.

And Sabine. All the way home from New York he had played over and over what he would say to her, to convince her that they should take a chance. He wanted her to know the truth. But she was so determined to keep him at arm's length. What did she mean, he wasn't free? She just had to stop and listen for one minute.

"Sabine, hear me out."

But Sabine was gone.

"I warned him about hurting you."

"He hasn't hurt me."

"Sabine. Give it up."

Ruby watched closely as Sabine willed herself into control. She'd always been this way, fighting emotion off like insects. In the illusory privacy of the thin-walled tent, Ruby wouldn't press Sabine. But she did caution her to handle the cups more gently. "Sabine, go home. I can attend to this."

"No, it's okay. I don't mind."

"Sabine." Ruby caught her daughter's hand, pulling it away before she could pick up the endangered teacup. "I can manage. Arthur's coming to help me."

"Oh? Oh. Great." Sabine zipped up her jacket and gave Ruby a peck on the cheek. "Good for you, Mom."

"Don't you be reading anything into this. He simply offered to help me put things away."

"I won't wait up."

"I'm not going back to your place, Sabine. I'm going back to mine."

"So late?"

"It's not that far and, well, I think that I need to give you some space."

"You don't . . ." Sabine stopped herself. "Call me when you get home?"

"I will."

A whiff of masculine air disturbed the atmosphere in the small tent. "Am I interrupting?"

"Here, Arthur, would you empty out this pot?" Ruby handed him the still-warm tea water. As he left, Ruby waggled her eyebrows at Sabine to beat it.

Arthur took the box with its fragile cups back to her bus for safekeeping. Pausing for a moment before tying shut the tent flaps, Ruby took a great breath of air. She felt as if all the signs and portents in the world were fore-gathering and yet she was blind to their implications. Something was happening, not only to Sabine but, equally, to her.

Dan Smith's stricken face hovered in the background of her mind. Her words, as true a reading as she had ever done, echoed in her ears. It had been as if she had been reading her own palms, her words spoken to herself.

You'll keep running until you face this secret, this fact, which has kept you running for a long time.

Two

Sabine drove home faster than she should have, taking the three winding curves in Windsor Farm Road much too recklessly. Never before had any guy gotten to her this way. That damned click. She couldn't let him touch her; one touch would be her undoing. She had lied to Ruby. He had hurt her by running off to New York. He continued to hurt her by trying to explain why he had. Things have changed. It didn't take a psychic to know that he'd been with Karen. That they probably hadn't patched it up. But as an intuitive, Sabine saw right through Dan Smith. To allow the relationship to grow was futile. In the end, he would leave. And she would not.

"Nip it in the bud." Sabine yanked open the storm door, and a small FedEx package dropped out. As good as her word, Loozy had sent the key to the house on Lower Ridge Road.

Sabine stood for a long time holding that key, wondering if she had the guts to do what Loozy was asking. Not because she thought the entities would hurt her, but because of what had hurt them. Alone in her own place, without the sounding board of Ruby, without the self-protection of her own skepticism, Sabine knew that what had been revealed to her in the writing was deeply sad. *Hide, the babe, they come. Punishment. Jacob's History of Windsorville* had not explained anything. The scattered words on the yellow-lined page were what convinced Sabine that an injustice had been done. One that kept these unhappy spirits calling out from the abyss. Perhaps an injustice as profound as that done to Goodwife Mayton, when they banished her from the village in punishment for her accusation against the magistrate, a man named Windsor. That incident did make it into the *History,* as an example of justice.

Sabine thought about calling Ruby on her cell phone, then remembered Arthur Bean. Who knew what might come of that? Wouldn't it be wonderful for Ruby to find a man with whom to finally settle down? Especially one right here in MRJ. Sabine quickly chided herself; no use jumping to conclusions. And that idea was too much of a leap.

No, the choice was hers; no input or advice from others. To stay here, warm up under her quilt and watch a little late TV, or go. Sit alone in a house that kept its owners awake at night. Go see what stories might be told. Decide once and for all if her insight was simply imagination. The key warmed itself in her hand.

Gathering up overnight things, changing the cat box, and filling the food and water bowls, Sabine locked her own door behind her and headed off to the Atchesons' house. The full harvest moon was struggling to carry its weight overhead. A nestling-in time of year, Sabine had always thought. Harvest in, sweaters pulled out of storage, time for winter projects to start, quilting and reading good books. In Loozy's house Sabine would settle in, protected from her own unruly thoughts by the unfamiliar walls and waiting spirit. She decided not to do anything this night but listen. She'd listen to hear the noises that frightened Loozy so much, to see if they were spirit-caused, or of this world. Without the distraction of living people, she could open herself up to other possibilities. Hauling on her skepticism like armor, Sabine added a cheap gold cross just to be on the safe side. Raised without religion, Sabine nevertheless felt better having the Christian symbol around her neck and beneath her sweater.

The house was cold, and Sabine twisted various thermostats in the upstairs and downstairs zones. Coming into the den, she spotted the wood stove and decided to treat herself to an evening by the fire. There was a neat pile of newspapers and scrap wood from the building project, pine ends and splinters of wood shingle as kindling. Out back was a large stack of split, seasoned hardwood, and Sabine brought in an armload to feed the flame as the night wore on. She didn't know a lot about loading wood stoves, only that you worked up: paper, kindling, bigger kindling, wood; stacking each combustible element like a four-layer cake, then tucking the burning tip of a wooden match under the crumpled newspaper and standing back. It took five tries before the paper ignited the splinters of shingle, but eventually it all took. Sabine shoved more of the pine ends in, determined to warm the chill room quickly, although she knew it was her heart that was icy. It had seemed the right thing to do, to keep Dan at arm's length, but in the soft quiet of the strange surroundings, her decision gave her no satisfaction.

The snap and crackle of fast-burning kindling was the loudest sound Sabine heard as she nodded off in the warming room, the weight of her unhappiness carrying her down before she thought to adjust the damper on the stove to slow the rate of burn.

Like a narcotic, the warmth eased itself through her bones, warming her almost into a sweat. Briefly she dreamed she was in a sweat lodge, surrounded by half-naked men, streaks of ocher, black, and red on their cheeks, anger in their snapping black eyes. She could nearly smell them, the pungent odor of unwashed, hungry men. She heard their voices, unintelligible cadenced words, a chant underscored by pulsing drum. The fire in the pit suddenly rose higher and higher, roaring like a furnace.

Sabine woke with a start to hear a crackling sound. The ceiling snapped loudly, as if giant footsteps were treading upstairs. Sitting up, she heard the distinct roar from her dream. Her heart beating in her ears, she first thought that the ghost was manifesting itself; then, with greater horror, realized the truth. The wood stove was out of control and the chimney on fire. The great heat was expanding the flue with acoustic dramatics. Quickly closing the stove's dampers, Sabine grabbed the phone and dialed nine-one-one.

She stood outside in the sharp cold night air, clutching her fleece jacket around her and listening for the sirens that grew louder as they approached. For reasons she couldn't fathom, the communications center seemed to have sent every truck the fire department had, along with an ambulance and assorted police. She felt more than a little embarrassed at the show of force. The difficult dogleg in the driveway made it interesting to watch the long ladder truck maneuver its way to the house. Flashing lights strobed the darkness, briefly revealing familiar faces under helmets. Otherwise they all looked alike in their heavy rubberized black coats with the broad bands of reflective tape across shoulders and cuffs, M. R. J. V. F. D. painted in yellow on their backs.

Someone climbed the ladder to the roof and began banging around inside the chimney with a chain to break up the creosote. In the darkness, the reflective letters appeared to float above the chimney until the spotlight caught and focused on the man.

"Happens every time some idiot thinks pine is a good-burning wood," Sabine overheard Amos Anthony mutter as he stood watching the ladder climber go up.

"I only used what the owners had put in the wood box," Sabine felt compelled to explain.

"Exactly what I mean. Happens a lot with new houses—all those lovely leftover ends just crying out to be used. Bad idea, especially if you don't burn hot enough to get rid of the creosote. Pine tar. Remember that stuff as a kid, always getting on your hands when you climbed trees?"

"Umm. No. Not really." Sabine's city-centered childhood had been absent of tree-climbing experience.

"Well, the stuff would stick for days, despite your mother going at you with a vengeance." Amos wandered off.

The lieutenant fire chief spotted her and came to question her about the house. Sabine gave him the information he needed to finish his report, and was relieved when he told her she could go back in. "No more fires, though, young lady. Not till the owners tend to that chimney."

Sabine went back into the open door of the house, following the tracks of the firemen's boots as they had checked on the stove, then into the basement to the cleanout.

"When was the last time you got that chimney cleaned?" A fireman she didn't recognize was scooping out the broken bits of blackened material into a metal bucket. He sat back on his legs and gestured to Sabine to observe the heavy amount of soot he was digging out.

"It's not my house. And the people who own it have only stayed in it a few weekends a year, mostly this summer. It's a new house."

"Odd. This chimney looks like it's had steady use for a hundred years. Weird. They must keep slow fires going, with nothing but pine."

"I don't know. I just know I won't be using it again."

Sabine left the fireman on his knees scooping the debris. Getting the same feeling she always got when she watched a mechanic check over her car, something between curiosity and boredom, she decided to go back outside to watch the fireman on the roof. As easily balanced as a chimney sweep, he stood over the center chimney, his face soot-covered from the occasional puff of smoke from the now-dead fire. Periodically he raised his face to the starry sky, and seemed to be enjoying his lofty view. It was only when he shouted down to a companion that Sabine realized it was Dan beneath the heavy helmet. Finally satisfied that the situation was under control, he gathered the long, heavy chain into a metal lariat and began to back down the extended ladder with the insouciance of long experience. Sabine had never before seen this incarnation of Dan, this calm, almost casual manner in which he'd climbed off the roof and down the ladder.

She stood, the lone female figure, clutching her jacket around herself, the shadows half-hiding her as the firemen busily gathered their equipment back into the trucks. Sabine stood in an anguish of indecision. Should she approach Dan, thank him, pretend everything was normal; or stay here in the shadows, wishing he'd go away and she could creep back into the disturbed house, hoping he'd never know it was she who had made the call?

As these things often play out, it was someone else who made the decision for her.

"Sabine, the owners can get my report tomorrow." Ted Francis, the fire lieutenant, scrawled his signature on a piece of paper held to a clipboard.

"They're in New Zealand."

"Then whenever they get back."

Behind Ted, Sabine could see Dan, see him startle at the sound of her name.

"Sabine?" Dan removed his helmet, his forehead white against the chalky black of his sooty face. He strode up to her before she could duck away. "I had no idea you were here. What are you doing?"

"Evidently setting chimney fires. I'm sort of house-sitting for the Atchesons."

"Alone?"

"Yes."

"I think maybe you shouldn't be alone. I'm sure everything is okay, but it might be a good idea to go home."

"Thanks for the advice. But I've got work to do." Sabine did not look at him, uncomfortably attracted to this new manifestation, Dan as fireman. She did not want to desire him today. Yet she was desperate to wipe the smudge from his cheek.

"Ghost hunting?" He didn't sound derisive, only concerned.

Damn his concern. "No. I have to clean up this mess."

"Sabine." Dan suddenly had her face in his hands, making her look at him as the garish strobing of the fire engine lights played off his face. He smelled pungently of wood smoke and this time Sabine knew that she wasn't imagining it. "Let me stay with you."

Sabine laid her hands on his, removing them from her face. "No."

The house stank of wood smoke. The expensive carpet was tracked with soot and dirt. Sabine flung herself onto the couch and let the rage run hot in the tears that burned her eyes and scalded her cheeks. She knew he shouldn't touch her. In his touch had been an image that swelled around all the others, an aura glowing red with passion, blue with conflict. She finally sat up and dried her eyes. She would not let him break her resolve. It would only hurt more later if she let him become part of her life now.

Subverting anger into action, she vacuumed and scrubbed, dusting the various objects in the den, and mopping the kitchen floor where the sooty footprints of the fireman from the basement had gone through. Twice she reached for the phone to call Ruby, and twice she changed her mind. It was after one in the morning and she didn't want to startle Ruby out of sleep. It could wait, this festering pain, wait till tomorrow to be relieved by whatever sympathetic nonsense her mother would use to make her feel better. Like an ice-cream cone after vaccinations. Or the promise of a new toy when they reached the latest destination. *Make it feel better, Mommy. A kiss on the boo-boo. Tell me I'm doing the right thing.*

To take on a relationship with a man so close to moving out of her life would be foolishness.

All at once, the adrenaline rush of the fire and of seeing Dan faded away and the exhaustion of earlier in the evening returned. She rinsed out the mop and drained the bucket. Too tired suddenly to find the guest room or brush her teeth, she wrapped a handmade afghan around herself and lay down on the rumpled old couch in the den. She still smelled the wood smoke and the foul creosote smell.

Tomorrow she'd call Loozy's answering machine and leave a message about the chimney fire. Tomorrow she'd also tell her that her ghost was probably the unsafe chimney, making noises as they burned their pine fires. Tomorrow she'd go home and tear up the yellow sheets, which, she was now convinced, were emanations of her own imagination. Tucking her nose beneath the afghan, she quickly fell deeply asleep, her hand clutching the small gold cross.

Three
❧

Sabine slept, dreaming the dream she had dreamed for many years. The same dream, with minor variations, that she had had since she began menstruating. The same dream she'd had since she began to see ghosts.

It was all so familiar: the dimly lit room, warmed by an inadequate fire. Birth pain without pain. The infant emerging, quickly vanished. The man, faceless as ever, bending to receive the infant, then to enter her.

Sabine woke with a panicked start. The room, still warm from the overheated wood stove, was dark, though she didn't remember shutting off the light before dozing off. Slowly her eyes adjusted and Sabine saw that the room was completely barren, like the room in her dream. She was lying down in a corner, on the bare wooden floor. Quiet voices told her that there were others in the room. Their soft voices muttered with foreign words, foreign until Sabine realized that they were speaking English, but with an antique accent complicating her understanding. She sat up slowly so as not to disturb the scene.

As in a play, the light in the room, a small fire in a hearth, slowly illuminates the pair sitting on a settle beside it. That they are a couple is easy to see in their closeness; the young man's arm holding the girl close to him, his free hand covering hers. They are in weighty conversation, their tones intense and solemn. In the same way that she could make out only a few words from the writing, at first Sabine could hear only a few distinct words spoken.

"*You've nothing to fear. I won't abandon you.*" The young man's voice is just past the first breaks of adolescence, a reedy whisper. "*Your home is here.*"

"*I have no home.*" The girl's voice bears a different intonation, another kind of accent.

Sabine leaned forward a little more to see through the gloaming what this girl looks like. She saw a slim young woman, dark visaged, sharp features softened by a sweet and mobile mouth.

"*My people are scattered. Your family took me.*"

"*They were wrong to do so. Vengeance is mine, saith the Lord. They should not have sought vengeance on your people, at least not in taking you from them. But, Sally, they were not unkind to you.*"

"*How is it ever kind to separate a child from its parents?*"

"*You would have been raised in heathen ignorance of the Lord. You and I would not . . . not know each other. Love each other as we do.*"

"*It isn't natural, our loving each other. I should hate you.*"

"*Darling Sarah, we were destined to be together.*"

"*My name is not Sarah. You cannot even say my real name, Christopher Windsor. I cannot even remember my Indian name.*"

"You're a baptized Christian, and our child will be a baptized Christian. You must forsake your birth, Sarah Indian. You are Sarah Windsor now."

"Only to you. No banns were read, no book signed. No one will ever pronounce our union as true."

"In time, dear Sally. In time they will accept. They must. After all, I am Robert Windsor's son. And he is . . ."

"I know who he is. But some things a leader must especially not condone."

"This is his grandchild." Christopher Windsor places a hand on Sarah's belly, suddenly prominent and immense. His voice, too, has changed, deepened, as if in the few minutes Sabine has watched, he'd moved from boyhood to manhood. Their words are now distinct; Sabine could understand each one and with each one, an underlying comprehension. She felt as if she knew them, knew their anguish, felt their commitment to one another and the great love which crosses the bounds of propriety in their world. It isn't an aging maturity that deepens his voice, it is the weight of his undertaking.

Sabine watched enrapt, unable to move, unaware of her own physicality in that room. She didn't feel the hard wooden floor beneath her, nor the cold against her back where the chinks in the shabbily built cabin let in the October air. It was as if she were the ghost in that place, and these two unhappy people the haunted. Eyes wide open, Sabine watched them as they slowly dissolved, the dim hearth light fading away. As if her eyes hurt from it, Sabine closed them to temper the fathomless darkness of the empty room.

At once the room blazed with light, and Sabine opened her eyes to see everything as it had been, in the strong light from the lamp she had left on.

Throwing back the tangled afghan, she leaped from

the couch and into the small bathroom nearby, where she retched into the toilet. She shook so hard that she thought she might crack her head against the sink, uncontrollably shaking as she tried to get off her knees. Dragging herself into the narrow passageway between the den and the kitchen, she curled up in a ball on the rug. She couldn't lift her head for the dizzying vertigo of animal fear.

"It was a dream. A dream. A dream." Even as she whispered the only logical explanation for such a powerful vision, Sabine knew that it had not been a dream. She tried to get to her feet, but the struggle overwhelmed her.

"Ruby. Help me," she uttered before losing consciousness.

Four
❧

A relentless pounding. The sudden touch of human hands. Slowly Sabine roused to realize Dan was lifting her, testing her pulse, gently wiping away the traces of sick from her lips. "Sabine, come on, honey. Can you look at me?"

Sabine tried to focus on his face, but it blurred and wavered in front of her like a phantom. With a tremendous effort she managed, and by focusing, the dizziness dropped away. "Dan, why are you here?" Her voice sounded miles away.

"What happened?"

"I saw them. I saw them." Sabine struggled to sit up, but Dan held her down with gentle restraint. "They were here. I know who they are now."

"Who? Did someone break in here? Did they hurt you?"

"No. The ghosts. Christopher and Sarah. They have names. I heard their voices. Saw their faces." Even speaking out loud took strength Sabine didn't have, and she felt the swoon come upon her.

Dan refreshed the wet cloth he'd used on her face and placed it on her forehead, trying to cool her hallucinations. Tucking the afghan around her, he lifted her up and carried her outside into his truck.

"Where are you taking me?" Once out of the house, Sabine came to herself and pushed away from Dan's side.

"To the hospital. You've been overcome by something, carbon monoxide probably. Did the furnace run last night?"

A rational explanation for an impossible event. Sabine leaned forward in the cab of the truck and raked her fingers through her tangled hair. "It was so real. It answered so many questions."

"It certainly does. The Atchesons are probably being slowly poisoned in their own house."

"No. I mean about the haunting." There it was, the H-word. She'd assiduously avoided using it, determined to be rational. Yet now, faced with a plausible explanation, she rejected it. What she'd witnessed in the night was too compelling to be chemically induced. Too solid. Even as the figures dissolved, they were detailed. A thread caught in the rough wool fabric of Sarah's dark brown dress, Christopher's stockings, a tiny hole in the calf of one. Sarah's eyes filled at once with fear and love. How they both knew they were doomed, and clung together on the hard wooden settle beside the dying fire.

Sabine shook her head. "No, it was real. You won't find anything amiss with the house. These things happen to people like me."

Dan shoved the key into the ignition. "People like you?"

"Sensitives. Psychics. Soothsayers." Sabine unbuckled the seat belt Dan had wrapped around her. "Call it what you like. I know what I saw, and it scared me half to death. But I'm all right." Sabine ignored the weakness in her legs as she climbed down from the truck. Dan reached out to stop her but she shook him off. What was he doing here, anyway? He had no right to worry about her. "Why are you here?"

"I . . . I had to make sure everything was all right." Dan gripped the steering wheel of the truck with both hands, as if he was piloting it down a steep grade. "With the house, I mean."

"Do you normally check on extinguished chimney fires?"

"No."

"I need some air." Sabine kept the afghan wrapped around herself as she went into the backyard. She wasn't conscious of heading for the cellar hole, but her random march took her there. It was barely light out, but the depression behind the stone wall was clear and into it Sabine went, sitting down on a soft tussock of wild grass, pressing her back against the stone. She pressed her eyes closed with her fingertips, not blocking out the images which had been shown to her, but looking at them carefully.

They *were* doomed, this young couple. She had seen their premature death hover above them in the dim glow of the fireplace. Though they were three hundred years dead, the shock of it, the certainty of it, was as if they were living beings, friends for whom she had divined death. Grief shook her; tears leaked out from beneath her fingers.

Then Dan's arms were around her and for once she didn't fight him. Sabine allowed him to press her close, to encompass her trembling body with his, until she was unsure where the border between them lay. His chin rested on the top of her head, and from time to time he gently rubbed his cheek against her hair. Sabine wept, grieving for the doomed lovers, grieving for a love that could not be. She grieved for Dan, that he could not accept this place as home.

He rocked her, and slowed her gasping breaths with his lips on hers. Then Sabine felt the grieving leave her and passion swoop in to replace it. Her mouth opened to accept the exploration of his agile tongue. She reciprocated. All good intentions were abandoned; all determination to keep Dan Smith at a distance exploded with the sizzle of his touch. It was like being held by fire. He was consuming her with his pent-up passion, filling her with the physicality of his need.

His long fingers opened her shirt front, his lips grazed the soft skin above her bra, then eased her breast out of its shelter and into his mouth. Quick little darts of his tongue sent strokes of heat into Sabine's belly, coursing downward and into her sex like lightning. He laid her down on the afghan and covered her, holding himself above her with his arms. She reached for his shirt, tugging it out of his jeans, then stroked his flat belly with curious fingers. Together they worked to undress each other. They tugged at each other's jeans, wriggling out of them, their shirts still on but open, exposing bare skin to the cool October morning air. Still above her, Dan worked magic on her rising nipples. Sabine stroked his long back, cupping her hands against his perfect buttocks, then moving to the front, where she found his erection. Dan slid off of her, pulling her on top of him. She sat up and he found new places to use his tongue, driving her nearly mad.

Autumn leaves clung to Sabine's hair, her Egyptian brown eyes widened, and her skin took on a rosy flush that descended from cheek to throat to breast. Her round breasts dangled like Aesop's mythic grapes over his face, tempting and sweet, but not as sweet as that elixir between her legs. Dan placed her on the afghan, stroked back her tangled hair, and kissed her gently on the lips. The more he touched her, the more he had the oddest sense that he'd touched her in just such a way before. This wasn't new territory but familiar ground. It felt more like a reunion than any first-time lovemaking should. Slowly, he entered her. Her legs encircled him and her hands traced maddening circles on his back. He thrust, once, twice, and the still morning air was rent with their passionate duet.

First light was going fast from dim gray to yellow, revealing a cloudy day. Setting the coffeemaker to drip, Sabine leaned against the island counter. What a funny, mundane thing to be doing, after all that had happened. She touched her lips with fingers still trembling, her belly still soft with a warm, satisfied feeling. They'd lain on the afghan for a little while as their bodies cooled from the heat of their lovemaking. They didn't speak, knowing words would shatter the spell. Sabine felt as if she'd entered a second trance, this one as powerful as the first. Images of fire filled her mind at Dan's touch, as if he was formed of those elements. The wood smoke of his clothes was real. The heat of his passion true. Except she hadn't been able to see their future. Surely with a connection so powerful, it would have been obvious.

Dan was checking for a possible source of carbon monoxide, still determined that was the cause of her vision. She remembered everything of it. What they looked like and their names. The sudden imposition of full-term pregnancy on the girl, Sarah, whom Christopher lovingly called Sally. She remembered the retching illness and shakes, as her body reacted physically to the powerful vision. Sabine couldn't say her fear had receded, but she did not allow it to overtake her in the light of day. However, she wasn't staying any longer in that house than she had to, finishing up the cleaning left over from last night's more ordinary adventure. Then she'd call Ruby. She had a lot to tell Ruby. Not just about the vision, but about Dan. There was no way she could keep this sweet interlude a secret from her mother.

Sabine thought about how Sarah and Christopher had had a terrible difference between them, and yet they were so in love. Like Romeo and Juliet, or Tristan and Isolde, Sarah and Christopher defied convention and family to be together. The profound willingness of this young couple to cling to each other was so compelling, it felt as if she had been experiencing their emotions.

Pouring out two cups of coffee, Sabine sat down at the table.

But what had happened to them? History had excluded them, ignored them. Skipped over young Christopher, made no mention of Sarah except for the celebrated victory over Sarah's people in the so-called defense of Windsorville.

Windsor. This land had been Windsor land. This land might have belonged to Beatrice Danforth before being sold off.

Dan came into the kitchen. "This place is heated with electric. Couldn't have been carbon monoxide. You win."

"You're a Windsor, aren't you?"

"On my mother's side, yeah. Gran was a Windsor before she married Frederick. Last of the line, no males to carry the name into the twenty-first century."

"But the bloodline runs direct to you."

"I thought you knew that. Danforth W-for-Windsor Smith."

"I confess, I hadn't made the connection."

Dan came up beside Sabine. "Does it matter?"

"I think these may have been your ancestors. The only Windsor male to survive of Robert Windsor's brood was Christopher. He's a cipher in the history books. Yet he had a son, also Robert, and he's got to be your ancestor."

"There were other Windsors. A whole extended clan of them. They feuded relentlessly for two centuries. Maybe I'm from that side of the family." Dan helped himself to more coffee, kissing the back of Sabine's neck as he did.

The house still smelled smoky to Sabine, but with a secondary pungency to the wood smoke and creosote, as if she had roasted meat last night. The same lamb smell as that night Loozy had given her dinner. Once it had caught her attention, it vanished. Synesthesia, Sabine thought, the smelling of something that isn't there, prompted by another stimulus, in this case, memory.

"No. I think that these are your people, Dan."

"Did I tell you that this property was in the family until Gran sold it to the people who then sold it to the Atchesons?"

"Then you are connected to this thing."

"How?"

"I don't know yet."

Dan set his coffee cup down and took Sabine's face in his hands. He kissed her and the newly satisfied was suddenly hungry again. More decorous, more comfortable on Drake's den couch, they took slow measure of one another. In the broad daylight, Sabine fleetingly wished she'd shaved her armpits, but then discovered the delight of a man's tongue tickling through those fine hairs. She made Dan lie flat as she examined his body, rough hewn and lightly haired, with her tongue and fingers while his fingers thumbed at her nipples. She admired his erection even as she teased it into extremis. The scent of pure wood smoke wafted through the air, and Sabine knew that it was the scent of Dan's arousal. *He was born of fire.* The words seemed almost spoken aloud and she pulled her mouth away from his. His hand settled her back to him, and no thoughts further intruded.

Five

c&

"Sabine, don't you think it's a little significant that you've had a major psychic experience, but the focus of this conversation has been Dan Smith?"

Sabine had to laugh a little at her mother's observation. "I'm a woman first, psychic second."

"Have you done his cards?"

"No. And I'm not going to. I need to keep that part of my life out of this thing. He knows I'm a little wacko; I don't want to exacerbate the image."

"Don't be silly. It can only help in the end."

"Mom, I am trying hard not to have any illusions about this relationship. I'm doing what I should have done in the first place, just let myself enjoy it." Dan had told her everything about Karen and his trip to New York as they'd had breakfast. Sabine felt a little sheepish about imagining that he'd gone back to make it up with Karen. Still, it could have happened. Karen might have rushed down those stairs and asked him to forgive her.

"I'm happy for you, Sabine. He's a nice man."

"Speaking of nice men, what's up with you and Chief Bean?"

"Nothing in the same league as you and Mr. Smith, but we had a nice chat last night."

"And?"

"We might have dinner some night next week."

"Mom, to paraphrase something I just heard: I'm happy for you."

"Thanks. Now, about this vision."

"Right. Why don't you come by after the carnival ends and I'll give you all the details." Hanging up the phone, Sabine had to smile. Not once, in her memory, had Ruby expressed anything but disdain for the opposite sex. Arthur Bean must have something special about him to have breached Ruby's fortifications.

Sabine stared at herself in the bathroom mirror, mascara wand suspended between the mirror image and her lashes. Her reflection dissolved and in her mind's eye she saw Dan's face over hers, blurry and concerned, calling her back from unconsciousness, calling her "honey." Still, their conversation over breakfast at the coffee shop this morning lingered like a sticky residue to what should have been perfectly happy.

They were opening up the closets and drawers of their lives, letting those things be held up and shown that constituted important details for the other to know.

Dan had spoken about Beatrice. "My grandmother was a powerful woman, not like Wonder Woman, but powerful in spirit. To see her lying weakly on the bed she shared with my grandfather, one feeble little hand in the air reaching out for me as if I were the star she was determined to catch . . ." Dan's voice slowly drew down into his throat. Sabine leaned across the table to hear it. "You tell me, how could I move her out of her house and into a nursing home?"

"Of course you couldn't." Sabine knew she was only Greek Chorus to his story.

"So I kept her at home. And she got better."

Sabine sat back. "One doesn't generally hear that ending to this sort of story."

"Well, better in that just being here, just promising she wouldn't have to go to a hospital, made all the difference and we had a good few months together. We waited together for her spirit to choose to depart."

"She was pretty strong to the end, wasn't she?"

"Yeah, she was still mobile in the spring, and in the summer was sitting outside in the back garden, scolding Nagy, directing me about which plants needed what attention. It wasn't until the end of summer that she began to fade away. Still, until the end she was in charge."

Sabine stroked the smooth skin of Dan's hand. "She's still in charge, isn't she?"

"This must be an example of your psychic abilities."

"No, it's just obvious that you're being faithful to her wishes. Keeping the theatre open, and Nagy at home."

"For now." Abruptly, Dan pulled his hand away from Sabine. They were quiet for a moment, aware of the elephant in the parlor.

The waitress set their pancakes in front of them.

"Dan, I'm not going to ask that you change your plans for me."

"I'm not going anywhere right now."

It was the phrase *right now* that lingered. Eventually he would be gone. Did she really want to invest herself in a transient relationship?

Sabine was frustrated with herself. When she should be thinking about the vision, thoughts of Dan intruded at every turn. It was as she'd joked to Ruby, she was a woman first, a psychic with an extraordinary vision, second. She capped the mascara. Dan was due to pick her up in ten minutes for their first real date.

Taking the yellow pad down from the shelf where she'd stuck it, she began writing down everything she could remember from the moment she fell asleep until she came back into the real world retching. As she wrote, things she hadn't been aware of came to her. A china dog on the mantel. A pair of boots leaning against the settle, warming before the fire. The scent of herbs from the black kettle suspended by an iron hook over the fire. This was a complete and marvelously detailed vision. Sabine tested to see if there had been anything she would not have known about from history lessons or trips to Sturbridge Village, some evidence that she had not made up any of this disturbing and tender scene. She closed her eyes and mentally looked around the room, most of it darkly obscure, as the small space was lighted only by the hearth fire. Sabine realized she was self-hypnotizing and let herself go. Only by going deep within would she bring out unconsciously observed detail. And there it was: a book, leather bound and titled *Carruther's Remedies and Midwifery Instructions,* the lettering bearing all the oddities of seventeenth-century printing. The book lay on the mantel beside the ink pot.

Her trance fell away and Sabine felt oddly refreshed.

Six

November 2000

"I love your house," Sabine said. They had been wandering all over it, Dan acting as docent, pointing out various historical and familial quirks of the place. They had ended up in the parlor Dan used as his favorite space. In the last few weeks Sabine and Dan had spent increasing amounts of time together, but this was the first time she'd come to his house for dinner.

"Any ghosts here?" Dan smiled as he decanted a bottle of wine.

"Maybe." Sabine refused to rise to the good-humored bait, seating herself in a wing-back chair beside the fireplace. Dan started a fire and it snapped at the splinters of kindling as it took hold. Sabine watched as Dan bent to poke at the logs. She liked the way his long back tapered down from his broad shoulders. She moved her gaze back to the fire and suddenly felt as if she was being reminded of something. She couldn't pull the thought into focus and for an instant felt disoriented.

With an effort, she looked away from the fire. A residual feeling of déjà vu made her take a deep breath.

"What's the matter?" Dan had heard her involuntary gasp.

"I think I shouldn't be drinking on an empty stomach." Yet she didn't feel like the wine had touched her at all.

"You sounded like you'd seen a ghost."

"Well, I do write for them." Sabine wanted to make a joke for him, wanted to see his dimples in the firelight.

"Ghost writer, huh?" Dan was close to her, sitting on the embroidered footstool at her feet.

The firelight danced against the wall in the shadowed room. Sabine leaned forward and was met by Dan's lips. Flavored with wine, sweet with new passion. A long tongue-sweet exploration of each other's mouth. Sabine felt a diffuse warmth slide from her lips to her belly and the fire in the fireplace leaped high to see it.

Dan was gentle. Gentle in that he was sure of Sabine's pleasure, taking a slow journey over her body, using tongue and fingertips to excite familiar sensations, to create new, never-before-experienced sensations. Ringing in her head like a chime were the words *this is making love, this is making love*. Different from having sex.

From the chair and footstool, they moved to the oriental rug in front of the fire. The heat touched them, the fire outside and the fire within combining until they craved relief. The moment before climax, Sabine had the oddest thought: *With this I am truly cemented to this place*. She came in radiating waves, believing for an instant that they would never cease. Dan came a moment later, so close they might have come together.

They lay together, pleased in some lovers' conceit that their first time in his house had been in front of the fire, passion overruling comfort. The case clock in the front hallway chimed the hour of nine.

"Don't you have to go back to the theatre tonight?"

"I've asked Maisie to do the deposit and they can call me if there's an emergency. Walt will bring Nagy home." Dan stroked her bare back, gliding his hand smoothly along her spine to her buttocks, which he cupped. Unbidden comparisons fluttered around the edges of his consciousness. Sabine's soft willingness was so different from Karen's rigid get-it-over-with style. Sabine made him feel like he was a good lover. A desirable lover, not a convenience. Forcibly blocking the thoughts, Dan bent and kissed Sabine's perfect behind. The smoke detector detonated the quiet air. "Shit! I forgot dinner." Dan grabbed his discarded jeans and ran for the kitchen.

Sabine spent the night, snuggled with Dan against the chill under piled blankets as they talked long into the night, whispering together like kids on a sleepover so as not to alert Nagy. The old house creaked and groaned like a ship at sea, its spars and timbers complaining against the wind. Sabine awoke from a light sleep, instantly aware of her surroundings and the man next to her. She listened to the soft sounds he made, and then to the sounds of an unfamiliar house. They had talked and talked, reluctant to give in to the separation sleep would require. Then suddenly the hour seemed very late, and they were both filled with a torpor brought on by the long evening's tutelage in body and mind. There was so much more to say, but Morpheus demanded obedience. Sabine slept lightly, dreaming her old dream of fire and birth. She woke only for a moment, adjusting her sleeping mind to her surroundings. The creak of the house's joists soothed her and she went back to sleep, her arm around Dan, his fingers holding hers.

In the morning, Dan got the coffeemaker going and sat down at the little kitchen table with Sabine. Nagy came into the kitchen just then.

"Nagy, say hello to Sabine."

Nagy rubbed his chest where his pajama top was open. Sparse gray hairs stuck out from between his fingers, matching the ones on his head. "I know you. You come to the movies."

"Yes, you do, Nagy. You always make sure I have my ticket stub."

Sabine felt a little awkward in a way she couldn't quite put a finger on. Almost like shyness. She didn't want to speak to Nagy as if he were a child, but didn't really know how else to talk to him.

"Dan, I'll make us some French toast if you want." Nagy bent down under the counter to pull out a griddle. "We have lots of bread."

"Sabine, would you like some?" Dan asked, although it was obvious Nagy was going to do it whether she did or not.

"I'd love some."

Nagy turned around and wagged a finger at Sabine. "You're just saying that to be kind."

Nonplussed, Sabine could only shake her head.

"Nagy, Sabine isn't being kind to you, she's being kind to me. She's really hungry."

"That's right. I'm really hungry." They had only heated a can of soup last night, unwilling to break the spell for more than a few minutes. She wore one of Dan's T-shirts, an obscure film title faded on the overwashed blue jersey. A pair of his socks and a chenille housecoat left over from his grandmother completed her ensemble. She felt cozy and at home. She looked at the mug of coffee Dan handed her and enjoyed a frisson of excitement at touching his fingers as she took it from him. She didn't need coffee to feel jazzed up; she didn't think she'd ever get her heart rate back to normal.

Nagy kept glancing back at the two of them, raising an eyebrow as he noted the proximity of their elbows on the table.

"Did you sleep together?"

"Why, yes, Nagy. Yes we did."

"Did you have sex?"

Sabine felt her cheeks redden, but Dan seemed unconcerned. "Right again."

"Do you like wheat French toast or white?" This was addressed to Sabine.

"Umm, white."

"Okay." Nagy opened the loaf. "I like that, too."

Sabine shot a look at Dan, who handed her the front section of the *Boston Globe,* then shook open the sports section.

Maybe, like dealing with Ruby, one just had to be honest.

"So, you've had your first sleepover." Ruby's tone was only mildly teasing, over the phone.

"Something like that."

"Have you read him yet?"

"Ruby, no. I've told you, there's no way I want to anticipate the outcome of this thing." She didn't tell her mother that every time Dan touched her, she was filled with images of heat and fire; that she couldn't discern if it was the imagery of sexual attraction, or something more sinister.

"What are you afraid of?"

Sabine had been holding the phone between her shoulder and cheek. Now she took it in her hand. "Mom, listen to me. Every day that goes by, I feel like our connection is getting stronger. I don't need the cards to tell me that."

"They're a tool. A road map, a blueprint."

"Mom, your analogies are growing more inexplicable. Aren't blueprints and road maps essentially the same thing? They tell you what to do?"

"No. One is decision, one is choice."

"It's a little early in the relationship to be talking about either choices or decisions."

"I think that some have already been made."

Sabine knew instantly that her mother was right. She had made a choice to pursue a relationship that might soon end. Except that Dan hadn't mentioned going back to New York, or looking for a theatre manager. He'd let the ad in the *Pennywise Paper* lapse. And some devil in her had kept Sabine from reminding him to renew it. She'd also made the decision to believe that it didn't matter that Dan's previous relationship had ended so recently. She was content that theirs was new of itself and not the stepchild of a broken heart.

"I have to go to work; I'll call you tomorrow."

"Wait. Sabine, what about the house?"

Sabine felt that little twinge of guilt associated with neglected homework. "I've been busy."

"You have to go back."

"No, I don't. I left Loozy the message that it was probably her chimney."

"Beenie, this is your calling. Don't ignore it just because you're distracted."

"Is that what you call it?" Sabine nearly giggled.

"I'm serious. Until you get to the end of their story, these spirits will not rest."

She was going to be terribly late to work. "I'll go back one night this week. I promise. Are you sure you don't want to go with me?"

"Absolutely. But call me as soon as you get back."

Sabine had been meaning to go back to the house. Meaning to sit with her yellow pad and let the spirits or ghosts or imaginings work through her again. But every time she thought about being there, remembered the violent sickness that came of her tortured vision, she lost courage and made a lame excuse. Sabine knew that Ruby was sitting in judgment over her reluctance, and for penance, Sabine did go back to the Historical Society reading room and try to establish the existence of Sally Indian. The volunteer that Sunday afternoon was more familiar with the materials and quite helpful, pointing out small clues in the deed book and other official records.

"And it might be all right for you to look at this." The volunteer, Hattie, unlocked a glass-fronted display case. "We don't let many people handle this, but I think it might be helpful to you." Hattie knew Sabine a little from her friendship with Hattie's daughter, Deb. "Just don't let on you saw it."

"Thanks, Mrs. Field, I'll be very careful with it." Sabine took a thin, octavo-size leather-bound book from the woman's hands. She examined it for a title, found none, and opened it up. Marbleized end papers, vellum pages. No title page, either, and it wasn't until she turned to the first page that Sabine realized that the little tome was a personal diary. "Dghter Mary here. Looks well." "Son Hammond here, will stay till Michaelmas." Line by line, Sabine read the short diary of Susannah Howe.

Records of births and baptisms, huskings, and quiltings, visiting relations, and work finished. She'd recorded the barters that kept colonial households in goods and services, and the injuries she'd treated as a midwife and healer. Susannah had written with the same unruly spelling as she had written herself under the influence of the house, a word spelled one way in one sentence, and another way entirely in the next.

Threaded in between the daily tasks set and accomplished were bits of gossip. "Thankful North seen to walk out with John Fuller." "Mary Carter del'vd of still-born son." "Windsor son has got a child upon the savage girl Sally." "Windsor son house burnt last night. Child only survived. Taken into care by Robt and Mary Windsor."

Sabine left her finger on the sentence. "Windsor son house burnt last night." She felt the blood flow leave her face. *Burnt.* As if deliberate. She carefully turned the pages of Susannah Howe's diary, scanning for more information. "Robert Windsor this day did take the infant Robert as his son, giving him all rights of a legitimate heir."

Piece by piece, Sabine wrote down Susannah Howe's terse comments regarding Robert Windsor, the burning, and the infant. Looking at the copied sentences, she saw an echo of what she'd been discovering through her sessions at the house. Each sentence stated some fact that explained or substantiated the feelings and visions in her trances. The smell of smoke became "Windsor son house burnt last night." The pregnant belly on Sally Indian was undoubtedly the orphaned child, Robert, adopted by his grandfather. Oblivious to the presence of the volunteer, Sabine laid her hands on the diary and closed her eyes. The small volume gave nothing away beyond its painstakingly inked words. Sabine opened her eyes. The last page, the last comment for 1668, was, "Mrs. Windsor poorly. Greeves overmuch for son Christopher."

Sabine sat for a long time with the diary closed beneath her hands. It had given her much, but much more would remain a mystery. That the young man, Christopher Windsor, had had a child with the Native American girl, Sally, was clear. That they had perished in a fire was implied. That Robert and Mary Windsor, the grandparents of the surviving child, adopted him, was stated. But how the fire started, and why, troubled Sabine. Because nowhere in Susannah Howe's diary was there any mention of the townsfolk defending the town against Indian attack. She mentioned Mrs. Addison's piles, but not an attack. There was no mention of fortifying the household, only that John Fuller walked out with his girlfriend and the banns were called the next week.

Sabine stood up. Maybe the attack came after this volume. Or maybe it was too horrifying for Susannah to jot down in a daily record. Or maybe it wasn't quite an attack.

Seven

&

Sabine pushed the Atchesons' back door open and fished around for a light switch. The house had that stiff odor of undisturbed air. She carried her big handbag, in it her trusty yellow pad with its automatic writing and copious notes. The two coffee cups she and Dan had used were still sitting in the dish drain, testimony to at least one event that hadn't been her imagination. As she moved through the kitchen the still air began to stir, faintly sour in her nostrils.

"Well, let's get on with it," Sabine said to the room. She dropped the pad and a new Bic pen on the pine table, used the toilet off the back entryway, and then poured herself a glass of water. Sitting down, she took a sip, folded her hands, and started her trance.

It had been over three weeks since she'd last been in the house, since her vivid experience of Christopher and Sally. Three weeks since she and Dan had given in to nature and begun that slow sweet journey. She smiled, then returned to her focus. There seemed to be no question but that they were becoming a couple. A magic word, descriptive of their association and, frequently, their favorite activity. After that first week they'd wisely slowed the pace down; he had things to do and so did she. That's what she told Ruby was keeping her from going back to the house. "I've got quilting club and two readings at showers, I've got a backlog at work and . . ."

"Hours on the phone with Dan, dinner and movies, yada yada."

"Something like that."

"It won't go away."

Sabine opened her eyes and drank some water. This shouldn't be taking so long. She just wanted to drop into a trance, write whatever message the spirits needed to reveal, and go home. Maybe she needed some props. Sabine dug a stick of incense out of her bag, then lit it and the two candles on the table. Remembering Loozy's excited connection between the writing and the little ink pot, as well as its appearance in her vision of Christopher and Sally, Sabine got it down from the windowsill to set it in front of the pad. *There, that's better.* Sabine breathed deeply, let it out slowly, repeated, and waited for the slow darkness to encompass her. The clock on the wall ticked, the toilet gurgled a little. Outside, the wind was picking up; she could hear leaves scurrying across the blacktop of the back driveway. She entered a place of cottony warmth, silence, and utter emptiness.

Her neck hurt a little, and Sabine moved to rub away the crick. Her cheek rested on her folded hands, the yellow pad unsullied beneath them. She'd made the greatest mistake of a neophyte medium: she'd fallen asleep. Sabine rubbed her eyes and stretched. Not even a scribble marred the page. Maybe the spirits were gone, maybe all that was necessary was that last vision. A look at the banjo clock told Sabine that she'd dozed off for only a half hour at most. Still early in the evening, so she should try again.

Sabine straightened out the pad where her cheek had misaligned it, started another stick of incense, a different flavor, and placed one candle directly in front of her. This time she stared at the undulating flame, using its flicker as her hypnotic spot. *Breathe in, breathe out.*

The issue Dan and she had not thoroughly addressed was his future. Not the future Ruby would have liked to have read, but his real, concrete plans. Sabine told herself that nothing had changed; certainly he still wanted to return to his film career. But the longer they didn't speak of his inevitable move, the more confident Sabine felt that maybe Dan was finding what he needed with her. He'd even mentioned a contract renewal with some distribution company. Surely someone contemplating leaving wouldn't bind himself to a contract.

Sabine blinked hard and refocused on the flame. "Come on, Sabine," she admonished herself. "Relax. Focus."

They were good together. They had fun. The sex was great. Sabine stared at the little tongue of flame and smiled. There was definitely a click.

One more try. This time Sabine managed to arrive in that place where the weight of her arms and the slow beating of her heart told her that she had, at last, achieved a true trance. She waited, listening, breathing steadily in and out, her eyes at half-mast as the candlelight bent and twisted in the faint stirring of air. Her hands remained folded on top of the pad of yellow paper. The pen remained horizontal on the page. Nothing. They were gone.

A tinkling chime snapped Sabine out of the hypnotic state. Eleven o'clock. She'd given it her best shot. "Okay, my work here is done." Sabine stuffed the blank pad back into her bag, snuffed the candles, wiped up the debris from the incense, and locked the back door.

"Nothing?"

"Nada. No one home." Sabine slid her office chair back to snag a file folder on her credenza. "I think maybe the last time was, well, the last time."

"What's changed?"

"What do you mean?" Sabine opened the file folder, glanced up to make sure Moe was out of earshot and that Balto and Teddy were still at lunch.

"You're different."

"How so?"

She could hear Ruby on the other end of the line lighting a cigarette, and Sabine could see her standing outside her shop, royal blue caftan fluttering in the November breeze. She'd be standing with one toe cocked against the sidewalk, her left arm folded against the chill, her right hand holding the cigarette and the cell phone tucked under her chin. "You began to be able to connect with the spirits when you entered puberty. You lost that ability when, I assume, you became sexually active. Now, before Dan, you were open to the spirits. Since Dan, they won't speak to you."

"So, let me get this straight." Sabine looked once more over her divider. "You think that my getting regular sex is prohibiting communication with the ghosts?" She forced her laughter down.

"Yes. No. Not the sex, Beenie. The love. You are so full of your own emotion, they can't get through."

"Busy signal?"

"Exactly."

"You're making this up."

"It's conventional wisdom."

"Mom, in no way is any of this conventional." Sabine spotted Moe. "Look, gotta go. And, by the way, Dan and I have yet to use the L-word."

"Oh, you don't have to."

Eight

✺

Dan set the phone into its cradle and sat down in his lop-sided desk chair. The unexpected call had stunned him. He almost hadn't answered the phone, anxious to get home to shower before heading out to Sabine's place for dinner. He had almost let it ring until the answering machine picked it up, with his own voice intoning the feature of the week, no message capability. He would have missed the most important call in his recent life. These sorts of calls don't get repeated.

"Smith?"

"Yes."

"Malcolm Drexel here. We met at my son's premiere party."

"Of course." Dan felt a Christmas-quality excitement begin to accelerate his pulse. "It was a terrific debut for him."

"Are you available?"

Oh, what amazing words were those.

"What do you have in mind?"

"I fired the assistant director off my new project. Don't press me for details, just know I'll never hire him again. So, the job is yours if you want it."

Drexel went on to describe a feature film with big-name actors, a massive budget, and one of the best cameramen in the business. "We're heading for location in Mexico the week after Thanksgiving. We've lost huge amounts of time already, so we're on a grueling schedule and won't even break for the holidays."

No one had answered Dan's ad for a theatre manager. He would have to simply close the Palace down. Maybe Ralph and Maisie could run it, but it wouldn't be fair to saddle them with the maintenance as well as their nightly duties while he was so far away. As for Nagy, maybe there was still space in the group home. God, what was he thinking?

Drexel, hearing the hesitation on the line, named a dollar amount.

"That sounds fine, but I'll need a couple of days to mull it over."

"Smith, I don't have a couple of days. Yes or no."

"Yes."

"Good man. I've seen your work, your documentaries. Let's see how we mesh with you as second chair. Who knows, maybe next time we'll put you at the helm."

"Thanks. Thanks a lot, Malcolm. I really appreciate this chance."

"Don't thank me, thank your girlfriend. Karen Whitcomb put your name up."

Dan settled the phone back in the cradle, and sat with his head in his hands. What was that story, "The Lady or the Tiger?" He felt as if whatever decision he made he'd end up eaten alive. It was everything he wanted, but at

the wrong time. He had Sabine, their relationship growing stronger every day. Yet if he was to be the man she
fell in love with, he needed to be true to his dreams.

"What you doin', Danny?" Nagy startled Dan out of
his thoughts.

"Oh, thinking." Dan looked at Nagy, taking in his
misaligned buttons, the stained and baggy trousers, and
his spiky unkempt hair. He wasn't taking very good care
of Nagy, not the sort of care Gran had given him. "Nagy,
let's fix your buttons." Dan got up and began undoing
the sweater.

"I can do it." Nagy pushed Dan's hands away. "I just
got mixed up."

"I know you can. Hey, Nagy?"

Nagy looked up from under bushy eyebrows, his
upper lip caught beneath the lower one in concentration.

"I have to talk to you about something really important." It hurt Dan a little to see the childish excitement
in Nagy's eyes. Dan realized that Gran had often used
those words to Nagy when she had a surprise for him,
or a special task. She'd never broken his heart with
them. Even when she got sick, she never used those
words. She'd said, "When I'm gone Dan will take care
of you," the importance of those words needing no pro-
logue. Suddenly Dan felt as if he didn't have the
strength to crest this particular hill. "Nagy, you know
how I've talked about doing something else besides the
theatre?"

Nagy didn't release his grip on his upper lip, only
dropped his eyes to better concentrate on the buttons.

"Nagy, look at me."

Nagy shook his head. "No."

"Then listen without looking."

"Are you going to tell me I'm fired?"

Dan laughed in spite of himself. "God, no. Not fired. Retired."

"What's the difference?"

Semantics. He was playing semantics with a mentally challenged old man. "Well, when you're retired you get to do anything you want to do. Fish; you like to fish. Sleep late. Go to the resource center."

"They're all dummies there. They're reeetards."

"Nagy!"

The resource center had always been a bone of contention between Gran and himself. He'd felt that Nagy would benefit from making friends at the center, where other adults with Nagy's limitations got to do things like take day trips to Sturbridge Village or the Norman Rockwell Museum. Where they played games or learned songs. Gran had always maintained that Nagy got all of that with her, that he needn't be exposed to such people. He needed the bar to be raised up, not lowered. In her own way, Gran was a colossal snob. Dan had argued that making friends he could relate to on an intellectual level, as low as it was, was just as important as either of them having equal friends. But Gran had poisoned Nagy's mind against the resource center and this was the result.

"I'm older than you. You can't make me go. I don't want to retire."

"Nagy. I have a new job."

Nagy did look up at him then, upper lip still sucked in, his knotty hands dabbing the last button into the hole. "What job?"

"A man wants me to help direct his new movie. It means I have to go to Mexico."

"Today?"

"No. But soon. Next week. After Thanksgiving."

"For how long? A couple of days?"

"No, more like a lot of months."

Nagy stood apart from Dan, his hands loose by his sides, his eyes downcast and his lips moving with his unexpressed thoughts. He didn't ask, "What about me?" He didn't cry as Dan thought he might. Nagy stood there in some dignity and waited for Dan to finish explaining. Finally, as Dan sat back down on the old office chair his grandfather had owned, Nagy asked his questions.

"Will you like your new job?"

"I think I will, Nagy."

"Will you be happy not to have to take care of me?"

"I'll miss you. Very much."

"Will you ever come back?"

"Of course, when I'm done with the job." Dan got up and reached his arm around Nagy's shoulders. "You have to understand that sometimes a man has to do hard things to get what he wants. Make hard choices. It would be easy to stay. But I would always have a sense that I blew it, that I let sentiment and history hold me back." Dan couldn't know how much of what he said made sense to Nagy, but he felt compelled to go on. "You see, the worst feeling is to regret what you haven't done. To be sorry for not doing something."

"What if you're sorry for *doing* something? Isn't that bad?"

"Yes, doing something wrong is certainly something to regret. But it feels the same: you wish things were different."

"I know." Two words, spoken softly, as if Nagy Danforth understood from experience what regret was. He pulled away from Dan's arm and turned his face to the open door. "I have to sweep now."

"You go ahead. We still have a movie to show tonight."

As the office door shut, Dan rested his forehead on the bridge of his hands and let the wave of emotion shudder through him. Rehearsing the conversation, he wondered, how could Nagy understand regret? What had he ever done to be sorry for except eat the last cookie or forget to wear his gloves? How could a simple old soul like Nagy understand the vast pit of regret Dan faced now? And yet in those two words, *I know,* Nagy offered an empathy Dan took as absolution. If Nagy understood the difficulty of this life choice, then he, Dan, could move ahead with it.

"Keep moving, Danforth." Dan spoke aloud to break the smothering thoughts. He could hear Nagy's broom snicking at the threadbare carpet of the hallway. Every day he did this, yet the dust of ages always rose up, an unlimited supply of old dirt. The boyhood odor of dust, of being close to the floor. A memory, vague in form, rose from the scent of dust. Playing with Matchbox cars on the hallway runner. Making motor noises. Louder and louder as voices from this office grew in volume, in tension. His grandmother and his father arguing. The office door with its frosted glass window bursting open and his father storming out.

"Come on, boy." His father scooping him up by one hand, the Matchbox car clutched in the other. "Whatever you do, Danny, when you grow up, promise me you'll get away from this place."

A fleeting glimpse of memory. His father and Gran arguing. Nagy standing nearby. Gran had seldom spoken of his father, of Gary Smith. A little light dawned on Dan, remembering now the long-buried moment with an adult's perspective. Beatrice had not liked Gary Smith, not liked the man who, in her world, was beneath her daughter. A common man, a projectionist and handyman. Sometimes it had been painful to hear her denigrate his dead father, as if by marrying her daughter, Gary Smith had doomed her.

Nagy moved down the hallway, the sound of the broom against the carpet fading away. Dan examined the memory for veracity. Had that actually happened? He had so little memory of his father, just an image of a man with a Fu Manchu mustache that tickled when his father kissed him. He had more memories of his mother. Domestic memories. Ironing in front of the television, poking around in the garden, filling the bird feeder. Ruby had told him he would keep running until he faced his misplaced guilt. He'd killed his parents; the lie he lived was in pretending it hadn't happened.

Sabine talked about ghosts in the Atcheson house. She should come here and visit the ghosts in the Palace Theatre. The place was filled with them.

Sabine. What was he going to tell her?

Sabine peeked in at the pork roast just beginning to brown. Time enough to jump in the shower and then get the vegetables going. This was the first real dinner she was making for Dan. They'd been out to the Blue Moose several times, and that once to his house. Sabine had loved it that Dan had tried to cook for her first, even though their ill-timed lovemaking had nearly caused a disaster. The lasagna had dried out to an Italian tortilla crisp.

A nice bottle of wine chilled in the fridge; some Celtic music played on the CD player. With Ruby's stuff out of the corners, her apartment looked tidy and welcoming on this cold November night. Except for Dan's theatre curfew, it would be a lovely evening. She might go with him to the Palace. Maybe they could come back here later, and in the morning she'd make him breakfast.

Her bathroom mirror gave Sabine back the face of a happy woman. A thought, a passing fancy: he's happy too. At first, with every breath he took, Sabine feared that he would not stay. Tonight, in spite of herself, Sabine hoped that he would not go.

Footsteps on the outside stairs. Slow ones, as if the climber carried a great weight. Jerry jumped off the bed to greet Dan as he let himself in.

Dan handed her a bouquet of flowers. "They're not much, just from the grocery store, but they were pretty."

"Thank you. I'll just put them in water." Sabine opened one of her glass-fronted cupboards and pulled out a cut-glass vase.

"My grandmother had a vase like that. Waterford."

"Tag sale. Probably incredibly valuable; I got it for a buck." Sabine filled the vase with water and settled the flowers in. His aura was almost navy blue with tension. Sabine physically felt a shift of outlook within herself, from contentment to wariness.

Then Dan was behind her, but not touching, as if he knew that his touch would reveal his state of mind. He wasn't ready yet to tell her what was going on, but he would. There was something else too, behind the tension. An excitement. Maybe he had a surprise for her. Not all tension was bad.

"So, how was your day?" Sabine turned to face him.

Dan's face was a map of turmoil, his eyes brimming with excitement, his lips tensed in pain. "Unbelievable."

Sabine knew then that their romantic interlude had been only that: a short, entertaining episode between the acts of their separate lives.

• • •

"I'll have to close the theatre; I don't think that I can saddle the Ralstons with its operation." Dan swirled the wine left in his glass. "At least until I come back. The good news is, I'll have plenty of money to sink into it."

"But then you'll be hired for another job and take off again."

Dan threw back the last gulp of wine. "That's what a career is built on."

"And what about Nagy?"

Dan looked down at his knees, a shrug. "I don't know. I've got a call in to that group home on Weymouth Street. They have a nice setup, lots of activity. They even get the residents little jobs at the Holiday Crafts and Hobbies to give them some independence. It's a good place."

"It's an institution."

"No, no, it's not. I promised Gran that would never happen. There are no bars, no guards, just counselors."

"You're very defensive about that. Why?"

"Gran was. Sabine, this is a good solution. It was always my intention to return to my career. You knew that and so does Nagy. You both just have to let it happen. Life changes, Sabine." His voice was husky with conviction, with the need to convince her it was the right thing to do.

"This is a dream come true for you, isn't it?" Sabine could no longer sit next to Dan, and got up to pull the roast out of the oven. "Your dream, and no one should deny it to you."

"Thank you."

"You met this guy, Drexel, at the same party where you last saw Karen?"

Momentarily fooled by Sabine's interest in the details,

Dan never saw what was coming. "Yeah, actually Karen was the one who suggested that he use me."

"Let me guess—she's one of the actors in this movie."

Dan set his glass down on the coffee table and got up. "She means nothing to me anymore."

"Yet she gets you the biggest job of your career. The one she knew you most wanted."

"We ended amicably."

"I see. So you'll spend, what, six months directing her, making her career grow?"

"Where is this going, Sabine?"

Sabine stuck a fork in the small pork roast and dumped it into the garbage. "Nowhere. Just like us."

"That's not fair, Sabine."

"What's not fair is sticking Nagy away, closing the town's only source of entertainment, and leading me to believe you cared for me."

"I do. I, Sabine, I . . ."

"Please, don't."

"I will come back. It's only temporary. Six months, nine at the outside."

"Ruby wanted me to read your cards. I wouldn't. Why? Because I knew that in the end it would be the story of your leaving, and I couldn't bear to know it in advance. I lied to myself. I won't lie to you. Go, prosper. Enjoy. Just let me go back to my comfortable life."

Dan stepped to where Sabine had cornered herself in the kitchen. "Sabine, I have never done anything so difficult as taking this opportunity. You can't think that closing the Palace and finding a place for Nagy is anything but grievingly difficult for me. But," Dan took Sabine by the arms, "it's the thought of leaving you behind that's killing me."

"Don't, Dan. Don't say any more."

"I know that if I have chosen wrong in taking this job, I will only blame myself. If I choose otherwise, it would always be between us."

"The wondering if you'd done the right thing? Blaming me for your failure to succeed?"

"I don't want what we have to become resentment."

"Dan, you've made the correct choice. I know that and I'll get over it. But I'd like you to go now."

Dan bent to kiss her, but Sabine's hand stayed him. "Go."

"Mom?"

"I'm on my way."

"No, you don't have to come. I just wanted to tell you, you were right. I should have read his cards."

"Beenie, you need me."

"I do, but I'm a grown-up. I'll recover. I have work tomorrow, so do you. Come for the weekend."

"Look, things are, shall we say, quiet here. Why don't I come for a little visit. We can stay in the house together and . . ."

"Mom, you don't have to hold my hand."

There was a gentle pause on the line. "But Sabine, who else's hand have I got to hold?"

She wanted to ask, Why is that, Ruby? Why have you so carefully kept yourself aloof from the rest of the world, caring only about me? But there would be no answer that bore even the slightest resemblance to the truth. "So you'll come for the weekend?"

"I'd like to stay longer, if I might."

"What's going on, Ruby?" Sabine heard the sound of imminent departure in her mother's voice.

"I can't make this month's rent."

"Ruby, I thought things were going well."

"So did I, but the owner of the crystal shop where I set up my business didn't tell me he was on the verge of bankruptcy. He told me this morning he was closing up for the winter. My landlord won't allow a home business. I'm looking for a new rental, but . . ."

"Ruby. Come stay with me. Springfield was never the right place for you. Maybe Moose River Junction is. At least for the winter."

"You don't have room."

"Mom, it's enough. We'll make do."

"That would be nice."

Sabine hung up and lay down on the futon. She would not give over to weeping. It was her own fault for believing she could change a man's heart.

Nine

❧

Greta Sutler brought a blast of chilly late afternoon air into the newspaper office. She'd cut all of her blond fluffy hair off. She looked older, more sophisticated with it short, gelled locks angling along her cheeks. "Here's the ad for next week." Greta didn't sound as hostile as she'd been the last couple of weeks since her blowup at Dan and Sabine.

"Thanks. Looks good." Sabine smiled. "So, how are things?"

"Good. Arnie and I had a good talk the other night. We've decided to slow things down. We're just not ready to get married." Greta returned to Sabine's desk. "I'm sorry how I acted about it. You were right. I should have believed you."

"You were right to be mad. Neither of us had any business interfering in your life."

"That's what friends do, Sabine." Greta poked her

fingers into her hair. "So, tell me about this thing with you and Dan."

"It's over."

"Already?"

"Yeah. He's got a big directing job out west and he's out of here soon."

"Doesn't mean you've got to break up."

"Well, we weren't officially . . ." Sabine etched air quotes around the word, "together, so it's a good time to stop."

Greta reached over the counter and patted Sabine on the shoulder. "Keep telling yourself that and maybe you'll believe it." She tootled her fingers at Sabine. "See you next week."

With so much going on in her mind, it was a relief to focus on work, and Sabine bent to the tasks of her day. It seemed only moments had gone by when she looked up to see Moe, Balto, and Teddy shrugging into coats and shutting off desk lamps. "I'll stick around a little, Moe." Sabine gestured to the stack of ads she was sorting through.

"Not too long, okay?" Sometimes Moe acted like a dad. At least that's how fatherless Sabine interpreted his gruffness, and chose to think it charming.

"No, just long enough to get these in order." She waved a sheaf of papers over the top of her divider.

The office door shut with a glassy rattle. Sabine got up and lowered the shade. With her hand still on the shade pull, Sabine suddenly felt the presence of someone approaching the door. Standing very still, she listened, sensing that whoever it was, was standing in hesitation. She supposed that the drawn shade was causing the person to rethink his plans. *I could make it easy on him and open the door, or be very quiet and hope whoever it is will come back when we're open.* Sabine checked on her charitability and found it lacking. She turned away from the door just as there was a quiet tap. Probably someone with a wedding announcement five minutes too late for the deadline. Damn. *Who am I to disappoint the bride?* Sabine opened the door. Nagy Danforth stood there.

"Nagy? Why are you here?"

"I know you work here. I didn't see you come out."

"You've been standing there?"

"I'm going to work."

"But it's only five o'clock. You have to eat dinner first."

"I ate at the diner. Dan's not home."

"Do you want to sit down?" Sabine patted the back of the side chair in her cubicle. Sitting heavily down in the chair, Nagy was obviously deeply distressed. He wore a poplin jacket, too light for the cold November night. In one hand he clutched a baseball cap, the name of a film emblazoned on the crown. Over and over he rubbed at his nose, until Sabine handed him a tissue and he blew it loudly. He seemed to be waiting to be asked a question, and Sabine realized that he seldom initiated conversation, and was uncomfortable in that role. "Nagy, what's bothering you? Why did you come see me?"

"Will you tell my fortune?"

Sabine sat back in her chair, causing it to roll away from the desk. She wheeled it closer to Nagy. "Why do you want me to do that?"

"I don't know." Nagy could not put into words the fear of the unknown Dan's news had caused him. He looked up at Sabine with his muddy blue eyes, red-rimmed from anxiety, and shrugged with eloquent confusion.

"I don't know . . ."

"You don't know what to expect."

Nagy nodded.

"Okay. But you must understand that I don't always know for sure what's going to happen. That I'm making guesses."

Nagy nodded, his rubbery lips pinched together in determined agreement.

"Give me one hand." Sabine usually liked to let the client choose which hand to give, then read the other. This time she took the right hand Nagy offered her and closed her eyes.

"You look like you're praying."

Sabine opened her eyes, gave Nagy a little admonitory scowl, and closed them again. Settled into her near-trance state for reading, she opened her eyes to examine Nagy's palm. She expected the short lifeline. People like Nagy didn't live into old age. At fifty-something, he was already beating odds. The lines that indicated love were strong, and she understood that he was capable of deep and enduring love. For his mother. For Dan. Sabine never knew what modality her readings would take, what path they would follow. She entered into a deeper place where conscious decision was absent. Of their own volition, her hands surrounded Nagy's right hand and she let his images, his emotions, his fears and hopes seep into her mind. Complicated images of a tall man appeared, his arm wrapped around a pregnant blond woman. An old woman who could only be Beatrice, a small boy crying. Fire, orange and yellow flames billowing, sparkling against night darkness. She had no way of knowing whether those images were Nagy's fears or memories. Fire could represent both. Dan was a fireman; maybe Nagy feared for him.

"Did you see my future?" Nagy had settled back into the chair, calmer but no less distressed.

"What do you think I saw?" Sabine turned the question back on Nagy, as she often did to get happier endings for her clients.

"I don't know. I want you to say."

Sabine realized he had little capacity for picturing the future. His was an existential life. "I saw some upset, but then I saw happiness."

"Is Danny really going away?" Nagy wanted specifics.

"Yes. But you know that."

"Is he going to put me in that group home?"

"Nagy, I don't know. I just see that you'll be happy, but unhappy first."

Nagy heaved himself out of the low side chair and walked away, his sloping shoulders drooping even more, his hands heavy at his sides. Sabine got up to unlock the door and let him out. "Nagy, cheer up. Dan only wants to do right by you."

"His idea of right." Nagy left the office and left Sabine stunned at the perception in his words.

It was impossible for her to go back to work; she was agitated with the vision Nagy's palm had induced. It was so similar to the vision she'd had at the Atchesons' house. A pregnant couple, obviously distressed, holding onto one another. The pervasive imagery of fire.

The meeting took longer than usual. Although he'd already given Chief Bean his resignation, Dan was nervous about having to announce it in front of his comrades. It was a surprisingly hard thing to do. Even though he'd never had any intention of rejoining the department, being on it had been a good thing for him all these months, providing him with an outlet.

Dan made his report on the fund-raising for the portable defibrillator. He was pleased to report that the carnival had netted almost half the amount needed, and he'd managed to eke out nearly half of the remaining cost from a few calls to local businesses. One or two major donors would put them over the top.

Then Arthur asked for new business. One or two items were discussed. Dan kept his mouth shut up till the last minute, when the chief called on him.

"Dan, don't you have something to say?"

"Yeah. Arthur, guys, effective next Friday, I'm resigning from the department."

Murmurs, then the direct questions. Why? Where? The expected felicitations, then, from Amos Anthony, "Does this mean we can have a going-away party?"

"Absolutely not." Dan held up his hands as if to ward off any idea of such a thing. "Just hang my number up and don't use it."

After locking up after the meeting, Dan walked down the wooded slope to Windsor's Brook. He often did this on meeting nights to shake the cobwebs out before heading to the theatre, mentally changing gears. The tributary gurgled prosaically, although he could only see it in the bits of moonlight reflected in its surface. Directly across, he could see Sabine's back light. Funny how he'd never noticed that before. Never looked across the stream hoping to see someone.

He breathed deeply of the night air and smelled the stream, with its muddy odor of leaf mold. Dan shivered. He'd spent a boyhood on the banks of this stream. He'd fished in it, skipped stones across its glassy surface where the stream widened and flattened out just past the cemetery. He'd skinny-dipped on prom night, and nearly drowned in it with an ill-conceived idea of rafting down it. It separated the Windsorville of his ancestors from the Moose River Junction of modern times. At the confluence of where Windsor's Brook emptied into the Moose River, his parents' home had stood.

Six years old. He'd been six years old and rambunctious. One of those boys who never cease moving except in sleep, always looking for the next adventure. A kind person would call their balloon frame house a fixer-upper, others might call it ramshackle and a comedown for his blue-blood mother. Fredericka was pregnant, though he didn't know that until years later. He'd been sent to bed earlier than usual. Nagy was sleeping in the other bed in his room. He and Nagy had been in the basement that day, playing with the lighter his grandfather had used. Nagy was so proud of having been given the memento of his father. *Flick, flick, flick.* A tiny yellow flame, burning off the sweetish odor of the lighter fluid. Dan didn't remember spilling the lighter fluid, but that's what must have happened. The lighter fluid must have spilled, and hours after they'd been sent to his second-floor bedroom, the house was in flames.

The day after Dan turned seventeen, he'd joined the volunteer fire department as a junior member. It was a natural extension of his Explorer Scout Search and Rescue experience, and a couple of his friends had joined as well. But Dan had also joined because he felt a moral imperative to do so. His personal tragedy had stunned the town; the death of the daughter of one of Moose River Junction's leading families had been taken as a loss for everyone. His own father, Gary, had been a fireman until he'd injured his back. Joining was as much a part of Dan's emotional makeup as his plans to go to college in New York. Something he had felt deeply.

Standing on the banks of Windsor's Brook sixteen

years later, Dan still felt that imperative, still felt as if he needed to give the department as much of his attention as he could before he left.

The day he'd joined the department, he and his friends had been given a tour of the original fire barn, the new warehouse-size barn as yet unimagined. Chief Murphy, long since gone to his reward, had taken them into the back room where five-drawer file cabinets were lined from wall to wall.

"These are where all our reports are filed." Chief Murphy thumped the top of one of the dusty cabinets. "From our incorporation in 1902 until today. Every report, numerically, by year." All three of the new recruits noticed the heap of unfiled reports balanced at a tilt on a wooden chair. "You'll learn how to write them. And file them." As a junior fireman that's what Dan did, quickly sucking away the fun and romance out of being a fireman.

The locked drawer marked 1965–75 had caught his eye. Filing away all the other reports, he imagined opening that drawer and finding the file with the Maple Street fire inside. Once, he screwed up his courage to ask Arthur to look at that file.

Arthur had shaken his head. "No, son. There are things best left alone. The past is one of them."

Going through his grandmother's things right after she'd died, Dan had come upon a tin Schrafft's box filled with clippings about the fire. He hadn't thought it odd that Gran would save each article, only that she'd stored them almost carelessly in this bent-edged box stuck on the top of her bedroom shelf. She had always been so meticulous about clippings. A dozen scrapbooks held engagements, weddings, birth announcements, and obituaries; every article or review of performances at the

Palace had been preserved; even his own high school career as it was printed in the *Pennywise Paper* had been lovingly snipped and glued to the black sheets. Baseball games and scholarships, his walk-on role in the school play, his Scout troop's successful bottle drive, anyplace his name appeared. More organized than photos, certainly more numerous, these bits of paper chronicled what had been important to Beatrice Windsor Danforth all of her life. But the fire that had changed their lives forever had been stuffed in a tin box like shame.

Dan hadn't looked any farther in the box than the first headline. He knew they were there, but he'd never read through them, as if she would know he'd been snooping. These articles would flesh out a terror he and his grandmother had implicitly never revisited.

Sabine's back light snapped off. He could see her in the light of the kitchen, her upper body moving rhythmically, doing the dishes. He could hear the clattery little tink of glass tapping the faucet as she rinsed. Her head was tilted a little, her hair bundled into a self-knotted bun. She looked, even from this distance, very beautiful. Dan was glad that she was angry with him. It had been such a close thing, staying because of her. What he'd said was true: he feared less losing her to anger than resenting her later on. The Road Not Taken. Better anger than hurt. He couldn't bear hurting anyone else as he had hurt Nagy.

Nagy had carried him out of the burning house. Sometimes Dan thought it was the one competent act of Nagy's life, understanding that he needed to do that. All around him had been the garish light and crackling sound of the fire. Even before the trucks arrived, they were audible, wailing, crying creatures making their slow way down Maple Street. Nagy had been crying, too.

So rapidly had the fire consumed the walls of the house, fed lusciously by the air between them, that it had already begun to crumble as the trucks pulled into the street.

"Mommy!" A little boy's cry.

Then Arthur Bean's arms enfolding him, rushing him to the running board of the truck. Over Arthur's shoulder, the vivid scene of flames and smoke, the skeleton of the house gold against the black sky. His fault.

Suddenly the strength of his recollections caught deep within his breast like a gripping hand. Dan turned too quickly on the slippery bank, and stumbled. Everything fell away as he tumbled down the steep bank. The dry autumn had lowered the level of the brook, and there was little water to cushion his fall. Dan banged his cheek against a rock. When he tried to get up, he nearly passed out with the pain in his right ankle. He sat down hard in the cold water with a reflexive cry of pain. To his own ears, the sound was as much soul-sickness as physical anguish, and he couldn't separate the two. The darkness softened and he fell back against the embankment.

Sabine heard the sound of crashing in the undergrowth, assumed a raccoon was running from a dog, and went back to washing her dishes. Jerry meowed at the back door, as he always did when her hands were dripping soapsuds. As she opened the door she heard the unmistakable sound of a human in pain. She grabbed her yellow emergency lantern and her fleece jacket and raced down the outside stairs. Everything was quiet again. Sabine held the lantern down and listened, hearing only the soft, guttural sound of the low brook bubbling along the rock-strewn bed. She was certain of it. Someone had cried out. Bundling her courage as she bundled her jacket close, Sabine picked her way down the leafy path that led from her small backyard to the embankment. Across from her she could see the firehouse, the only light, the big spotlights in front of the two bays. Angled to cast light downward, they shed no light on the area immediately in front of her. Sabine held up the big boxy lantern and methodically swept the woods with its light.

She missed him the first time her light passed over him, the dark form against the bank. The second time, she realized that what she saw was not a random pile of leaves, but a figure. As she steadied the light on him, she recognized the barn coat as Dan's. Even as she held the light, he began to come to. His slow attempt to rise sent her splashing across the brook, heedless of her sneakers in the icy water.

"Dan, what happened?" She knelt beside him, helping him to get into a sitting position.

"Damnedest thing, I just slipped. When I went to get up, well, I guess I've sprained my ankle but good."

"Let's get that boot off." Sabine set the flashlight down to illuminate his leg and began to unlace the heavy work boot he wore. "You don't want to have it cut off if that ankle swells." In a curiously intimate gesture, she slid his sock down. With tender fingers Sabine touched the wounded area, pressing carefully to determine if it had already begun to swell. There was heat radiating from Dan's leg, and she knew he was struggling not to yelp when she pressed a little harder. She tested her conscience. Had she really needed to press that hard? A little flush of doubt. "Let's get you to the hospital."

"I'm sure it'll be all right. Just help me to my truck." The last thing Dan wanted at this moment was to be weak in front of this woman. Her gentle probing had sent streaks of desire through him, his male body forgetting its wound for a moment in the natural and sudden response to her hand until she'd pressed too hard. When Sabine stood to take his weight, they both nearly toppled back into the brook. To rebalance, Dan set his right foot on the ground and nearly fainted again. "Oh, God. Maybe the hospital is a good idea. Can you drive my truck?"

"If I get you up to the firehouse, I can call an ambulance."

"If you get me up there, you could drive the ambulance. That's where it lives."

Sabine chuckled in spite of herself. "Okay. Can you get up?"

"Just give me your arm." Dan pulled himself up onto his good foot, using Sabine as a lever. She let him lean against her and the two made their slow, painful way to the top of the embankment. Once there, Sabine left Dan sitting in the truck while she used his key to go into the firehouse and find an EMT kit with an ice pack. It was exactly where he'd told her she'd find it, and she came running out in a couple of minutes.

"Sabine, can you stop by the theatre for a minute so I can tell Nagy . . ." Dan held his breath against a new jolt of pain as he tried to find a good way to support his ankle with the blue pack on it.

"Let's just get you to the hospital and get that ankle taken care of."

"Please. I don't want him to worry."

Sabine gripped the wheel of the big Ford truck. "Of course. You wouldn't want him to worry about you. To miss you."

Dan shot her a glance. "Sabine, please. I can't talk about this right now."

"I'm sorry. I'll keep my mouth shut."

"Thank you."

Sabine backed out of the parking space and heard the loose stones spit out from under the back wheels as she sped away from the firehouse.

She pulled up in front of the Palace Theatre. The first show was well under way. Maisie Ralston still sat in the glass booth, tallying ticket sales. "First show's started, second show in an hour."

"No, no ticket. I need to talk to Nagy. I've got Dan in the truck with a bad ankle." Sabine explained the problem quickly and Maisie nodded.

"You get him to the hospital; I'll take care of Nagy. I'll stay with him tonight, so if Dan gets back late, he won't have to worry."

"Thank you so much, Maisie. I know they both depend on you too much, but they appreciate it." Sabine had no idea where that came from, but it seemed quite true so she felt all right in expressing it.

The hospital was twenty minutes away from rural Moose River Junction. It might as well have been an eternity, so uncomfortable were the two in the cab of the pickup. Driving a little fast, without her glasses, in an unfamiliar and much larger vehicle than she was used to, Sabine kept her hands on the wheel and her jaw a little more forward in concentration. Dan was quiet, staring ahead, only his occasional grunt indicating he was still in great pain.

She didn't want to look at him. She didn't want to feel sorry for him. It was hard enough pretending to Ruby and Greta that she and Dan hadn't been serious, but she couldn't carry it off in front of him. He'd held her heart in his hands and then cast it away.

Ten

Ruby thought she'd be at Sabine's by midnight. It had taken a long time to pack up the old VW van, scattered as her things were between the shop and the two rooms she'd rented deeper in the bowels of darkest Springfield. The truth was, this was probably the VW's final trip. After so many years of faithful service, Ruby knew the lime green bus was at the end of its extraordinarily long life. Twenty-seven years and more than 300,000 miles, in a car that had been bought used. Thank God she'd made mechanic friends everywhere they'd gone. More than a means of transportation, the VW bus was home when no place else ever had been. More than once she'd opened it up as a mobile parlor, setting up shop in campgrounds and shopping malls till the police drifted by to see what was going on. In it, Ruby Heartwood felt as though she led a charmed life. Not once stopped for speeding, never breaking down except where help was handy, dodging those same curious patrol cars with what Ruby called her cloak of invisibility in the lime green and highly noticeable bus. In the same way, Ruby had managed to avoid jail when caught setting up shop without a business license. She claimed it was her third eye that kept her ahead of danger. To little Sabine, it was just time to move on. Greener pastures. Sights to see. Sabine, so tiny and helpless in her portable bassinet strapped to the backseat bench. Nowadays she'd be arrested as a neglectful parent for driving around with a baby so poorly restrained. Then, she just kept on the road, her third eye recognizing the right place to stop for a while.

Memories seemed so prominent lately. After years of repression, every little thing swept Ruby back in time. Passing a school built of those same pale bricks the orphanage was built of, hearing a song on the radio that had played so loudly over the carnival midway speakers. The smell of fried dough at the Firemen's Carnival. All of these things brought images and emotions up from the burial ground of her memory.

Oddly enough, it was Arthur Bean's slow, sweet overtures at befriending her that had triggered random memories. No one had ever treated her so respectfully. The few men she'd attracted were drawn by her exoticness, not her true self. They had assumed a free-spiritedness that, despite appearances, was only an act. Arthur understood the difference.

Ruby spoke to the dark interior of the bus. "It's time to face your demons, Mary Jones."

Jones because, like in a Dickens novel, she was named by the nuns. Mary because all foundlings were given saint names. Baptized Mary Jones, Ruby had shed that name the moment she'd hidden herself in the straw of the animal trailer of the carnival in the parking lot of the school. The parish held a carnival and fun fair annually to raise money to support the orphanage. Every year after age ten Ruby had been put to work, along with the other older girls, to help pick up litter and sell tickets. All year she waited for the return of the carnival and the sparkle its presence lent the faded and dark life of the convent orphanage. Lights and noise and exotic-looking people. At night, the carny workers camped a little ways off in the empty lot across the street from the dorm. From her window, Ruby could see the trailers, warmly lighted, whiffs of cooking drifting across the street. They looked like miniature homes, with happy families tucked inside. At least to an orphan girl who had never seen the inside of a house, these little homes looked wonderful. She heard laughter.

How do you know a fantasy exists until you seek its fulfillment? Ruby hadn't known what she planned until she crept out of that dormitory, dressed in donated blue jeans and sweatshirt, the sneakers on her feet the castoffs of some slightly bigger girl. She carried nothing with her, owning nothing. Pure and untouched by any emotion that might cause her to turn around, Ruby slipped down the metal backstairs and out the open laundry room window. *Hurry, hurry,* her heart told her. To be caught would incur the wrath of the superior; to fail would cause her heart to break. It pounded so hard that the image of Christ's Sacred Heart exploding in her oxygen-deprived chest came to her. In the sanctuary of the church there was a painted wooden statue of Christ, His fingers touching that garish orb. From the time she was a little girl, Ruby saw God that way, a rock-hard figure with a heart of wood. How could he love the little children, when his minions tortured them so? Having no reference for parental love, Ruby could not imagine receiving love.

Over the years, she'd been trotted out annually for inspection by potential parents. Each time, for no explained reason, Mary Jones failed to come up to some expectation and never made the cut. Like being left off a team. Her infancy had been an unattractive one of runny noses and ear infections. Her toddlerhood had not measured up to that of the golden-haired girls who snuggled up to prospective adopters, beaming baby smiles. Mary Jones had been reserved, shy, and, ultimately, unadoptable. Now, at fourteen, she was long past the age when people wanted to adopt. She was told repeatedly that she was a far luckier girl than those who went from foster home to foster home. At least she had continuity and an education. She didn't argue the point. Instead she ran away. The soft lights of the carnival workers' trailers had seduced her with the idea of home.

The only vehicles on the Pike were the massive semis that blew by the lime green bus with tooth-shaking velocity. Ruby clung to the wheel, energized by her thoughts. Letting the old memories surface after all these years was like a release of energy. It had taken so much strength to keep them in check. Ruby smiled ruefully. She had told Sabine so many tales, would her daughter believe the truth? Would she believe that after all these years of protest, Ruby would just suddenly give up the story? How do you explain to someone that, for certain stories, there is only one right time?

The emergency room of the small hospital was busy and understaffed. Sabine and Dan had sat in the waiting room chairs for an hour before even getting through the initial check-in process. The cold pack from the firehouse was long since tepid gel. Sabine did manage to snag a wheelchair with an elevated footrest so that Dan was more comfortable during the wait. Twice ambulances came in, bullying Dan back in the long line of noncritical supplicants.

"Look, this is going to take all night, Sabine. Why don't you take the truck home and get some rest? I'll get a cab."

Sabine was feigning a deep interest in the art on the walls of the waiting room. The magazines were backdated half a decade and either sports or housewife oriented. Sabine had found the vending machines and Dan had dug up enough change to buy them both a candy bar. Once the topic of his accident had been beaten to death, they had only the silence of their discomfort with one another to think about.

"That probably makes sense. Can you get a cab to Moose River Junction?"

"Sure. I'm sure I can."

Sabine had the advantage of Dan, standing above him as she was, and a little behind. His voice had in it the tension of pain, and he shifted against it.

"Dan, they'll give you something for that pain pretty soon, and I'm sure you're next. Why don't I wait a little longer?"

"You don't have to."

"No. I certainly don't. But I will." Sabine wasn't going to let him think she was soft. But she had brought him here and it would be hard for him to get home in the middle of the night. This wasn't New York, where a guy on crutches could flag a cab with one hand.

They resumed their silent wait.

Dan hadn't described to Sabine his state of mind when he stumbled and fell, relating the story as just a little evening appreciation of the air and stars before going to the theatre. "I can't believe I was so stupid as to stumble over that root like I did. I've been down that path a hundred times. It was like I was flying; there was no stopping my trajectory." Despite the growing pain in his ankle, Dan tried to keep the incident light, even laughable—if only the pain would go away. Sabine had seen the bruise on his cheek and gotten a second ice pack from a nurse. "Good thing the water level was so low, or I'd probably have drowned."

"Were you unconscious?"

"I think so. I don't remember."

"Be sure to tell the nurse that. They might want to check for concussion."

"How do you know so much about it?"

"I watch *ER.*"

Sabine drifted off to reexamine the artwork, clearly not interested in idle chitchat with him. Dan noticed that her feet were still wet from her sprint across Windsor's Brook. Had she known that it was him lying there? If she had, would she have just dialed up nine-one-one and let someone else handle it? Dan could sense Sabine's distaste for being with him, and knew he deserved it. Still, she'd been a good rescuer, a good neighbor. In staying here with him, was she just being a Samaritan? He watched her squint at a tacky sunset painting. She leaned a little forward, myopic without her glasses. Without her glasses? Cripe, she'd driven him to the hospital without them. Because he'd asked her to.

Watching Sabine from the distance of the long waiting room, Dan felt as though his heart was cracking. When they examined his ankle, they would find that it was nothing compared to the sundering of his unruly heart.

"Okay, Mr. Smith, let's get you to X ray." A scrub-suited nurse grabbed the handles of the wheelchair and spun him around toward the double doors that separated the waiting room from the examining area.

"Sabine?" He didn't know why he called her name. She was watching the nurse take him.

"I'll be here, Dan."

Sabine watched the nurse push Dan through the automatic doors, which opened at the last possible moment before his elevated ankle hit them. She winced at the narrow miss. "What am I doing here?" She fished around in her jeans pocket for change. Coming up with a tattered dollar bill, she attempted to get the vending machine to accept it. Failing that, she wandered out to the covered docking area where an ambulance sat, its back door open. She should have insisted on calling for an ambulance. It wouldn't necessarily have been faster getting Dan here, but it was obvious that those who arrived by ambulance got faster service. The drive had been unnerving, especially as she'd left her glasses and license at home, too. Dan probably thought she'd hunched over the wheel because she was anxious to get him here; the truth was, she was terrified she wouldn't see something dangerous in front of her, like a deer.

The stars were stifled by the parking lot lights, the air near the running ambulance was tainted, and Sabine went back inside. She wasn't hopeful that Dan would be whisked through and they could go home anytime soon. Bundling up her fleece jacket under her cheek, Sabine closed her eyes and tried to pretend she was sleeping in the lime green bus. How many times had she done that, refusing to sleep in the back while her mother drove through midnight towns? Sitting bolt upright in the passenger's seat, her cheek supported by her little pink satin pillow some landlady had made for her. *When I open my eyes, I'll be home.* Sabine never asked, when will we be there, how much farther? She knew her mother rarely chose a destination. "My destination will choose me."

"Moose River Junction chose me," Sabine had said to Ruby. Just like that. A call, a sense of place, of home. *Here is where I lay my hat. Here is where I rest my head.* Some song had those words. *This is where they know my name.* It was very late, and she was very tired. That must be why the sudden tears threatened to leak out from under her closed eyelids. Under them, the image of the two ghost lovers, side by side on the settle, telling each other that what they were doing, what they had, was right. Outside forces had taken that away from them. Destroyed them rather than let their love flower.

"Mrs. Smith, you can come in now."

"What?" Sabine pulled herself out of her drowse. "I'm not Mrs. Smith."

"Sorry, I said I'd go get his wife and he didn't correct me."

"I'm his . . ." Sabine hunted for a descriptive term that would cover the whole of their abortive association. ". . . His neighbor."

"Whatever. He's ready to go."

Sabine met Dan in the examining room. His ankle was taped and he'd been given a pair of hospital-issue crutches. "Just a bad sprain. I'll be tap dancing in a week."

"You tap-dance?"

"There's a lot you don't know about me." It was meant as a joke, but his timing was off.

All Sabine knew was that Dan had gotten a good dose of pain medication. In view of his unpracticed crutch-walking abilities, Sabine insisted he sit in the wheelchair again and get rolled out to the car. "I can't pick you up again, Smith. You can practice walking on your own tomorrow."

"Anything you say, Sabine. You're the best."

Oh, yes. The pain meds had helped greatly. Dan talked nonstop for ten minutes of the twenty-minute ride home. "Sabine, I can't thank you enough for helping me. I don't deserve it, I know that. You have to understand that I can't turn my back on this opportunity. If you'd let me explain." His words began to drift onto their beam ends as the drugs took effect. "You're the best. I can't do it anymore. Nagy deserves better. His buttons were all mixed-up. I'm not a good caretaker. I wish . . ."

"Dan, shut up." Sabine clenched the wheel in her hands, wanting him to stop trying to convince her he was doing the right thing.

With a last grasp on clear thinking, Dan touched Sabine's arm. "I just want you to understand that it isn't you I'm leaving."

"Dan, you aren't going to remember tomorrow what you've said or what I'll say, so I'll say it. I think you're a grown-up and you have to do what's right for you. But that doesn't mean anyone else has to like it. Or that it isn't going to affect anyone else, or be right for anyone else, and I mean Nagy, not me. As for me, you can go take a flying leap." There, she'd said it.

But Dan was asleep, oblivious to her words.

She pulled up into the driveway of his house and shut the truck off. Dan's head was back against the seat. Even in repose he looked sad. "Dan, we're home." She shook him a little.

Dan eased himself upright and looked at Sabine. In the shadows of the fading night, he could see a difference in her eyes. She looked at him without anger. But also, without love. He'd lost her. Pushed her away when she was the one person who might love him, not as a successful director or the dutiful grandson, not as a New

York player or a small town businessman, but as a man.

"Sabine. Thank you. For helping me out."

"Now we're even."

"How?"

"For the morning when you pulled me out of the house, when you thought I was overcome by carbon monoxide." Sabine opened her door to help Dan get out of the truck. "Can you get inside on your own?"

"Yeah. Wait, how are you getting home? Take the truck. I'll get it tomorrow."

"I can walk. It's not that far."

"Sabine. It's the middle of the night. Take the damn truck."

Sabine saw the wisdom in that, despite feeling only good friends loaned vehicles, and that driving a guy's truck was tantamount to being his girlfriend. False impressions were a better risk than walking along a dark country road in the middle of the night. "All right. I'll leave it here in the morning and walk to work."

They both felt the awkwardness of the moment. They both felt a need to say more, and the deeper imperative not to.

Dan broke first. "Thank you again, Sabine. I think I'd have been spending the night in the woods if you hadn't come along."

"Dan, I didn't just 'come along,' I heard you cry out."

"You did? I don't remember crying out."

"Like a banshee, but less girlie."

Dan looked puzzled.

"A banshee is a female spirit, generally believed to be calling out a death."

A death. He had been thinking about death, hadn't he? Though long ago and remote to him, the death of his parents had been on his mind, jumbled together with his current stresses. Dan propped himself up on the crutches and made a staggering attempt at a first step. The combination of exhaustion, pain, and medication made each step a challenge, but he wouldn't let Sabine do anything more for him. Then she was there and opening the clumsy arrangement of storm and back door for him.

"Is there anything I can say to make you not hate me?"

Sabine tossed back her loosened hair and shook her head. "I don't hate you, Dan. I'm happy for you. We should all get what we want."

Ruby Heartwood pulled into the driveway behind Sabine's car at a quarter past one in the morning. She was surprised to see the lights still on, more surprised to not find Sabine there. She sat for a minute, gathering her panicky thoughts, and then smiled. Of course, she was with Dan. A sudden reconciliation perhaps?

Ruby took in the sink of soapy water and the unlocked back door. No. Something had happened. She went out onto the back porch, wrapped herself in a quilt, and sat in the plastic deck chair. She lit a cigarette and waited, staring across at the little fire barn and wondering absently if it would be appropriate to give Arthur a call tomorrow. Just to tell him she was back in town. Just to say hello.

Buzzed from the long drive and the flashes of intensive memory, Ruby felt wide awake and agitated. As she had always feared, once the floodgates of memory were opened, they were hard to close. She dragged deeply on the cigarette, coughed, and stubbed it out. One of these days she'd quit.

Eleven

Everyone at the carnival had smoked. And drank and played cards and lived like folks everywhere, except that they carried their neighbors with them and there were some peculiar neighbors. The Allen Brothers Carnival was too small to have a true collection of freaks, and none were terribly grotesque. Ruby soon grew oblivious to Johnny Tat's thousand tattoos and Madame Desdemona's prodigious size and beard. They simply became Johnny and Desi, good-hearted folks with savings in the bank and hopes for a Florida retirement.

Ruby had come out of hiding at the next performance location, a small city a hundred miles away from the orphanage. She pretended, as all runaways do, to be older, wiser, and employable. The manager, wiser and older and infinitely less gullible than Ruby, had seen a day laborer, nothing more. "Okay, you can work with the grounds crew. Five bucks and a meal." Doing essentially what she'd done when the carny had been at the orphanage, Ruby picked up litter, dumped garbage, and ran errands at the beck and call of the rides operators and the ticket sellers. It was hot and she was soon coated in dust and stickiness. Ten times she passed by the circular tent of MADAME FONTAINE, SEER AND PSYCHIC, PALMS AND TAROT READ, FORTUNES INTERPRETED. On the eleventh pass, a voice called out to her.

"Miss. Come here." The accent was blended European, entirely fake. Madame Fontaine beckoned Ruby in with glittering hands. The soft light of the sun through the beribboned tent glanced off the ten glass-jeweled rings on Madame Fontaine's red-tipped fingers. "Child. I need a favor."

"Okay."

"It's been a slow morning. Sit here and pretend to be having your fortune told."

"Sure." Ruby sat down on the cushions in front of Madame Fontaine's cushioned banquette. "Shouldn't I open the curtains more so that people can see what's going on?"

"Yes. I was going to say that."

"I know."

Madame Fontaine raised a painted eyebrow. "Are you being flippant?"

That word was so evocative of the sisters. Ruby shook her head. "No. It just made sense."

Clearing her throat dramatically, Madame Fontaine took Ruby's slightly sticky hand in a businesslike fashion. "Hmmm, let me see . . ." Her voice was directed toward the opened curtain. "I see a long life . . . many love affairs. No, only one." Madame Fontaine rambled on, her eyes not on Ruby's hand but on the doorway. The ploy attracted a couple of teenagers. "I'll be right with you," she called out cheerily in her phony European accent. "I see a handsome man, no, wait . . . you will have two handsome men to choose from."

"Thank you, Madame Fontaine, thank you so very, very much!" Ruby clasped her hands to her chest in mock appreciation and sauntered out past the waiting girls. "You won't be disappointed," she stage-whispered to them.

At the end of the night, as the merry-go-round and the Tilt-A-Whirl each ground to a halt, Ruby went back to Madame Fontaine. Shyly, and with great apprehension, Ruby gave the old woman her made-up name, Ruby Heartwood, and then said something she'd never admitted even to herself. "Madame, sometimes I see things. I feel things."

Through the gauzy film of years, and in spite of what happened, Ruby still remembered Phyllis Fontana's gruff kindness with gratitude. The old woman was quick to recognize Ruby's talents and exploit them to her own advantage. But she was fair, making sure Ruby got fed and had a bed to sleep in. She gave Ruby a percentage of the door. Phyllis taught her the tricks of the trade—how to extract information from the unsuspecting client, how to present a foreign flavor to a reading. "Above all, they are here to be entertained. Never forget that. Even an inaccurate reading will be enjoyable if you put on a good show." Phyllis Fontana failed only in protecting her protégée from Buck Fontana, her middle-aged son.

Buck was a roustabout, doing the heavy manual labor required to set up and move the small carnival. Sometimes he'd fill in for a rides operator or a barker. Mostly, though, he found a quiet corner and drank.

Tacked to the wall of the Fontana's trailer was a black-and-white school photograph of a good-looking boy about her own age. His curly black hair was scraped back in the style of the forties, his angular features highlighted by piercing black eyes beneath perfect brows on a high, white forehead. Phyllis saw that the old photograph had caught Ruby's eye. "Buck's high school picture. Handsome boy, looked like his dad. His dad was a true Romany. A Spanish Gypsy. That picture is just before Buck went away to the war." Phyllis turned away from the photo and sat heavily down on the only chair in the tiny space. "War turned him to drink. It didn't come on him natural. He saw things."

"What things?"

"Death."

"He was at war; of course he saw death."

"No, he saw death on the shoulders of those who would perish the next day. He said he saw it like a shadow. The others were quite afraid of him in the end."

Buck might have been good-looking in youth, but that penchant for drink had long-sinced erased the steely cut of his jaw and bloated his belly, despite the roustabout's hard labor. He might have been forty or fifty to Ruby's young eyes. Now she remembered little of his face and everything about his reaching hands, bristle-roughened lips, and self-inflicted tattoos.

She hadn't dared complain to Madame Fontaine. With the treachery of the years, Ruby couldn't figure out why she had been so reluctant to tell Phyllis that her middle-aged alcoholic son was constantly making advances on the young Ruby. Maybe she had been afraid that, like with the sisters, her story would be proof of her sinning ways. No matter what the complaint within the confines of the school, it had been turned upon her: "You've brought this on yourself." Ruby knew nothing about the ways of men and at first thought that Buck was a funny teaser, trying to tickle her. Then he began to fondle her breasts and try to sneak his stringy hands between her legs. She avoided him, going out of her way to be sure she was never alone in his company. She stayed outside the trailer as long as Phyllis was elsewhere.

Ruby shook off the memory, deeming it unworthy of a star-laden night, sitting in the quiet safety of her daughter's back porch. Waiting for dawn or waiting for Sabine. Yes, she'd tell Sabine the story, edited down, revised a little to make it more palatable in the telling. She didn't need to go over every detail. She would tell Sabine a story of an orphan, twice abandoned. Tell her that she hadn't lied when she told Sabine she was a Gypsy. Her grandfather had been a Romany. Her grandmother a Romany Rye, the Gypsy word for an outsider. Phyllis had fallen hard in love with the father of her son. "Three nights of raucous lovemaking and I never saw him again. But I loved him and kept his child under my breast. Such romantic nonsense." Phyllis liked her drop or two, and in the late night, after the carnival lights were cut and the families snug in their trailers, Madame Fontaine would speak of things locked away in her heart. "I sometimes think that's what's the matter with Buck. He has the Gypsy blood mixing around with my French—too volatile a mix for an ordinary man."

Volatile indeed.

Suddenly Ruby was filled with a certainty. It no longer mattered that she'd suffered the harm and dislocation of her early life. She'd raised a good and sensible child into adulthood. Buck was no longer alive. At least not to her. What was past must be acknowledged, but then left behind. There was a future here, in this place and time. She was still young enough to embrace it. For too long, she had lived her life in reaction.

The clarity of her thoughts forced Ruby to her feet. She pounded the rail of the landing with one fist: the past was done. As surely as a veil had been torn away, Ruby saw that her future no longer needed the fat padding of an unhappy past. First she needed to tell Sabine everything—an act of exorcism. Then she needed to unpack.

Parked behind her car, the lime green bus filled the driveway, so Sabine pulled the big pick-up truck, with its roof rack of emergency lights, off the road across the street. Now everyone who passed would think she and Dan were still a number. Sabine locked the truck and crept quietly up the back stairs. She needn't have bothered being quiet; Ruby was wide-awake and waiting for her on the futon. She held Sabine's latest notes from her research. "This is very interesting."

"I'll tell you all about everything in the morning."

"About this or about what's kept you out all night?"

"Both."

"Good night, Beenie."

"Good night, Mom."

Ruby wrapped the quilt around herself but lay awake for a long time on the futon. Sabine positively projected conflict. If she believed in such nonsense, she'd imagine a dark-colored aura over her daughter. Stress, disappointment, anger, even a little jealousy mixed all around into a darkening palette of emotional color. It didn't take a psychic to figure out that the cause was Dan Smith. It took a mother's intuition, and noticing that Sabine drove home in his truck. Alone. No scent of sex or happiness on her, either. Ruby had sniffed as she'd taken Sabine's good night kiss.

Sabine lay awake, too. Too tired to sleep, it seemed. Her mind circled the last hours, teasing her in its unruliness in thinking about Dan. Why did she feel as if she was shivering internally? Maybe it was just that she was cold. She gathered a second quilt over herself and patted the bed for Jerry to join her.

She wanted to feel cold toward Dan. She wanted to be able to shake off the incipient caring feeling that he woke in her. Sabine refused to fall easily into the buddy trap men liked so much to spring. *Be just friends; let him off the hook so that his male conscience was clear. Off to Mexico with the ex-girlfriend? That's nice, dear.*

No. She had too much pride.

Twelve

Sabine stumbled out of bed, pleased to find Ruby already up and breakfast made.

"Coffee?"

"Please." Sabine looked at her mother, a little surprised to see Ruby's natural hair. It had been years since she'd seen it. Without the mass of black curls, her mother looked smaller and, in the ordinary flannel pajamas she wore, quite normal. Her hair was stylishly short and nearly all gray. Instead of making her look older, it had the opposite effect and she looked quite youthful. "You always say you can tell when something's on my mind. Why do I have the feeling something's on yours?"

"Because you are a true seer."

"I know. I think I'm just coming to terms with it. I've seen things, Ruby, I've seen things so real . . ." Sabine felt a sudden welling in her eyes. She brushed them away. "Are you going to ask me to travel with you again?"

Ruby sat down at the counter, hooking her sock-covered toes onto the rungs of the bar stool. She kept her eyes on the black coffee in the mug with yellow balloons on it. "No. This is your home, Sabine, and you're all I have."

It was as if the mountain had, at long last, come to Mohammed. Sabine placed her hand over her mother's. "We're all either of us has." Impulsively, she then turned her mother's hand over and ran a finger along the lines there. "You've come here to tell me something. So tell."

"I should have said it long ago."

"What have you come to tell me, Ruby?" Sabine still held her mother's hand, a hand that was growing warm in hers. There was a vibration coming from one of them, but Sabine couldn't decide if it was from Ruby, anxious about what she was going to say, or from herself, fearful of hearing it.

"The truth."

"Why now?"

"Because you should know something of your history in order to address your future."

"You're speaking in fortune-teller-eze."

"What I mean to say is, that if you are going to marry and have children, you should be able to tell them where you came from."

"I don't think that's going to happen anytime soon."

"But it is time for me to tell you my story."

"Have the cards told you so?"

"No. My heart."

Sabine smiled and took a deep breath. "Then I think I'm ready."

The two women remained at the kitchen counter, but Ruby's words took them back to a distant time and place. Ruby kept one hand on Sabine's as she began her story.

"Sabine, I don't know who my mother was. But I

imagine she was a young girl, like I was fifteen years later, who got knocked up, either by force or foolishness. Perhaps her parents hid her in a room until she delivered, then dropped the unwanted bundle off with the sisters at the orphanage. Maybe the girl gave birth behind a Dumpster, then had a change of heart. I don't know. All I do know is that if you go to the convent there, you'll find a record of a Mary Jones. That's the name they gave me. The clothes on my back, a basic education, and nothing else.

"I ran away, then found myself in exactly the same position as my own mother had been. For years, I wanted to protect you from making that mistake. I kept you moving when you were a baby so that no one could ever take you away from me, no misguided social service agency could put you in foster care. Then it became a habit, the moving. And I realized that I was as much Gypsy as the man who fathered you." Ruby heard the words coming out of her mouth, but felt little connection to them. She had been rehearsing them most of the night, and now, spoken, they seemed tinny and unemotional. Which was good; she was desperate to keep this story in an unemotional framework.

Sabine sat in a kind of horrified fascination, incapable of turning away from her mother's daunting words. She kept thinking, *I know all this. None of this is a surprise.* And yet, the actual confirmation of her suspicion regarding her own conception startled and pained her. Ruby was blunt and seemed to have forgotten that Sabine was the product of the rape she now described in detail.

In spite of her determination to keep herself at a distance, Ruby's eyes began to fill with the return of bitter emotion. It was almost as if she was hearing the story herself for the first time. How a heavy, stinking drunk forced himself on her, the feel of the rough ground beneath her back where his scrabbling fingers had found her shirt and pulled it up to squeeze her adolescent breasts, baring her back to the harsh ground. The pressure of his jerking movements against her fragile bones. Ruby spoke in an uneven cadence, speeding up and slowing down as her inner eye witnessed this scene. The moment of cruel penetration, excruciating pain as he hammered away, his dirty, rough hand over her mouth to prevent her screams from being heard over the loud noise of the generator.

"His hands were all over me. His breath reeked of onion and beer. He'd always pestered me, touching me and all, but that night was different. For a long time, I tried to figure out what I did wrong, to place myself in such a dangerous position, but I realize now that it was inevitable. You can't put a nubile fifteen-year-old in a trailer with a middle-aged bachelor and not expect some trouble.

"He caught me behind the animal trailer. I was taking a shortcut from Madame Fontaine's booth to the trailers. It was dark and I was being stupid. Buck must have seen me leave his mother's booth, and followed me. I still had only the clothes I'd left the convent in, used blue jeans and a sweatshirt. My first reaction to his grabbing me and throwing me down on the ground between the trailers was, *my God don't rip my clothes.* He kept saying, "Come on girlie, you know you want it." I fought him, punching and scratching, but he was very heavy and very determined. Out of fear that he would break the zipper in the only pants I had, I undid it myself. An action he took to mean compliance. An action he used as a weapon after the fact. 'I'll tell my mother you led me on. She'll throw you out like the little slut you are.'"

Ruby took a sharp breath. Then she would once again become a homeless orphan. She needed Phyllis, even loved her. Buck knew that and used it as a weapon to ensure his domination of her over the course of several months.

"Sabine, I had nowhere to go but that little carnival. I actually felt at home there. Phyllis Fontana, Madame Fontaine, was as close to a mother as I had ever had. You'll never know what it was like to grow up as if there were no families in the world, only classmates, teachers, and disciplinarians. Phyllis took me under her wing, made sure that I had a place to sleep and food to eat. She was hardened by her life, but still had a gentle decency that showed up every now and then in a hug, in her praise for a good reading, in bragging about me to the others. Phyllis called me her *protégée*. She was a pudgy little crone with a theatrical bent and decent divination abilities. When I came along, also with the gift, well, I became the daughter she'd never had. Except for Buck, I might have stayed a long time with her.

"When it became obvious that my belly wasn't a result of her good cooking, she left me. Left me standing on a sidewalk in Cincinnati. Despite her psychic abilities, she never doubted Buck's story that I had seduced him. Mother love blinds us. What's that expression? Blood is thicker than water?" Ruby had entered that place where the present fades and the past becomes alive. "I promised you, right then and there, I'd never abandon you."

Sabine reached for a tissue, took one, and handed another to Ruby. "Mom, how did you ever survive?"

"Because I had you to love."

• • •

When Sabine had been a little girl, she'd often fantasized about her father. One day he might be a tall knight on a coal black charger, the next he was a tennis pro, or that handsome businessman with the briefcase riding to work on the subway. He'd see her from across a room, or on a city street, or at the beach, and know her. He'd raise her up in his arms and swear he'd been looking for her all her life.

The truth, that her father was a half-Gypsy, alcoholic, carnival-roustabout rapist seemed more fictional than her childhood imaginings. It was hard to reconcile the daydream with the reality, and Sabine swallowed hard trying to adjust her thoughts to it. She slid off the bar stool and went into the bathroom to stare at herself in the mirror, trying to subvert the fear that her bad blood would show up on her face. Ruby had said he'd been handsome as a boy, it was the war and seeing death on the shoulders of others that turned him so evil. That, and bad living. Bad living? Was moving from town to town with a carnival any different from moving from town to town without one?

She put her hand to her cheek. Was there some hidden genetic marker that would appear in the next decade as alcoholism or brutality? She, too, had seen death shadowing people. Or was her curly hair the only heritage from this man, this Buck Fontana? Spanish Gypsy and French.

"Mom?"

Ruby was rinsing the breakfast plates off. From the back she looked like a small boy.

"Mom. Do you think that maybe Phyllis left you on the sidewalk to save you from Buck?"

Ruby turned around, incredulity oh-ing her mouth. "What?"

"Madame Fontaine. I'm her grandchild. It doesn't make sense that a woman who bore an illegitimate child of her own would be so intolerant." Sabine took the dripping plate from her mother and set it back in the sink. "She had to know what he was, what he'd done. If she had the sight, she would be able to see in your heart that you were innocent. For better or worse, maybe she thought you'd be better off away from that environment. That I'd be better off."

"Sabine, you can't romanticize what happened. You can't know what it felt like to have the only family you'd ever known turn its back on you and drive you away."

"And what did you do?"

"Slept in abandoned cars. Ate out of a Dumpster. Washed dishes in a Chinese restaurant until my water broke." Ruby pulled the drain plug out of the sink. The water gurgled into a tiny vortex. "I delivered in the emergency room in some Cincinnati hospital, and while they were distracted with other patients, I left with you bundled in stolen diapers and blankets. I knew they had called social service. Within twenty-four hours you'd be ripped from my arms and I'd be in foster care myself. Oh, there was that part of me which thought that might be a good idea, but there was a deeper part of me which knew that for the first time in my life, I had a family. Flesh and blood. Mother love. I would not do to you what my mother had done to me. I would not abandon you 'for your own good.' That's what the nuns always told me. I had been abandoned for my own good. And now you're telling me that maybe Phyllis abandoned me for my own good. There is no such thing. No good ever comes out of leaving someone with no explanation."

"I only meant . . ."

"I know what you meant. It's incredibly hard to

believe oneself the product of such a misalliance. No, I assure you, I was an unwelcome burden, you were an unwelcome burden, in a tiny tagalong trailer."

"How did you manage after I was born?"

"I was lucky; your birth was uncomplicated and I recovered quickly. I realized that my best hope was to exploit my abilities. That's when I started with the curly wigs, in an effort to look older and exotic. I hid beneath them, beneath the caftans."

"And we kept moving because no place was safe."

Ruby sat down on one of the stools, her almond eyes filled with overrunning tears. "It became a habit. For years, I kept moving to confound the authorities who might take you. Then I ran because I could never make enough to pay my bills. Then I ran because I was afraid not to."

"You can stop running now, Mom. You're safe here with me."

Tears now rolled unchecked down Ruby's smooth cheeks. "I know, Sabine. I know."

As Sabine embraced her mother, she felt a loosening of the twisted strand of tension that had connected them as surely as the umbilical cord had. The truth was harsh, but behind the fan of emotion Ruby had produced in telling her story, lay hidden something of another sort. A happiness that Sabine understood to be outside of herself, yet familiar. Her mother projected the same sort of happiness she herself had known only a short time ago. Maybe Ruby's would prove less illusory.

Thirteen

They'd insisted on giving him a farewell send-off. Nothing fancy, just a potluck and a few bad jokes at the old firehouse. Arnie had picked him up, since it was still too uncomfortable for him to drive.

"Hey, Arnie. How's it going?" Dan felt awkward letting the young man open the car door for him and hold the crutches. It was an unexpected blow to his self-esteem to have anyone help him. It hadn't bothered him as a boy, the time he'd been casted with a broken leg. Of course, that had come from sliding foot first into second base on a stolen base run. He'd been safe, but hadn't played the rest of the season. Then it was kind of cool to be the wounded hero. Now he just felt foolish.

"I'm okay, Dan. Just fine." Arnie pulled away from the curb carefully, as if he might hurt Dan otherwise. "By the way, I've been meaning to thank you."

"What for?"

"For your advice about, well, about marriage."

Dan looked at Arnie. Was he to be haunted by that ill-considered remark? "I'm sorry, Arnie. Greta is pretty mad at me."

"No, you don't understand. We've come to an arrangement. It's okay." Arnie was still nattering on about the great relationship he now had with Greta. They saw each other just as much, but the pressure had been removed.

Dan was only half listening.

Is she the love of your life?

I think she could be.

Not Karen. Never Karen. Sabine.

The party was crowded with firemen and their wives and girlfriends. Kids ran around everywhere. Tons of food was set out on six-foot folding tables. Pumpkin and apple pies, all manner of casseroles. A veritable harvest feast. Dan sat at the front of the room, his bad ankle elevated on another folding chair, for all the world like some gouty monarch giving audience. He felt a little silly, but subdued. Here was his going-away party, and he still hadn't met Nagy's needs, the distribution company wasn't willing to let him out of the contract, and Maisie cried every time she saw him.

At first he thought it was Sabine standing in the open bay door, but then he realized it was Ruby. To his surprise, Chief Bean rushed over to greet her, bringing her along to meet various people. But as she got closer, it seemed as if she had been looking for him.

"Dan Smith. How are you? Oh, silly question, obviously very uncomfortable. Come along, I'll take you home."

Dan didn't question that she offered without being asked, that she knew he needed to leave. He didn't question that this sprite of a woman might know vital things about him, things her daughter would have complained to her of.

Across the brook, Dan saw Sabine's lights.

Ruby nodded. "I was sitting over there watching all the activity, and knew I had to come see it up close. What a fun party! I just love the things small towns do for their favorite sons." She held his crutches while he jockeyed himself into the bus. "You hurt on the inside, too."

"How do you know that?"

"Because I feel a lot of the time like you do right now. I'm a mover, Dan. As I'm sure Sabine has told you. I can't sit still in one place too long for fear of suffocation."

"That's exactly how I feel, Ruby. Like if I were to stay here, I would suffocate from three hundred years of habit. My grandfather actually wanted to build the theatre in Springfield. But my grandmother wouldn't hear of leaving Moose River Junction. That's a little-known secret in my family. Everyone thinks he just loved her so much, he built it here."

"Which is the same thing that kept you here."

"My grandmother?"

"In a way. Your love of her, your duty to her. A not unattractive loyalty to family tradition."

"You make it sound like I should run for my life."

"Maybe you should. Before you fall in love with a woman who will keep you here. You'll grow bitter, like your grandfather did."

"I'm not sure he was bitter."

"He was dead before you were born. Everyone tinkers with the dead to make their memory pure. Your grandmother wouldn't have been any different."

"So you give me your blessing to leave this town and your daughter?"

"You can't leave what you don't have." Ruby started

the bus. "Besides, you aren't responsible for all the decisions. Sometimes things just happen. As I've said to Sabine, you can't duck your fate."

Dan had no reply. He felt emptied of thought. Sitting next to this odd woman, he felt as though he couldn't locate the right reaction—bemusement, amusement, or denial. So he sat quietly and spoke only to direct her to his house. To Nagy's house.

Ruby swung into the narrow driveway. She shut the bus off and touched his arm. "Dan, maybe I can help you."

"How so?"

"I'm, shall we say, unencumbered right now. I can stay with Nagy. He can stay at the theatre."

"I need a theatre manager."

"I can do that. I've taken bookkeeping courses over the years. Being self-employed, I've had to."

"Why would you do this for me?"

"I'm doing it for me. I need the money, although I won't gouge you. And I can't stay with Sabine too long. It isn't healthy for either of us."

"She did tell you we'd been dating?"

"Yes, of course. Though I have another name for it."

Dan had the good grace to blush. "Did she tell you that we broke it off?"

"Of course."

"So why are you doing this for me?"

"Don't look a gift horse in the mouth."

"Ruby, you have to know that the last thing I wanted was to hurt Sabine."

"Dan. It's what people do to each other."

"You can't be serious!" Sabine didn't know whether to be mad or laugh at Ruby's bizarre declaration that she was to take up residence in Dan Smith's house and care-take his uncle and manage his theatre. "Why would you do that?"

"To help him out."

"And this is a good idea, why?"

"It's time for that man to fish or cut bait."

"You expect that he'll come running home with his tail between his legs."

"I'm not predicting his future."

"Or mine."

"Only my own. I need a job and a place to live. He's got both for me."

"Okay. Suit yourself, but don't for one minute enter-tain the notion that I'll be happy to see him fail. Or to see him back here. We're through."

"Never crossed my mind."

Sabine decided not to get annoyed with the situation. Ruby had her own life to live, and she would do as she pleased. It was a far better idea than traveling to yet another distant town to set up shop. Once Dan was gone, it would be pleasant to drop by and have a cup of coffee with her mother. To say nothing of lowering those long-distance bills by 90 percent. It was comforting to think that she, like everyone she knew around her, would have family in town. In fact, except that it was owing to Dan Smith's need, Sabine was thrilled with the arrangement.

The Atchesons were due back from New Zealand in a few days. Loozy had e-mailed a postcard to Sabine from Hawaii, where they had spent the last of their extended vacation, breaking up the long journey. She'd said that they intended to come up the first weekend in December, and how were things? She'd underscored *things,* leaving Sabine no doubt as to what Loozy was hoping she'd tell them upon their return to Moose River Junction. She would love to come home to an empty house.

What could she tell them? That she'd experienced a powerful vision, but that she'd fallen in love and become deaf to the spirits? Well, now she wasn't in love. Maybe she should go back before they arrived and give it one more try. She still wanted to do some more research on the case, too. There were a couple of other diaries in the glass case at the Historical Society; maybe Mrs. Field would let her look at those.

"Ruby, does this mean you aren't going to be around to help me with the Atchesons' house?"

"I'll have my days. Are you thinking about another visit?"

"I am. Maybe we can go over Thursday, while the turkey is cooking."

"We?"

"I need someone else to put me under. I didn't do so well by myself last time."

"You do know why."

"I know. I know. But that doesn't hold true anymore."

Ruby's lips made a little doubtful curl. "Fine. What time are you putting the bird in?"

"I thought we'd eat around three. So, with my little bird, go there at eleven?"

"Oh, did I mention I invited Arthur Bean to Thanksgiving?"

This offhand announcement threw Sabine completely. She didn't know whether to make a big deal of it or play it cool.

"Say something, Sabine." Ruby was hunting for matches. "His kids are all at their in-laws for the day.

He'd go with them, but he's volunteered to be on call that day. I didn't think you'd mind."

"Mind? That you have a friend?" Sabine found a booklet of matches in a drawer. "You go, girl."

"Stop that." Ruby took the matches and went out onto the landing. In a moment, she was back. Without a word, she opened the under-sink door and tossed the packet of cigarettes into the trash.

Fourteen

❧

When Nagy got to the theatre Dan and Ruby were there. Dan was showing her around, pointing out things a manager should pay attention to. He saw Nagy come in and waved him over. "Nagy, can you show Ruby the back room? I've got to return a phone call I should have made an hour ago."

"Sure." Nagy didn't know why he should show Ruby his office, but he guessed he'd better if Danny asked him to. "It's behind the screen."

Although Danny had told him that the Palace would stay open and he could live at home, things were still going to change, and Nagy hated change. When Mommy died, he'd hated having Dan tell him what to do. Then he got used to it. Now he wouldn't have Dan telling him what to do, but Ruby. He wondered if she would take him out to the cemetery on Sundays, too. Maybe this is what Sabine had meant when she'd told him he would be unhappy at first, then happy. Maybe Ruby would make him happy.

Every night when they said good night, Nagy told Dan that he would miss him. Every night Dan said he'd miss Nagy too, that he'd send him a sombrero from Mexico. Lying under his covers, staring at the fluorescent stars pasted to his ceiling, Nagy doubted Dan. When he went away to college, Dan had said he'd miss Nagy, but he'd come home. Then he said he couldn't because he had important stuff to do. Then he said he'd be home a lot after he moved to New York, but, until Mommy got sick, he only came once in a while. Now he said he'd be home in six months. Maybe longer. But he'd call. Calls were okay, but it wasn't the same as having Danny across the kitchen table from him, reading his papers or talking about his new girlfriend. Sabine. She was nice, but she was getting left behind, too.

"This is exciting, Nagy. I've never been in a projection booth or behind a screen before." Ruby linked her arm under his, making him suddenly feel very sophisticated. Very few women ever touched him. Just his mother and his teachers in the special class. He liked being touched. It made him feel like he wasn't any different from anyone else. Ruby's arm linked with his made him feel very special and not in the way that word was so often used in his world. Not different, or stupid, or handicapped, but cherished. Even though he knew that Ruby was younger than he, it reminded Nagy of being with his mother. Ruby liked him for himself. As they climbed the short flight of steps to the room behind the screen, Nagy decided to show her his collection.

"So, what do you do in here, Nagy?"

"I fix things. I unroll the posters for the next day, roll

up the old ones, and put them in these." He pointed out the cardboard tubes. "And I think."

"What do you think about, Nagy?"

"I think about the movies. I think about the ones I've seen."

Ruby surprised him when she didn't ask the obvious question: which was his favorite? He was always asked that question, mostly by people who didn't know what else to say to him. Instead, Ruby pointed to the poster of *Jaws*. "That's one of my favorites. That and *E.T.*"

"Those are my favorites, too. 'Elliott, phone home.'" Nagy put on a shaky extraterrestrial voice. Ruby laughed.

"Sabine was a little girl when that movie came out, maybe eight years old. She made me go see it five times."

"When you own a movie theatre, you see all the movies more than five times."

"Then I guess I'll be watching a lot of movies, now."

"You don't have to watch them all. I don't watch the ones I don't like. I sit in the office and play with my Game Boy. Can I show you something?"

"Sure."

Nagy slid open a long drawer beneath the work table. He removed a cigar box with what Ruby thought could only be reverence, like a priest and his chalice, or an archeologist with a relic. "This is my collection. I look at these a lot when I don't like a movie." Nagy handed the heavy box to Ruby.

"May I?"

Nagy nodded, his bottom lip drawn under his upper in anxious anticipation of her response.

Ruby opened the lid and looked at the cigarette lighters. There had to be a hundred of them. All types, colors, imprints, and sizes. "This is quite a collection, Nagy. What do you do with them?" Though she asked the question, she knew what he'd say.

"I only look at them." Implicit in his response, the following of orders. "Only look."

"They're very nice, Nagy. Did you find them all?"

"Most. Not this one." He held up the lighter that had belonged to his father, Frederick. Gently, he placed it in her hand.

Ruby knew immediately as she held the lighter that it had special significance, that it had featured in a deep memory of Nagy's. Impulsively, she put the lighter in Nagy's hand and then covered his hand with both of hers. She closed her eyes and let the images pass through. "This was your father's."

"Yes." Nagy's eyes lit up with surprise.

"It means a lot to you, doesn't it?"

"I have to keep it here. I can't use it."

It had been a long time since she'd gotten such a strong emanation from anyone; true psychic moments were rare now. But she was getting very strong impressions. "No one knows you have this, do they? They think it's gone."

Nagy jerked his hands away. "You can't tell them."

She wanted to touch him, to calm him down, but put her hands at her sides. "I won't."

"Mommy gave it to me."

"I know, Nagy. You didn't steal it. It belongs to you."

"I didn't do anything bad."

Ruby did come up to Nagy now, putting her arms around him. "Why would I think you'd ever done anything bad?"

"They put bad people away."

"Nagy." Ruby hugged him tight, then turned him to

look her in the eyes. "Nagy, no one is going to put you away."

His eyes brimmed with frustrated tears, frustrated by his limited capacity to express what really was on his mind. Ruby felt the frustration, sensed the underlying insecurities that Dan's departure represented to this fragile soul.

Nagy had never been left alone before. Always, there had been Beatrice. Then Dan. Ruby pulled an unused tissue out of her caftan pocket, flourishing it like a magician's scarf. She understood exactly how he felt. It was how she'd felt when Sabine had chosen to make a life on her own. Nagy wiped his eyes and handed the tissue back to Ruby.

With Arthur Bean coming to dinner, Sabine decided that her little ten-pounder was probably inadequate. Perrotti's had only eighteen- to twenty-pound turkeys, so it looked like they'd be eating a lot of bird for the next few days. Maybe she should invite someone else to dinner. A week ago it would have been the most natural thing to invite Dan and Nagy, but Sabine shuddered the thought back. No more dwelling. Though Ruby's revelations had distracted her from thinking too much about how she almost lost her heart to a man predestined to break it, her mother had reversed the good by helping him do the job.

Sabine hefted the fresh turkey into the backseat of her car. Two more errands, and she could go back to work. Lacking a roasting pan big enough for this turkey, she had called Marge Davey at South Congregational to see if she could borrow one from the church. Sabine walked across the green to fetch it now. In going to the parish hall, she chanced to look in the direction of the old burying ground and saw Dan and Nagy at the family plot.

It was a reminder of that first Sunday when Dan had gestured toward the ancient cemetery, explaining that he and Nagy tended the graves every couple of weeks. That it helped Nagy to accept Beatrice's death, knowing she was close by and that he could still talk to her. They kept the plot clear of windblown debris and would often have lunch there, as if the three of them were picnicking. What would Nagy do now, with Dan gone?

Sabine wouldn't let the thought form, wouldn't allow herself to wish it was otherwise. Theirs had been a brief fling, a good time. She wouldn't regret that it had happened, or dwell on wishing it could have been more. She'd be over it in another week.

Using one crutch, Dan walked with his other hand on Nagy's shoulder, companionable, comforting. She knew that Nagy must be feeling unhappy with Dan's decision. As she watched them walk slowly away, she spotted something on the ground, something Nagy must have dropped as they walked back to their house.

They were too far away to shout after, so she entered the burying ground through the gate bordering the church and bent to pick up the glove. She'd give it to Ruby to return to Nagy. She wandered around the fenced plot, reading the headstones, amazed that within this raised square of ground lay three centuries of Dan's ancestors. How miraculous to be able to come and touch the mementos of one's past. To know their names and their dates, the summary of their existences. The graves were laid out in a rough quadrangle, and Sabine paused before each one, the more recent graves in front of the older graves in the interior of the square.

Sabine then bent to read the most recent double gravestone. FREDERICK MICHAEL DANFORTH 1900–1954.

BEATRICE WINDSOR DANFORTH 1904–2000. Suddenly curious, Sabine turned around and looked at the oldest of the headstones, all the lettering faint, the stones flinty. ROBERT WINDSOR B. 1668 D. 1737 AGED 69 YEARS THREE MONTHS. Etched below that, MARTHA, HIS WIFE. Sabine touched the fragile gravestone and felt her legs begin to tremble. She knew without looking that the even older stone beside this one would be this Robert's grandfather. His adopted father. Although the ravages of the harsh climate had all but erased the carving, Sabine could feel the grooves with the tips of her bare fingers. The barely decipherable numerals, D. 1701. Sabine realized she had come to the end of the gravestones, and knew that nowhere in this family plot had Christopher or Sally been buried. He had been excluded from mention in virtually all records. And even his body was excluded from the family plot.

There was another granite double gravestone, and Sabine leaned closer to read it: FREDERICKA DANFORTH SMITH 1938–1973, GARY ALDEN SMITH 1935–1973. Sabine squatted to examine the dates more closely, surprised at the coincidence of the same death year. Dan would have been a little boy. She hadn't realized.

"You found Nagy's glove. Thank you." Dan's voice startled Sabine.

"Yes. Here." She stretched her arm out, still keeping her other hand on the polished headstone.

Dan's fingers touched hers as he took the glove from her hand.

"I'm going Saturday."

"I know. Good luck." Sabine couldn't quite make herself raise her eyes to his.

"Sabine, I have to do this."

"I wouldn't have it any other way." Still, she could not

bring herself to look at him, desperately afraid that she would give lie to her assurances. "It's not like we were like you and Karen had been."

"Karen?"

"Seriously involved."

"That's over, Sabine. You know that. This is business."

"Give her my best." Ah, refreshing venom. "Dan . . ."

Dan turned back to Sabine, his eyes raking over her as if he'd some need to memorize her standing there in his family plot. "Sabine?"

"How did your parents die? How is it they died in the same year, coincidence or accident?"

Dan didn't answer her at first, "No one has asked me that question in years. You see, everyone in this town knows how they died."

Sabine felt a quick regret that she'd blurted that question out. She knew that she was being rude, and that there was some part of her that wanted to exact a little hurt. She was still coming to terms with the revelations Ruby had laid on her about her own parentage, and suddenly it seemed as though Dan should come clean about his own. If she had been standing closer to him, she would have grabbed his hand and let his conflicted thoughts enter her, reveal to her the truth of his childhood. In the next instant she banished the urge and apologized. "I'm sorry, I shouldn't have said anything. Obviously something horrible happened."

Dan was standing outside the family plot with his eyes on the double headstone of his parents, as if trying to remember their faces. Finally he looked up at Sabine. "They died in a fire."

"I'm sorry . . . I shouldn't . . ." Sabine backed away from the granite marker, bumping into Robert Windsor's crumbling slate headstone.

"I was six. It was a famous fire in these parts. Big and hot and fatal." Dan rebalanced himself on the crutch.

"Dan, I'm so sorry. I had no idea." Sabine stepped forward then, but the fence around the plot separated them. She reached out to touch him over it, but he stepped away.

"I started it."

Sabine stood in horrified silence. It explained so much. The pervasive odor of wood smoke came from his memory, the essence of his deepest secret.

"I'm surprised you hadn't divined it before this. You seem to know so much more about me than anyone." Dan turned and limped away from the family plot, heading to where Nagy waited in the car. He had never, ever, said those words out loud before. He had promised his grandmother years ago that he never would.

Sabine dashed for her car, forgetting the roasting pan as she ran to get away from her own cruelty, ashamed at having provoked such an admission from Dan. She had wanted to hurt him, but had no idea what a burden he carried. It was patently obvious, in the unrehearsed way it came out, that he'd never made that admission to anyone before. His pained expression, the ragged breath that followed. Sabine pressed her forehead against the steering wheel and fought back guilty tears. How horrible to grow up with that guilty secret. How horrible that she'd made him give it up.

When Dan had held her in his arms, she had seen the colors of conflict; she had smelled the dusky scent of old smoke. The odor of memory. Like his ancestor Robert Windsor, Dan had suffered the loss of his parents by fire, and the raising up by a stern grandparent. And the suppression of secrets.

Fifteen

The Macy's Thanksgiving Day Parade was nearly to Santa Claus by the time Sabine got their turkey stuffed and in the roaster. Potatoes were peeled and sitting in water. She was cheating and had bought frozen squash and turnip. Ruby had made the pies, one apple and one squash for the three of them, and an extra squash that she'd bring over to Dan.

"For Nagy, it's his first Thanksgiving without his mother."

"Right. Fine." Sabine was still shaken from her encounter with Dan in the burying ground. "That's a nice thing to do."

Last night Ruby had picked up on her agitation immediately, and Sabine had related the sorry tale, finally feeling better when Ruby reminded her that it was like hesitating to speak of the recently departed, as if not speaking of them would make it easier on the bereaved.

"You may have brought the idea to the fore, but, believe me, he carries it around with him all the time."

Sabine nodded and wiped her eyes. "I was so mean."

"You were venting. It's understandable."

By eleven o'clock, they were ready to drive to the Atchesons' house. Sabine was not in the mood for a reading and warned Ruby that she didn't hold out much hope anything worthwhile would happen.

"I read your notes again, the ones from the diary. Very interesting. What do you make of them?"

"I think there was a terrible accident. Buried in Susannah's terse little entries are these tantalizing hints. I didn't write them all down, but she alludes to the infamous Windsor feud. Property lines, hereditary issues, and the like. All of the clues about the burning lead me to think that it was a deliberate act. Seeing Christopher and Sally, overhearing them lament their position, well, it was clear they were flying in the face of society with their love. People back then were hardly tolerant."

"So you think that someone, maybe a relative, burned down their house, with them in it?"

"What I don't know is if the arsonists knew the house was occupied. It's possible Christopher and Sally were just supposed to be scared, not murdered. They were hiding inside, probably not imagining that the mob would burn the house down with them in it."

"What do you think you'll get today?"

"You know better than to ask that. If I harbor any preconceived notions, I'll get them."

Ruby was impressed with the house. "It's like *Architectural Digest* meets Martha Stewart."

"That's what I thought. Loozy is obsessed with home decorating. You should go into the upstairs bathroom;

every magazine there is a bible of decorating suggestions."

"Where do we begin?"

"I had the most vivid experience in the den. Which I like to think of as the only real room in the house."

As Sabine led the way, Ruby oohed and aahed at the grapevine and baby's breath wreaths, the tiny framed quilt squares, and the teddy bear collection perched on stenciled shelves.

"Maybe the ghosts hate the decor. Too cute."

"Funny, Ruby."

"Oh, this is better. Move the coffee table and let's set up on the rug."

They slid the low table aside to make room for the large circle of fabric stenciled with the moon and stars. In the middle of that, Ruby set a fat white candle, then sprinkled crushed herbs around it. She handed Sabine a chain with a crystal suspended from it.

"Wear that."

"Why?"

"Can't hurt. My bankrupt landlord gave it to me before I left. A consolation prize."

Sabine and Ruby sat opposite one another, Ruby facing the east, Sabine facing the west. Ruby lit the candle, and immediately it gave off a pungent scent. "Let's do it." They joined hands.

Sabine felt the tingling in her fingertips, a slight buzzing that threaded through her veins and into her spine. Focusing on the candle flame, she let herself relax, finding it easier this time. The rolling thoughts that had kept her blocked last time seemed tempered now; having Ruby's steady hand in hers helped to keep them at bay. She did not think of Dan and his leaving. She was empty of jealousy, anger, hurt, and regret. All that entered into her mind was that she was open, ready to hear what the spirits wanted her to know.

A light rain moistened her face as she held it to the sky. Sabine opened her eyes and saw a small cluster of huts. Smoke issued from the tops, peaceful wisps of cooking fires. Women called to children, concern making their voices sharp, though Sabine could not understand their words. The children came, naked, frightened. One child stood apart, a girl old enough to wear a dress, yet young enough to be intent on her berrying and ignore the summons. Sabine blinked and the girl was gone. Her berry basket lay on the ground, the blueberries scattered.

Ruby watched Sabine carefully, judging the quality of the trance by her rapid breathing and fluttering eyes, her head swaying on her long neck. "Sabine, come back," she said sharply.

"I will." Still entranced, Sabine spoke with thick drowsiness. "I cannot come. They take me."

"Who?"

Sabine let go of Ruby's hand and pointed, her forefinger accusing someone. "Windsor."

"Are you Sarah?" Ruby gripped Sabine's hands in hers.

"That is what they call me."

"Do you want to go home?"

"I cannot."

"Why, Sarah?" Ruby felt the great sadness come through Sabine's hands into her heart.

"Because I have become too white."

Ruby shifted a little on the floor. Her derriere was becoming numb, but she dared not move too much for fear of frightening off the spirit of Sarah. She waited, watching Sabine's face to see if the trance was lessening.

Her daughter's face was dark, her closed eyes moving rapidly beneath their lids.

"I carry his child."

"Whose, Sarah?" Ruby wanted to hear her say it.

"Christopher's. They will punish us."

"Who?"

"Windsor. They mean to punish me. They will punish us."

"Sarah, did they know you were in the house?"

Suddenly Sabine's eyes opened, and she shook her head to clear away the fuzziness. "What happened?"

"She spoke through you." Even Ruby seemed shaken by the visitation. The voice coming out of Sabine's mouth bore no resemblance to Sabine's own. "A very soft, frightened voice. A girl's voice, really."

"What did she say?" Sabine placed her hands flat on the floor to keep from toppling over with the dizziness that worsened as the trance diminished.

"She's very frightened."

As with the first vision, Sabine suddenly felt overwhelming nausea and ran for the bathroom. She recovered better this time and was able to walk back to the den.

Ruby had blown out the candle and collected the cloth and herbs back into her bag. She had equally collected herself, and no longer shook with the reality of a foreign voice emanating out of her daughter. "As you've figured out by your earlier work, and your research, Sarah was a captive of someone she calls simply Windsor. She was pregnant with Christopher's child. She said that they meant to punish her, but they punished them. Thoughts?"

Sabine was lying on the couch, one foot on the floor to still the waves of vertigo. "We need to go baste the turkey."

• • •

Arthur Bean arrived with flowers and a bottle of wine. Sabine thought he looked very nice in his dark corduroy pants and obviously new plaid shirt. He'd put on a tie, which didn't quite match. Sabine took the wine and tried not to be too obvious as she watched him kiss Ruby and give her the flowers. Seeing them, even surreptitiously, gave Sabine an oddly twisted blend of satisfaction and jealousy. Maybe it wasn't too late; maybe she should call Dan and Nagy. If he'd ever speak to her again after yesterday. Squelching the notion, Sabine opened the oven door.

"We have pop-up."

With all of the food set out on the counter, there was more than enough room for the three of them at the drop leaf table set up in the middle of the living room. Arthur took over the carving duties with obvious skill, doling out perfect slices of white meat to them. Conversation rambled around from politics to sports, Arthur declining to let Sabine turn on the game while they ate.

"No, I'll catch the fourth quarter with pie."

"So how long have you been on the fire department, Arthur?" Ruby scooped another spoonful of mashed potatoes onto his plate.

"All my life. Well, let's see," Arthur toted it up on his fingers, "Nearly forty years, if you add in my years in the service. I was seventeen when I joined."

"So, you were around for the fire which killed Dan Smith's parents?" Ruby seemed nonchalant, and oblivious to Sabine's kick under the table.

"Terrible thing, that blaze. I'll never forget it. You don't get many conflagrations like that, wind-whipped and dry as tinder. Gary was, to put it kindly, not very good about the house. Things were in poor repair. Not that that would have prevented the fire. It was the piles of stuff in the basement—cans of paint, rags, papers. An absolutely textbook case of tragedy in the making."

"What started it?" Sabine couldn't stop the question.

"Kid and a lighter. Equally textbook."

"He set the fire?"

"No, no. We think he probably was in the basement trying to smoke a cigarette. He either dropped it and thought he'd stomped it out, or tossed it away and it landed in a pile of old newspapers. Could have smoldered for days."

"He was smoking?" Sabine felt a slight disbelief grow.

"Hey, kids try it all the time."

"I didn't think six-year-olds ever did."

Arthur set his fork down. "Six? Nagy was twenty-six if he was a day."

"Oh my God. Arthur," Sabine pressed her forehead into her hands, "Dan thinks he started the fire."

Arthur stood up as if hearing an alarm, then sat back down. Folding his hands together in a posture of deep prayer, he rested his forehead against his knuckles. Then Arthur raised his face to look at Ruby and Sabine. "The truth is that Beatrice Danforth always hinted that she thought Dan was responsible, but that he would be forgiven because of his age. But I knew better. She would do anything to protect that son of hers, and she fretted a lot that Nagy would get put away. It seemed the lesser harm, to let the world think it was an innocent child's action. If Nagy had been blamed, he might have actually been arrested. He was over twenty-one."

"They'd have arrested a mentally challenged man?"

"With Fredericka dead, Beatrice only had Nagy left.

And Dan. But to take Nagy away would have been cruel. I couldn't do it, so I ..." Arthur stared at his hands. "I let the myth live. But mind you, I never falsified anything. I simply reported it as children playing with a lighter."

Ruby reached out and rubbed Arthur's shoulder. "Nagy still has that lighter. He keeps it hidden in the drawer of his table behind the screen at the theatre."

Arthur looked up at Ruby and smiled a little. "Do me a favor, and take it away from him?"

"Sure."

Sabine got up and started to clear the table, her hands shaking a little. "Someone should tell Dan. Tell him before he leaves."

Ruby and Arthur just looked at her.

"No. I've done enough damage to him by getting him to reveal his secret."

"Sabine, in that case, it would be best coming from you." Ruby gently touched Sabine's cheek.

Jacob's History of Windsorville sat on the coffee table. Sabine slowly went over to it and picked up the narrow volume. "I should return this."

Maisie, wearing Gran's gift of the diamond brooch, had pulled out all the stops for Thanksgiving dinner at her house. Dan and Nagy had been sent home with more leftovers than either of them could do justice to. Besides, he was less than forty-eight hours from leaving. Thank God, Ruby was coming to stay; she'd make sure those leftovers made it out of the refrigerator before they became unidentifiable.

It had been good to be at the Ralstons'. Maisie's constant chatter and Ralph's insistence that they watch the football game in near silence helped immeasurably to keep his mind off the knot in his chest, which seemed to grow heavier each hour. There was a moment when he wondered if he was having a heart attack, it seemed so real. But he knew quite well that it wasn't.

Once home, the sleepiness that had followed dinner fell away and he decided to pack. He pulled six flannel shirts out of the laundry basket, then figured he wouldn't need those where he was going. Dan felt as if he was moving through water, as if someone else was stuffing those faithful shirts into the drawer.

He'd had this strange feeling of being separate from himself ever since his encounter with Sabine, like the weird sense of being in a dream. She'd gotten him to say out loud words no one, ever, had heard him say. Only once had he heard them spoken.

"Danny, my little one. You must not blame yourself for what happened. Always remember, it was an accident." Gran's soothing voice. Growing up, he always wondered at her love for him, that she so quickly forgave him for the fire. "We shall never speak of it again."

Most of the time he was able to keep those words and the thoughts surrounding them in check. But lately— and maybe it was all Sabine's talk of ghosts and smoke— lately he'd been unable to keep them at bay. And yesterday, whatever possessed her to push those words out of his mouth? Was she so angry with him that she'd used the very thing he couldn't forgive himself for as a weapon? It didn't seem like the Sabine he'd danced with on the Palace stage. The Sabine who'd taken him to the hospital, or the woman he'd made love to.

"I'm going to bed, Danny."

"Okay, Nagy. Sleep tight."

"Don't let the bedbugs bite." Nagy stood in Dan's bedroom doorway, no robe on in the cool house, his pajamas rumpled and too short for him. Dan felt an overwhelming protectiveness toward him, and limped over to give Nagy a hug. "I love you, Nagy."

"I know you do." Nagy pulled away and went off to bed.

Dan was still standing there, stuck in some unreasoning state of suspended animation. He couldn't make himself continue to pack; he couldn't seem to make himself move. He heard the back storm door open on its squeaky hinges, followed by a rapid knock. It was enough to restart him, and he hobbled downstairs to answer the door.

"Sabine? What are you doing here?"

She held out *Jacob's History of Windsorville*. "I needed to return this."

"No, you don't have to. I meant you to keep it."

"Dan, I have to talk to you." Sabine stood at the bottom of the steps, looking up at him with her Egyptian brown eyes. They glittered in the porch light.

He hoped that his expression didn't betray his confusion. "Come in." He held the storm door open, reflexively breathing in her scent as she passed in front of him.

Inside, Sabine set the volume down on the cluttered kitchen table. She turned to face him, her gloved hands clasped tightly together. "Dan, I am so sorry for what I said to you in the graveyard. I had no idea."

"There was no reason you should. It's all right." How far from the truth could he go before she caught him at it?

"The thing is—and you have to believe me—you didn't cause the fire. It wasn't your fault."

Dan felt the constriction in his chest renew itself. "You can't know that." Fighting the urge to pick up the leather-bound volume and pitch it against the wall, he allowed only his voice to betray his anger. "Is this some example of your clairvoyance? Some fortune teller's misguided attempt to make me feel better?"

Sabine shook her head. "No, not at all. It's . . ."

"So first you make me reveal my deepest secret, and now you're telling me that the central truth of my life is a lie?"

"Yes. No. It's not true. Arthur Bean told us the story."

The sense that he'd been pushing himself through water suddenly became drowning. The knot in his heart constricted and for a moment he thought he would be sick. "No. Why would my grandmother tell me it was my fault, when it wasn't?" He had to grip the back of a kitchen chair to prevent himself from swaying.

"Because of Nagy."

"Nagy?"

"Yes, to protect him." Sabine was weeping to see Dan's horrified face. Weeping to know that her well-intentioned words had hurt him so much. "Nagy was smoking. He dropped a cigarette into papers or rags in the basement. That's why you don't remember it. You weren't there."

"Please get out of my house."

"I thought you should know. This thing you've been carrying around all these years is . . ." Sabine hunted for the right words, afraid of the look on his face, ". . . is misplaced guilt."

"Out."

On the shelf in the closet in his grandmother's bedroom, Dan found the old Schrafft's tin stuffed with clippings. He took it down and placed it on the bed. He seldom came into this room. In the soft lamplight, it looked a little dusty, and there was a cobweb dangling above the bed. He reached up and brushed it away, then sat on the bed and began to read.

Six times, the story ran: three articles in the *Pennywise Paper,* and one in each of the Boston, Springfield, and Hartford papers. The heroic efforts of the local fire department were lauded, the loss of life lamented. "The fire has been ruled accidental." A sidebar about not keeping rags and old papers in basements was clipped, as well. The truth of Sabine's story did not reside in these clippings.

Dan stuffed the articles with their black-and-white photos of the burning house back into the box and, heedless of the pain in his ankle, headed downstairs. There was only one place he might find the truth. He jammed the Ford into reverse and tore out of the driveway, his mind on the locked file cabinets at the old firehouse. He wouldn't let himself think what it would mean to find out whatever truth he was meant to know.

Once at the firehouse, Dan fumbled a little with the keys, and he breathed deeply to calm himself. Inside, he went into the back room where the records prior to the new firehouse were kept. Years 1902 through 1990. The yellowed cardboard in the metal slot reading 1965–1975 was in the middle of the line of file cabinets. Dan grabbed a fire ax and drove it against the edge of the cabinet. The little metal lock popped under his blow, and Dan dropped the ax. For a moment he hesitated, then opened the drawer.

Never had his hands shaken like this, not even when crawling through a burning house, knocking down the doors to see if anyone was within. Not when faced with removing a decapitated victim from a car crash. Not even when grieving.

The report was held in the file folder by a two-prong

metal clasp, otherwise the papers would have spilled out onto the floor of the firehouse. Dan studied the dry words through a blur, as if his eyes could not focus. At last he sat on the floor, closed the file, and let the tears come.

Arthur Bean stood on the landing, his elbows leaning on the rail. Beside him, Ruby Heartwood rested her cheek against his arm. "He's over there."

"Are you going to stop him?"

"No. I feel bad enough about being a part of this in the first place. I should never have let Beatrice talk me into it. It was a breach of public trust."

"Arthur, don't blame yourself. The will of a mother to protect her child is the most powerful instinct of all. I've been doing it all my life."

Arthur felt Ruby's arm go around his waist and he turned into her arms.

After a moment he asked, "So, where's Sabine?"

"She'll go to the Atchesons' tonight. There's unfinished business there."

"So . . ."

Ruby led Arthur back into the apartment.

Sixteen

❧

The key to the Atchesons' Lower Ridge Road house was still in her bag. Real ghosts seemed more comfortable than the haunting memory of Dan's face. She'd made a hash out of helping him. She was an idiot for letting Ruby talk her into telling him without thinking out the consequences. Of course it hurt him to think his grandmother, whom he adored, had used him so cruelly. At least here, she might put something to rest, rectify someone else's wrong.

The one question that remained was whether Christopher and Sally's deaths were deliberate. Or had the villagers made a terrible mistake, one they had covered up with the fiction of a defense?

The den had been the locus of her most vivid sightings. Eschewing any props, Sabine went into the small, cozy room and sat on the couch. "I'm here," she called out loud to the still house. "Come talk to me."

Sabine knew she sounded a little hysterical, but then,

wasn't that what paranormal experiences were thought to be? Manifestations of hysteria? Well, she was nearly there. With everything in her own life in disarray, the unhappy ghosts would make good company. Except that, in her agitation, they would not come. As silent as death, the house remained still, undisturbed except by her own quiet weeping. Ultimately exhaustion overruled, and she drifted off to sleep.

Sabine woke suddenly with a powerful thirst. She pulled herself off the couch where her intended trance had become nightmarish sleep. Not bothering to find a light, she went into the kitchen for a glass of juice to quench the dryness in her mouth.

She found her way to the pantry. In the dark her sense of smell was more acute, and the small room seemed very pungent with the smell of food and wood, an earthy smell like apples close to bad. The pantry was very cool. Sabine fumbled for the refrigerator door, but her hand only touched wood. Knobs stuck out here and there, and shelves with rough surfaces, like burlap.

"Hide in here."

"Why are they doing this to us?"

"Don't fear; you are my wife. Your child is mine."

"Don't let them hurt him."

"Put him under the floorboards. He'll be safe."

"Don't let them hurt my baby."

"Darling Sally, I won't let them hurt any of us."

"They come."

"My God, my God, they've set the house alight! Do they not know we're within?"

The smoke filled Sabine's nostrils, stinging her eyes. A relentless and panicked pounding echoed in the small windowless space, Christopher hammering uselessly against the barricaded door. There was silence as the smoke suffocated them. Sabine screamed. The smoke blinded her and she waved her hands to move it aside. Outside, angry voices called for justice. *"Punish them."* Didn't they know there was a child in here? Sabine coughed and stumbled against the wooden shelves, struggling to find her way out. With every move, she felt the heat of the flames against the wall. She heard the squalling baby. Other voices. *"What have you done? What have you done? You've killed Windsor's son."*

Commotion all around as voices in the night cried out for the doomed pair. Then, the muttered words, hissed in collusion: *"We must pledge this act to secrecy. We will say we came upon the scene. Say naught else."*

Sabine raised her hands. "I will tell the world what you've done!" She banged her open palms against the rough boards. "Your lies are exposed."

Suddenly rough arms lifted her away. She struggled, afraid that the same forces that had driven the ghosts of Sally and Christopher into the buttery were clutching at her. She kicked and squirmed, but the arms were strong and lifted her away.

"Sabine, it's me. It's Dan." Dan's hands were on her arms, gently pulling her back to the modern kitchen. "It's okay; nothing is going to harm you. There's no fire. Come back, Sabine." His voice sounded like Christopher's, his anxiety pitching it the same. The other voices, the panicked, horrified lamentations, the horrific calls for justice, began to recede, until only a muttering was discernible to Sabine.

As she woke from the trance to reality, Sabine felt as if she were being held by Christopher's ghost, that she could smell the smoke of the fire that had killed him. Shuddering with the last of the spell, Sabine knew that the arms that held her were Dan's, the calming words his, the very timbre of them stretching like a bridge between the two realms to bring her back into his world.

The spell dropped away and Sabine opened her eyes in the brightly lit kitchen, Dan Smith's arms wrapped around her. They stood for a long time, not speaking, just holding each other, taking comfort in the close human contact.

The horror of what had gone on three centuries before began to fall away from Sabine. The fact of Dan's arms surrounding her moved to the forefront of her consciousness.

"It was a horrible accident. They burned the house without knowing Christopher and Sally were in it. They covered it up by lying about the defense. The whole story is a lie."

"It would seem as though history has repeated itself in me. Fires, cover-ups, and lies. My whole life is a lie."

Sabine wanted to respond but felt herself swoon, powerless to stop herself. As if she weighed nothing, Dan lifted her up and brought her into the den, laying her down on the couch. He sat beside her, chafing her hand as if to bring it to life.

Her focus slowly returned and she felt her hand in his. She left it there. "Why are you here?" Sabine hated that her voice was shaky.

"To apologize."

"For what? I'm the one who . . ." Sabine was suddenly gripped with the usual nausea from her trance, and she pulled away from him and ran to the bathroom. He waited outside the door. When she came out, a damp washcloth to her mouth, he handed her her jacket.

"You need some air."

The night was cold, the stars brilliant, and for one

moment she remembered that night a bare month back when she'd stood in her own backyard and felt happy at the life she was leading. Now, she'd had her heart broken and her mind disturbed with this haunted place; she had the awful answers to her lifelong questions. None of it felt like happiness.

"Sabine." Dan paused, and in the darkness she couldn't tell if he was trying to compose himself or waiting for her to say something. "I read the clippings. Then I broke into the firehouse files and read the original report." When he paused again, she was certain it was to compose himself. "You were right. My grandmother did let everyone think I was responsible for the fire so that no one would blame Nagy. Certainly she convinced Arthur it was preferable. It would have meant that Nagy would have been institutionalized. She fought her whole life to prevent that."

Sabine reached out to touch him. "Oh, Dan." Her fingers found his face and she cupped it. "Didn't she see what guilt that placed on you?"

"Nagy was her son." Dan took the hand that touched his face, and held it. "I understand why it was better for her to place the blame on me. No one would have put me away. But you see, it really doesn't make any difference. I wouldn't love either of them any less for having known the truth."

Sabine pulled her hand from Dan's. It was no good to let herself feel gentle about this man. His power lay in making her care about him.

"Sabine, Ruby told me you were here."

"Why were you looking for me?"

"I've come to ask if you'll go with me."

Sabine stepped back, her hand covering her mouth in surprise. Dawn was beginning to lighten the sky, and she could see the outlines of trees and the heavier weight of the hillside behind the house. A solitary crow cawed and flew out from a pine. In the vague light, Dan looked no more substantial than Christopher or Sally had in the buttery of her mind's eye.

"Why? Why ask me now, Dan?" Sabine shook off the sense that he was a ghost haunting her present.

"Because I know that nothing makes sense in my life anymore except that I love you."

Sabine closed her eyes, suddenly afraid that she was still entranced and that none of this was happening. "And so you want me to go with you?"

"Yes."

Images of impermanence flashed through her mind. The years of moving from place to place, the friendlessness. This was her safe harbor after all those years. This was where she wanted to be, and this man wanted her to let go of the ropes and sail back into the unknown.

"I can't." The words wrenched themselves out of her mouth as if spoken by another. "I can't leave my home. I've only just found it." Sabine ran into the house, leaving Dan behind.

Inside, leaning her full weight against the door as if Dan would break it down to get her, Sabine felt the same tingling exhaustion as she felt after witnessing the ghosts in their extremity of fear. It was as if his ghosts and hers and the ghosts of the forgotten pair stood outside, corralling Dan and Sabine in with their knowledge of the past and the unknown future. All around, Gypsies danced in the firelight and lovers perished in it. As she had allowed herself to be held by Dan, she had seen the colors of his past, augmented by the images she had witnessed. Fire and fear, love and violence. Terror.

Dan had been terrified as a child, a terror that had

etched itself onto his heart like a permanent scar. To believe himself guilty of the death of his parents, a second deep scar. To understand now that Nagy had been responsible and that his grandmother had allowed such a fiction to live, laid a third one on his heart.

Sabine covered her own heart with the flat of her hand. Her own scars were there, created by the constant uprootedness. Scars scratched on her heart by the rough fabric of her mother's fears. Under her palm, Sabine felt a new scar being made. This one would be deep and would take a long time to heal.

Its heat against her hand, her bumptious heart spoke the truth. *If you loved him, you would go with him. Might he not be your home?*

Seventeen

‎࿂

December 2000

Sabine met with Loozy and Drake at the house on
Lower Ridge Road. The past week had been like being
ill.

The rift with Dan, coupled with witnessing the final
chapter in Sarah and Christopher's tragedy, had physically weakened her. It hadn't helped that Ruby was now
living with Nagy, and finding a new life with Arthur
Bean. Sabine dreamed that she was alone on a promon-
tory, like Indian Maiden Rock, with nothing above or
below her.

"Here's what I know." Sabine sat with the Atchesons
at their kitchen table. "My research has been helpful, and
I have been here four times to see if I could put the clues
together."

Drake, in his classic pose of skepticism, motioned for
her to continue.

"I believe that Christopher Windsor had an illicit but
loving relationship with a girl who was a captive Indian.

They called her Sarah, and he called her Sally as an affectionate nickname."

"Keep going."

"Sally was a slave, for all intents and purposes, so the son of one of the wealthiest and most influential men in the settlement would not be allowed to marry her. Nonetheless, they set up housekeeping, angering the family and the neighbors. These were unenlightened times."

"And . . ."

"I believe that the villagers only meant to scare Christopher into coming to his senses. They thought that if they burned down their house, that would be message enough. They didn't know that Sally, Christopher, and their infant were inside the building. When it came to light that the adults had perished, the child surviving only because his mother had put him in the root cellar, they covered it up. Hence, the so-called defense of Windsorville. They blamed the tribe Sally had been stolen from."

"And how do you know all of this?"

Sabine smiled. "Three-parts research. The story is well documented outside of Moose River Junction's Historical Society. I took a day off last week and went to the state archives."

"And the fourth part?"

"They told me."

Loozy wiped at her eyes. "That's so sad. And it all happened here?"

"Yes. This land was in Windsor hands, undisturbed for three hundred years. There is a cellar hole out back, behind your stone wall. It's more than likely that was the site."

"What do we do about it?"

"I don't know." Sabine felt so tired, a weariness that leadened her whole body. Was she turning into stone? Her feelings were so blunted, she could barely hear Loozy's plaint.

"Is there really nothing we can do?"

"Try finding their graves. I've checked and they're not in any of the consecrated graveyards within the town. But there are half a dozen private burying grounds in the area. You could start there."

"And what will that do?"

"Remind them that they're dead."

Loozy's fair skin paled further. Sabine felt sorry for her brusqueness and leaned in to hug Loozy. "It'll be fine. Just acknowledge them; that they lived, loved, and died."

Loozy returned Sabine's hug. "Imagine loving someone so much you'd do anything to be with them."

Sabine felt her face tense with the need to fight back tears, and was glad that in hugging her, Loozy faced away from the raw pain Sabine knew she couldn't hide.

Drake Atcheson was not satisfied with her story, but he handed her a nice check for all her work.

On her way out to the car, Sabine was stopped by Loozy. Hugging herself against the cold air, Loozy called out, "Wait, Sabine. I want to thank you. You've really helped me. Just knowing that I'm not crazy is comforting."

"No, I think now Drake thinks I'm the crazy one." Sabine stood quietly for a moment. "What will you do now?"

"I think we have no choice. We'll sell the house. Maybe we can find a Windsor descendant to buy it."

"That's really too bad." Sabine looked out toward the hills behind the house. "It won't solve anything for

Christopher and Sally. They will continue to relive their tragedy until something releases them."

"Like finding their graves?"

"I think so." Sabine pulled open her car door. "They need some sort of consecration."

"A blessing?"

"Loozy, I have no idea. I'm just the messenger. They spoke through me, but they only told me what was happening, not how to release them from it." Sabine suddenly remembered that she still had Loozy's house key. She rooted around in her bag for it.

"Sabine, keep the key. It'll be a while before anyone wants this place, so feel free to visit it if you want."

"I don't think I can." But it wasn't the ghosts that would keep her away. It was the haunting memory of the last time she saw Dan.

Eighteen

&

May 2001

Sabine stuffed her hands into the pockets of her shorts. As often happened this time of year, the valley was enjoying a false blast of summer. Even before she'd began climbing uphill, she was perspiring. The house below was still for sale. A lonesome real estate sign waggled in the breeze, creaking a little on unoiled hinges. The economic downturn had kept the Atchesons in possession, if not in residence. Sabine hadn't been on the property since December, but the warmth and sunshine of this perfect May afternoon had given her an impulsive desire to go for a hike, and the trail above the Lower Ridge Road property had come to mind.

She hadn't been up this obscure path since she and Dan had climbed it on that brilliant fall day, when the air was chilled and they discovered the cellar hole. How close they had felt, she remembered; the warmth of his nearness on that cool day. She hated those unbidden memories, hated herself for letting them run their course without suppression.

The path seemed far steeper than in the fall, and far lonelier. As she came near the top of the hill, the spring-thickened underbrush cleared out and the tall silver birch and pine stood prominent. To make this place immune to her own ghosts, Sabine deliberately moved to the rock where Dan had pointed out landmarks far below. What had he called it? Indian Maiden Rock? A hawk worked the sky above her in a languid spiral. Sabine stood on the boulder they had stood on and listened, as Dan had instructed, to the sound of silence. Silence bounded them now. They had not breached that silence since Thanksgiving night, each afraid that to break it would imply capitulation to the other's desires. She would not go; he would not stay.

"I will get over him," Sabine said to herself, recognizing that, of all the people in the world, she would be happiest to see him come into a room. She bullied herself, believing that she should not feel that way and daily she tried to wither the desire and the affection she felt into a dry, tolerable future friendship. But she dared not speak to him yet; she hadn't quite gotten to that point. She dared not speak of him, either, and pushed Ruby's concern away with abrupt refusals to detail what had happened.

What was hardest was that she knew he loved her. If he hadn't voiced it, if it had remained only a potentiality, she could have easily transformed this limbo of feeling into something passionless and ordinary. No, what was hardest was that she loved him. The past months had not diminished her heavy sense of having made a bad decision, but only increased it with each moving hour. The happiness she had enjoyed before meeting Danforth

Smith seemed empty and simplistic. The unhappiness of being settled in this place without him mocked the whole reason she had rooted herself in Moose River Junction. She had her place, but no heart to keep in it.

Sabine stood on the boulder and looked down on the town. The clouds scudded quickly overhead and for a moment she felt as if she were moving, a slight vertigo grabbing at her feet. She sat to recover her equilibrium, but the truth would not be vanquished. *My God, I've chosen a place over a person.* She had mistaken security for happiness.

Tears endangered Sabine as she scrambled down the side of the rock. She found the path and began to run.

It might not be too late.

Ruby would have his number.

She'd call and . . . and what?

Breathing heavily, she slowed down and began the arduous task of rejecting her burgeoning desire to hear his voice, to compromise herself. She walked the rest of the way down the path.

The low stone wall, lichen-covered and pearly green in the warm May sunshine, beckoned to her. Sabine went over and sat on the side where the depression may have been a foundation. It was cool there under the shade of the trees. Here, as above, it was preternaturally quiet. No birds sang, not even the noisy crows, which had kept the woods animated throughout her walk. She closed her eyes and let the coolness refresh her. A drifting scent of wood smoke tickled her nose, and she opened her eyes.

Dan Smith walked toward her. So deep in unbidden trance, so immediate in her thoughts, Sabine was unsure if he was real or conjured.

Then he spoke and the spell dropped from her. "Sabine."

"Why are you here?"

"Ruby told me you were here today."

"I mean, why aren't you in Mexico?"

"Ruby is terribly worried about you. She called me."

"And you came?"

"And I came."

"Dan, can you ever forgive me?" Sabine felt warm tears roll down her chilled cheeks. "I've complicated your life so much."

"What good is a life not complicated?"

"I couldn't live with myself if I thought you were here to give up your dream."

His hand grasped hers and pulled her gently off the ground. His arms around her melted the cold stiffness from her, his lips on hers fired the icy lump of her heart. "I'm here to ask you once again, will you go back with me?"

Sabine's face lay against his chest. She was shivering and she didn't know if it was from the breeze on her damp skin, or fear. She knew that he'd never ask her again. She knew that what he was suggesting was not the same as Ruby announcing a sudden move to an unknown place. He wasn't asking her to compromise her permanence, only to compromise her stubbornness.

Dan led her out of the cellar hole, into the lee of the wall. He echoed her thoughts. "It's just a trip, Sabine, not a permanent move. The filming is almost done; we're only reshooting some scenery. The actors are gone. You and I would be home, home in Moose River Junction, in a couple of weeks." He kissed her forehead. "I'm not asking you to give up your home here." He raised her chin with his forefinger. "I'll never ask that of you. I'm just asking that you be with me somewhere else for a little while."

Sabine felt herself forsake her prideful anger. His tongue and hands, his very scent, and the touch of his fine hair against her cheek blasted her reserve, and she met his passion with passion equal. "Yes."

The rocks formed a perfect screen and the soft, mossy ground outside of the wall a perfect couch. Wordless, savoring their desire by slowing it down, Sabine and Dan made love. Lightly dressed in the spring warmth, it was easy to suddenly be naked, and they reached for each other, their bodies remembering the passionate choreography of earlier days. Wood smoke permeated the air; voices all around hummed in wordless approbation. Sabine felt the power of her human passion augmented by the desires of long-dead lovers. She knew then that their couch was a grave, and that their love-making not their own, but belonging to Sally and Christopher. At the moment of climax, their physical release, powerful and intense, became metaphysical, pouring out of their linked bodies and into the ether.

The ghosts were finally put to rest.

Epilogue
❧

July 2002

South Congregational Church was rapidly filling up. Sabine Heartwood stood at the back of the church and smoothed the folds of her watered silk dress. Her palms felt a little moist, her mouth dry with nervousness.

The sunlight played along the walls of the church, smooth yellow light glowing against the pearl gray walls. The candles were lit, two eight-taper brass floor candelabra sending a slightly smoky scent into the air. Sabine took a deep breath and let it out. Today she could detect no ghostly faces streaming across the smooth walls. All the ghosts were gone, their corporeal remains now laying in the consecrated earth of the old burying ground outside these church walls, where their descendants rested. The plaque on the town green commemorating the "Defense of Windsorville" had mysteriously disappeared shortly afterward.

From her vantage point, she could pick out the heads of all those people she knew. Moe and his wife, Balto and Teddy. Maisie and Ralph sat close to the front; Maisie had on a vintage blue pillbox hat. Arnie and Greta. And Greta's new boyfriend, whom she'd met at Greenfield Community College.

It was such a rare thing to get Ruby into a church. Only the most solemn of occasions could induce her. But there she was in the front row, her natural silver-streaked hair shining in the sunlight, slender and beautiful in a new teal green suit. She looked, even from the back, young and contented; happy, perhaps for the first time perfectly at home in her surroundings.

Things suddenly took on speed. The prelude now over, the organ began the first chords of Pachelbel's Canon. Then Arthur Bean was beside her, gently offering his arm. Lynn Miller was slowly moving ahead of her, to lead her to the others at the rail. Even from the distance of the long aisle, she could see Nagy's happy grin. Sabine took Arthur's arm and moved forward.

There, waiting for her, was Danforth Windsor Smith. Her lover, her friend, her groom.

Her home.

ATRIA BOOKS
PROUDLY PRESENTS

SUMMER HARBOR

SUSAN WILSON

Available in hardcover August 2003
from Atria Books

Turn the page for a preview of
Summer Harbor. . . .

Chapter One

At the foot of the porch steps, the metal FOR SALE sign clattered in the breeze off the water. A discreet sign, with letters overarching a stylized lighthouse, all done in blue and white, advertising the local agency that handled important real estate: "Seacoast Properties, Ltd."

"Limited to what?" Will asked.

"Limited to the wealthy."

"Like Pop and Nana?"

"Only in the old days of yacht club cotillions and madras shorts. Today's wealthy, the ones who survived the downturn, they put Pop's money in the chump-change category."

"Chump enough to send me to Cornell."

"This house is sending you to Cornell." Kiley immediately regretted her sharpness. She hadn't meant to snap at him, but the impact of seeing the house, so eerily unchanged from her memory of it, was like grit against polished wood.

Kiley bent over to snag a drifting piece of paper from where it had become tangled in a rosa rugosa bush. Nowadays, the owners of these shingle-style summer-houses had landscape architects swarming over the small yards to install "native" plantings and cottage gardens. Her father had stuck in a hedge of old-fashioned privet, a couple of spiky yuccas, a scattering of lace-cap hydrangeas, rosa rugosa bordering the cement path to the front door, and let the yellowish grass do as it pleased. "This is a summer place, if I wanted a fussy garden, I'd stay home in Southton," he'd said. It would probably be a selling point—not much to tear up, and the rosa rugosas were native.

It was frustrating, how every little action prompted a memory. A piece of litter extracted the echo of an off-hand remark from her father. Even the key in her hand prompted a vivid memory of it hanging on the hook by the back door, the seashell key chain exactly as memory served. In her eighteen-year moratorium from Hawke's Cove, the house had remained inviolate in her thoughts, pristine and untouchable, and today verified her chosen memories.

Kiley had never forbidden herself memory. Some-times, in the early morning hours when the infant Will suckled on her breast, refusing to go back to sleep, or when a Don Henley song would come on the radio, which so clearly brought back the feel of sand beneath her feet, Kiley relished the companionship of her two best friends, even if they were only embodied in selec-tive memory.

It was out of a great need to keep this place and the good memories in the vault of sanctity, that she had refused ever to come back. Nothing remains the same once reality has overridden the imaginary. How could she keep separate the cherished youth of summers in Hawke's Cove, with the tragic end to those days, if she were to actually set foot where it had all happened?

It had come as a mild shock that her parents wanted to sell the Hawke's Cove house. Her grandfather had purchased it for a song in 1933, and it had been the sum-mer focal point of the Harris family ever since. Kiley had paid little heed to her parents' frequent conversations about the place's disposition; she always assumed that, ultimately, it would come to her. The idea of actually sell-ing it out of the family hurt her in a place she had long kept apart from her adult self. Intellectually, Kiley knew that the place was beyond her parents, as her mother lost skirmish after skirmish with brittle bones and her father struggled for air against the emphysema slowly choking him. Childishly, she had pushed forward the hope that her parents would neglect to really do anything at all about the house, and that at some magical and ill-defined point, she would find herself suddenly able to go back to it.

When her parents abruptly announced that they had decided that the house would be sold, and the proceeds would fund Will's education, the irony was not lost on Kiley. By his very existence, Will had cost her Hawke's Cove. Now Hawke's Cove would pay for his absence. Before her parents' offer to pay for Cornell, Kiley had expected that Will would stay closer to home and go to a state college where she could afford his tuition. The sheer distance between Southton, Massachusetts and Cornell in New York State made Kiley weak with knowing she'd see her son only rarely once he left for school in the fall. Unbearably proud that he had been accepted at Cornell, and unbearably sad about letting him go, Kiley covered her maternal angst with busyness. She focused on the minutia of preparing for college, and pushed away the distant day in September when he would leave her behind. Maybe it was easier for parents with spouses and other children. But Will, he was her world.

Now her parents had said they wanted her to go and inventory the place, ready it for sale, as if they could order her to break her moratorium against being in Hawke's Cove with the task.

"Mother, why don't you just have the agency hire someone to pack it up, or, better yet, just sell it with the contents?"

"Kiley, I will not have strangers stealing from me."

Lydia Bowman Harris, now in her seventies, was obsessive about theft. Their Southton home had all kinds of burglar deterrents, which on average were accidentally set off once a week by her father's slowness in getting the right buttons disarmed. It was kind of a family joke.

"I can't just up and take off for Hawke's Cove. I don't know when I can get free, and certainly not for long enough to get the job done."

"You have vacation time."

"Yes, and I was planning on going to Cameo Lake with Will. It's our last—"

Her father stood up, then took a moment to pull in sufficient breath to add weight to his words. "Kiley, we buried the past, got on with our lives. There's nothing there which is going to change anything, or revive anything, or matter much any more. We need you to do this for us. We don't ask much of you, but this, we're asking." Merriwell Harris walked with slow dignity out of the parlor.

"Don't mind him, Kiley." Lydia Harris waved a still-elegant hand in the air in dismissal of her husband's remarks. "He's not happy about having to give up the place. It was in his family for seventy years."

"Then don't."

"Why should we hang on to the place when there's no one to use it? You won't go."

"Mother, you know the memories would choke me."

"Kiley Anne Harris, for eighteen years you've done well, made a good life for you and the boy. I know we were uncompromising in the beginning, but what's done is done. I don't think that any of us would wish things had been different." Meaning that Will had not been born.

"No. Of course not. But I can only keep focused on the good things if I can keep the past out of sight."

"It was your own doing. Until you face that, you'll never grow up."

Lydia's sharpness only set Kiley's back up. No, she would *not* cross that little bridge over the wetlands that separated Hawke's Cove from Great Harbor. In some ways, she was the opposite of that old guy who took tickets at the theatre when she and the boys were kids. Joe Green, it was said, could not leave Hawke's Cove, even to bring home his own boy's body for burial. They said it had cost him his wife.

She, on the other hand, couldn't return. As long as Kiley remained on this side of the bridge, she could choose idealized memories that were harmless.

At night, sometimes, she would wake from dreams of water. Complicated dreams that left her sad. For a short while Kiley had gone to a counselor, a recommendation from a nursing school classmate. All the counselor could tell her was that she needed to get a hobby; she was too concerned with serious matters. She hadn't told him anything of the past, only of her present: school, working full time, raising a toddler single-handedly. The rift with her parents over Will's existence.

"You need a break, Kiley. Find some time for yourself. Go to the shore."

Kiley stopped seeing him after that.

The dreams were cyclical and her journal noted that they most often appeared when not she, but Will, faced a life change. When he was being toilet trained, or trying out for youth soccer; when she went out with someone for more than two consecutive dates. Even as he entered high school. Periods when she worried more about him. About how she was raising him.

In her dreams Kiley never saw Mack or Grainger, but the constant of water in these dreams always woke in her the sensation that she'd been with them. Hawke's Cove, a place surrounded on three sides by the sea, providing years of summers together on the beach and in the water.

The sailboat that they lovingly made seaworthy. And, of course, the insoluble association of water and the way things had ended between them.

Kiley could imagine no circumstance that would induce her to abandon her eighteen-year prohibition against going back to Hawke's Cove. It was her self-punishment. She would forever deny herself the thing she most wanted in the belief that she deserved no less.

And that belief had held up, until Will and two of his pals got caught with marijuana.

The second most dreaded phone call in a parent's life: "Come down to the station." Kiley felt detached, as if she did this every day of her life. She brushed her teeth and combed her hair, pulled on a clean sweatshirt over her pajama top and sweatpants over the bottoms. Normally she'd never go out in such an outfit, but this seemed all right under these circumstances. No one would know her. She found her car keys and remembered to set the house alarm. She drove slowly the few miles to the police station, the radio off, as if music would be inappropriate. All the way there, she spoke aloud to herself. "At least he's not dead." If anyone had asked, she would have been unable to pinpoint her emotions. Part relief it wasn't worse, part anger. Certainly the shame would emerge, the hunt for a one-line acknowledgment of parental mortification to hand to those people who studied the police blotter and would casually ask about the situation, masking their curiosity with concern. It was almost like déjà vu. So clearly, Kiley remembered the raised eyebrows as she appeared in the market with her blooming belly. The "how are you feeling dear" code for "what a shame, the Harris girl knocked up, and no father."

As the parent of a teenage boy in a moderately well-to-do town, there was a certain expectation that this might happen. Perhaps this was an initiation rite. "Come join those of us whose children have destroyed our credibility. You bring the coffee and we can share our disappointments." A twelve-step program for failed parents. Hadn't she played with him, taken him sledding and to minature golf? Hadn't she made him sit at the table to do his homework, even when he'd preferred to do it slouched across his bed? Hadn't she made him dinner every single night of his life? But she had left him in the care of babysitters while she pursued her certification as a physician's assistant. She had declined membership in the PTA because she didn't have time in the evening to go to meetings that weren't part of her education. Suddenly Kiley couldn't remember laughing with him.

The parking lot was empty of civilian cars, the station house door wide open in the late June night. Kiley rested her forehead on the steering wheel, her thoughts swirling. She took a deep breath and drew on her professional reserve.

That Will was exceedingly lucky not to have had the stuff on his person, and that the arresting officer had chosen to charge only one of the three boys, was almost no consolation. Will's action, whether the first and only time as he claimed, or one of many never discovered, meant that somewhere, somehow, she'd deluded herself into thinking she'd successfully raised this boy by herself. That all the long talks they'd had, all the rules she'd imposed, were laughable. In one night, he had proved that she was not the paragon of single motherhood she had occasionally thought herself, now that he was about to be launched into independent adulthood.

What had seemed, nineteen years ago, to be the hardest decision she would ever face in her life, had paled in comparison to the daily diet of hard decisions that rearing this boy had fostered. Even now, those interminable nights of wakeful debate while lying in her dorm room bed, could startle her with a clarity of memory. As if those circling thoughts had been physical, as physical as Will's first kick in utero or the labor pains of his birth. Those pains she had forgotten: not so the pangs of struggling to tell her parents she was, at eighteen and almost through her first semester of Smith College, pregnant. She deliberately told them after the sixteen week mark; deliberately and resolutely never told them who had fathered the child.

The drive home from the police station, deep into the predawn darkness, theirs the only car on the winding country route, was in a silence so extraordinary Kiley felt as if she could touch it. Will stared out the passenger window. His form filled the small space with coltish length, accentuated by the baggy jeans. There was so much Kiley wanted to say: you could lose your place at Cornell, you are risking your life, what in God's name were you thinking? But she kept silent, afraid that she would be unable to stop once she got started, and the last thing she wanted was to become the shrieking banshee of his expectations. Often enough he'd accused her of "screaming" at him when she had reprimanded him in a deliberately level voice. This time the potential for her voice to rise into a penetrating howl was so strong she would not let herself even speak. She simply told Will to go to bed; they'd talk in the morning.

A trace of gray appeared beneath the edge of her shade. Kiley watched the darkness with open eyes, unable to sleep. In that first notion of dawn, her bedroom door opened and Will stepped in.

"Are you awake, Mom?"

She heard his snuffling and sat up. At once her big, bright and independent boy was in her arms, crying out his shame and regret and pleading for her forgiveness. She rocked him, resting his head on her shoulder, wondering how he could feel so much like the little boy who once cried with the same heartsick intensity when he'd broken her favorite antique vase.

The last few months had been a tug of war between them as never before. His natural demand for independence and her equally natural desire to remain part of his life had warred mightily. Was she powerless to keep him from repeating his mistake? Despite his tears and apology, how could she really trust him not to do the same thing if peer pressure and opportunity offered?

Kiley was shocked at how damaged her trust in him was. In her predawn imagination she saw him selling his blood to support his habit, then closed her eyes against the lurid image. It was only pot, and only once—or so he said. The fact she doubted him pained her, and Kiley knew that this loss of trust between them might only be healed by separating Will from the source of his temptation, in particular, those friends of his. They weren't kids she'd known since Will had been in grade school. These were kids from one of the other towns that made up the regional school district. She barely knew their names, much less who their parents were or how much supervision they got.

What Will needed was a safe place. They both needed an interim resting place where they could mend this rent in the fabric of their relationship before he was launched on his final lap to adulthood.

Hawke's Cove had always been her place of refuge. When schoolwork, or arguments with her parents, or spats with girlfriends made Southton oppressive, she would think of Hawke's Cove, of the predictable routine of beach and reading on the porch, of the scent of damp air and hot sand. The peace that comes with being in the place you are the most happy. The friendship of Mack and Grainger.

"Will, I think maybe we should go to Hawke's Cove."

Will sat up and pulled away from her, his eyes glittering with spent tears in the strengthening light of day. "I thought you wouldn't go."

"I don't want to, but I think that we need the time away."

Will pulled away from her arms, a rapid flat-palmed rub of his eyes wiping away the small boy who'd just been there. His jaw flexed. "You know I won't do it again, I promise. Swear to God."

Kiley took the corner of the sheet and wiped her own tears from the corners of her eyes. "So you're promising to keep away from D.C. and Mike? All summer?"

There was exactly enough hesitation in Will's answer. "It wasn't their fault. I mean, it was my choice, I did it. No one put a gun to my head."

"You bought it?"

"No. I just smoked it."

"If I take the car away from you, you can't work. You're too old to ground, and I don't want to spend the last summer we're together worrying every night that, deliberately or not, you're in the wrong company."

"Don't you trust me?"

Kiley's eyes drifted to the light bordering the edges of the drawn shade. Over the years, parenting had taught her to temper her words. She knew how harsh words, even justifiably provoked, could be soul-breaking to young ears. Reprimands were always based on anger at behavior, not him. Never ad hominem, always a little retractable. Until now, when there were no words for how betrayed she felt by his behavior. By him. He had done the one thing they had discussed and agreed on time and again. If he could fail her so easily in this, would mere words repair the damage? Talk, as her mother often said, is cheap.

"No, Will. Frankly, I don't."

Will stood up and gathered his dignity around him. "I really am sorry, Mom. I know that I screwed up. It was a mistake in judgment but, whether you believe me or not, it won't happen again. It was stupid."

"So why did you do it?"

"I can't tell you."

Echoes of her own words nineteen years before. *I can't tell you.* She understood that there were times when it was enough to admit error, if not reason.

"I understand why you might not believe that I won't ever do it again, but taking me away won't give me the chance to show you that you can trust me." Will's voice had taken on his most reasonable tone, the voice he used to convince her to give him permission to do something against her better judgment. Like let him attend that party at Lori's.

"Going away will give us both a little distance from this incident, Will. We need that." Kiley hoped he didn't see that she was convincing herself with her words.

"So, if we go, how long do we stay?" Will's tone verged on curious as he capitulated.

"I'm not sure. A couple of weeks, three maybe." Kiley threw back the bedclothes and sat on the edge of the bed. Sleep was out of the question. "I have a month coming to me and July is a good time to go. The doctor is taking his vacation then, too, so things will be slow at the office." Kiley found her slippers and pulled on her housecoat. "Let's have breakfast."

Will shook his head. "Not for me. I'm going back to bed."

"We aren't done talking about this, you know."

Will stood in the doorway and shrugged a silent "Whatever," and Kiley knew that she'd made the right decision. He thought that his tears and apologies were enough. In that still childlike, solipsistic world he inhabited, Will believed that he had smoothed things over. That she was his mother and, therefore, she must forgive him. Kiley remembered how that felt. If only tears and remorse could smooth away the mistakes of youth. This indiscretion would not affect the rest of his life in the way hers had, neither would it go away.

"Tell me something." Will remained in the doorway, his hands pressed against the doorjamb.

Kiley pulled the belt of her housecoat tighter around her waist. "What?"

"What is it about Hawke's Cove that scares you so much?"

"Stuff."

"Like my father?" One last arrow fired.

Kiley knotted the belt, not looking up at Will. "Your father was the love of my life."

That was all she would ever say. That his father was someone who was kind, and handsome, and clever, whom she loved, and was now gone.

The truth was, she didn't know who his father was. Long ago she had loved two boys equally, only to find that that wasn't possible. In love, there can never be three. The uncanny part was that every now and then Will betrayed some characteristic of the one, and then of the other, as if the two had joined together to create this child; that her love had somehow caused the impossible to happen, and Will was part of all three of them.

The old summer place was so like she remembered it that for an instant upon opening the double front door, Kiley half expected Mortie the cocker spaniel to greet her. Mortie had been her dog as a child, a golden tan color which had faded as he aged, peacefully dying in his sleep right there in the corner beside the hearth in the summer of her seventeenth year. Kiley glanced at the corner, almost surprised that there was no dog bed still there. Stifling the temptation to abandon unpacking in order to tour the house as a memory museum, Kiley called to Will to start unloading the suitcases from the car.

Kiley's parents hadn't been back to the place since her mother's first fall. A shattered hip and the diagnosis of advanced osteoporosis had ended their summer pilgrimage to Hawke's Cove, despite the encouragement of Lydia's physical therapist to keep doing what she had always done. Any thought of going was compromised as Merriwell's lungs began to lose their battle against his lifetime of smoking. So, the Harris house had stood empty last summer for the first time in nearly seventy summers. No Harris had lounged on the front porch, morning coffee in hand, surveying the magnificent seascape that, no matter how often it was viewed, never failed to amaze. A three generation continuum had been broken, aided by her refusal to come back.

Now there was Will, representing the fourth generation at Hawke's Cove, standing on the broad verandah, staring out across the short yard to the intense blue of the summer ocean. His ball cap was twisted around backward, his baggy jeans exposed his boxers, and his face was glowing with that first view of the cove which lent its name to the town. Will hitched up his jeans and turned to face his mother. "No one ever said it was this beautiful."

"It's even more beautiful during storms. The sea becomes this gray-green color and the whitecaps are like cream. You can't see across to Great Harbor, because the sky and the sea become the same color. When I was a girl we'd sit out here to watch the storms come and go, like our own private show." She let Will imagine she meant herself and her parents. But it was Mack and Grainger with whom she'd sit, enraptured by the dramatic sky, jumping and grasping hands at each bolt of lightning spearing from the black clouds into the roiling sea, like Neptune's tridents.

"Do you think we'll get any thunderstorms while we're here?"

"This is New England seacoast, so anything's possible."

Kiley grasped the handle of her suitcase and climbed up the steep and narrow stairs to the second floor. She breathed in the slightly musty salt-and-wood smell of long-closed summerhouse. The scent acted like a door to the memories of other summer arrivals, made tangible by the same awkward weight of the overpacked suitcases, and the familiar sound of her sandals on wood floors. She half tasted the homemade chowder always left for them by the woman who used to open the house when she was a girl.

The wash of homesickness brought sharp tears to her eyes.

"Mom, are you all right?" Will's voice betrayed his surprise at his mother's quiet weeping.

"I never realized how much I missed it." Kiley laughed at herself and brushed away the tears. "Oh, I feel so foolish." But was it the foolishness of sentimentality, or the foolishness of having stayed away for so long?